Mighty Mary

Mighty Mary

Max Davine

TAMARiND HiLL
.PRESS

For Crystal and Sunny

ACKNOWLEDGEMENT

"Mighty Mary" is a work of fiction, but given the gravity of historical events which inspired it, I felt that hefty research into Mary's final hours were an absolute necessity. This would not have been possible without the excellent records kept by Craig Dominey of The Moonlit Road, a website chock full of strange tales from the American South. Thank you and thank you as well for keeping obscure pieces of Americana alive. There are so many untold stories out there and you provide a wealth of insight. Also, thanks to Krissy Howard for her 2016 article and the photograph that moved me to tears and then to inspiration.

On a more personal level, I owe the fondest thanks to my supervisor at Deakin University, Doctor Gary Smith, for his tireless work in shaping me as an author to bring the very best out of my story. Peter Kalos of The Melbourne Actor's Lab, whose voice still rings in my head daily – "put your characters up a tree and throw rocks at them" – "do your work!" – etc. Dina Gavrilova for never letting me be mediocre in anything. Diana Leshcheva for the brief but insistent support she offered. To the firefighters of the Belgrave Fire Brigade for their encouragement and for continuing to allow me to serve amongst them. To my workmates at Holmsglen Institute for never letting my feet leave the ground. Lastly, to Crystal, to whom the book is half-dedicated, for her early encouragement.

CHAPTER 1

At first, there was only light and sound. Bright, dazzling yellow that shone through the formless void of darkness and a cacophony of tuneless, unintelligible noise that frightened and confused her. The warmth of the sun was heavy and strong, and it burned. A sudden, brisk breeze cut through it, and her whole little body shivered. She curled into a ball. The noises were deep and resonant. There was thudding on the ground all around her and long, consistent growls from every direction. She opened her eyes and in the blur of yellow, she began to see the great, blue sheet above and the endless, dusty ground below. Shadows loomed around her. Gigantic forms that blocked out the light and the heat. They reached out toward her, touched her. Finally, the sensory overload became too much. The bolts of panic shooting through her quivering flesh took hold. She raised her trunk into the air and screamed out...

Out from the chaos arose a familiar sound. She'd never heard anything before, but she knew this sound. She knew the shadow that fell upon her from behind. She knew the soft, gentle touch of the trunk that curled around her and warmed her. On her wobbly legs, she scurried closer to it. Deeper into the folds of flesh that she knew would protect her from all this strange and terrifying world. The rhythmic breathing and low growling settled in her ears and melted the fear from her heart. The trunk curled around her back in an embrace. The great legs were like pillars of a fortress. She knew this was her mother.

The baby dared to look out into the vast space she'd been plunged into once her eyes adjusted. She saw the green of long, waving grass that rustled and hissed and the billowing canopies of the lonely trees which were scattered all around them. In one direction, she could see the land reach all the way out to the blue sky and touch it. She saw the rest of the herd as they walked through that grass, or idled beneath the lonely trees, reaching out now and then to pluck the greenery from their brown branches and shovel it into their mouths. She recognized their long legs, their floppy grey skin, their floppy ears, their dexterous trunks and their big, friendly brown eyes as her own. They were her family. Around their ankles scampered others, some only a little bigger than the baby, some considerably bigger, but still only calves next to the full-grown cows. They chased each other, playfully frolicked in the grass, or chased the little squealing pigs that tried to hide in the thickets. One young cow stumbled on her uncertain feet, still covered in the furry down that the baby felt all over her own body and shook her trunk rigorously and honked with laughter.

It looked fun. The baby decided to try it for herself. She shook her head about, which sent her trunk flopping into her mother's legs. More room was needed. She took a few happy paces out into the world and shook her head. Her trunk whipped and flew about and knocked her softly on the head. She honked joyfully. The other calf honked as well. The two babies shook their trunks and honked and chased each other through the shallow water on the edge of the pond and over the muddy banks of its edges. Both babies warmed when they touched their trunks together or rested against each other until their breath caught up with them.

Soon the baby felt tired. She quickly returned to her mother and reached up to suckle her milk until she felt heavy and sleepy. The bright yellow light in the sky had sunk down behind the tall grass, the clouds had turned into wispy shadows and the day's great dome of blue had opened up to show the infinite space of twinkling lights. All the vastness around them was plunged into night. It was calm and peaceful, and the baby felt the warmth and closeness of the herd as they gathered around and heaved onto their sides or knees, lowered their heads down, and dozed off. Her mother huddled around her. It was the cosiest, safest place in all the world. The baby felt gentle and soft, and she slipped off into sleep.

They woke again and, under the serene starlight, continued their grazing. The cows moaned and grumbled as they climbed back up onto their feet, but the calves and newborns were up and yelping and frolicking already. By day, the baby found her friend and they played, but by night, all the calves stayed close to their mothers. Other babies began to join in with the games. Even older calves joined in the game of shaking their trunks around. Some of the calves had different smells and presences to them. These were the males. They were often first to start headbutting, usually each other, and knocking one another into the sparkling water of the pond. The baby liked watching that. She liked the way the drops of water flung up in droplets and shimmered in the sunlight. She tried to catch them with her trunk. One day, one of the males sucked the water of the pond into his trunk and shot it into the air. Beneath the sunlight, the droplets showered over a spectral arch of colour. Enchanted, the other calves quickly sucked water into their trunks and shot jets into the air to make their own rainbows.

The baby tried. She put her trunk in the water and tensed her muscles, but she couldn't breathe in. She was too afraid she'd choke. The others stopped playing and just watched her struggling. As she tried and failed, a cold jet of muddy water slapped against her side. The calves all honked and shook their trunks at the joke, but the baby felt cold sinking through her. She didn't feel like one of them anymore. She retreated to her mother's shadow and suckled, feeling the sting of scorn.

Before long, the cows started to issue low growls, and each calf followed the familiar tone to its mother. The baby wasn't far from her mother, who led the herd along from the grass, out into the expanse where the trees stood. They walked on and on, though the baby felt tired and weak. Sometimes they'd pause, and the baby would suckle, while the other calves played, but it was never enough to reenergize her. She was always tired when they started walking again and didn't want to join the other calves. The sting in her heart reminded her of their scorn. She didn't want to feel it again.

One day, a terrible, bitter odour carried on the light, chilly breeze that met their faces. The cows grunted and growled and called their calves to stay close. More of the larger cows moved to the front of the herd, forming a barrier of mighty flesh as they walked. Soon enough, they came upon the source of the smell. The cows formed a circle around the dead creature, which the baby recognized as one of their own. The deep grey of his flesh had paled, and raw meat sat rotting in the sun where parts of his face had been torn away. A cold shiver ran through the baby as she looked. It was so still. Even when they slept, the others were bursting with the aura and signals of life; the pulses, the throbbing and flickering, the breathing and

5

sighing, the warmth and the presence of sentience. All of it was gone from this one. He was a rock. The baby felt tears burning at her eyes as the cows touched the cold body with their trunks. She reached out to do the same, but with a firm flick, her mother pushed her back down beneath her belly. The baby felt how unsettled the cows were. She saw how they inspected the deep red wounds on either side of the trunk, where some of the cows, like her mother, had tusks. They touched two holes in the dead buck's forehead. Black dots where his red life had seeped out of him and stained his face.

The trunks quickly withdrew. The growls became frantic, and the calves were quickly gathered up. Icy tendrils of fear crept through the baby's flesh. She didn't understand why the cows were so disturbed. She knew mortality. She had seen one of the mothers step on a little furry creature accidentally, and it had burst open and spilled all its red life out and been still. She knew it was dead like this buck was dead. Birds had come to eat what was left of the furry creature. There were no birds to peck at the buck. The buzzing urgency she felt from the cows confused and frightened her.

Still, she understood the needs of predators. They killed to eat, and this young buck had been killed and had not died by misadventure or thirst. He'd died violently but had not been eaten. The baby did not see this as significant, but it disturbed the others.

They walked quicker, after that, and rested less often. The weight of her own body was nearly unbearable, but the cows remained wary and impatient. The baby wanted to get as far away from the dead buck as possible, and quickly, so things could go back to normal and she could feel warm and at ease with her herd again. But the fright lingered, even when she couldn't see the body behind them anymore. When they did stop to rest and eat, the calves stayed with their mothers. None of them played.

Nights grew cold. Though the herd huddled together, the baby could feel the numbing air on any of her skin that was exposed from her mother's embrace and she feared this would go on forever. Clouds covered the sky, they turned the blue dome white and sometimes deep grey. The world remained in toneless shadows and she missed the vibrancy of the sun. Then, the clouds wept, and heavy, drenching torrents of cold water pelted them through the night. She was glad when that was over. Though the herd huddled together, the baby still felt the loneliness of her alienation. The other calves seemed to have developed their own language that the baby couldn't understand. Even while they weren't playing together she'd see them looking or honking at each other, but never at her.

On and on they walked, past the last of the lonely trees and into a plain where the grass grew up to the baby's ankles and the ground squelched when she stepped on it. Streams of water were spread across the plain like the branches of trees. Their edges had swollen right over the banks and formed a huge swamp. The water was icy on the baby's feet, and she squealed every time her foot sank too deeply. The baby felt faint, as though she might collapse, but the cold ground startled her and kept her upright.

In the distance loomed giant forms, which intimidated the baby with their sheer size. They rose up silently out of the earth and blocked out the sky with their fat, cold grey flanks, so high that their peaks seemed to scrape the bottoms of the fluffy clouds, which bled white over their tops. But they never moved. They just stood there in silent watchfulness with the steady assurance of eternity. The baby could see that there was no way of getting to those giant forms, for across the plain through which the herd was walking there stood a formidable wall of trees. A huge, thick forest with an endless night beneath its greenery.

The herd was walking on unsteady feet. Their wariness was disheartening, so the baby kept focused on the forest edge until the day grew hot beneath the finally shining sun and they could finally smell rich, lush food. At last, the nightmare vision of the dead buck faded from the minds of the cows, the baby felt its spectre fade like the memory of a bad dream, and the herd was peaceful again. Still, the baby did not want to leave her mother's side. She wanted to be near the steady watchfulness of her eyes, the warmth, and security of her size and the affections of her caresses. A bastion of safety, in a world of disturbingly dead bucks and scornful calves. But she saw the calves playing again. They were splashing in the water, spraying mud and trying to make rainbows again. The female baby, who'd lost much of her furry down, found her way back to her first friend. She shook her trunk.

The baby's stomach was fluttering. Though those sweet brown eyes beckoned her to come play again, her heart hadn't forgotten how quickly they had turned cold to her. But the other baby had forgotten all about it. She was shaking her trunk, then staring expectantly. The baby began to feel bad, as though she herself was scorning now, and so she shook her trunk in response. Before long, she'd left her mother's side and was playing with her friends again.

Then, the other baby stopped at a fallen branch with some green leaves left on it. With her trunk, she picked up a bunch, tore them from the branches, and stuffed them into her mouth. The baby was feeling empty in her stomach. It rumbled, and she knew it was hunger. Her mother's milk had stopped filling her the way it had. She copied her new friend and tore off some leaves, then put them in her mouth to chew. For the first time, she felt the bursting sweetness of greens, and she loved it. She hurried over to the grass to try that. It was dirtier, rougher, but she loved it anyway. She forgot all about the vastness, the fear. The barrier of flesh that was her herd, kept her safe and enclosed. She felt secure, so she ate. Then she drank the cold water.

Other calves would continue their play of squirting water at each other, but they took little notice of whether the baby could do it or not. She was glad for the anonymity. She'd learned to headbutt and took to taking on the largest of the male calves. The others would honk and squeal excitedly each time she did it, so she was sure to do it often. The male calves would play right back, but the baby could hold her own. On green food and fresh water, she was becoming dexterous with her trunk and powerful in her body. Sometimes she'd go back to her mother at night with tender spots, but they only meant that she'd have to play harder the next day.

Gradually, the cold lifted and the clouds parted to show the bluest dome of the sky again. The muddy water receded from the ground, which became dry and the grass browned. The herd stayed near the forest edge, but the calves got thirsty. Their play took them further and further away from the cows, as they chased the water. The baby noticed how small her mother and the rest of the herd looked from where they were, and it frightened her, so she grunted and grumbled to call them back. They ignored her, but once the cows started making sound, the calves returned.

The air grew thicker and heavier. One morning, the baby felt her tongue was almost sticking to the top of her mouth. She wanted water. The other calves were already walking out to where they'd last seen some, so she hurried to catch up to them, but there was no more water. It had moved back even further. Before them, blocking the calves' way, was a wall of tall reeds which reached high over the heads of even the biggest male calf. All the calves could smell the water on the other side. It wasn't far.

The baby looked back. The cows were already small, their growls and groans sounded faint in the distance. She didn't want to go any further or have reeds blocking her view of them. She could see her mother amongst them, which comforted her. She didn't want to lose sight. But the male calves were already pushing their way through the reeds. Some of the larger female calves were with them and the babies were following. The baby looked back at her mother. Her tongue was so dry, and her head was beginning to ache. The smell of the water was becoming overpowering, the distance back to the cows was intimidating for her to walk it alone and she felt alone without the calves nearby. So, she followed them into the reeds. Their storks were rough and thick to push through and for a moment she felt like she was alone. Fear began to prickle up inside her, so she hurried through the path of disturbed reeds until she could hear the calves playing and splashing in a stony clearing at the river's edge.

They'd found the water. The baby drank and felt the cooling relief work its way through her entire body. Other calves started spraying each other with water or knocking each other into the shallows. None of them dared to go too far out; the rushing surface, the terrifying breadth and the bleakness of the river's depths were too frightening. The baby drank some more, then rushed over to headbutt one of the males. A female headbutted her. They squealed and played together.

Over the rustle of the reeds came the low growl of the baby's mother, calling the calves back. It was stiflingly hot out there, so the calves quickly crawled into the water for one last cool off. Some of the larger calves were spraying themselves with mud. The younger calves copied their elders, but the baby still hadn't figured out how to do it. While the others were distracted, she dipped her trunk into the brown water at the river's edge. She heard her mother calling, but she wanted to get it right. So, she sucked in and felt the cold mud gurgle up her trunk. Quickly, she stopped before it stung her sinus, and she was able to lift her trunk without spilling any. She blew with all her might and sprayed the cooling mud over her back.

Excited, the baby quickly filled her trunk again and sprayed mud over the others. They honked with glee and sprayed her back. They played and splashed about until the baby was knocked into the shallows by a boisterous male. As she happily climbed back to her feet, she noticed the silence. Behind the splashing and the squelching and the bellowing of the calves, there had been the rustle of the reeds, the incessant buzzing of insects, and the chirping and cooing of birdsong. All were suddenly silent. As they sensed the baby's fear, the other calves settled and heard the silence as well. They listened, but the only thing to hear was the running water and the distant bellows of their mothers. They could hear their own heartbeats.

A gentle breeze was cool against their wet skin, as though the mountains had breathed on them, and the baby felt the icy tendrils of fear creeping through her flesh and up her spine again. The reeds were still and close, but like curtains, they covered the silent world surrounding the calves. It got too much. The baby started crying out for her mother. She raised her trunk high in the air and screamed with all her might. The other calves joined in. They all huddled together, fearful of some phantom that seemed to be stalking the silence. It was as though eyes were watching them. Cold, cruel eyes piercing the baby, not watching, but deciding. She called louder, as did her friends, but their cries seemed to fall faint as soon as they left their mouths, as though they were being sucked up into the sky and dissipated on the breeze.

One of the larger males stepped away from the others. Without a sound, it leaped upon him. A flash of orange against the yellowed green of the reeds. A long, agile and powerful body, with its limbs spread out to its sides, latched onto the male's back, while a gaping mouth opened and plunged yellow fangs deep into his flesh. He screamed and staggered about while the predator, orange with black stripes, kicked wildly at his stomach. White horror paralyzed the baby as she saw the clawed feet rip the skin away from the male's belly and expose the red, bloody rags of flesh beneath.

A deafening bellow blasted from above. The predator fell from the young one, folded its ears flat back against its neck, and hissed with its fangs bearing through its bloodied lips. Thunder filled the ground, as the cows charged. The little ones scampered from the path, as the giant bodies formed a wall around them. The predator crouched low to the ground and swiped the air with its huge paw but dared not attack. Barely missed by the sharp swing of her mother's trunk, the animal fled into the reeds.

The baby trembled as her mother stood over her and touched her and spoke to her. She felt like she might collapse. The other adults gathered around the wounded male. Deep scratches leaked red over his skin and he cried from the pain.

A sudden jolt from the side startled her. Her mother had struck her with her trunk! She grumbled, angrily, before shoving her away from the scene. Flooded with sadness and shame, she hurried to her mother's feet and wrapped her trunk around one and cried for forgiveness. Softer, then, the mother nudged her. One more affectionate caress and the herd had to be on their way.

CHAPTER 2

They were moving again. The baby recognized the path they'd come along and knew they were going back to their warm-season feeding grounds. Only this time something was very wrong. The herd moved slowly, even by day. The mother of the wounded calf was all the way at the back, trying to push him along, but he cried, and his flesh quivered, and he just couldn't seem to get his feet moving. In fits and starts, he tried to keep pace but would stop each time and moan agonizingly. He'd collapse and cry, and the herd would have to stop to wait for him. The baby shivered as she saw his skin turn ashen, like the dead buck they'd seen on their way to the plain. The sight made her stomach churn. All the while, she knew they weren't moving fast enough, and though the cows would keep vigil and form circles around the calves whenever the wounded male's strength failed him, she couldn't shake the prickling feeling that the predator was still stalking. Watching with those cold, cruel eyes. Indifferent to suffering. The wounded male's bloodstains had turned purple and his exposed tissue had turned grey and developed yellow sores which leaked fluid and smelled sour and pungent. It wasn't hard to imagine that the predator was drawn to that smell.

Night fell again, but the herd was restless. The calves were all moved to the centre of the cluster, while the cows remained on the outside. The smell that issued from the wounded calf was overpowering. It not only filled the baby's gullet with slimy bile and made her eyes water, but the worry for the wounded male pierced her heart and her stomach turned slowly.

The clouds had formed a thick sheet over the sky and by nightfall, the world was plunged into a darkness so thick it felt as though the baby could reach out and touch its inky surface. But she didn't dare reach into it. She was afraid of what was lurking behind its pitch-black veil. All she could hear were the moaning cries of the wounded male. Each night felt longer than the last, but this night felt longest of all; though she was so tired her legs throbbed, her eyes itched and her back ached and the mercy of sleep alluded her. She could sense the trembling hearts of the other calves and the adults watching over them. The night was so dark they stayed until morning came. To the baby, it felt like the darkness would never leave the world.

Relief finally came with the whistle of a nearby flock of birds, and the golden line shimmered on the flat horizon ahead and the cotton-clouds which streaked the sky seemed to flush with blood. The cows growled and gathered their calves, and the baby's mother was leading them again. The wounded male struggled to his feet. His eyes seemed distant and glassy. As the day went on, the clouds dissipated, the sun's heat intensified, and the air became dense and muggy. The baby felt herself gasping for air, as though she'd been running or playing.

She knew their surroundings though. She could see the scattered lonely trees and the distant forest beyond them and could smell the water she knew when she first entered the world. But there was no sign of the grass. It should have been just ahead. The squeals of the little pigs should be welcoming the herd home. All was silent. Instead of the richness of greenery, the air was tainted with a strange, acrid smell that alighted instincts inside the baby to turn and run away.

Her mother halted the herd with a great and urgent bellow.

Ahead was the sight that sent shivers through them all; where once there had been a field of grass so long the adult cows could hide in it and stands of trees that could feed them all with their lush, green canopies, there now stood something the baby could never have imagined. Rows upon rows of odd shapes, some like the silvery mountain peaks back across the plains, but smaller than an adult cow, while others were large and had sharp corners and straight, symmetrical walls. She could see that the smaller structures were flimsy, with walls like skin, while the larger ones were solid, and were clustered in the centre of the strange new jungle, where nothing roamed but small upright creatures. They were like the apes that lived in the trees, but hairless except for on their heads, and with loose skins wrapped around their bodies. They were far away, so the baby could not see them properly, but from the cold fear radiating from her mother and all the other adults, she knew she didn't want to be any closer.

They were sick. Even the baby could tell. She knew from their scent secreted into the still air and the laborious effort of their standing upright and moving about. They were not plump with flesh, like her kind, or taut with muscle, like the apes which lived in the trees and were similar to them. They were hungry. Wasting away. Their bodies were thin and beneath their second skins their bones showed through. She could sense their sorrow. Their suffering. The baby knew, like the rest of her herd, that the only thing more dangerous than a hungry predator was a sick or wounded predator. These creatures didn't seem like predators, but the threat which radiated from their mechanical indifference warned the herd of enemies.

The smoke was billowing in gigantic columns up from the large structures and from various spots around the smaller skin structures. The baby knew the fire was a lethal force of nature, but with a shudder, she realized that these little upright beings, controlled fire. They lived amongst it. Even created it. Then, she saw what was left of the stands of trees that once stood

19

beyond the grass, just beyond the edges of the skin village. There were only a few of them left, and they were surrounded by the creatures, who moved thin sheets of hard, grey material between them back and forth, sawing into the trunk of the trees, until they groaned and heaved and fell with an earth-shaking crash. The other creatures moved in and beat at the wood with sticks that chipped chunks of it away. Then they carried them back towards the large central structures.

Her mother growled, calling the herd toward her as she quickly retreated from the bizarre and terrifying sight. The other cows acknowledged with moans, but they couldn't tear their eyes away from the casual, calculated destruction being wrought on their feeding ground. The baby's mother trumpeted loudly and startled the adult cows, who quickly fell into line and started following her. For one heart-stopping moment, the baby was separated from her mother's shadow and hurried to catch up. As she did, she caught sight of the wounded male.

He was trembling on his flimsy feet and she could see his bones sticking out through his wasted skin, as though he was slowly fading into nothing. His trunk hung limp and his head was held low, his body lacked the strength to lift it. He leaned on his mother's leg and she urged him to continue. They had to keep moving. The baby caught up with her mother and they kept walking. Her mother would know the way to food and water. She would save them. The baby knew it. With a stout heart, she stayed by her mother's side, believing that they would lead the herd to the nourishment that the wounded male needed to heal.

The alpha female led the herd down a slight slope. The baby could sense their subtle descent. Ahead, in the distance, there stood an oasis of green, divided in two by a snaking river. But the distance was far. Leeward of the wounded male, the baby could smell his wound more strongly than ever. She craned her neck to look back at him and whimpered at the sight of him leaned on his mother's leg as she took slow and careful steps, while the distance between herself and the others grew with every pace. She wrapped her trunk around him and he fought with all his might to carry on. A gust of wind blasted the baby with the odour of his injuries. Bitter and foul. She looked ahead again. It was a hopeless distance. She heard the footsteps of the herd behind them and felt her mother leading them, a sentinel of endless strength. All the knowledge of the world was centred in her wise and watchful gaze. All the horror that lurked in the shadows would be deflected off her powerful frame. She knew the way.

They would make it, the baby thought. They would.

A rumbling came through the earth. It was gentle at first, barely stronger than the parading footsteps of the herd. But it grew quickly, and even in the heat of the day, that seemed to thicken the air to syrup. The baby felt her blood run cold as it rumbled closer and closer. Shrieks and cries issued from the herd behind them. Still, her mother did not stop. She trumpeted loudly and urged the others to keep moving, to keep together but when the baby looked behind her, she could see that the herd were scattering. Fear sent them into a state of delirium. They bellowed defensively, they pushed their young toward the centre of the group and they flapped their ears and raised their trunks high. Finally, her mother relented, and the baby found herself being pushed roughly into the centre of the cluster. The cows formed a tight circle around the calves and blocked out much of the world. They bellowed and trumpeted and kicked up the dust to form massive clouds around themselves. The noise was rattling and thunderous. The vibration in the earth grew and grew, until it felt as though the ground itself might split open and swallow them all. As it got louder, its rhythm became definable; a steady, constant chugging.

The cows' aggression escalated, and they roared and lowered their heads threateningly. The calves were screaming and crying. The baby peeked between her mother's legs, out past her shaking trunk and through the thick dust cloud. She

22

saw it. It moved faster than a river runs. At first, she thought
she saw a giant snake, but it was too big, and had no eyes or
mouth. The long, black monster chugged so loudly her bones
rattled. From its head spewed a thick stream of white mist that
burned her nostrils and made her eyes water and she coughed.
It even smothered the smell of the male calf's injuries. The
earth shook as it rolled past, on and on and on its body went.
When the last portion of it finally rumbled past, leaving only
the acidic smoke in its wake, the baby heard the crying of the
calves and the tense breathing of the startled cows. That
frightened her most of all; that their giant, formidable
protectors could be as frightened as they were. The baby burst
with frightful emotion and wept into her mother's leg. A high
whistle resonated in her ears, and the dulling vibration in the
earth lingered long after the chugging had faded into the
distance.

It was no creature; the baby knew this. It moved, but there
was no life to it. Like the structures and the sheets that sliced
into trees, it was something unnatural. Something that
belonged to the apes that walked on the ground.

The baby's mother was the first to break from the circle.
She quickly moved around to the wounded calf and touched
his head with her trunk while his mother looked on. Slowly,
the smell of his wounds replaced the acrid scent left by the

monster and the urgency of their situation returned to their beating hearts. With a heavy grumble, the baby's mother called the others back into line and led them toward the green oasis in the distance.

She led them on, in the direction the chugging thing had travelled. They moved so close the baby saw the two thin, parallel lines left on the earth where the beast had travelled. They chilled her blood. It was the perfection of them; two lines, side by side, bridged by pieces of fashioned wood, was an unearthly sight. Something altogether alien and nightmarish to the baby. She couldn't comprehend symmetry. Once they'd seen them, the herd kept their distance.

It was visible, the oasis, but every step the herd took towards it seemed to push the sight of it, and the scent of the water running through it, further back. The herd was weak with fear, hunger, and thirst. The baby's whole mouth felt gluey and stiff, like moving her tongue might cause it to crack and shatter to million pieces and turn to dust. As the day wore on, the clouds ahead, looming over the oasis, grew dark and rumbled angrily. A soft electrical current flowed through the air from ahead. Behind them, the sun was setting beyond their decimated feeding ground, and bathed the far-off mountains in copper tinted light. Shadows grew sudden and dark and stretched out before them, seeming to drive the oasis even further from their reach.

Even the baby's mother was panting, and white foam had gathered around her mouth, as it had the other cows and even the calves. It dawned on them they would have to stop. One of the lonely trees stood not far from their path, so the baby's mother deviated toward it and quickly set about reaching her trunk into its canopy and stripping the branches, which sent the leaves fluttering down to the needy calves below. They bustled and fought over the greenery, while the adults went hungry. Even the baby launched herself in, driven by a desperate need to taste, to chew and to fill her roiling belly. It was only after there was nothing left that she realized the wounded male had got nothing. He was still far behind, lingering while his mother urged him on. By the time they arrived, they could only rest in the shadow of a naked tree.

Dark clouds rumbled in the distance as the world plunged into night. The herd gathered together and huddled up to sleep for a while. The baby fought to catch the sleep that continued to outrun her, and she heard the restlessness of the others as they stirred in the darkness, until the clouds were above them. A few pitters, a few patters, and they opened to unleash a heavy, pounding rain. The herd huddled closer for another restless night.

CHAPTER 3

The sheets of water cascaded down over the carriage windows. The long, lean figure of Mister Villiers hunched over the drawing desk, swirling a coffee and watching it, intently. 'Any chance this mess will smudge up our trail, Henry old boy?'

'Not to worry, m'lad,' Atkinson assured him. 'Our railway line, however...'

'Oh, never mind that, Henry,' Villiers muttered.

'I do mind that, Mister Villiers,' Atkinson quipped. 'They're not paying us to hunt big game.'

'They're not paying us to fret, either, old boy,' Villiers said, as he shone a persuasive smile over Atkinson. 'I tell you it will be done.'

Atkinson shifted in his seat and looked down into the black sludge that was left of his own coffee. He knew it was hopeless by the way young Villiers' back had arched and his predatory eyes had widened at the sight of the elephant herd they'd passed on the way in. The East India Company's newest railroad executive, Walton's replacement, was no more concerned with the besieged line between Patna and Bhagalpur, or whether Calcutta got their silk and potassium nitrate on time or ever than his predecessor had been. And for much the same reason.

'It will be done,' Villiers said under his breath as he stared into the black sheet that night had made the carriage windows, watching the ripples run down one after the other.

They'd arrived at their station late, but due to the deluge, had not even bothered to disembark the carriage. The bunks were more comfortable when the train was still anyway, so there was no need to rouse the workers from their shanty village. For Atkinson, however, it meant remaining stuck alone with the newcomer at least until the rains let up.

'Well, you won't complain about the weather back home, after a year or two of this,' Atkinson said, trying to break the silence between them. 'Six months, we haven't even got halfway.'

'Walton must have been laying the sleepers himself,' Villiers said, still staring at whatever the blank, wet glass showed him. 'The locals should be used to this.'

Atkinson ran out of energy for the young man's conversation. Precious few were the intervals in which Villiers had actually engaged in conversation about the railway, on their way here. Always technical matters, though. Never the labour force. Never their unwillingness to work in the monsoons. Again, and again, all Villiers would say of it was 'It will be done.' No sooner had Villiers stepped off the steamer ramp in Calcutta, than he was talking about bagging a 'buck'. It was the undoing of the privileged. Atkinson had spent enough time working around them to spot them a mile away, and this thin, fair young man with a pencil moustache and a red cravat beneath his khakis was born to title rather than toil.

'I tell you, Henry, you should have seen the one that got away in Rhodesia,' Villiers was ranting. Atkinson was lost in watching the black sludge in his coffee cup swirl around until the young man sat right in front of him. 'Big as a house, it was! Not to worry. I'm certain I saw one or two amongst that herd who was twice as big!'

Atkinson opened his mouth, meaning to inform the young man that Asian elephants don't grow as big as African. But he thought better of it. The sooner John Villiers could sate his bloodlust, the sooner they could get the Company out of his ears, he thought.

'I met a very peculiar fellow, on safari, you know?' Villiers said. He eased back in his seat and turned his legs out from under the table in order to cross them. 'Called himself a Colonel. He didn't depart the lodge with us, this fellow. An American. We met him out in the savannah. All alone, he was. Without a round of buckshot to his name. Just a pair of binoculars and a knife. I tell you, he must be a tough chap, this one. He joined the group, but he expressed no interest in hunting. Would you believe it? To go all that way and not go hunting. Odd fellow. In more ways than just that. Kept quiet. I never saw him eat a thing, but he was big, I tell you. Burly. Ugly as they come. I say, do you have any idea in which direction those elephants might have been headed?'

Atkinson looked up from his vile looking coffee and thought for a moment. 'There's a river near here. The local labour force wanted to camp near it.'

'What on Earth for? Don't they get enough water from the sky?'

Atkinson shook his head and set his coffee cup aside.

'Anyway, this fellow...have you ever been on safari?' Atkinson shook his head again. 'This fellow, he wasn't interested in hunting, but he wanted animals all the same. Said he'd pay top dollar to anyone who could bring him back a live one. Can you imagine? Bring him back a live lion, what do you say?'

Villiers laughed heartily.

'Have you ever been to the zoo, Mister Villiers?' Atkinson asked. He leaned forward and spoke slowly. Villiers nodded.

'Well, where do you think those animals came from? The lions and tigers and such?'

A great light illuminated Villiers' face, while the condescending tone of Atkinson seemed to bounce off him, undetected. 'So, it can be done!'

Atkinson clicked his tongue and sat back in his seat.

#

Sleep was ripped away from the baby by the sudden, ear-splitting, heart-rattling shriek that sent shattering tremors through the whole herd and seemed ready to rip the sky above in two. She wasn't sure if she'd been sleeping or not. She found herself hovering in a dazed state between desperate hunger and dry thirst, battered all the while by the constant rain that was quickly turning the ground beneath them to slush. But her eyes were already filled with the hot tears of grief before she heard that one, horrifying cry.

The clouds must have moved toward them while they slept because the world was again in pitch-darkness and the electrical current in the air had become tense and strong. Panicked bodies heaved themselves from the dirt and hurried toward the source of the noise. The baby's mother hauled herself upright and the awful smell struck them both, so terrible it made the baby wretch. The baby blinked and squinted as her eyes slowly adjusted. The cows spread out, parting around the howling adult, who stood over the withered, still form of her calf. It was the wounded male.

He was laying on his side in a growing pool of water. His mouth hung open and let the muddy water in and he was not responding to the rough caresses of his howling mother's trunk as she stood over him and tried to shelter him from the downpour. With a chill, the baby realized how still he was. Like the buck on the trail, the signals of life, however faint they'd been by sunset, were flickered out. He was as stone. Dead.

With their calves between their feet, the cows gathered around the baby and with their trunks they patted his cold little body, as well as his trembling, crying mother. The baby hurried to be beneath her mother's belly but found that she was getting too big to fit under there. Still, she squeezed in, hiding from the rain and staring with morbid fixation at her friend. A horrible ache pierced her heart and seemed to weigh her body down as she remembered him alive; the way his eyes had moved, the way his warmth had radiated from his being, the way the comforting aura of life had beat inside him. To see it gone, and just his lifeless matter remains, made tears run from the baby's eyes. Just like that, all he was, was gone. A void was left in the earth, filled only by a corpse; and as one, the herd felt the painful, gaping wound whence he'd been ripped from them.

Slowly, soft grey light shone through the shimmering rainfall and dull, washed-out colour returned to grassland. The baby looked on, in the direction they'd been headed. The forest was so near she could discern the leaves upon the nearest tree, so much closer than it had seemed yesterday. The cruelty of life made her forget her own aching hunger pangs.

He'd almost made it, she thought as she wept.

At the sight of the greenery, the herd broke apart. Their hunger and exhaustion were greater than their grief and they charged for the lush forest with their calves. The baby moved to follow them, innate urges pulled her along. But her mother wasn't leaving. The mother of the dead calf was stuck with her baby, and was nudging it with her trunk, trying to make him stand up and come along. There was manic delirium shining in her eyes that frightened the baby. But her mother, alpha female, would never leave one behind. The baby wandered a few paces toward the forest, which was quickly blanketed in a heavy mist that obscured the bases of the trees, the shrubs, and the giant grey bodies of the cows as they quickly disappeared behind the shimmering sheets of rainfall. They could taste the greenery, it tingled on her tongue. The smell of it was overpowering. But through the beguiling call of her senses, the baby felt something else. Something familiar.

That icy presence had returned and cut through her intentions like a cold blade every time she tried to run from her mother's side. She could feel those cold eyes watching, waiting. She ran back to her mother, who was stomping her feet and issuing a commanding growl for the grieving mother to leave the corpse and rejoin the herd.

There was no getting through. The bereaved cow would not abandon her child, even though he was dead. The baby saw the water bubble around his mouth as his mother pushed at his body. He seemed less and less flesh and blood by the moment, more and more just mineral matter.

Suddenly the dead calf's mother let out a frightening bellow that jolted the baby away from her mother's side. Her mother turned from the dead calf and lowered her head, swiped her trunk from side to side, and kicked clumps of mud into the air. Behind her, the baby saw the predator. It had followed them all this way! It hunched low, its ears flattened, and opened that gaping mouth to let out a ragged, bone-chilling roar. The baby's mother quickly stepped in front of her, each cow defending her young, but for the baby, it was too much. While the enraged mothers made their stand and matched the predator's rattling roars and swiped their trunks at its clinging claws, the baby turned and ran for the forest. Whether her mind made a conscious decision or not, her body carried her toward the safety of the others.

She ran across the open field toward the forest edge. The sparseness around her sent her heart aflutter with cold fear. Her eyes darted around wildly, at every plop in every puddle, at every rustle in the soaked treetops, she felt the predator's presence behind her. It wasn't stronger than the cows, but it was faster. If it saw her, it could dart around them and chase her down. She knew this. She ran through the pounding rain with all her might. Her flesh prickled, and her mind seared with terror. The roars of the cows faded behind her, with them the ragged roars of the predator.

It could still get her, she thought. Or there could be others...

Phlegm burned the back of her throat. The baby grew short of breath. Ahead, she could hear the moans and crackles of the trees put under immense stress as giant bodies leaned against them or tore branches from their canopies. She could follow the scent of her herd. It drove her through the forest as the trees and shrubs enclosed her and the thick, white mist-veiled all but the chaotic chorus life issued around her. She heard the screech of monkeys in the trees, the deafening chatter of birds as they sheltered from the deluge, and the casual moans and grumbles of her herd in the distance behind it. Even the towering trees became shadows behind the wall of suffocating cloud.

Anything could hide behind this, she thought. Images of yellow fangs bearing from gaping mouths, or staring eyes which steered them through the mist, of monsters that stalked the waterways silently as driftwood, of creatures large enough to snare her in their mouths, pierce her body through with their sharp teeth, and carry her away, all flashed through her mind and with every glance she saw them crouching in the shadows of the brushes or slinking low and fast behind the silhouettes of the tree trunks. The rumble and clamber of the herd drew her onward, but her flesh tensed from the terror her imagination inflicted upon her and the mist was so hot and dense she could hear herself wheezing.

She heard the babble of a river quickly rippling and stirring beneath the bombardment of rain, and quickly swelling over grass and shrub. It was just ahead, winding through the forest and seeming to carry the mist on its surface and spread it into the trees.

From upriver came the sounds of the herd. As she peered toward them, the baby saw the silhouettes of their bodies which wafted through the fog and the treetops jerked and swayed as whole portions of their canopies were stripped bare. She mustered what was left of her strength and ran with all her might. By the time she reached them she was reduced to a stagger, but she felt the trunks of the cows brushing her flanks with concern as she hurried past them. They comforted her and stilled the fear pulsing and pounding inside. She passed through the outer circle of cows and found her friend happily chewing on the leaves of a fallen branch. Driven by need, she dove in and joined the other calf. The baby felt her strength restored with every trunkful she shovelled into her mouth. The euphoria was intoxicating.

The other calves, who'd eaten their fill, already played their water games in a hollow carved by the swelling river while the shadows of their parents loomed in the gloomy forest around them. The baby could see them, and it warmed her. But she could also see one less. Amongst the cows keeping watch, she knew the absence of their alpha more immediately than the others. They might have considered it, but for her daughter, it was alarmingly apparent that she was gone. Her friend shook her trunk and yelped, calling the baby to join the other calves by the river. But the baby was still eating and felt numb towards her friends. She was thinking about her mother. Thoughts stirred inside her. She knew absolutely that the predator was no risk to their alpha female, but nevertheless, she didn't like being separated from her. Not while fog enshrouded what surrounded them. Not while the absence of one male calf was as obvious and painful as a scar on her heart.

CHAPTER 4

The day wore on and the sky drew up its drenching deluge before sunbeams began to shine through the slowly parting clouds. The electrical current remained in the air and warned that the relief would not last long, but the birds took the opportunity to flutter off into the distance anyway, and the monkeys quieted down while the herd continued to loiter in the clearing by the swollen river. Having eaten her fill, the baby watched as the other calves played and the adults kept vigil, all waiting for the call to reunite the herd. But the call wasn't coming. The alpha female, the baby's mother, had still not returned.

Though the mist had not yet dissipated, the baby could see the way the adults foraged, and the calves played with frustrating indifference to their situation. They knew that if their alpha did not return, another would step up and take her place. The baby grew frustrated with them. For the second time in her life, she felt shut off and isolated from the warmth and the harmony that had welcomed her into the world. But she was not sad this time. This time, she was angry. She wanted to leave them and go back to her mother alone. Only the innate voices inside which warned her of the danger in doing so kept her from abandoning them. The other baby female waddled over to her, while she lay down between the constant hum of the cows and the yelping and splashing of the calves and shook her trunk and squealed to beckon her over to the fun. But the baby didn't feel any reservation about scorning her this time. She didn't want to play. She wanted to feel the rigid organization of her herd again, guided by the strength of their leader. She wanted to feel the powerful and watchful but loving and wise and formidable presence of her mother back with them again. If that was impossible for now, she at least wanted her friends and the other cows to notice with as much worry as she felt that their alpha was gone. She wanted them to feel the sickly roiling in her belly and the pain in her heart for their dead friend. The tense worry that her mother wouldn't be back for a long time.

What could be keeping her? Surely the predator was not putting up that much of a fight? Surely the heartbroken mother could gather enough sense to leave her dead child by now?

The baby's heartbeat as loud and sharp as the cracking sounds of the heavy drops that fell from the trees and splattered on the low broadleaves of the undergrowth. Yet the others took no notice. They were worried about themselves. It was as though the baby had plummeted into some crevasse and the herd were enjoying themselves just above her but couldn't see or hear her.

Her friend toddled back over to her and sprayed her with a cool trunkful of river water. It was some slight relief to the heavy humidity that was like trying to breathe through hot mud. The detached child in her mind urged her to go play in the river, told her that worrying would not conjure her mother any quicker, and complained of the stifling atmosphere. The baby forced herself to her feet and laboured over to the river's edge, a few lengths from the squealing, trumpeting rabble of calves, and eased herself into the water. The others quickly hurried over to her, following like the herd always did her mother. They sprayed her with water, they knocked her about with headbutts and they hooted at her joyfully. But the baby could not get away from herself. Even surrounded by them, she felt wreathed in shadow. Utterly alone. Their play only aggravated her more. She wanted to remind them of their dead friend, somehow. To remind them of her mother. She wanted to make them aware of how fragile they were, that such life could be stricken from their bodies in an instant, and they, like their friend, would become inert, rotting matter. But the wild ignorance in their eyes and the energy of their play barricaded any such dampening thoughts and they played on without the baby.

Suddenly a sound pierced through the sky and sent white currents of fear shuddering through her. The calves stopped their play and the cows stopped their feeding. They all looked in different directions, unable to tell from whence the sound had originated. It had been a sharp crack, which was followed by a heavy, resonant whoosh that seemed to vibrate in the air, and suddenly the baby's heart filled with horror as she thought about her mother. Images and emotions burned inside her mind and her blood turned cold.

The urge was sudden and absolute; she had to return to her mother. Fear compelled her, but something greater made her climb out of the river and start running back along the path she'd followed to find the herd. She'd never have been able to ignore their calls for her to return, otherwise. The fear of isolation was greater than her imagination. But she wasn't imagining, she knew she had to be with her mother. Something about the ignorant play of the calves after such a tragedy, and the nonchalant feeding of the calves, had made her feel unsafe with them, even a stranger to them, and the baby knew like nothing she'd ever known before that the sound she'd just heard was danger, and she'd known all her life that the only true safety from danger was her mother.

The adults started calling their calves to them and they formed their protective circle, but the baby had not heard the low growl of her own mother, so she ran along the river until their cries for her faded behind the thinning wall of mist. Panic threatened her with every breath, and tears clouded her vision, but she kept running. Her body ached to have that protective gaze cast over it like the flowers longed for the sunlight: her heart raged to feel the beating of her mother's nearby, and her flesh felt a chilling cold.

A gentle breeze flowed from the land of the mountains and carried the mist away. The baby could see her way, but the excited screams of monkeys and the screeches of birds in the trees drowned out her squeals and trumpets for her mother, and she could not hear if her mother was responding.

Like a sharp whipping, the second cracking sound slapped against the baby's ears, sent a shiver through her, and stopped her in her tracks. Immediately the monkeys and birds fell silent and from beneath resurged the blood-curdling "whoosh" like the one that had followed the first. The baby heard herself scream.

Then, in response, she heard the growl of her mother. The tune reached into her heart and held her like a tether, and the baby ran with all her might toward the source of it. Before the monkeys and the birds stole all sound away again. The baby heard another call, only it was distressingly rugged and shredded with urgency. Her gut churned to know her mother was suffering. She ran and ran. Terror forced her feet.

A third cracking sounded out, but she didn't stop. Not even as the silence fell upon her, and the scream of a cow filled it.

She wasn't thinking. She didn't hear the echoes, the whoosh, or the exploding cracking sound that sounded out immediately after it. The baby didn't care. She'd heard her mother and was blind and deaf to all but it.

The trees and translucent mist parted before her, and the baby found herself looking back over the fields with the lonely trees. The sight that met her there defied her understanding. She froze still, eyes wide with the cold captivation of sheer horror.

Life haemorrhaged in crimson fountains from the dead calf's mother, only a few long strides away, as she keeled over. Her thick, powerful legs were propped and trembling beneath her, trying to keep her up, but her body became too heavy, and she collapsed with an earth-shattering thud that sent mud splattering out in all directions. Her head stayed up, but the blood cascading from the holes in her face filled her eyes and the baby could tell she was blinded by it, for she waved her trunk about with directionless aggression. The roaring sounds she made never stopped until her body crumpled, and her head splatted down on the ground. Then, all that moved were the ribs that peeked up from the skin of her flank, rising and falling steadily.

The baby's mother stood behind her, trying to rouse her with sharp whips from her trunk. The look in her eyes was

alien to her own calf, who had never seen such blazing, red
fury blasting from them. Her mother was looking out past the
fallen cow and issuing ferocious battle cries that shook the
baby's bones. But something else caught the baby's eye as well;
her mother had a wound on her shoulder and it too seeped
red down the length of her leg. Seeing it, the baby squealed to
her, but her mother was possessed with her fight reflex.
Something in the field had drawn her wrath.

It was the upright apes. They were a distance away, but the
baby could see they were different to the ones which had
browner skin and were sickly and lived in the village of little
peaks. There were two of these ones, fairer in colour and with
their second skins covering them more completely than their
browner counterparts, and more tightly. One stood behind the
other. The first held something long and thin in his hands,
which he cracked open and fiddled with, before fixing again.
The baby could see the energy of their movements; they were
healthy creatures, not like the others. They had full frames and
plump flesh. They were predators on the hunt. The one with
the long, black object propped one end against his shoulder
and raised the other. It was pointed at the baby's mother.

The giant, enraged form he was pointing at let out another
jarring roar before leaping from her fallen companion's side
and charging headlong toward them. The baby ran towards her

mother. There was no consciousness to it; she just started running for her. She was screaming. She knew she'd never catch her. At full flight, her mother was incredibly fast. But she ran for her. Screaming. Somehow, she knew what was about to happen.

With another almighty crack that thudded against the baby's flesh the stick in the ape's hands let out a cloud of white smoke. It didn't seem to have worked, the baby's mother kept charging. The two apes quickly ran out of her path, recovered themselves, and gave her another blast of the white smoke. Her mother ran on past them and the baby followed. She saw as her mother's feet buckled and she lost momentum. Stumbling on uncertain footing, her mother slowed her pace, and turned back to face her aggressors...

...the baby saw her face.

The bloody holes had formed, one above her eye, the other in her cheek. But the vengeful fury remained; like the red blaze of a giant forest fire, they roared silently at the two apes, before she raised her trunk and howled at them. Another blast startled the baby into dizziness and sent her mother recoiling. Her legs began to wobble, as the dead calf's mother had. Red fountains gushed from the wounds, but she didn't fall. A burst of strength fortified her, and she took a few paces toward the apes. Another blast stopped her still. She stood for a moment, swaying side to side, before she crumpled onto her belly.

The terror released the baby and sent her plummeting into a well of grief. She squealed as her heart felt crushed as though in the talons of an eagle and she ran toward the failing giant. The fury faded from her mother's eyes as the strength seeped from her body in the red rivers which coursed over her skin and she recognized the squeals of her calf. The baby pressed her face against her mother's and felt the warm blood cool as she touched it. Once more, that warmth that came from the inside filled her as her mother wound her trunk around the baby's and held her in close embrace, before a painful moan rolled out of her and the baby felt her mother's great trunk go limp in her grip as the warmth of her face left her own. Her head crashed down into the wet grass.

For a moment the baby stood shivering before her mother as the brown puddles flushed red and she lay with her mouth slightly open, jaw askew as it hung limply, her trunk curled in front of her face, the stillness in her eyes and of her body and the shining, flickering, pulsing signs of life gone from her body. Life seemed to leave her flesh in an instant. The wounds on her face stopped bursting blood with her heartbeat and it simply ran like droplets down the trunks of trees after the rains have ceased. Like the calf had been, like the buck had been, she was still. That nightmarish, awful, heartbreaking still that only the dead assume.

The baby knew what had happened, but she could not comprehend her grief. The great surge of fire and ice that exploded from her heart and pierced through her body all over was too much. She flung herself into the limp folds of her mother's flesh, seeking out the residue of her life, the warmth, a twitch, something, anything...but she was overcome with tears and she howled and cried. All at once, all of what her world had been until that moment was suddenly stolen from her smashed and destroyed before her eyes. The watchful gaze she knew first and knew best was gone. The warmth that kept her from the sparsity and cruelty of the open wilderness was gone. The calm and serenity that tempered the chaos and violence raging in every direction, every moment of every day for all eternity could no longer protect her. The world had fallen away from her and chaos had returned. She was adrift. There was nothing but this dead matter left of what was. All she could do was cry into it. Cry so whatever vestiges of life might have remained inside the corpse could hear her.

That all she could wish: that her mother was dead still eluded her comprehension. She only knew she was alone and vulnerable, and all she could do was cry out 'come back, come back...'

It was to no avail. No racket could cure what the apes had done. Apes the baby forgot about or didn't care about. She couldn't do anything against them anyway. She couldn't defend herself. She couldn't call on the herd, they were too far away. She could only cry to her mother.

'Come back.'

CHAPTER 5

'Did you see that, old boy!' Villiers shouted, excitedly, as he cracked open his smoking Holland and Holland 2-bore shotgun and let the two empty Schroeder and Hetzendorfer cartridges slide out and fall to the ground. 'Two brutes with three shots! And a tiger!'

Atkinson watched the young fool's arm go limp as he transferred the shotgun to one hand. The pain in his shoulder was just taking hold. His knees were beginning to tremble as well. Yet, the enthusiasm never left his face.

'I say,' Villiers finally said, looking questioningly at the monster gun he held in his shaky hand. 'Lucky you had that sidearm...I dare say this thing would have cut that tiger in two! Imagine, that beautiful fur, ruined!'

With a disapproving shake of his head, Atkinson touched the butt of the Remington which had saved their lives. Villiers had proven to be clumsy with his shotgun at the worst possible time; they were being charged by an already frazzled, two-hundred-pound Royal Bengal Tiger. Fortunately, he'd managed to keep his composure as...

The ring in their ears was dying down, and something else caught Atkinson's attention. A high-pitched, distressed wailing was issuing from beside the larger of the fallen elephants. He looked at Villiers, who was clutching his now doubtless throbbing arm, as the awful realization dawned on him.

The little elephant, not more than three years to his life, was curled up beneath his dead mother's ear, crying out toward the forest.

'What's that awful racket?' Villiers asked, turning pale.

'A baby,' Atkinson breathed. He pointed to the wretched little creature.

'But you said that the bulls didn't watch over the babies!'

'They're not bulls, obviously!' Atkinson snapped.

'You mean I wasted four shots on cows?' Villiers scoffed. 'Females? What good is that, old boy? Do you know how much these bloody cartridges cost?'

Atkinson took his helmet off and covered his frustration beneath wiping the sweat off his brow. 'Do you fancy chasing down the bulls, in your state?'

'What state?' Villiers retorted, defying himself to stand upright. 'I'm fit as a fiddle, old boy! I can't bring back the heads of two female elephants! I'd be laughed at!'

'Mister Villiers," Atkinson seethed. 'Can any of your friends tell the difference between a male and a female Indian elephant, just from the head?'

Villiers looked off into the distance, lost in thought. Then, as the idea popped into his head, Atkinson saw him alight again. 'Well, then. Shall we set back, and fetch a few of the rail crews to retrieve my prizes?'

'We'll have to take the little one with us,' Atkinson said, watching the calf nuzzle his mother's cheek. Silent, for the moment.

'What on earth for?'

'He's calling to something, Mister Villiers,' Atkinson warned. 'Either the rest of the herd will heed him, or whatever predators are within earshot.'

Villiers again fell into thought. Atkinson was beginning to enjoy the effect his simple reasoning could have on the young hunter. Perhaps having him for a supervisor wouldn't be so bad after all...

'I say!' Villiers finally declared. He clicked the fingers on his good hand. 'I'll bet that American chap would fancy a baby Indian elephant!'

'There you go, Mister Villiers, that's thinking on your feet!' Atkinson patted the young man's sore shoulder, eliciting a wince of pain. He hid his chuckle behind a wave back towards their guides.

#

When the baby's voice finally ran out and all she could do was sigh and sob, she became aware of the two upright apes watching over her. She was afraid of them, but the sorrow that hung over her heart fatigued her body to the point that she could no longer resist whatever they were going to do to her. As she curled up beside her mother's still face and rested her head on the limp, cold trunk, she stared back toward the forest. Some faint survival mechanism gave one last flicker of hope that the herd might come running, having heard her cries, and then extinguished. Despair melted over her in the form of wistful longing; she'd never be as big as the cows, never reach the size of her mother, never know her years or see the vistas onto which she looked. She would never feel the company of a bull or understand what it was that happened between them and cows. Her life was only her infancy. Already, it was over.

Tears ran heavily, and her breaths were stammered, but the baby felt no more urges. Her heart was as convinced as her mind that the two apes would, any second, turn their death stick upon her, and blast the life out of her. She lay still and waited for the agony she couldn't imagine.

The dead calf lay near them. Beyond him, the chest of his mother still rose and fell, ever so faintly, as life clung to her.

Buzzing sounds issued from behind the baby. She turned
and saw the flies accumulating around the darkening holes in
her mother's face. There remained just strength enough to
swat them away with her trunk, but they only whipped about in
circles before landing back where they were. The baby kept
swatting. She didn't want them there.

The apes had come closer. Their sudden presence right
beside her startled the baby and she retreated deeper into the
hollow of her mother's shoulder. A group of their darker-
skinned cousins had joined them, wearing their looser clothes
around their thinner frames. The two pale apes were watching
her with predatory intensity, while the darker-skinned ones
simply watched with blank indifference.

Beyond them, back at the trees, the baby felt for a moment
that the herd was watching, that they had followed her cries,
and come to save her, but had stopped just behind the forest's
edge, and was watching. 'Your mother died,' their scornful
looks seemed to say, though the baby only imagined them.
'You lost your mother.'

Of the two pale apes, one was elder and much shorter than
the other. He didn't carry the death stick, but for some reason,
the baby couldn't stop staring at him in utter fear. He stepped
toward her with assurance, before he turned toward the
darker-skinned creatures, and made a series of complicated

sounds at low volume to them. Immediately, the darker-skinned creatures began to move toward the baby.

She knew the elder pale creature was their alpha. He commanded them. She watched him, waiting for the death-blow to be ordered by him, and found herself growing frustrated that instead his darker-skinned servants merely surrounded her. She'd become impatient for the abyss beyond life. She just wanted to be blind to the accusing glares from the forest, deaf to the thunder of murder and immune to the heartache of living.

The darker-skinned apes spread out and crouched low. They advanced on her slowly, on light feet, as though the baby hadn't seen them, and they wanted to sneak up on her. She barked at them, as though to let them know there was no point in prowling, but that only made them jump back, then they advanced even slower.

She looked at the death stick in the young pale ape's hands and remembered how her mother had charged, and how he had responded. She felt a fever kicking up inside her heart, as her frustration and confusion sweltered, and she leaped toward him, screaming. Immediately, she felt the darker-skinned apes swarm her and a rough vine was suddenly looped around her neck. For a moment, the world was a blur of bodies surrounding her and hands touching her. She wanted to knock one over, to hurt one, but she couldn't decide which one to move towards. She screamed and darted about, feeling the rough vine getting tighter around her neck.

Suddenly, the darker-skinned apes parted, and the elder pale ape was moving toward her. He spoke very soothingly and slowly and reached one white, delicate looking hand out toward her. Her rage calmed immediately, though her heart pounded so hard she could feel its pulse on her burning tongue. The baby wanted to cower, to retreat to her mother. In an instant, she regretted her momentary lapse; now they were separated. The darker-skinned creatures pressed against her from behind and to her flanks, keeping her still, until the elder pale ape had his hand softly on her forehead. He made a low, sweet, shushing sound. She noticed, in his other hand, he was holding a long, thick, smooth and straight stick. Like the death stick.

She knew these were the creatures who changed their landscape to suit them and built structures with straight lines and parallel features. The baby didn't know how, but she knew they were associated with the giant, chugging snake that shook the earth as it rolled along two shiny tracks. They commanded it like they commanded each other, and now they wanted to command her. Fear held her so steady she could not but submit, while the elder pale ape continued to stroke her head with his little hand. He was speaking, softly and gently. But she couldn't feel any comfort. There were too many things too unnatural about these apes, from their second skins to their devices and tools, they had an aura of cruelty and alien aspect about them that made them feel like something from inside a nightmare, but the baby couldn't wake up and escape them. They were real. It just didn't seem possible.

She couldn't understand why they would kill her mother, then try to soothe and comfort her. The confusion of it was what froze her. She found mercy from the aliens, but she couldn't grasp why, or why they weren't eating her mother.

Finally, the monster relented his stroking, took a few steps back, and pointed his stick off into the distance. He barked some sharp orders to the darker-skinned apes, and they moved out, walking in the direction their master had pointed. The baby felt a firm tug on the vine around her neck, but she wouldn't budge. Her mother was just behind her. She turned and tried to move back toward the body. Another sharp jerk made her gag. She began to sob again. They wanted to take her away from her mother. Flies were gathering on her mother's wounds again; she had to clean them! She tried to run toward it. Another sharp jerk tore her off her feet. She staggered. The elder pale creature was near her again. She felt

a sharp thwack in her side that felt as though it tore right
through her skin. She cried out.

The elder pale ape had hit her with his stick!

The pain seared and simmered, and the baby cried. But she
understood the message. Another sharp jerk on the vine and
the baby followed the darker-skinned creatures. Through the
blur of her tears, she saw the giant, chugging snake waiting for
them far ahead.

The pale apes stayed behind, along with some of their
darker-skinned servants, and the baby felt a sudden surge of
panic that she was leaving her mother with them. She squealed
and shook her head against the vine around her neck. With
her trunk, she felt it out and tried to loosen it, but the darker-
skinned apes pulled and tightened it more and more.

Twice more, the thwacking sounds and the streaks of fire
slashed across her backside. The baby screamed and hurried
to catch up to the darker-skinned creatures who towed her
along with their vine. She looked back, tearily seeing the elder
pale-skinned ape standing behind her with his stick while the
younger pale-skinned ape watched the rest of his servants
working away around her mother's face.

The sight of the dead buck they'd found so many seasons
ago, his tusks torn out, flashed across the baby's mind, and

suddenly she knew the heinous ritual they were conducting. She bellowed with the eruption of fury and tried again to charge back. But she could not withstand the whips. It seemed to cut her to the bone, without ever breaking her skin, and though she wanted to protect her mother, her instincts refused to do anything but obey the tugs on the vine, for that was how she knew to avoid the pain.

Her mind repeated it, over and over, until it drowned out all but her complacent sorrow; avoid the pain.

Before long, they reached the giant, chugging snake as it sat still on its parallel tracks. The baby could smell the acrid scent of its breath, but up close she could sense its lifelessness. Its body was constructed of wood cut from trees, cut the way she'd seen the upright apes cutting wood from trees, and fashioned the same way she'd seen them fashioning their dens and structures. She could see that the head of it lacked eyes, a nose or a mouth. It was just a solid, black material that was hard and firm. They didn't get close enough for her to touch it. Instead, the darker-skinned apes led her alongside it, to where its long body broke into several compartments, all made of tree flesh, and they opened one of them up.

No blood spilled out. There was no life inside; it was hollow and dark. The apes rested the part of its hide on the ground, so they could walk it up, into the empty viscera of the beast, and with a few tugs of their vine they dragged the baby up with them. Inside was hot and dusty, she could barely breathe. The apes led her to the corner of the structure and tied the vine around her neck to a loop in the wall. Then, they left her and closed the body of the beast up around her, plunging her into darkness.

The floor was hard. She'd never felt anything so oppressively hard in all her life. The baby couldn't be comfortable, she couldn't even rest in her grief, which she felt was draining her of all her energy, even her flesh and blood. She wanted her mother. She wanted sunlight. Despairingly, she knew both were gone until these strange alien apes saw fit to return the sunlight, and nothing could bring back her mother. They'd taken her to where she could never be retrieved from. Gone into the darkness between dreams, or the eternity beyond twinkling stars. She hated the symmetry and straightness of her chamber. It made her sick. It didn't belong.

The baby curled up as tight as she could into the corner and tried to sleep. She wanted the refuge of sleep, the dreams in which her mother could return to her, or in which she could imagine that she'd never left the herd, or that the predator had never attacked her friend. She tried to wonder what had become of her other friends, but she knew they were probably playing. Oblivious. The cows were probably feeding. Still waiting for their alpha to return or, having replaced her already, gone off to find new feeding grounds. The thought broke her heart all over again; her mother should be missed! They should wonder what became of the baby! But she remembered how grief or worry had passed in favour of food and play, to return another day, when everything else was satisfied. She knew she could never get to them, to warn them or lead them to the upright apes, whose delicate bodies they would crush beneath their fury and strength.

So, she chased sleep. She chased dreams where she could be home with them all again.

CHAPTER 6

'Fine specimen!' Villiers gushed, as he rapped with an open-palm on the carriage that housed the little elephant. 'He must weigh half a ton already! What a mighty beast he'll make, eh, old boy?'

Atkinson shook his head as he watched Villiers stop rotating his sore shoulder to wipe the cascading sweat off his brow again. His face was bright red and blotchy, and he seemed worryingly faint. For that reason, Atkinson didn't have the heart to voice his suspicions that the baby elephant was, in fact, also a female. He was too frustrated, anyway.

The workers, who should have been laying railway sleepers, were busy hauling the immense tiger corpse into the carriage behind the elephant, having carried it across the fields in a canvas bag. Meanwhile, cotton-ball clouds littered the clear, azure sky.

'Fine way to waste a day's labour,' Atkinson said, staring skyward. 'We won't get another twelve hours like this for some time, I assure you.'

'Oh, what does the Company need saltpeter for anyway?' Villiers waved it off as he leaned against the edge of the carriage. 'Black powder is out of fashion and besides, they know they can make it themselves. By the way the old buggers in Deli swill on their brandy all day, they should be able to make enough to tide the redcoats over into the new century.'

The labourers managed to get the tiger up the ramp and into the carriage.

'You should have skinned it out here, taken the pelt,' Atkinson said.

'Nonsense, old boy,' Villiers retorted.

'No stomach for it?'

'I don't want to see it damaged.'

'It's more likely to be damaged while it's still attached to the animal, m'lad.'

'I'd just rather it be done back at the village,' Villiers said. He pushed himself upright and started walking toward the passenger carriage. Atkinson followed, slowly. The old veteran could tell the young lad hadn't the stomach for skinning his own kills, and likely had a paid professional waiting back at the village to do it for him, but he knew that suggesting such a thing would only bring denial of a more and more unbelievable nature. Besides, Atkinson had other business to attend to, if this "Colonel" of Villiers' was not a figment of his youthful imagination.

'So, of the sale for the elephant?' Atkinson began.

'I'm a fair man, you did your bit to help in the capture,' Villiers said, quickly and suddenly alert. 'What do you say to twenty per cent?'

'Fifty, of course, Mister Villiers, is all I'll accept,' Atkinson said.

'Fif... - Fifty!' Villiers halted, eyes wide with outrage. 'I shot both of those monsters down, I tell you and damn near lost my arm in the process. What, fifty? Good God, man!'

'What would that bloody tiger have done, then?' Atkinson said, raising an eyebrow.

'I'd have seen him before he pounced,' Villiers said, with a raised finger. 'If you'd only given me another second!'

'He wasn't giving any more seconds, m'lad,' Atkinson assured the youthful hothead. 'He'd have killed you with a swipe of his paw, and I'd have shot him and claimed the whole thing for myself.'

'I...' Villiers ejaculated, but quickly lost his train of thought. He looked back at the carriage for the elephant, as though it would give him some inspiration, then turned back, even more enraged. 'You cannot compare that bloody cat to two giant elephants!'

'The elephants would have left us alone, if not for you drawing the attention of the "cat", m'lad.'

'Those brutes were out for a fight, I tell you! I've seen that look in their eyes before!'

'Fifty per cent,' Atkinson cut him off. 'I might also resist reporting this flagrant expenditure of time and labour to Deli, old chap.'

The older man looked at the younger with the contented smirk of victory, as he held out his hand to close the deal. Villiers, though still flushed red with outrage, choked on his retort and begrudgingly shook it.

'Fifty bloody per cent,' he grumbled and shoved past Atkinson to get back to the passenger carriage.

Atkinson sighed, serenely, and walked at his steady pace after Villiers. The wetland before him shone beneath the radiant sunlight and the large scavenger birds circled the two giant bodies left out there. In seconds, the exposed remains were blanketed with buzzards. The workers had already loaded their ivory, much smaller than it would have been on bucks, onto the train.

#

A heavy chug startled the baby from her daze. Around her was darkness, broken only by thin shafts of light that shone through the gaps in the construction. The world buckled, slid, jolted and began to move. The baby felt sick instantly, her stomach felt like it was turning inside out, so she squeezed herself even tighter into the corner and covered her eyes with her trunk. She couldn't remember whether she was asleep properly, but she started to imagine the warm, soothing, gentle sensation of her mother's trunk binding her and protecting her in a loving embrace. There was a fresh, painful, bleeding wound whence the dream had been ripped from her and she cried, though she felt like she was out of tears. It hurts too much. Her mother, the grief, was like a noxious cloud that filled her whole body and swallowed her mind.

The chugging was rapid and constant. It kept her suspended between sleep and wake, at best, but mostly she lay there awake, moaning to try to ease some of the pressure that seemed to build inside her heart. It threatened to make her body explode. She knew the chugs mean she was being taken away. There was no more home. To where she was being taken, the baby didn't have the imagination to suspect. Something from a nightmare was all she could think.

As they gathered speed, the baby felt herself falling out of her corner. She tensed and tried to keep herself from rolling into the darkness around her. The shafts of light flicked on and off. She felt the distance between herself and her herd growing as the space they held in the hollow of her heart shrank painfully until she knew there would be nothing thenceforth but figments of her imagination. Brief moments of foolhardiness cut through her resignation and she stood and rammed the flimsy wall of the structure, but it only hurt her head. There was no breaking the planks. Even if she could, the vine wouldn't allow her. It was itchy against her skin. Growing frantic, she tried to pull at it with her trunk, but that only seemed to make it tighter. It became uncomfortable for her to swallow, it was so tight. She grabbed it in her trunk and tried to pull it off the loop on the wall but with each tug, she heard it crackling and tautening. It was not like the soft creeper vines of the forest; it was not like anything in the forest. Again, she knew she was dealing with something of manufacture. The apes made this vine and it seemed to grow stronger the harder she pulled on it.

A sudden force knocked her to one side. She screamed as her body hit the wall, but the thought that she might fall out encouraged her growing fever. She threw herself against the wall again and again, until it hurt too much to continue. Then the despair set in again. The baby liked the fits of madness that overcame her, even though her attacks on the walls left her tender and sore. Her delirium kept the heavy feeling in her heart at bay, and clouded thoughts of her mother which seemed only there to torment her as a constant reminder of what was lost forever.

Her belly groaned, and she made a mess where she'd been curled up. The baby tried to move away from it and curl up in the other corner, but the vine wasn't long enough. The delirium set in again. She charged the walls, she screamed, she tried to loosen the coarse vine around her neck. Then the pain again. Then despair. She moved as far as she could from her corner to cry. She pressed herself against the wall and the floor. Amidst her sobs, she heard the chugging begin to slow and felt the inertia pressing against her flesh begin to let up.

The sickness in her belly made her insides flush and pulse with hot discomfort. The pressure was building up and slime filled the baby's gullet. She whimpered with each shallow breath. For a while, it felt as though she might pass out, though she welcomed the thought because then she could sleep. Instead, like the taut vine, her belly tensed painfully, and she vomited onto the floor.

The baby gave up on corners and just flopped onto the hard timber, dizzy, exhausted and swirling with the black, poisonous mists of grief and sorrow inside. She heard her little voice calling for her mother, pathetically. There was no point in giving volume to her cries; she knew only the upright apes would hear her now, but her mind could think of no other form of release, so she called and called under her breath, as though to conjure her in a dream or vision. The baby turned on the floor to face the direction of her herd, or what she thought was close enough. She wanted to face her mother, as though it would somehow bring them closer. She wanted to crawl into the corner of the carriage that was closest to her, but the vine kept her, so she crawled as close as she could. It felt like a betrayal that she couldn't. The ice of guilt prickled up her spine and added frost to the storm of grief.

She'd just gone. She'd left her mother. The thoughts beat against her and chilled her more and more. The baby hated herself. She wanted to rip through her skin and flesh and escape from herself, or for the world to open up beneath her and swallow her, crush her, or just drop her into nothingness.

'How could you lose her?' she kept thinking to herself, on behalf of her herd and out of vengeful hatred. She thought of her mother, lost in the ether, crying to her the way the baby had cried to her. 'How could you be the one calling for help? Look at what you allowed to happen!'

Her fault. All her fault. Now the baby heard her mother's cries and could do nothing to help her. She cried back, but her mother couldn't hear. She howled apologetically and wished she could feel the reproach of her mother's trunk again and be forgiven.

Outside, the chugging stopped. A hideous screeching sound issued from somewhere below and the inertia suddenly pressed in the other direction, which snapped the vine even tighter around the baby's neck. She wished it would snap shut and cut her head off, so she could crawl out of herself and disappear into the nothing that had consumed all the life in her mother's body. But all it did was make her more uncomfortable. Again, she was left to the mercy of the apes.

Another series of sharp jolts and clangs and the baby felt that she was still again. She could hear the apes outside, making their complex sounds and moving about, shouting sharply at each other or half-mumbling. With two clicks, the wall opened up again, and the light and heat of day fell upon the baby and dazzled her eyes and scorched her skin. Two of the darker-skinned apes entered. The delirium sizzled briefly beneath the baby's surface; she wanted to leap up, charge them, knock them over, and run away. But her body was flat with exhaustion. She felt flaccid and wobbly. Even as one of the apes undid her vine from the wall, she could barely muster the strength to stand...until the elder pale ape appeared at the door, carrying his stick. The baby remembered the horrible, stinging, searing pain he could cause with that. She quickly staggered upright and laboured herself alongside the two darker-skinned apes toward the opening in the structure's wall.

The baby's stomach growled, and her mouth tasted salty and bitter from the vomit. She was out of breath before she got down the ramp and the sight of what was before her startled her.

Other darker-skinned apes were waiting for her on the solid platform of wood, while around them seemed to be a living, breathing entity of structures, both skin and solid tree wood. They stretched on as far as she could see, swallowing the openness in their streets and avenues. The baby knew she'd seen this before; she was inside one of the villages that the upright apes made from the forest and wilds around them. There were structures and sections of ground flattened out into streets. There was symmetry and straightness everywhere. The skin structures sat on grass that was short and level, without tufts or ragged edges. No grass seemed able to live at the feet of the solid structures. But all around were creatures. Mostly the darker-skinned apes, but amongst them walked four-legged creatures with muscular little bodies, stumpy legs and long ears, which laboured beneath mountains of bags and objects lashed to them, as darker-skinned apes guided them around. The apes used other animals as carriers! Some even carried them! The baby saw other creatures, like the little stumpy ones but tall and elegant, with coats of fur that shone, carrying the apes around, as they sat on their backs! They were the pale-skinned apes, who rode them, all males, all watching over the others with disturbing authority in their little, piercing eyes. But everything seemed alive. The structures had apes moving around inside them, the baby could see them through glossy holes in the walls. The crowds flowed through the streets like blood through veins. Machines, like the chugging snake, buzzed and moved and performed functions the baby could not comprehend.

A few taps to the baby's backside reminded her of the awful fire stick and she quickly stumbled down the ramp to the platform, where the darker-skinned creatures again surrounded her. They guided her down another ramp to the dirt, where there was water. The baby lost all awareness of anything but her intense thirst and plunged her face into it, guzzling the stagnant, slimy water down her throat. The apes escorting her waited.

She stopped for a moment and checked to see where the elder pale ape was. He watched, but the stick was by his side. He was patient for her. So, she drank more. She felt the sickliness in her stomach doused and the acidity in her gullet wash away.

Then, those icy spikes of guilt pierced her spine again. The baby stopped drinking and looked at the elder pale creature. He watched her calmly. There was no malice to him, no cruelty; just simple neutrality. It unnerved and confused her. He raised his stick. The baby shivered with fear and quickly started walking, right into the hip of one of the darker-skinned apes. She didn't hit him hard, so he didn't move. He didn't even flinch. He shoved her back, weakly. She howled with distress, tried to make him understand that the pale ape was going to hit her if he didn't let her walk.

The pale ape muttered a few orders and the darker-skinned apes led her again. Her stomach rumbled with hunger, but the guilt had taken hold again, and all she could think of yet another betrayal of her mother. She'd run away with these apes, who'd slaughtered her mother, and now she took water from them. How she hated herself! She started to dawdle. The darker-skinned apes tried to pull her rope and push her flanks, but she was lost, searching the mists of grief to find the spirit of her mother again, searching for the one who could hold her accountable and punish her. She felt the stick tapping against her back leg. The baby ignored it. The next she felt of it was another searing crack and she screamed and caught up with the darker-skinned apes. Her senses were shocked. The mists cleared. The guilt vanished. It hurt, but she felt right that it hurt. She deserved to be hurt.

The baby was led through the middle of the alien world which continued to bustle and flow all around her. They passed the solid structures quickly and soon were weaving through a jungle of canvas dens, where the darker-skinned apes lived. The baby could tell they were mostly female. They toiled around and remained close to the dens made of skins, where they put objects on top of open flames and dropped plants and roots into the water that boiled inside them, or they dipped wet second skins in and out of water that they held in objects made of the strange, stone-like substance that made up the head of the chugging snake, or they watched over their children, who either stayed by their side and helped them, or played in the grass.

Firstly, the baby noticed the children. They knocked each other over, found mud and threw it at each other, they chased one another and yelped and squealed and tackled their friends to the ground. Amidst all her fear and grief, all her confusion and beguilement at the state of this strange place that she couldn't believe existed on the same plane as her own, the baby felt a confronting fondness swell inside her, for here were little apes that were just like her friends and played just the same way.

Secondly, she noticed the adults. The females, like the cows of her own species, kept vigil over their little ones, but the severity of their gazes narrowed, and the relaxed posture of their weak, malnourished bodies tensed when they set eyes on the elder pale ape who walked behind the baby.

A number of the children ran towards the baby. They were screaming and waving their arms in the air. She recognized the innocent gesture of play but was startled anyway. She had seen their innocence, but she also had observed the gentle side of the elder pale ape while he'd watched her drink and the soothing tone he'd used to try to talk to her. This monster who had killed her mother was speaking to her in a lullaby. She knew how deceiving these things could be. She knew the rules her instincts set out for things in the wild did not apply here. These apes were something else. She was afraid, but she soon learned that the children's mothers were more than afraid. As would the sentries of her own herd, they leaped up and grabbed their children as they ran or called some of the larger ones back with a series of short, sharp yaps. The baby recognized the tone and tremor of fear in their authority. They were afraid of the elder pale ape as well.

The baby began to wonder why. Had he beaten them all with sticks? There seemed so many of them. Why were they so thin and frail, while he was so strong and fit? Then, she remembered how he'd allowed her to drink. So, he controlled the water. He controlled the food. They feared him because he could take it away. He was the law of nature. But how? How could such a frail little animal have such power of mercy and cruelty? How did he make the tall creatures carry the pale apes about? How did he make the stubby creatures carry things? Then, she realized she too was under his control. She was walking because he wanted her to. She was walking exactly where he wanted her to.

The frosty guilt crept through her again.

Gradually the skin structures around them spread out and before long they were walking through an open field, through grass that had been permitted to grow with its normal rugged and wild chaos. The baby took a deep breath. Beyond the darker-skinned apes which surrounded her, she could see the space through which they walked, the trees far beyond and even the rising hills in the distance. She could feel the soft caress of the evening breeze and sense the openness and freedom that were just beyond the escort that guided her and the terrible barrier of pain that the elder pale ape controlled by his hand. She spread her ears and listened to the symphony of the wilderness; the birdsong, the rustling treetops, the swishing of the grass they walked through and the chorus of insects that came alive as the sun reached for the far west where the hot earth kissed the clear blue sky. She dreamed of her kind lumbering through it. Herds where calves played in the safety of their mothers' gazes. She dreamed of that warmth again. Into the vastness, her heart tried to pull her, but the back of leg still stung as a reminder of the consequences and besides, there was danger out there and she was far from her herd. There would be no escape for her. She wished she could have the energetic delirium back, but she was carrying the weight of despair but resigned to her fate. So, all that she saw and felt, she took in. She knew she'd need to reach into it later. She knew, in her heart, she'd find her mother there.

In the field was another structure, but it was not entirely enclosed like those back in the village. Whole sections of walls were missing and let the air blow through, but a thin roof kept the extremity of the sun out. It did not have wheels or tracks like the chugging snake and wasn't accessed via a ramp. She figured it didn't move. Around it was a large patch of grass sectioned off by a perimeter of wood fashioned into three planks supported by thick stumps, so the baby could see through but never climb out.

They wanted to keep her. This was her herd, so they thought. Had they killed her mother to steal her baby? She didn't understand why creatures would kill other creatures, but to eat them. She certainly couldn't comprehend why they would take a calf like her and keep her alive. She wasn't tall and regal like the creatures they rode on, and she doubted she could carry all the weight she saw piled on the stumpy creatures.

The baby knew, as well, that she would get bigger as time went by. Stronger. Then, she could carry things. Her heart broke to pieces all over again as they led her through a section of the perimeter that swung aside to allow them access, as it dawned on her that here was where they intended to keep her. All her life. This was it. She wished she could die. She wished she could escape herself and be as a bird; just flap right out of her own mouth and leave this body behind to fly out into the infinite sky and find her herd again.

There was another vat, this one full of dried greens, and the baby ate. She was too hungry to resist. She sobbed as she ate as the shame burned and roiled under her flesh. But she was hungry. She was awful. A weak, sad creature who couldn't even make herself die to escape her captors.

By the time she finished eating the apes were all gone, and the sun had reached its most intense angle of the day. The baby had become so heavy she couldn't hold herself up. She wanted to get out of the sun, so she went inside the structure and flopped onto the dirt floor. She cried until the purgatory of sleep and wake hovered in her mind. She searched it for her mother, but there was nothing there. Her mother had left her.

'I deserve for her to leave me,' she huffed to herself. 'I am awful. Evil. How could I?'

A horrible, awful, evil creature.

CHAPTER 7

'My luck!' cried Villiers, as he paced around the drawing room of his station. 'This is just my luck!'

Atkinson couldn't help but chuckle as he flicked some of the drying mud caked onto his boots off onto the fine Turkish carpet. The young man was marching about in an office built from what was practically slave labour, adorned as it was with fine finishes, polished English furniture, elegant paintings of the Indian landscape predicting the success of their railway line, and staffed with English chefs stocked with French claret and all the luxuries he'd find in his London tenancies, and all the while he cursed his ill-fortune. Less than a year in this place, the seasoned veteran thought, and Villiers would break. He'd be home in time for next Christmas.

'Is it insane, or what?' Villiers demanded. He'd stopped in front of Atkinson with a childish stomp of his foot.

'Hm?'

'The elephant, man!'

'Oh, no. Not at all,' Atkinson waved him off and took a brandy balloon from the decanter tray offered by the liveried servant. 'Distressed, that's all. The train, you know, they don't understand motion. They're not used to riding in vehicles.'

'Well, how much longer will it be like that? Can't you beat it, until it gets up and does something?'

'It's too much afraid of me already. Give it another few days.'

'Now they tell me "the ivory isn't worth much"!' Villiers said.

'You're lucky they had ivory at all,' Atkinson said. 'Females don't tend to grow tusks.'

'Oh, blast,' Villiers said. He'd stopped at his drawing desk as Atkinson had spoken, and hunched over it, hands clasping either side, angrily. 'Sunday!' he called.

'Sanday,' Atkinson corrected, into his brandy.

The servant returned regardless. Villiers quickly struck a match, and melted wax over the fold, before stamping it with his seal. He handed the finished letter to the servant. 'Very careful with that.'

Sanday obediently bowed and carried the letter from the room.

'Almost forgot the purpose of the bloody infant,' Villiers snickered.

'Ah, the Colonel,' Atkinson mocked.

He wanted to say more but Villiers was taking measurements off the map. A rare enough sight that even sarcasm was not cause enough to distract him.

'The skies are pleasant, these past two days,' Atkinson said instead.

'Hmmm,' Villiers stared down at the map, brow furrowed. 'We have lost two good days, though. And it seems we're quite a few miles behind schedule. I can see why the Company brought me out here, old boy.'

'Well, sir,' Atkinson said. He downed his brandy in one gulp and stood upright to light a cigar. 'What would the Company's prodigal son have us do?'

'I forgive your insolence, because of your experience,' Villiers said, smiling with a sudden gravitas Atkinson hadn't expected. 'I want all the workers on double-shifts until the rains come back.'

'We shall have to apply to increase their wages,' Atkinson suggested.

'Absolutely not!' Villiers spat. 'Where is that written down as law? They're paid what they're paid. How is it calculated, hourly?'

'No, sir,' Atkinson said, almost disturbed. 'Weekly.'

'Well, then, why worry? They still work the same number of weeks a year, we're just increasing the time they spend each day working.'

'Very good, sir,' Atkinson said. He took a shallow bow and hurried out the door to relay the order to the station masters. It happened quickly and unexpectedly, but Atkinson suddenly felt a swell of respect for the newcomer.

Perhaps they'd get everything done after all and still have time for an elephant.

#

A soft nudge to her belly woke her. She'd lost the will to dream, but still somewhere on the threshold of every sunrise the baby's mind wandered back to the hours spent sleeping in the fields or plains or the valleys with her herd, and waking to their presence all around her, all beneath the loving shadow of her mother. Every time she woke, reality had to dawn again, and the baby would swing from a silent surge of rage, then plummet back into the deep abyss of despair that kept her heavy against the enclosure floor. So heavy that she'd watched the days go by, watched the sun rise and fall, watched the stars and the moon alight the night, watched the clouds come and the hammering torrents of rainfall, without the will to run into any of it. There it was, wilderness, as close as she thought she'd ever come to it again, and yet her heart couldn't be moved. Like a ball of granite inside her, she couldn't lift it.

It was night still, unusually luminous. A full moon. A few of the canvas structures glowed with amber firelight from within, while the eerie, still lights that burn soft yellow at night inside the solid structures in the distance were all out. None of the apes, pale or darker, were to be seen.

Another nudge and the baby became suddenly aware of the horse standing over her. She shuddered with fright, at first, but staring past the big, soft, fuzzy nose into the huge, innocent eyes calmed her instantly. All the while, she'd shared the enclosure with the tall, regal, muscular looking creatures that carried the apes on their backs or towed them in wagons on wheels behind them. They mostly galloped about in the paddock or stayed at the back of the enclosure where their hay was. They ignored her. This was the first time one of them had approached her. She tried to read the big, brown, vacant eyes staring at her, but couldn't figure what it wanted.

Then, as she watched, it nudged her again. Same spot, right on the belly. She reached up with her trunk and touched the side of the horse's neck, where the long hairs of its mane streaked across the fur. It shook its head and clopped one of its hoofs on the floor.

A dark-skinned ape boy always came to feed and wash them and remove the waste from their part of the enclosure. He'd remove the baby's waste as well but wouldn't touch her. He'd talk to all of them in his language, which was far too complicated and noisy for the baby to understand, but she'd picked a few sounds and managed to identify what they belonged to, over the days. Horse was one. Wagon was another. The skin structures were tents, the solid ones were houses or stations. The chugging snake, which had come past as he'd been talking once, was a train.

The horse, one the other hand, was far too basic for the baby to understand. He snorted, clopped his hoof, or shook his head. That was it. No growls, no trumpets, no signs with a trunk because he didn't have one, and no signals with his ears.

'What do you want?' she touched the horse's neck again.

It shook its head, clopped. She gave up, wanting to be alone, to sleep more. She covered her eyes with her trunk.

Softly, ever so gently, she felt the soft, fuzzy snout touch her side again. She looked up again in frustration, but suddenly caught something in those eyes that had meaning to her.

'Get up.'

'I don't want to.'

'Get up!'

'I can't! It's too much! I'm so scared and sad and alone...my heart is broken.'

'...get up.'

Unable not to giggle, the baby heaved up to her feet and tried to force herself to remain sad and angry by trumpeting at the horse. It took a few bounding leaps backward and joined the others at the rear of the enclosure, where all of them stared, dumbly, at her. She couldn't help but stare back. Their big eyes held no secrets and had a strange way of melting her defences. She felt as though they were looking inside her, albeit without comprehension.

'You don't understand what's happened to me,' she tried to signal them. The horse which had woke her, a brown one, took a few short steps toward her, stopped its foot, raised its upper lip to show its buck teeth and gums, and made a long chortling sound.

'You're up,' was all the baby could make of it.

She tried to copy the gesture; she raised her trunk and tried to show her gums. The horse stepped a little closer, its head held low. It came close enough for her to touch it with her trunk.

'I'm so sad,' she tried to sign, shunning it. But she couldn't deny the warmth she felt towards it. The simple happiness she felt beginning to glow inside her. She couldn't allow it. Couldn't feel okay. Had to be sad. Had to wallow in despair. The baby turned away and went back to her spot, but before she could lie down, she saw the horse was still standing there with its head held low. The baby lay down and turned away. With her eyes closed, she heard the horse's hoofs clopping slowly back to the others.

More than sorrow and coldness filled her. She felt the scorn she'd just dished out. In the darkness she missed the warm honesty of those vacant eyes. Before the tears came, she was upright again. The horse had joined the others at the haystack and was ignorantly chewing on golden strands as though it had forgotten everything already. The baby moved back toward the floor, but her heart raged inside. It had felt light for the first time in days, and there she was trying to burden it with weight.

But she deserved it! Didn't she?

The baby found herself meekly approaching the horse. 'I'm sorry.'

The horse kept eating. The baby got closer.

'I'm sorry.'

The horse couldn't see her. She took a few more steps and gently prodded its belly with her trunk. It looked at her, chortled, and stomped its foot.

'I'm sorry. Please understand me.'

It turned, chortled, stomped its foot, and held its head low. The baby reached up and touched the horse between the ears, right on the tuft of mane that hung over its brow. Its whole body shifted, and it made a satisfied grumbling sound.

Suddenly, it pulled its head away and charged out into the paddock, crossing over the baby's spot in a single bound. It galloped out over the grass, kicked up clumps of dirt as it went, then stopped, turned, and gave her another chortle and shake of its head. The baby moved to the edge of the hard floor of the enclosure and looked out into the oily grass, which seemed silvery blue in the ample moonlight. A soft breeze cut across and made it rustle. She could resist no more. She ran out after the horse, which took off and galloped right across the paddock. The baby followed but could only watch as the tall creature shrank away from her vision and crossed to the far fence in a few seconds, while she could only amble in comparison. The baby squealed out to the horse, which she could just see pacing around the far end of the paddock, while the forest stood tall and the canopies wafted in the breeze behind it. She heard her own cry echo back at her. As though carried by it, the horse was quickly back to her. It galloped up, nudged her side and ran back toward the enclosure. She turned and ran after it, able to keep pace this time.

She gargled joyfully. It was holding back for her!

'Come play with me!'

'I will! We'll play together!'

The horse stopped and leaped toward her, stopped short and with a jerking motion leaped back again. The baby raised her trunk and hooted affectionately. It did it again, kicking up mud toward her. The baby hurried over to the water troth, filled her trunk, and sprayed the horse. It leaped back under the sprinkle of water, shook its head, opened its lips to show its teeth, and chortled in a way that the baby knew was laughter. She quickly filled her trunk again and sprayed. The horse leaped to one side, then back again, cutting through her brief shower of water which cast a silvery, shadowy rainbow in the pure moonlight.

The horse ran again, slowly this time, allowing the baby to run alongside it. It stopped and darted back. She shook her trunk and followed it.

Another warm breeze caressed them. It blew the horse's mane up and rustled the grass and distant treetops again. For a moment, with the dull glow of the firelight in the tents going out one by one and the forest edge, the village, the train, and its tracks and the distant mountains all faded behind the veil of night, the baby was happy again. For a moment, she could forget that there was any danger. That monsters surrounded them, held them captive, and used them. She just had fun with her new friend.

They didn't even notice the red streak alighting the eastern horizon, announcing the new day.

CHAPTER 8

Two perfect days were enough, or so it seemed Providence had decided. Atkinson awoke to the dull grey sunrise, heard the deluge thundering down on the iron roof of his cottage, and rolled over in frustration. Life beyond the window was completely lost behind the sheets of water rolling down the glass. Thunder rumbled behind a brief electric flash.

He pushed off the sweaty sheets and sat up to stuff his pipe. His servant, whom he'd nicknamed Simon out of frustration over the pronunciation of his real name, entered with a broad smile. He brought Atkinson's tea tray. 'Good morning, sir.'

'For you, perhaps,' Atkinson coughed, gesturing the window. There was a note on his tray. He picked it up and read, with a heave of fury, that Villiers had ordered in new labour from Bombay. 'That damn fool!'

'What is it now, sir?' Simon asked.

'Not you, Simon,' Atkinson said. He screwed up the note. He didn't like to admit it, but he was still uncomfortable touching on the topic of dead labourers in Simon's presence. Other Indians were fine to him, but Simon had access to Atkinson while he slept. 'I'll have to rush breakfast. Have my clothes laid out immediately.'

Simon bowed and hurried to the servant's wardrobe. Atkinson emptied his pipe into the tray, rushed through his breakfast and quickly dressed. He pulled on his raincoat and, with the note, ran across the outpost to the stationmaster's lodge, where he'd seen the lights on through the last three rainless nights. Even with the raincoat, he felt his clothes soaked through and his skin wet before he took three strides, and the note liquified in his hand. By the time he arrived at Villiers' door, he felt as though he had swum there.

One day, he thought, a consulate position in Uganda. Enough servants that he'd only ever have to leave to go on safari. He knew he'd proven himself to Her Majesty, many times over, but in India, he was in the Company's hands. They put him in the rain, only they could get him out.

'Good morning, sir,' Sanday said when he finally opened the door. Atkinson pushed past him and stormed into Villiers' drawing room. He shoved the door open but stopped short of the Turkish rug.

The young man was pale and intensely focused on his drawing board, with dark rings around his eyes and a slight tremor in his hands. 'Good morning, old chap!' he said, without looking up.

'I must urge you to reroute the replacement labour, sir,' Atkinson growled.

'Fifteen men died of exhaustion on my railroad, old boy, I can't do without them.'

'Sir, there was a terrible outbreak amongst the labourers in Bombay late last year. We can't risk it infecting our station.'

'I know about the outbreak,' Villiers said. 'Have Ogilvy relight the distance markers within the hour, there's a good fellow.'

'The rain, sir.'

'Use the kerosene lamps. We'll work in the rain.'

'Sir, the outbreak!'

'Symptoms took three weeks to set in, for Bombay, I read about it.'

'So?'

'So, we'll be done in two,' Villiers said. 'Provided we can replace dead labourers quickly. We'll be gone before the plague starts knocking them off, old boy, don't fret.'

Atkinson wanted to speak, but his words got lost.

'Better to work in the rain,' Villiers was muttering. 'Fewer predators are on the prowl in the rain, are they not, old boy?'

'I suppose so, sir,' Atkinson admitted, then turned to get the supervisors up.

'Oh, Mister Atkinson!' Villiers called, stopping him. The young man tapped a manila envelope next to his drawing board. 'Down payment from our friend the Colonel. I'd hate to have to send it back...how is our elephant?'

'I haven't checked for some days, sir,' Atkinson said. Before the days of pristine weather, and the resulting push to get as many miles of train line down as possible, the decision to shoot the elephant had been floating about. 'Shall I check today?'

'Get Ogilvy up first,' Villiers said, darkly.

Atkinson dawdled in the rain, figuring he was wet as he could be anyway, and got Ogilvy to work. With the elephant on his mind, he trudged out through the village toward the paddocks to check on it. He bit his lip in frustration, anticipating the elephant to be laying down in the corner of the stables still, if not dead from its own neglect than close enough to it.

An opaque mist streaked across the field and slightly obscured the stables. One of the horses, it looked like Bailey, came thundering out and galloped across the grass. His hoofs sent up muddy spray and his body cut through the rain at such speed that a trail of droplets trailed ins his wake. He cut hard about and galloped back to the stables, where he stomped his foot and shook his head impatiently. Atkinson picked up his pace, perplexed by the sight.

Then, right in front of him, the little elephant emerged, and shook its trunk joyfully and greeted the horse with an energetic hooting sound.

Atkinson paused. His mouth hung open and quickly filled with rain. But his spirits lifted quickly; at last, the elephant's spirits had lifted! He turned and hurried toward home to get his cane.

#

The baby gasped for air as she hurried back to the shelter of the stables, trembling with exhaustion. The horse galloped up behind her and seemed not to have exerted itself in the slightest. But she was feeling their playtimes growing longer as she slowly recovered her strength and she was buzzing with pleasure to feel the refreshing hammer of rainfall all over her skin.

The horse continued to stomp its foot and snort impatiently while she drank and ate. The baby didn't know how to tell him she was tired and needed a moment's rest. As far as he was concerned, she realized, they were one and the same species; she was just smaller than he was. He expected her to have the same energy as he did. Though she was catching up, she knew she'd never keep pace with him. She just wished she could tell him so.

As the baby chewed on her hay, she heard the click of the latch on the gate. The horse leaped from her side and hurried to the back of the stables to rejoin the others. The sudden movement frightened the baby. She looked back at him and saw that he was staring out into the rain. His eyes remained as placid and open as ever, but his body had changed. His muscles seemed to have tightened and his movements stiffened. He'd suddenly become cold and timid.

The baby turned back, and a cold shiver ran through her. The first thing she saw was that stick. Immediately phantom pains flashed across her back and legs where she'd been struck, flooding her with painful reminders of what it could do, and she held her head low in trembling, terrified subservience.

All she knew to do was to avoid the pain. That became the instinct that took over all others. Avoid the pain.

The ape holding it was showing his teeth to her and staring. It was the elder pale-skinned ape. His second skins hung heavy from his body with the weight of the water they'd absorbed, but still, he stood upright and imposing.

He tapped the stick gently against his ankle and said a word she recognized. 'Come.'

She wanted to. She wanted to avoid the pain. But the baby couldn't reconcile moving toward the stick with doing so. She couldn't lift her feet off the floor to walk. Her heart began to thud sharply. Tears stung her eyes. He tapped his ankle again. 'Come.' She moaned at him, trying to make him understand that she was too afraid of him.

It didn't matter. He made a clicking sound and stormed toward her, and in an instant, she felt the searing touch of that stick against her backside again. The baby screamed and hurried out into the rain. The elder ape's voice barked behind her.

'Halt!' he said. 'Halt!'

She didn't understand. The baby was running from the pain, but the pale ape ran faster, and suddenly the stick was right in front of her face. She tucked her trunk in and pulled her head away. The elder ape tapped her flank to stop her running away. She froze. The terror seized her. She held her head low, the only way she could express to him that she was subservient and didn't want to be hit again.

He tapped his own ankle again. 'Come.'

The baby started walking. He walked beside her. She flinched with the flashes of fear that shot through her heart every time she felt that stick brush against her back leg.

95

'Halt!' he said. The baby froze. She knew what each word meant now.

He tapped again. 'Come.'

She kept walking out into the paddock. The elder ape hurried around to her other side and touched the stick to the side of her face. She kept walking, not knowing what that meant.

'Turn,' he said. A foreign word to her. He said it a few more times. She hurried her pace. Suddenly, the whole side of her face exploded in paralyzing pain. She squealed as the world throbbed before her eyes. Her jaw buzzed with agony. 'Halt!'

The baby stopped and blinked through the tears and trembled with terror.

He tapped again. 'Come.'

She walked. Then, yet again, she felt the stick pressing against the side of her face.

'Turn,' she turned away from it. He didn't hit her.

They walked, and they walked. The rain softened and eventually dulled to a drizzle, the ground was squelching beneath their feet and the mud swallowed the baby's feet up to her ankles, but still they walked. Beneath the heavy grey clouds, the world plunged quickly into darkness and still, they

96

walked. The baby learned what 'Turn' meant so she could do it with only a gentle touch on her ear from the stick to indicate which direction. The elder ape walked her in countless circles until she was dry in the mouth and ready to collapse. He stopped twice, both times he took one of the horses and rode it off into the village, allowing her a little time to eat and drink and rest. But he was back quickly, and the baby would resume walking.

In darkness, he finally left without a horse. The baby defied her crushing fatigue to hurry to the water troth and drink heartily. Her stomach ached with hunger, so she ate quickly, thinking that the ape would return. She didn't like the hay. It was coarse and dry and didn't keep her full like the green food she got in the wild used to, or her mother's milk would. But she knew she'd never taste that again. So, having eaten, she felt little more energized than she had before, and waited for the ape to return.

Time passed. He didn't come. The baby's eyelids grew heavy. She hadn't had time to grab her usual quick naps between playing with the horse and being forced to walk around the paddocks with the ape. But she didn't dare drift off now. The fear of being awoken by the slash of that stick kept her alert.

Her body couldn't hold her. She lay down but remained determined to stay awake. She knew for certain that if the elder ape came back and found her sleeping, he'd beat her. The baby blinked hard and bit her tongue to keep her eyes from closing. She couldn't hold it off. The darkness swept in and took her without her even noticing.

When she did wake, it was slow and laborious. She couldn't remember waking with such difficulty; like her eyes had plastered shut in her sleep and she couldn't move them, or her brain had shut down entirely, and needed blood to pump through it to bring it back to life. She raised herself up with a groan, the lethargy gripped her like weights latched to her limbs and body. It was daylight. The baby had never slept so long in her life, to go from night to day. It was not her species' way.

The horse wanted to play again. The baby didn't want to hurt his feelings, so she tried to frolic with it in the still mushy ground, beneath the cream-coloured morning sky. The air felt still and heavy as death, every breath was long and difficult, and walking through the light fog felt like trying to walk underwater. Still, it wasn't long before the horse hurried back to the stables in fear and left the baby to the elder ape, who returned with the stick in his hand.

'Come,' he ordered when he reached her, and they walked in the paddock again. The baby was so sore, every motion ached and ground beneath her skin, but the fear pulsing and pounding through her heart kept her walking, even though she had to gasp for air. 'Halt.'

Through the mists, the forest's edge peeked. The baby could see the giant trunks of the trees standing guard against the openness of the fields and the village beyond. There were no creatures around. In the distance, the birds chirped, and the monkeys screamed, but nothing showed itself. The baby had not seen any animal but those the upright apes commanded, but for the faint silhouettes of birds high overhead, since she was brought to this place. It didn't make sense. There was always life where she was from. It only felt more isolating. While they walked, the baby felt as though the land had broken off around her and the elder ape, which left them both alone and adrift in the sparkling clouds that coloured the night skies beyond the stars. Impossibly far from home, from anyone, and with this cruel, heartless creature that did things that no creatures do. It killed for the sake of killing. It tortured. It enslaved. It used pain to coerce. The more the baby observed and became aware of, the more horror she felt rotting inside her at the thought of the upright ape, particularly this elder one.

They turned away from the forest and walked. Then, turned again, and walked. Then, turned again, and walked. Then, the forest again.

The baby could daydream. What her mind could conjure for her had been both a source of torment and relief, so she was careful when she chose to retreat into it, and careful not to go so far that she couldn't avoid the pain of the stick. She began to imagine the enormous, lumbering grey bodies of her herd moving along the forest edge, harvesting the greens of the undergrowth or stripping the lower branches for their calves. She fantasized about calling to them, catching their attention, and having them charge up to the paddock. The fences would be nothing against their weight and strength. They'd smash through the wood and charge the elder ape down. He'd strike and swipe with his stick, but it would be useless against the thrashing of their trunks and stomping of their feet. She imagined them ripping his fragile little body off the ground and slamming him into the mud. Trampling him. Smashing his bones and grinding his organs into jelly. Turning him into a pile of red pulp.

Hot rage began to pump through her veins and abate the icy fear that gripped her. The baby drew strength from it. She was small now. But she knew one day she'd be bigger. Where would this ape be, with his stick, then? She'd make him walk around in circles first before she tore his body to pieces.

'Halt!' he called. She stopped. Her veins ran cold again.

He stood in front of her eyes and started gesturing her. The baby trembled, eyes squeezed shut, waiting for the lightning bolt of blazing agony to shoot through her flesh again. But it didn't come. She slowly opened her eyes. She saw his broad features, his silver-coloured hair, his sharp little nose, and his thin, stiff-lipped mouth. The crown of her head was roughly level with his chest. He held his head back, and his eyes were squinted with authoritarian annoyance. He was raising his hand to his chest and lowering it. The stick was gripped in his other hand. But she didn't understand. He tried again. The baby's heart raced. She didn't know what he wanted, but she knew the pain was coming if he didn't get it. He gestured again, and the baby saw his frustration was making his hand tremble. She panted, crying, and was seized by jolting panic. She turned her face toward the stable and cried out for her tall companion. Immediately, she felt the horrible cane slash across her ear. The searing pain rang out inside her skull, and her vision blurred for a moment.

When she regained her senses, he was standing there still, gesturing just the same. The baby shrieked pathetically, pleading for mercy, or some kind of an explanation. But he only raised the cane again, holding it across her front. So, she stayed quiet. Her ear was burning, like tongues of flame were licking at it. She studied the gesture. What could it mean? Panic began to spark through her. The baby didn't understand. She didn't know what to do. But he continued holding his hand before him, raising and lowering it. The cane was ever at the ready. She saw the hand that gripped it tighten. The knuckles flushed white. The baby didn't think. She never made a decision. All of its own, her trunk shot out before her. She grabbed at the cane.

The elder ape withdrew it and struck her hard, right across her trunk. She cried and quickly recoiled. He didn't stop. He stepped in and struck her across the face. The baby closed her eyes, screaming as the red lashings of electrifying pain burst through her head, trunk and face. She curled back and crouched on her hind legs. Crying.

It stopped. The burning, throbbing pain persisted, but he stopped hitting her. She heard herself wailing and forced herself to stop. With a tremor in her heart, the baby knew her tall companion was not coming to help her.

Afraid that she was making him impatient, the baby slowly opened her blurry eyes. He was standing before her, stick held down by his side. Her skin felt as though it had been torn through, but she couldn't smell blood. She was trembling, crouched on her hindlimbs, head bowed subserviently. Both of them were stinging.

The elder ape curled his lip and ran his eyes over her thoughtfully. The baby read that he was thinking. His shoulders shrugged, and his eyebrows raised. He gave a short sigh.

'Come,' he said. The baby walked.

CHAPTER 9

Atkinson smiled proudly as Villiers approached, torn away
from his work at long last by Sanday and the stable boy, both
of whom followed him. Sanday held his umbrella up against
the unrelenting drizzle.

'Henry, old man,' Villiers called, as soon as he got close
enough. Atkinson bit his tongue. 'Is that my elephant, up and
about?'

'More than that, sir! Look at this.' Atkinson said. He turned
to the baby elephant and tapped the rim of his boot with the
cane. 'Come.'

The elephant started walking.

'Halt!' she stopped. He quickly moved to her front. 'Sit!'

The baby crouched on its hindlimbs and sat as would a dog.
Atkinson raised his hand before her face, and she lifted her
trunk and eased upright, her two forelimbs waved free in the
air.

'Marvellous!' he heard Villiers say.

'Down,' Atkinson said, and the elephant eased back onto its
feet, standing naturally.

'Just in time, I say, just in time,' Villiers said. He was nodding his head and smiling excitedly.

'You tell that Colonel that this was all in less than fourteen days! It learns remarkably quickly, I should say.'

'How long does it normally take?' Villiers asked.

'Well, I don't rightly know,' Atkinson said, looking at the elephant to hide his embarrassment. 'I've not done this with an elephant before. But I dare say it takes the average calf more than two weeks to pick up all that!'

'Will she respond if I try?' Villiers asked. His hand reached out for the cane in Atkinson's hand.

'I don't see why not!' Atkinson handed Villiers the cane and stepped out of the way.

'Come,' Villiers said.

The elephant didn't respond.

'If it's not going to listen to me, it might not listen to the Colonel, old boy,' Villiers said, but as he did so, he missed the elephant walking away from him. Atkinson quickly gestured the young man's attention back to the creature. 'Halt!'

It stopped walking.

'Excellent! Brilliant!' Villiers cried. The elephant ducked its head, shivering.

'It doesn't recognize those commands,' Atkinson said.

'I'm not giving it commands!' Villiers said, waving the cane erratically.

'Here, give me the thing, before you cause it to panic!' Atkinson said. He snatched the cane back from Villiers. 'It seems to be a touch neurotic. If you give it commands it doesn't understand, it starts to get finicky.'

'You're talking about it as though it has emotions, old boy,' Villiers said, as he stepped back under Sanday's umbrella. 'It is just an elephant,' he turned to Sanday. 'How far off is the freighter?'

'Monday morning, sir,' Sanday answered.

'Excellent,' Villiers declared. 'I'll even concede that you've earned your fifty percent, Atkinson, old boy. Well done. Well done indeed.'

'Leaving Monday?' Atkinson said. He tapped the elephant's flank with the cane, gently. It flinched in panic. 'Time flies, hey? I should like to have seen what more we could teach it.'

'Judging by the way it shivers and cowers, it's due for a breakdown anyway,' Villiers said. 'I'll send a wire to the

Colonel with the commands you've taught her if you'll write them down for me, old boy, so he can be satisfied with his purchase at least until we're done here, and long since moved on.'

'Oh, I don't think it's all that bad,' Atkinson said. 'Time, m'lad, it's still a young beast.'

'If you don't want your money, old boy I'll keep it, but the elephant is going on Monday.'

'No, of course,' Atkinson said, and he turned away from the elephant. 'I merely conject.'

'You can start them packing down the village today,' Villiers said. 'We're on schedule to move to Bhagalpur by Wednesday. I want a whole new labour force. This one's infected.'

'Yes, sir,' Atkinson said. He hurried from the paddock to relay the orders.

#

The baby stood still while the younger pale ape inspected her. He didn't have the stick, nor did he have the elder ape's aura of serene menace, but she could see he had a greater command of the servile darker-skinned apes. No escort had carried a rain-sheltering device for the elder ape, whom the

107

baby had heard referred to as "Old Boy". The younger, she heard "Sir" applied to twice. So, Old Boy and Sir were the pale apes that controlled the darker-skinned apes, kept them sick and hungry, probably beat them like they did her when they failed to perform their silly tricks. She looked at the ape holding the rain-sheltering device. He seemed healthier than the others, but what did that mean, really? Had he endured the starvations, the beatings, and the pointless meandering about in paddocks longer than the others, and earned his place in the violent hierarchy? All thoughts the baby knew gave her feelings of anger and resentment, both of which cultivated a sleeping but aggressive fury inside her for the pale apes. But she swallowed them, deep down, hiding them. She couldn't let any pale ape see them yet.

Sir inspected her for some time, then turned his heel and walked off with his servant following behind him. The exhaustion finally set in, as the strain of discipline was allowed to subside, and the baby hobbled back to the stables where she lay down and watched the misty rain obscure the village beyond the fence posts.

She didn't realize she'd began to doze, when the baby found the soft muzzle of the horse started nudging her side again.

'I'm so tired,' she sighed.

'Get up,' the horse nudged her.

'I'm tired, and hurting,' she tried to express. She touched his leg with her trunk. 'I love to play with you. I love having you for a friend. You make this bearable. I love you. But I can't play now.'

She smarted over her thoughts. Could she love anything, since her heart had been so completely torn to pieces? Could so broken a thing ever love again? She didn't know. Nor did the baby know where the thought came from. She only wanted to make the horse understand that she appreciated him, and didn't mean to scorn him, and that expression 'I love you' fit perfectly.

She petted the horse's head again, without standing. Love had meant protection. In the wilderness she could remember how frightening the sparseness was, how dark the forest undergrowth, how things could hide in dark shadows, waiting to pounce. Love was the wall of flesh that the cows of her herd made around her and the other calves when they sensed such danger was near. A sensation without contact. Security while naked. Strength while weak. It was the unspoken assurance that she was never alone. Never exposed. Never vulnerable. The reminder that she had a home.

The baby petted the horse. 'I love you.'

Whatever went on in those big, innocent eyes, the baby couldn't tell, but the next thing she knew, he was easing himself down onto the floor beside her, his legs tucked under his powerful body, with his head rested across her back. For a moment she was teary-eyed. Then, she was asleep.

It was an open plain with long, yellow grass softly swaying in the sensuous warm breeze. The lonely trees spread all the way to the lips of the powdery blue sky, mottled with wispy clouds. In the distance, the silvery cliff sides kept silent vigil over all the world. The baby felt the soft earth under her feet and the serene comfort of knowing where she was and what she was. Gone were any thoughts of sticks that burned like fire or apes that walked upright. She forgot about walking, about stopping, about sitting or rearing up on her hindlimbs and waving her trunk in the air. She was just a free spirit, out in the world she belonged in, and never for a second thought she'd been taken out of it.

All around her, everywhere she went, she felt the watchful gaze of her mother. She couldn't see her; no matter how fast the baby turned, rolled or looked about, the shadow of her beloved protector, from which she drew life and knew love, was just beyond her periphery. But the baby knew her mother was there, and that was enough. She squealed with delighted as she frolicked in the grass. She growled low, so her mother would come after her, follow her as she ran through endless openness, towards lonely trees that stood since before her, and would long stand after her, and the mountains beyond, which had watched the land itself form and reform, and which saw the passing of time so infinite that the lifespan of any living thing was but the blinking of an eye. The rivers brought water to her as they had for generations before her and would for generations more. Nothing could change anything. It was the way it was, and so it would always be.

The hard floor of the stables surprised her, when the baby woke again. She'd been there for nigh countless days, but for a moment, she didn't know where she was. With a cold shudder it dawned on her and the baby curled up to cry as her heart roiled with sickly grief all over again and she realized the world in her mind and the love in her heart wasn't real.

Night had fallen. It had been another strangely long sleep and again the baby's head pounded, and her mouth was dry. She didn't want to get up just yet, though. She felt too weak. So instead, she lay there and cried.

...then, a soft, wet nudge to her side. The baby looked up into those staring eyes and her own flooded with tears all over again. She wrapped her trunk around the horse's leg and led herself close, then sobbed into his fur. She felt his nose touching her back and the top of her head. At last, it seemed he understood.

Daybreak came, and the baby's hunger and thirst became too much to ignore. The horse followed her as she hobbled out to the troth and drank, before going to the haystack to eat. The hay, as always, made her dry again, so she drank some more and, sure enough, no sooner had she finished than the horse was dancing about in the paddock, stomping his foot and chortling again. The baby couldn't help but be moved. Even giggle. She needed the lift in her heart. After all, the elder ape would no doubt be on his way.

They played together as the sun rose without the colourful drama of the past few days, but gently bathed the world in its brilliant glow to signify another turning of the season. They stopped to rest as the day grew hot and both needed shelter and water. They stopped for naps and short periods of sleep. They played some more. The elder ape didn't come. Night fell again. They played until fatigue took them. Another unnatural sleep overcame the baby. She didn't dream but did wonder if the sleeping patterns she'd adopted in captivity were influenced by the horses, or they too had been thrown off what was natural to them by these strange, artificial confines which were made of nature, but were sickeningly unnatural.

She'd never slept in such large blocks, that night seemed too brief. With her herd, they'd stop for quick naps here and there, whenever the mood took them, or their surroundings accommodated them. They didn't even lie down. But those little naps were getting harder and harder to snatch, and instead all her sleep was being lumped together. It was uncomfortable to go so long without food or water and took her much longer to recover from. The frustrated baby couldn't understand why it was happening!

Another day came and went, much the same as the last, and without the appearance of the elder ape. As they played together, the baby began to notice the children of the darker skinned apes, whom both of the pale-skinned apes referred to as "natives", were gathering along the fences and watching them. At first, they frightened her. She couldn't understand why they were watching so intently, bearing their little teeth. Then, during one of their breaks, she saw one of the boys half hanging over the fence as he began to wave one of his forelimbs in the air, like her calf friends would their trunks once, in a lifetime that was beginning to feel vague as a distant dream. Sensing the innocent fragility of the children, the baby shook her trunk in response. Other children started climbing the fence and waving. Each time, the baby would wave back. Before long, they started making noises at her that sounded chaotic and frightening, but they did it as they waved their hands and showed their teeth, so the baby felt that it was safe to wave back and hoot joyfully at.

The horse seemed ignorant of the natives. He didn't want to join in their waving, he just wanted to keep playing with the baby. She would join him, until he'd gallop off too far for her to pursue, having forgotten about her limitations, then she'd go back to the crowds. She didn't know what, but there was something she began to like about their attention.

As she went to get her big sleep after yet another day of playing and being watched by children, the baby went to sleep buzzing with excitement for another day. She never forgot the ache in her heart, and it never went away, but she had found a joy that could temper the agony. If life was to go on like this, she thought, it wouldn't be so bad. But as the soft blue morning twilight greeted her eyes the next morning, the baby heard the click of the gate and saw Old Boy approaching, his stick in his hand and a heavy looking device strapped to his hip.

'Good morning, then!' he said. 'Come!'

CHAPTER 10

All the pain and suffering this monster could inflict flooded back to the baby as she marched out into the paddock again for another pointless session of walking about, making poses and turning left or right. Only this time, the children had gathered at the fences again. She forgot herself, for a moment. Delirium swept in and seized her, and she saw them as the calves she'd grown up with, as fellows of her that she could call on for help, and she trumpeted to them with her highest distress cry.

The response was a swift slash from the searing stick to her thigh. She screamed out, her heart pounding painfully. The children kept waving and cheering. It was a moment of horrifying abandonment that filled her with that old chill of loneliness, that void of isolation, that ice of grief. The baby caught her breath and started walking.

'Halt!' the order came just as quickly. She stopped. The baby felt the stick touch her left ear. 'Turn!' she turned right. Her eyes passed the faces of all the smiling children who kept waving their hands at her and cheering, despite her suffering and stopped on the gate, which hung open. Beside it stood Sir, his servant, and the small team of natives who'd lashed her and stolen her from her mother's side in that nightmare that felt so far away when she played with the horse and was so immediate now. 'Come.'

The baby walked towards them. She could see the gate was open for her and she was being walked out and knew that last time she was taken suddenly it was to never be returned to where she came from, but still, she did not look into the stable to see the horse one last time. She felt the dark shadow of parting aching in her heart. She felt the tingle in her spin that assured her that love was again being ripped from her life. But the baby couldn't bring herself to deviate even a little bit. The fear of pain overwhelmed all. She passed by the stables without looking into where she knew her best friend in the whole world was standing, watching her go, his innocent, vacant eyes fluttering with bewilderment. The baby didn't look back.

At the gate, she felt that awful vine, that "rope", around her neck again. The natives tugged at her and she went with them out into the fields. The children swarmed her. She couldn't breathe. She felt their hands on her and their bodies crashed against her, they shoved bits of hay and grass at her mouth and splashed water over her trunk. The baby, terrified, just stared ahead and followed the rope, knowing Old Boy and Sir were just behind her. She couldn't understand why the children were shoving food at her, but she knew they were getting some kind of enjoyment out of it. They liked to watch her suffer with the same energy that they enjoyed watching her play with the horse. The thought haunted her. They were no less cruel and monstrous than their elders. They didn't care about her at all, they were just amused by her. Nothing else.

While the children swarmed her all the while, they retraced their steps back through the town toward the waiting train, and only as the houses began to flank her in solid rows did the baby finally realize that she wanted her horse companion to know of her. She bellowed with all her might, frightening the children a few paces back. A sharp thwack from the stick reminded her of her loneliness. She kept walking, up the ramp and back into the cavernous interior of the train carriage.

Before she was tethered to the wall again, the baby turned and looked back over the village, into the piercing, little eyes of Old Boy and Sir, and back toward the stables where her horse friend had probably already forgotten her. A faint light in her heart hoped bitterly that he wouldn't. That he'd remember her for as long as she'd remember him.

Then, she was closed in again. The chugging started. The jolting, the clanging, the squealing, and the train was carrying her along its tracks to whatever awaited her next.

#

The baby endured the ride until her delirium felt like it would never cease. In fits, she beat against the walls until it hurt, then fell to sobbing on the floor in between. Finally, she found solace in standing away from the walls and swaying gently, rolling her body from side to side, almost matching the buckling of the train as it rolled along its tracks. The baby found that doing that seemed to even out the distress of such close quarters, of symmetry and straight lines, and of the racket and the steam and the uncertainty and the grief, all of which seemed to hammer into her from all directions. Swaying her head lulled her into a sleepy state, in which she could escape into her imagination. She wanted her to see her mother, but forcing the image never worked. There would be times when she'd hover in the limbo between wake and sleep, and suddenly her mother would be there, in every detail, every wrinkle, every sag, every streak of colour through her eyes, even her smell and her comforting presence. Those moments would take her by surprise, and the baby would cry for her. But when she wanted them, when waking life became too much, and she'd want to escape into her mournful memories, her mother would never come. Not even the sight of her. Only when the baby swayed her head and forced out all the horror around her, she found herself coming close to her mother. Like a cloud billowing over the drought-scorched earth, but never quite releasing its rain. Still, the baby kept trying.

Suddenly, the floor kicked the baby over. She stumbled and hit the wall that leads the carriage along. The train jolted, rattled, and finally came to a stop. Already a foul smell wafted in through the loose boards of the carriage; like the rotting corpse of the buck they'd found in the field, yet somehow unnatural. It was acrid and stagnant. The baby knew she was smelling things that were not from the earth but created by these apes. The harsh miasma of manufacture was bitter and cruel, even in the smells it generated. Then, the door opened. The baby gasped and took in a whole lungful of the foul atmosphere.

An impregnable looking forest of structures, all different sizes, shapes and colours, all in rows and packed so tightly that air didn't seem able to escape the thin ravines which ran between them and were flooded with filthy, diseased-smelling and sickly-looking life. Like rivers, the bustling kaleidoscope of natives walked up and down the streets, while horses drew carts and donkeys carried loads amongst them. Between the buildings, the sky wasn't visible. The baby looked on with awe and terror beyond her most vivid nightmares; she'd never imagined such a growth could have formed and lived on her earth without her knowing until she was brought to it. That such decay, such filth, such crowded chaos, all held behind those bland, straight, symmetrical walls, could have been formed on the same ground on which she walked, could have polluted the same air she'd breathed all her life, startled and confused her. There was nothing natural here. She was already dizzy when the natives untied her from the wall and walked her down the ramp, onto the platform, then onto the streets.

Then, the baby walked amongst it.

Like thick undergrowth, the bodies enclosed around her. The heat was blinding. The sky ceased to exist, except for a thin blue line directly above, flanked by the tops of the structures. Horses clopped by with their eyes covered and with things in their mouths and natives on their backs or carried in wagons behind them. Donkeys wailed pathetically as they were whipped the same way the baby had been by Old Boy. Shallow trenches that ran alongside the roads reeked of omnivorous excrement. Children sat beside them, wasted to their bones and with their second skins hanging off their withered frames, holding objects in their hands and looking, pleadingly, at passers-by, who seemed ignorant of them. The baby had never seen an adult creature of any kind walk past a needy child without the slightest regard before. Amongst them walked a few of the pale apes, anomalies amongst the madness; they were straight, healthily plump, symmetrically clad in their second skins which looked clean and bright. They, in turn, ignored the natives around them.

Breathless, the baby tried to hurry along, but she didn't dare depart the escorts entirely. She quickened her step until the rope felt taut around her neck, and just hoped they would hurry along to keep up with her.

They passed through gardens of dead plants and dead fish and dead animals, all spread out across benches behind which the natives stood and called out to those who walked past. Every now and then, someone stopped, took a plucked root or dead animal, exchanged something small for it, and departed back into the crowds. For a few terrifying moments, the baby couldn't perceive a way forward. All she saw was a great encirclement of ape bodies, pale and darker-skinned, no passage through or around. She stopped and wailed. A firm tug of her rope brought her along, deeper into the crowds. She couldn't move without brushing against their oily second skins or their frail-feeling limbs. Some smelled strongly of bitter rot. Like the wounded calf had smelled, only without visible injuries.

Thicker than the miasma, the dense heat or the bustling crowd, though, was the overwhelming aura of misery. Everywhere, radiating off every being both four-legged and two, but for the pale apes. They moved amongst it all with the same serene cruelty and casual command that Old Boy had carried himself with, in the paddocks. The baby shivered with fright every time she saw them.

Finally, they broke through the columns of buildings and stood on elevated ground that overlooked wooden floors that extended over water that reached all the way to the fuzzy horizon. The baby had never seen such a sight, and it daunted her. The water was flat and calm, and all different shades of green until it reached out into the haze and became striking deep blue. Enormous machines, built of the same black, hard material as the trains that floated out on the water, were scattered across unfathomable distance. The baby could see from the giant leviathans that were silently tied up to the wooden platforms on the shoreline that they were enormous; enough to cast a shadow over an entire herd of her species. Those out on the water spewed the same dark clouds out of their chimneys as the train had.

It smelled of smoke and stagnation, and all across the wooded shoreline, the apes swarmed about, moving from floating machine to floating machine, wheeling wagons or carrying goods in their arms. The escorts dragged the baby down into it. She walked out over the wooded shoreline and could hear the edges of the giant water slushing and gulping not far below her feet. She could see apes of all different colours and shades, not just the pale or the brownish. There were stark white apes with fiery hair on their heads and faces, tan coloured apes wearing tight second skins and even a few that were browner than the natives, even black-skinned. Some looked at the baby as she scurried past them, head held low with her trunk tucked up under her chin, but she tried her best to ignore them and to keep walking with her escorts. She knew where she was going. Though it terrified her, she didn't want to be out amongst this. All around her, the sense of malaise and disease had taken a sharp turn toward danger. She sensed a threat from every ape she passed, regardless of their colour.

Between the towering machines, the wooden floor thinned and stretched out, and down one such corridor, the baby was taken. They found their way to a ramp, beside which a tan-coloured upright ape, wearing what seemed like too many layers of skins for such heat, was waiting. They exchanged a few sharp, complex vocalizations, and the baby was taken up the ramp.

Ahead, she could see that the entrance to the bowels of the giant mechanical beast was pitch dark, smelled hideous and yet, for the first time since she was put onto the train, natural. It was a wafting emittance of odours, many of which she recognized. There was the bittersweet stench of predators and the sweet, nutty smell of herbivores. Excrement. Water. Hay. Other things, she couldn't recognize. Then, closer to the small, black hole, she began to hear them. A maddening symphony of pain and suffering; cries from mighty bellows to wretched shrieks, all echoing off the hard, fleshless walls of the giant stomach in which they were imprisoned.

The baby trembled all over. Her eyes watered with fear. But there was no other way; she entered the hot, terrifying interior of the machine.

CHAPTER 11

Little glowing bulbs gave the cramped insides of the machine its only light. They emitted the same unearthly yellow as the lights that shone inside the houses. It took some time for the baby's eyes to adjust. She was walked along a narrow strip of rugged, hard material that she recognized the touch of from the head of the trains. All around her was screaming, such a convoluted racket that she couldn't tell one species from the next. She began to think they must have one or two of everything that lives in the whole world inside this giant monster's belly. As the rope tugged her along between the natives, the bars on the faces of their enclosures came into view. The baby could see the little boxes that held the creatures secure. Then, she began seeing the animals inside as they passed; a little monkey gripping the bars in his hands and feet and shrieking with fevered fury; a wolf that paced up and down, beating its head against the hard walls of its enclosure; a black panther, with its shiny, oil-like coat and striking green eyes full of calculating, predatory malice, laying against the bars so its skin bulged out, and licking them with its rough, spotty tongue...

...the baby trembled with fear. As they walked, she felt the knees of the natives behind her knocking against her backside. A sharp tug of the rope pulled her back between them, but she couldn't focus on keeping pace. The madness all around was disorientating. She forgot which foot to step with, which way they were going. She knocked her face against the back of the native in front of her. He yelped and jerked the rope. She squealed. A few sharp kicks came from behind. The baby was losing her breath. Her chest grew tight and her eyes watered. Screaming...the constant screaming! Her skull was pounding and felt like it might split up and fall to pieces. Her spine ached. She tasted bile in the back of her throat. Stiffness cramped up all her muscles. The natives grew angrier. She felt their feet and hands whacking against her skin and the rope tugging hard at her neck. All these animals, doing these unnatural things! What sort of wolf paced up and down, beating its head on things? Why were monkeys alone? They were never alone. Why was a black panther licking inedible bars? What was wrong in here? What was this place? Noises bounced off the walls, and everything seemed to be shrieking and crying all around her all the time, like a constant storm of suffering bombarding her as would the wind and the rain.

Then came a roar that turned her blood cold. Her survival instincts drew a sharp and sudden focus from her, and she was able to walk with the natives until they brought her to one enclosure that was still empty. But they also brought her closer to the source of the roar; beside the enclosure directly

opposite hers, there hunched and drooled and stared an
enormous tiger.

The baby stared back at it, at once haunted and hypnotized
by its huge, cruel, piercing eyes, the size of its body which filled
up the whole enclosure, and the fangs which peeked out from
the panting mouth. A mouth big enough to wrap around the
baby's neck. Its huge chest heaved up and down as it seemed
to struggle to breathe, just like her. Its huge paws flexed against
the oppressively hard floor. The baby realized it wasn't
interested in her. It was staring, but only because it was inside a
cage, and she was outside. It didn't look at the apes, it just
stared at the baby. She couldn't read its expression, that
predatory cruelty was constant, but she could see the signs of
fever and even fear all over its body, because they reflected her
own; the tightness of her muscles, the cramps, the inability to
breath without panting...

A sharp kick sent hot pain through her side. She squealed.
The ape with too many skins on, hit her with a thin sheet of
wood and she hurried into her cage, wanting relief from the
intense stare of the tiger. The bars closed in front of her with a
resonant clang and the lock clicked shut. The natives reached
in, pulled the rope off her neck, and in an instant were gone.
The ape in too many skins scratched his sheet of wood with a
little twig and began to walk off in the other direction.

Just then, the tiger bellowed again. Its forelimbs shot forward and its paws wrapped around the bars, and it started biting at them to no avail. The ape with too many skins paused in front of it, completely unmoved by the sudden ferocity, and kicked one of the paws. The tiger howled and pulled back into the cage, humbled.

Then, the ape was gone.

The tiger curled up against the back wall with its ears folded against its head and huffed. The baby blinked in disbelief. The upright apes could even subdue tigers. Those fragile looking, light, little creatures could command the greatest predator in all the world. She had witnessed examples of their power, but nothing like this. They'd only subdued her mother by killing her. This tiger, they didn't have to. They just had to put it in a cage and kick it. All the time she spent afraid of Old Boy, the beatings, the walking, the performing poses and tricks for him, came flooding back, and the baby felt an uncomfortable but certain swell of pity for the animal that she had learned to fear and hate.

'I understand,' she tried to communicate by raising her trunk up through the bars, tentatively. The thought of a passing foot kicking it kept her tense. But she wanted to talk to the tiger. She wanted peace with it, she couldn't quite understand why. A formidable ally? Or just another colleague in the life of suffering and servitude at the hands of these forces beyond nature, the upright apes? It didn't matter. Her heart ached to get a response from the tiger. It became the most important thing in the world. She wanted it to respond. 'I understand.'

It looked at her. She took a half-step back but held her ground. The heat was suffocating, coupled with the tension it was almost too much. But she held her ground. It was just looking. It looked cruel because it just looked that way, and the baby knew she had a fear of it that was innate and unconquerable, so the baby gave it a little hoot. 'I know you.'

The tiger opened its mouth and made a strange, guttural noise, then flopped its head against the wall of its cage so the baby couldn't see its face anymore. Then, it just lay there. The baby pulled her trunk back in and stepped backward, nothing more to do but sit in her painful discomfort. Her head was aching more and more, she thought it was going to explode! She wanted the tiger back. She wanted so much to talk with the tiger.

In the cage opposite hers was a strange looking animal. It was black, with tufts for fur puffing out from all over its fat, bulbous body. It wasn't like the other animals; there was something serene, even content, about its almost happy looking face and calm eyes. The baby couldn't believe what she was seeing; something so calm and peaceful amongst all this! But there it was, laying on its back with its head propped up against the back wall of its cage, watching her as though half asleep. She raised her trunk and shook it gently, lest it hit the walls of the cage. The roof was just above her head and the walls just far apart enough to give her room to sway. But the creature just stared back, scratched its belly, took a deep breath, and let out a short sigh.

It was a sloth bear. The baby knew their docile ways, but with the cries and the screams reaching such a pitch that she began to feel as though the giant machine might actually shake to pieces from the vibrations and let them all fall into the deep, forbidding depths of the water, she couldn't comprehend how an animal could not be terrified, disturbed, or at least lonely enough to want to engage with her, like her horse friend whom she knew for sure by now was gone from her life forever.

'I'm scared!' she wailed to the sloth bear.

It just stared at her dumbly, and took another exasperated breath, as though the shrieks and cries were becoming a mere annoyance.

'Please, I'm so afraid!' she found herself wailing. Hyperventilating, she tried to turn around. Tried to see something other than the cavernous viscera of the machine, but her face hit the wall of her cage. She couldn't turn. She found herself joining in the chorus. Screaming, nonsensically.

Not to the ignorant sloth bear, but just out into the ether. The baby heard herself be drowned out, but only screamed louder. Her legs grew weak and wobbly as jelly. But laying down was so hard! The cage was too small! She cried loudly as she eased herself down on her belly, and felt warm liquid running out under her that started to itch as it dried. She'd wet the floor of her cage, but she didn't care. All she wanted was to hear some kind of response to her cries or at least hear them over the cries of everything else.

'Quiet!' she heard the tiger's moan. She never heard such a sound issued from a tiger before, but there was no mistaking its meaning. The predator was upright again, hunched at the bars, staring at her. For a moment, it looked so strong and powerful that fear shot through her like a bolt, and she whined to her sloth bear for fear of how close he was to the beast. But she wasn't screaming. The fear froze her voice. The tiger, meanwhile, simply rolled itself up again and seemed to fall asleep. Clarity came over her like a blanket, and the baby thought about why the tiger might have done that. Why silence her, when the whole forest was howling?

The baby prepared herself to try to talk to the tiger again since the sloth bear wasn't interested, but a sudden rumble burst through the belly of the machine. A deafening noise shook the whole ship. Then, a gentle swaying. Easing, up and down. They were moving. It was one minor comfort for the baby; she was right about these machines being transports, like the trains, and that meant that like the trains they had destinations, and once they reached that destination she would be let off. This nightmare would end.

But when? And what would become of her amnesty with the tiger, if the upright apes let them all loose? Did the upright apes care if the tiger attacked her?

The screams escalated. The pain in the baby's head throbbed and felt blinding. Her stomach churned. The walls were so close! The swaying was so deep and constant and unrelenting! The roof was so low! The sickly smell of urine crept into her lungs and finally, she vomited. Her bowels gave out soon after. She had to stand up to keep clean. The pulls of motion went on and on. The screams would not stop. The baby fell into a state of delirious horror. A horror that would not stop.

From her breathing felt a haziness seep gently through her whole body until a hot flush shot over her and she passed out.

The baby felt the vibration of a thousand screams shooting through the darkness of her consciousness. She felt the hard floor beneath her and the hot air around her, and the swaying of the machine roiling through her, while sickly feelings swept about inside her like wraiths. Then, a blast of cold, and the baby shuddered awake with the sound of her own scream.

Two upright apes stood at the bars of her cage. One had a device; a cylinder with a pole on top which he pumped up and down, plunging it in and out, and that made water shoot out the end of a hose, like her trunk, but smaller. Cold jets of water sprayed her face and swept her mess across the floor until it clumped up at the back of her little cage. Satisfied, the ape heaved the cylinder aside, then threw a vessel of water into a little drinking trough that ran along one side of her cage. Most of it spilled over the floor.

Then, he threw a handful of dried greens through the bars of her cage, and moved along, pulling a trolley behind him. The other just watched. The baby heard them move from cage to cage, doing the same thing. She saw that the tiger was already wet, as was the sloth bear, but while the tiger stood upright, panting and glaring coldly after the apes, the sloth bear remained in the same recumbent position in which the baby had found him, staring into nothing. The tiger had already eaten whatever it had been fed, the baby could see the dried flecks of blood on the fur of its chin. But the sloth bear hadn't touched his branch of nuts and leaves.

The baby was hungry and felt desperately weak. The act of raising her trunk to wipe the water from her eyes had stolen her breath away. It was so hot the water made the air seem steamy and thick. The baby's eyes itched from tears she'd cried in her brief sleep. Water dripped on her skin from the roof and felt had and heavy, and loud, like explosions. But the machine was quieter. Much of the screaming had died down. Most of the animals must have been hungry. But the sloth bear wasn't eating or drinking.

That gave the baby an idea.

It dawned on her like a dark shadow. Cruel and heartbreaking, like a hard realization, rather than a means to an end, but the baby knew it was what she wanted. She didn't want to be the plaything of these apes anymore, or be their slave, or even go to wherever they were taking her. She'd lost her mother, and her best friend was back in the old land, there was nothing better coming. The ache in her heart assured her. It felt so easy to decide. As though she could just roll over and slip right in and be gone. Nothing. Just a dead form of useless matter, without the throb nor flicker of life, just like her mother and her friend. She wanted to be like them. If she didn't eat or sleep, she would be.

The baby decided not to eat or drink.

The pain in the baby's body, the faintness in her head and even the cloudy stinging in her eyes began to feel welcomed and relieving, because she recognized them as symptoms of dying. She even growled at the tiger, asserting her lack of fear.

'Come,' she said. 'Close your jaws around my neck until I'm dead and eat as much of me as you want. I don't care. Where we're going, I don't ever want to get there. Never ever get there.'

The baby backed into the cage and waited for the looming darkness to finally take her and set her free from this world of manufacture and of cruel, upright apes. This unnatural phantasmagoria she'd been swallowed by. She hated it. Life had become unbearable.

Screaming was issuing louder again. The other creatures had eaten and were back in their delirium.

Time seeped by so slowly. The baby wondered which sway would be the last, and how much they would slow down before she finally sunk down and never came back up again? She stopped thinking about the screaming. The baby wanted her mother. She wanted to be thinking of her, when the final darkness took her and let her sleep forever. She closed her eyes and tried to remember. Soon enough, the baby found herself swaying from side to side, forcing the image with all her might, trying to remember the lost images of tusks and watching eyes, the dreamlike emotions stirred up by a watchful shadow, the protective sentinel that would never let her go.

The screaming and the rocking gently sunk out of her mind. She was dying, she thought. Dying at last. The baby swayed and swayed, trying to make the image clearer. But she could barely remember the tone of grey her mother had.

All she could think about was her hunger and her thirst. The smell of the food and the water in her cage masked completely the smell of decay, of mist, of filth and waste. It was rich and overpowering. The baby forced herself to resist.

There was no telling night from day. The baby barely knew when she was sleeping or awake. She was always tired, and the sounds and sensations of the cage followed her into the shallow teases of unconsciousness. She couldn't recall her mother. The guilt set in and she wanted to die all the more. The baby's body felt on fire. It was enough to distract her from hunger and thirst, through by now her tongue was sticking to the roof of her mouth, and she felt painfully empty and dry. It was like the blood in her veins had congealed. She couldn't even breathe.

A drop of water ran down her flank and reminded the baby of the soft nose of the horse as it had nudged her awake back in her old enclosure. The baby closed her eyes and swayed and gently dreamed of his silhouette against the fiery sunsets as he ran up and down in the grassy paddock where the air was fresh, and the ground was soft and real. She watched him until he faded into the sunbeams. When she woke, though the baby hadn't realized she'd been sleeping, she felt a jolt of panic that she'd find Old Boy standing over her, ready for another exercise. But he wasn't there. She was in the water machine. The tiger was watching her, as was the sloth bear. Both seemed lazy and complacent.

The baby felt a surge of burning rage at both of them. So strong she could taste hatred. She wanted to kill them both. To snap the tiger's neck with a mighty trunk she'd never develop, like the one her mother had wielded. She wanted to pick up the sloth bear and throw him like her mother could have. Her teeth were grinding. The baby stomped her feet and growled at them. They didn't react. Her heart was pounding.

Suddenly, she found herself drinking greedily from her troth. She sucked it dry. She drank until she vomited again, then she drank that up. Then she ate. She ate until she was sick, then cried out for more because there was nothing left. Tensely, she waited for more. The baby howled for more food.

CHAPTER 12

It was after they had come to a stop that the baby noticed how still the sloth bear had become. Still, she hadn't accepted what had happened until the upright apes came with a large bag, opened his cage, and heaved his body into it. They hauled him onto one of their trolleys and wheeled him off, and he was gone. All the food they'd distributed to him on the long voyage, from the first day, was still there at the bottom of his cage. She shuddered. All that time, he'd been doing exactly as she'd tried to do over and over, quietly and determinedly and, at last, successfully.

The baby heard the cages being opened; the click, the whine of the bars swinging open, the grunting and gibberish of the apes and the jealous screeching of the other animals surrounding them, still locked in their cages. She stared into the empty cage left by the sloth bear. Like the whitening skeleton of an animal that died on the plains, it was a memorial that ached in the baby's heart and filled her with haunting shame that she'd lived while he'd died. It was unnatural. Sloth bears lived in caves and tree trunks and died in the wilderness, not in little straight, symmetrical compartments floating out in the furthest reaches of existence. They took him from home like they took her, and he died like that.

The baby wanted her friends near her. She wanted to touch them, and talk to them, and reassure them that she loved them and that they were safe together and at home. She wanted her mother there, to make her feel that way. But it wasn't that way. She was far from home. She could feel how far she was; if home was a star in the night sky, then it had fallen behind the curve of the earth. Or if it was the direction she'd once faced while she slept, then that direction now looked into meaningless abyss. It was like there was no home anymore. She cried and swayed her head, all she could do to pass the time until they got to her and let her out.

She felt the tiger watching her. It had sat up again and was staring through the bars with its long whiskers twitching back and forth. She stared back, still swaying her head. It felt like forever, while clicks, whines, squeals, gibberish and squawks sounded in time, seeming to get no closer to them. The baby felt no more threat from the tiger. She wasn't even intimidated by the glassy stare of those cruel eyes. It was just nothing. Like a shrub with two emerald lights pointed at her. Strange thoughts began to enter her mind; it wasn't real. It was just a dream. It was dead, but awake still, and watching her. Calling her to die with it. There was no reality. There was no wilderness. All that had been before was just a dream, and now she was waking up. Born into the world again, where her mother would greet her, and everything was cold and hard and smoky and steamy and smelled of acrid chemicals and excrement. Or space. She'd just float between two worlds. Voices would call from the phantasms that sparkled inside them. Accusing, angry voices; the baby had failed, the baby had lost, the baby hadn't been able to hold on. Leave her to float there.

'What do you want?' she huffed at it, calling back her sense of reality. She felt her mind emptying and stupid things floating about inside of it, and she didn't like it.

The tiger just stared.

Freshness began to waft gently through the giant chasm they'd been imprisoned in. Cool, light air that chilled her skin and awakened her stiff lungs from their agonizing slumber. Life began to flow through her veins again. 'What do you want?'

The tiger cocked its head. For a second, she thought it said, 'To eat you.' But then it made a strange huffing noise, throaty and rough, and she read something from it that she'd never expected: 'We made it.'

She touched her trunk gently to the nearest bar. 'I'm glad you're alive.'

A response never came. The apes were at its cage and opening it. The tiger let out a roar, but one of them flicked a long rope and it made a startling CRACK and the tiger ducked its head in submission, its ears tightly behind its head. With it like that, one of the apes was able to tie a rope around its neck and guide it out as though it was as harmless as the baby was. It was disturbing as it was unbelievable; she'd twice seen a tiger like that face off against an enraged herd of her giant kind, and there it was, again cowering under the hands of frail little apes.

They held the power of pain, the power of life and death, they could kill without touching, without even being near, and could cause agony with a stroke of their wrists. But there had to be something more, the baby thought. Some other unworldly power that she hadn't witnessed yet.

It was the longest time and the ridiculous thoughts again began to waft through the baby's mind. She couldn't even identify them, they were like clouds passing gently over the sky; formless and opaque. That was her mind, even to herself. Formless and opaque.

Finally, the apes were opening her cage. It had been so cramped for so long that when the bars swung open she felt herself fall out of the tiny space. Then, she had to walk again. The apes kicked and shoved her along on her wobbly legs, which directed her to the left and right as she more stumbled along than actually took steps. She couldn't figure which leg to put in front of the other and her mind remained a vacant fog.

Then, she was on the ramp. It was night-time, and the air was penetratingly cold, so the baby shivered. She hesitated at the top of the ramp, able to see over the side into the crashing, swirling waters which threatened to swallow her if her uncertain legs should have failed. The stars looked down with unrelenting twinkle, each one taunting her with a beauty she could never escape into, however much she wanted to. Around them, the great void of openness threatened to swallow her up and leave her adrift in its endlessness. She cried out from the frantic fear shuddering inside her. But the apes were growing tired; they kicked her harder and harder until she pitched forward and very nearly did fall over the edge of the ramp. Her whole body stiffened suddenly to catch her, and it hurt. But her senses aligned again, and she was able to calculate her steps more clearly. She walked down the ramp, one foot at a time.

At the bottom was more of the hard, cold ground that the apes paved over nature's earth, and all over it were towering structures, all symmetrical and wooden and narrow, too small to accommodate living things bigger than monkeys or birds. For a moment the baby decided that's what must be in them. Then, as the apes led her through them, she realized how silent they were, and began to shiver with fear. If there were monkeys and birds inside them, then they were dead.

They passed through a fence woven from the hard material that the apes made machines from, then passed over ground made of tiny stones and dust, before reaching a hillside covered in grass. Stolen for a moment from herself, the baby rolled over in the soft, damp, cool grass and squealed with delight as it tickled and caressed her body. More sharp kicks and grunts from the apes called her back, and she sorrowfully parted from it. Then, up the hill.

When they reached the crest, the baby saw the lights the apes made shining from inside a forest of towering structures that stole the breath from her. A giant, sprawling labyrinth of buildings plunged into the darkness of night and was relit by the unearthly, chilling yellow glow of their own creation. At the base of the hill was a mess of train tracks, all overlapping and running off in every which direction. Upon them were a few trains with the carriages open, waiting. The baby knew where she was going. But the cold was beginning the prickle against her skin, and the void was still intimidating, so she welcomed being inside again.

The apes led her hastily down the hill, across the tracks, and to a waiting train, where she climbed another ramp and again found herself tied up inside a wooden carriage, in pitch darkness once they closed the door. But this time, she felt the presence of other creatures. She smelled something familiar, something that seemed to recall a vague, distant mist that veiled a dream she couldn't remember having. The baby felt the warmth of other bodies all around her. As her eyes adjusted and absorbed what they could of the silver shafts of starlight piercing through the cracks in the carriage, she began to see the bulbous heads, the swinging trunks and the hulking bodies, none of them bigger than her own. Immediately, she started to cry, though they ignored her entirely.

They were others like her.

The baby wanted to touch them, to speak to them, to rouse them somehow...but all they did was stand there, gently swaying. She wanted to shake her trunk at one but couldn't decide which. So many ideas and urges ran through her so quickly, she didn't have time to catch them or make sense of anything. She could not think of a thing to say or anything to do! But there was a way of communicating, she knew it! A way of opening up...she tried to remember her friends in her herd. There was a friend she had. There were many, but one was special.

As the train buckled, chugged, and started along its way and the sun came up, the baby found herself an alien amongst her own kind, swaying on board a carriage full of strangers, unable to remember what to say or do.

Daylight warmed the inside of the carriage and the baby found a decent sized slit between the planks right near her head, where she could observe more closely this new world she'd been brought to. It both excited and daunted her, to think that these apes, who had come to her land as strangers from across the vast water, had a home somewhere, and that she was now in it. But, to her surprise, when she looked out into their world, she didn't see the labyrinth of structures that she'd first perceived in the night from the hilltop. That's all she'd expected. Instead, she saw trees. Golden-leafed trees with thick, rough branches and thinning canopies that stretched out as far as she could see. Their yellow colour was rich and warming beneath the crisp sunlight. Others were fat at the bottom and narrowed towards the top, instead of billowing outward in a green canopy, and instead of leaves, they had little green bristle. Others again were giant, towering monoliths with red trunks that reached so high that their tops seemed to sit amongst the clouds and their middles seemed too thick that they made even the body of the train seem like more of a worm than a giant snake. It was a wilderness again. Nothing like her wilderness, but natural nonetheless.

On and on it went. They went deeper into the forests, cutting up through them where the apes had cleared a path for their train. The baby felt them climbing higher, up to a greater altitude. When night came, the calves didn't huddle together as the baby had expected but held their lonely trances and continued their aimless staring, which the baby couldn't understand any more than she could think of a way to break it. So, she focused on the outside, which whipped by them as the train chugged and drew them on, deeper into the apes' world. The baby's flesh never stopped quivering, the heavy weight in her heart never ceased to remind her that this wasn't home and spike her every emotion with slivers of guilt that she wasn't collapsed in tears or dead in bereavement of all she'd lost. The shadow of her herd and her mother moved through every patch of wilderness outside, just beyond the field of vision afforded by the crack in the planks. But the baby was mesmerized as well. Daunted. Frightened. But mesmerized. It was all so different; different air, different temperature, different smells, different feelings.

She grew frustrated with the others. How could they not be enthralled, or at least terrified? How could they not be the least bit glad to have each other?

Ahead, there loomed a giant mountain range, which gave the baby some sense of ease. Although, it was not the familiarity of landmarks so similar to those she could remember seeing back in her old home, all the way to the beginning of her life, because these ones looked so different. They weren't coppery or silver like the ones at home. They were blueish, with shades of green where the forest seemed to be creeping up their flanks, and white all the way down to their middles.

It was the sight of the mountains themselves. That's why she as so comfortable. It was the sight of trees so tall that they made even the terrifying machines and disturbingly uniform structures the apes made seem tiny and insignificant. It was nature and chaos and asymmetry and beauty that the upright apes either hadn't, or couldn't, destroy. The baby felt as though as long as she could see giant trees, golden forests and blue mountains here, she would know that there were still large vestiges of wilderness back home. Even if they could lay a few train tracks through portions of it, they couldn't take away all of it. They couldn't kill and enslave her whole kind, as long as there were free animals here. It was just musing, she knew it, but she held on to whatever comforts she could, like little warm, glowing stars she could catch floating through her mind and keep inside her heart.

For the first time since she played with her horse friend in some other world that lived and breathed in a different sphere of existence altogether, the baby felt calm.

The train stopped in a small village of ape structures built in a clearing that divided a forest of the conical spine-trees. Waste had gathered on the floor of the carriage. The baby had shuffled to avoid it touching her feet but before long she couldn't. The smell was beginning to churn her stomach. The carriage door opened, and a few of the pale apes were standing on the platform, their black stains on their faces and all over their second skins. They watched as a line of dark-skinned apes entered the carriage with the tool they used to shovel the waste into bags. The baby again saw the signs of pale-ape dominance; these ones had darker skin again than the natives back in her old world, and their bodies seemed even more worn, malnourished and sickly. They were all males. Some of the older ones, with grey hair or none at all, had hunches in their bags and hands that seemed to be turning into the bark of the trees they'd passed by.

'Hello there, elephant!' one of them said, as he came near her. She recognized those words and raised her trunk in response. When she looked in his eyes, she felt warmth move through her. They were kind eyes. There was a pain in them like they'd cried too much, but there was no cruelty or deception in them. 'You need to step aside for me now!'

They talked to the elephants. That was what the baby's kind was called by these apes; elephants. She couldn't pronounce it herself. She hadn't yet figured out how to make sounds as they did, but she wanted to. Not for the pale-skinned apes, she didn't that they'd talk to her anyway, but for the dark-skinned apes, and the 'natives', if there was any in this new world. Like she'd tried to talk to the tiger. There was an undeniable kinship in the way they suffered at the whims of these mysterious pale-skinned apes, who the baby was becoming more and more convinced were not of any earth where things grew or the chaos that was nature existed, but some other place. Far, even from this one. Where everything was perfect and symmetrical, and life existed not by the hunt for food but by the will of one species to dominate another. A world where predators didn't kill for food but enslaved and used like their machinery. Some bizarre realm that had no comparison even in the nightmares the baby had since seeing their structures. A place that made them heartless and cruel, but deceptively friendly as well.

It was all beginning to make some kind of sense. They had conquered this world as they were conquering her world. They'd move on to another one, like an infection, and conquer that as well. Morbid fascination kept the baby thinking about what their original world was like. It felt okay being sickened and scared by her imagination. It kept her mind off the persisting ache in her heart, which now seemed to have no origin, but was just a scar upon a scar that bled into her veins became as much as part of her as her bones or her skin.

'That's enough!' the pale apes barked, when the dark-skinned apes had finished, and the floor was clean again.

They left as they came in; single file, the bags of waste slung over their shoulders. They stopped at the pale apes, who put little shiny things in their hands. 'Thanks, boss.'

It went on like this. They passed over tracks that skirted the edge of the mountains and felt, for a moment, like flying. The air was so cold and fresh that the baby shivered, and her teeth chattered. She heard the other elephant's teeth chattering as well. It was an opportunity to try to communicate with them again, but again it went ignored. On and on, they came down again, and passed by new types of tree; these ones had long, floppy branches that hung flaccid instead of reaching out into the sunrays. The ground changed; it became redder and dryer. They chugged through lowlands flanked by rolling hills which rose up from thick forests. The sun rose and set. The baby began to think that this might be the rest of her life but, though she was painfully bored and aching inside for too many things that she could prioritize, she didn't cry. She was free from the water machine.

To pass time, she swayed her head and daydreamed about her horse friend. How beautiful his eyes were. How tall and majestic his muscular body had been. It hurt because she wished she could see him, but it was a sweet hurt that kept her warm.

The train would stop, and dark-skinned apes would bring them feed and clean their waste and fill their water, before taking shiny things or fashioned leaves from the pale apes with a passing 'Thank you, boss,' and they'd be on their way again. Since passing the mountains, one of the pale apes carried the same tool that Sir had used to kill her mother. It struck her with a cold bolt of horror every time she saw it. But on they went again. Leaving on village or town behind for another. She learned the difference between the two. Towns were bigger; the buildings were more solid, and many were made of stronger material than just wood. They also had more apes in them, and unlike her old world, these ones were mostly pale-skinned. Their women walked in the big, frilly second skins with their broad hats on their heads and their little ones in tow, often with males to escort them, and sometimes in wagons pulled by horses. At one stop, the baby saw a wagon clicking along without a horse! Like the train, it left a trail of smoke behind it.

If there were dark-skinned apes, they were often alone, and busy staying out of people's way. Her heart swelled again for them; here they were fewer than the darker-skinned apes back home. Like her, they were outnumbered. How lonely it felt!

That was so much the darkness that ached inside her; her loneliness. She wanted all the more to reach out to them.

At one town, she saw one at the corner of the structure on the platform with something in his hands. He held it to his mouth and blew into it, and it made such a sweet, beautiful sound! The baby immediately trumpeted back at him, and he stopped, cackling. The pale-skinned apes and the dark-skinned servants cleaning her carriage all laughed like that as well. All looked at her, smiling and laughing like the children had back in the paddocks. It made her feel safer, to make them laugh. She wanted one of the objects that the dark-skinned ape was blowing into. If her own trumpet made them laugh, then his most certainly would!

Performing tricks had been her means of survival, with Old Boy. When she'd done as he wanted, he'd not hit her. A means of avoiding the pain. The baby knew she was figuring the apes out.

Then, one morning, when the skies were rolling with heavy grey clouds, the train stopped at a platform, the carriage door was opened, and there entered a line of dark-skinned apes without bags or tools for cleaning up waste. Instead, they unclicked the hard, cold, rattling ropes that held them in place, and clicked them one-to-the-other, so the elephants were free of the carriage, but were still tied together. They put a rope

152

around the baby's neck and led her to the ramp. She went with them, even though they didn't have sticks to beat her with. In the corner of her eye, she could see the pale ape that carried the weapon that could kill them from where he stood. That was enough to frighten her into obedience.

The pale apes in their fitted second skins and frilly dresses stepped aside as the elephants were led out onto the platform. They smiled and waved, and the children of those that had them squealed with excitement and stomped their feet. But their parents held them from coming too close. All in a row, the cold bonds tight against their itchy ankles, the elephants walked down another ramp and onto the stony dirt, where the baby saw the pale ape who was waiting for them.

He was high up on a horse, calmly watching and waiting. The baby stopped before him and he looked down at her with tiny, beady little eyes, even for a pale-skinned ape. Immediately her blood ran cold. These were not the deceptive, warm eyes of Old Boy or Sir, they were the cold, cruel, calculating eyes of a predator. He didn't smile, just sternly looked at her. His second skin was completely white, all the way down to the bottom of his feet. Even his hands were covered. Only his face showed his natural tone; less pale than pink in colour. His body bulged in the middle and around the face. In all this, the baby couldn't pick what, other than his eyes, made her so uneasy around him. Her heart skipped beats and her stomach felt like it wanted to turn around and run away. She even felt breathless.

But he just waited as the other elephants made their way down behind her until the last rattle finally stopped. In a flat voice, he uttered words softly. The dark-skinned ape that held her rope quickly gave his end to the ape on the horse, and he tied it to the thick skin that was draped over the horse's back. He didn't give the dark-skinned ape anything but whistled to the pale-skinned apes who stood behind them. The one without the weapon approached and he got a stack of fashioned leaves, from under the pink ape's second skin.

Without another word, the pink ape turned the horse and led the elephants away from the platform, towards the town. The baby was cold and terrified. Each step became laboured by the fear of where this ape was leading her.

Silently, she began to cry for home.

CHAPTER 13

She was led through the town, past structures she could see were made of fashioned stone. It daunted the baby all the more to know that the apes could shape stone. Wood, at least, was soft. Elephants could bend and snap wood. But stone! Nothing broke stone...

They moved down the middle of the path where wagons, both with and without horses travelled. On either side, people gathered and were waving and cheering. Children threw little nuts from bags at them. One got the baby in the eye and stung her terribly. The only dark-skinned apes she could see were walking alongside the row of elephants, keeping watch over them. It was more pale-skinned apes than the baby had ever seen, and it made her feel smaller than a mouse. Desperately, she tried trumpeting at them. They laughed, but the children threw more nuts at her, which stung both her eyes this time.

Punished! For performing a trick for them! Maybe she didn't understand the pale apes at all? But then, where were they going? And why?

The day seemed to grow darker every second as the pink ape led them from the town and out onto the grassy hills. Ahead of him, perched upon a flat-topped hill in a vast, grassy valley where structures stood scattered about like the lonely trees back home, the baby could see another paddock. But this one was different. Instead of one stable in the corner, it seemed to have many, and these were big. As they got closer, the baby realized a whole herd could fit inside them. They weren't big; they were enormous.

They dipped below the hillside and for a moment it was just grass and a soft electrical breeze preceding a storm. When they came back up they crossed a road and were at the gates of the paddock. More dark-skinned servants opened the gates, which creaked loudly, and the pink-skinned ape led them through. The baby saw the top arch of the gates pass over their heads as they stepped, one at a time, onto the stony dirt. It wasn't a paddock. There was no frolicking in this place.

With a squealing creak, the gates slammed shut behind them.

They were led between two of the enormous structures, which seemed to go on and on forever, through an empty space, and to the front of a third, which more servants opened. The pink-skinned ape handed his end of the rope to one of them, one who was carrying a stick like Old Boy's, and he tapped her flank with it, just like Old Boy used to. Jarring jolts of terror flashed through Mary's flesh like memories of the searing pain that sliced through her whenever Old Boy whipped her, and she cried out as she hurried into the structure.

Then, the smell hit her.

Sweet, dried grass. Leavy feed. Grain. Nuts. And elephants!

Rows upon rows of stables, just like the ones the horses had lived in, but with elephants in them! Elephants just like her!

The terror sank like the rolling tide and the baby felt a surge of calm. She was no longer in the frightening ape's company, but in the company of a whole herd's worth of elephants, and all close to her in age. They weren't standing still and subdued like the ones she was still tied to had on the train either; they were hollering, trumpeting, grunting, growling and even playing. The baby shuddered with excitement as they passed by a stable in which she saw one juvenile male headbutt another's flank and knock him a few paces. He was sprayed with water from the troth, in retaliation.

One by one, the elephants in the line were uncuffed and released into a stable, until finally it was just the baby. A gate was opened, and she found herself on a bed of hay with a full feed basket, a troth of pure water and another female elephant, the same shape and colour as her. The baby shook her trunk and gave an excited squeal.

'Hello.'

'Hello!' the other elephant said back.

The baby's eyes were watering. 'I've come so far!'

'I did too.'

They could say little more. The baby ran across to her, their trunks entwined, and she felt the warmth of an honest, sincere embrace from one of her own. The feeling buzzed inside her. A joy that reached out of her memories, across the great abyss of grief, of loss, of pain and terror and touched her heart right there where she thought she'd never feel any warmth again as long as she lived.

#

She woke with a violent shudder. It was night. The baby knew she heard screaming, but she couldn't remember if it was in her dream, or if it had woken her. She listened to the darkness in the stable. Other elephants breathing. Deeply, rhythmically. Sleeping. Sleeping long, un-elephant like sleeps. But none others heard the screaming. It must have been a dream.

#

It was 5 AM. Winter had melted into summer without much of a Spring. Philip Junor had to make sure he spent as much time with the young generation of elephants as he could before they had to be moved into Stable 6.

Stable 6 was just a sinister anomaly that he wished was Stable 4. But there was no stable four. It went; 1, 2, 3 and 6. It didn't make sense. He wished there was no stable 6. He wished there was no Colonel.

Sunrise breathed in through the open window and gently filled Philip's bedroom with the early-summer heat. He knew it was time to rise. It was not a Stable 6 day, and if anything, days that are Stable 6 days had only taught Philip to appreciate days that weren't even more. He knew he had to enjoy the elephants now, while they were young and innocent of the Colonel. Even more excitingly for the twelve-year-old, it was Monday, which meant it was Benjamin's day off from assisting the Colonel with the training as well!

He quickly pulled his pants on by the suspenders and threw a work shirt on over the top of them. They still smelled of hay and elephant dung from yesterday, but he liked that smell. With his straw hat on, he hurried into the hallway, carrying his socks. The next door down was Benjamin's. He pushed it open without knocking and seized his brother by the hair.

'Ah! Boy, I done told you not t'do that!' the sixteen-year-old mumbled into his pillow.

'C'mon, Benjamin!' Philip said, as he tugged his brother's hair.

'Dang it, I got to leak anyway,' Benjamin said. He beat his pillow with frustration and sat up.

Benjamin headed to the outhouse while Philip fired up some kindling in the stove and put on the coffee pot. Benjamin always took so long out there; the coffee was ready before he was back. They put their shoes on, just as old Ernie Grimes was riding his wagon, already with five workers sitting in the back of it, by the gate of their house. He pulled the horses up, put his feet up, and watched the sunrise.

The boys said hello to him and didn't mind that he was slow to respond. They knew old Mister Grimes loved the sunrise, and it did look beautiful in the springtime, on the road between their house and the facility. Though it was two days past spring, this morning was no exception. A fire-red sky, thinly dabbed with deep purple clouds with golden hems, lit the rolling countryside with a fine honey tint, and the trees across the heath cast brilliant shadows over the soft hills.

'Yes, sir,' old man Grimes' husky voice breathed, as Philip and Benjamin sat amongst the labourers. 'That be God's bestest gift fo' all mankind, right there.'

'Come on, Grimes, get it goin',' Jack Irish said, through a mouthful of stale bread. Grimes ignored him for a few seconds while he took a deep breath as though the scenery itself might fill his lungs. He stuffed a pipe with old corn shoots and lit it up.

'Why do you always stop to stare at the sunrise, Mister Grimes?' Philip asked, again. Benjamin shoved him in the ribs with his elbow.

'Don't be callin' no negro mister, boy!' he hissed.

'Grimes,' Philip corrected. He'd heard the answer before, but he wanted to hear the old man explain it again. 'Why?'

'Some folks be rich, some folks be poor,' Grimes answered. 'Some folks be men, some folks be women. Some folks be white, some folks be black. In all them ways, some folks got more'n the other folks. An' folks got more'n other folks like to keep them other folks from gettin' too much of anything, whether that be mo'money mo'food, or even mo'smarts. That's right, them folks in power, they can stop you gettin' thangs. Keeps 'em in power. You ain't got none, you can't have none. Got no smarts, can't get no money. Ain't got no money, can't get no food. Can't get no food, you ain't gon' be around too long. But folks learn how to get what they can. Poor folks work for rich folks, an' rich folks give'm a little money. Women marry men and get theyselves a share of that

161

money. Black folks work for poor folks, and it goes on...but there ain't nobody, not nobody in this world no-how, what can keep the stars from shinin' on a fella, or the sunrise from fillin' theys' heart. Theys God's way'a sayin' you is all men. You is all goin' t'heaven.'

'What a load of bull,' spat Brutus.

Old man Grimes exhaled the last of his corn shoot smoke and got the wagon rolling again.

Philip wondered if elephants could see the sunrise.

They arrived at the facility, and Grimes headed over to the fire pit to put some breakfast on. One or the other Mister Junor always gave Grimes a little extra on his pay to cook the labourers some breakfast. Sometimes it was bullied beef and beans. Sometimes he'd get out the hotplates and fry up a basket of eggs and a few pounds of bacon. Once he made pancakes with blueberry jam. Everyone figured he must have robbed a bank somewhere, but one of the labourers told Philip he'd saved up the extra money himself, and that was his sixtieth birthday, so he wanted to celebrate. Philip thought that was strange; who celebrates their birthday by cooking everyone else a special breakfast, and not mentioning why? But Grimes was always an interesting man. Someone once said he'd been born into slavery. That his mother had escaped an okra plantation in Georgia when he was just a baby, and she'd been

162

caught, and burned alive in front of him. Philip had got nightmares and hoped it wasn't true.

He watched Grimes firing up the kindling in the pit over his shoulder, as they headed for the grain and hay stocks. He had such a serene nature to him. A placid smile always on his face, even when he was getting yelled at by someone. Even when the Colonel called him 'nigger'. No, Philip thought. The story couldn't be true. That'd be just too horrible for a person. He put the thought out of his mind and let himself be excited instead.

He'd seen the hotplate in the back of Grimes' wagon.

They shovelled their stock into the stock bins and wheeled them into Stable 2. Philip and Benjamin took the same bin, which made Philip smile. It had been a long time since the brothers had worked the same stock bin. They wheeled it by the enclosures, while another two labourers followed with a cart full of buckets of water and started restocking their feeding trays. At this hour, the young elephants were dopey. They ignored the workers, mostly. A lot of them didn't even wake up when Philip entered, set down the new hay, and backed out again. He liked the elephants, but he'd been told since birth about never turning his back on them. He checked their charts. Their names, all given by Philip, and their ages. At four years, it was time to go over to Stable 6. Brady and Abraham were eight months. Peggy and Rachel were ten months and two years. Bill was one year, David was eighteen months. Amelia was seven months, Beatrice was two and a half years. On and on they went, he knew them all.

Benjamin didn't think it was worthwhile naming them. 'They're just dumb animals,' he'd say. Previously, they'd used a letter and number system. But they used Philip's names now. Philip even heard his brother talking to one of them, one day. Talking about the Parker's daughter, in town.

'Oh, Philip!' Benjamin snapped when he looked at the little chalkboard chart hung on the enclosure gate. 'Didn't I tell you to change that name?'

'Didn't you tell Mary Parker that she has an elephant named after her?' Philip said, having remembered only the parts of the conversation he liked. Namely, his and what he intended.

'No, I ain't gonna tell Miss Parker that she has an elephant named after her!'

'Why not?' Philip said. 'She'd think it's romantic.'

He made kissing sounds and hugged himself until Benjamin swatted him with the back of his hand.

'No,' Benjamin said. 'She would not.'

'Why?'

'You just don' unnerstand women, is all.'

'Mary Parker ain't no woman!' Philip argued. 'She's a girl. Mom's a woman.'

'Ain't no difference between a girl and a woman, boy!'

'Now who don' unnerstand women.'

'Change the elephant's name!' Benjamin pointed at Philip. 'I know enough to know there ain't no girl wants her name shared with no elephant!'

All the more now, since Mary had grown bigger than any other elephant her age. She was huge, already able to hang her trunk over the gate, or reach out and grab hay from the stock bin. Her chart said three years, eight months. The chalk was smeared, but Philip knew she was an Indian elephant, which aren't supposed to be as big as African elephants. But Mary was sizing up to be bigger than all of them. She was always friendly though, and abnormally obedient. Only once she'd taken hay from the stock bin, and when the labourer had swatted her trunk away, she'd never done it again. She was up already when they reached her. Standing in the back of her enclosure, swaying her head from side to side, like they did sometimes. Philip had asked the Colonel why they did that. All he'd answered that animals didn't have reasons to do anything, they just did it. Ernie Grimes, however, had said that's how

165

they dream when they're captive. They sway their heads, so they can remember the wild.

Old man Grimes probably didn't know anything about elephants, Philip thought, except how to shovel up their manure. Philip's father had always told him never to make the mistake of thinking animals have human thoughts, memories or emotions, and Philip figured there's no reason why Mister Grimes would know that. Nor would he know that people sometimes see their own emotions reflected back at them when they look at certain animals. That's a mistake too, though, Philip's father always said. God created mankind in His image. Only man has a soul.

'G'mornin', Mary.'

Philip opened Mary's gate. She shared her enclosure with Patricia, a two-year-old. But Patricia always overslept, while Mary was always up. She stopped swaying and watched Philip take some of the dregs out of the feeding tray and throw them on the floor. Or, Philip thought he saw her watching. Benjamin handed Philip a few handfuls of hay, and Philip spread it over the bottom of the feeding tray, then added another layer from Benjamin, and then a third. Mary waited until he was done. Philip backed up. Mary seemed to be watching him. He closed the gate.

No, he thought. Mary wasn't watching. You've got to think to want to watch. Otherwise, what would you be watching for? Mary was an elephant.

'Naming them's gone and got to your head, boy,' his father would say. Still, he couldn't help but wonder...if Mary was watching him...if...then would she to maybe want to watch the sunrise sometime?

He mustn't get attached, he thought. Four years, eight months. She'd been part of his life since he was twelve, and he admitted to himself that he had grown attached to her. She was different to the others. Aside from being bigger, she seemed more watchful. Like maybe only she had a special personality or something. But no, mustn't get attached. She was due for Stable 6 soon.

CHAPTER 14

Mary watched the scrawny pale apes refill her feed and
replenish her water from their buckets. She understood that
Mary was her title, her name, but not what she was. She was
not a Mary. She was an elephant. An elephant named Mary.
Philip was a pale ape named Philip, but they weren't called
pale apes, they were called people. So were the dark-skinned
apes. They were both people, but the dark-skinned people had
other names and were often referred to as "boy" or "workers".
The males were called men and the females were called girls
or women. Mary hadn't figured out, yet, what the difference
between the latter two was, but she had come to understand
that she never knew the names of the people who'd held her
captive back in her home. Sir was not a name, but just
something they called each other, while Old Boy was
something the people became with time.

Their language was complicated, but Mary enjoyed thinking
about it and deciphering it. Patricia did as well, and that made
Mary wish she had such an articulate mouth to communicate
with her fellow elephant in the people language. What she
couldn't understand, though, was why the people couldn't
seem to grasp elephant speak? She liked Philip, even though
he was a person. He wore his second skins ragged and loose,
like the workers, and she even saw them standing over him

168

and growling or barking at him, occasionally, which made her think that maybe she'd figured their hierarchies wrong. Either way, he was more like the workers than the other people. She thought that if she persisted, she might get through to him.

Mary shook her trunk at Philip and gave him a happy hoot. 'Hello!'

Philip clearly didn't understand, though he'd said, 'Good morning!'. He ducked his head and flinched. Mary knew she was bigger now. She was taller than most of the people, especially Philip. But she kept hope that either Philip or Benjamin would come to understand that it was not a threat. She was just saying hello.

Benjamin was watching her with that expression again. Mary kept still. He had an edge of cruelty that reminded her of the person who'd brought her to this place, the one on the horse's back. She never tried to talk to Benjamin.

'We'll be back soon, Mary,' Philip said, as he closed her gate behind him. 'Take you for a walk, okay?'

Mary forced herself not to respond, the only response that they were ever happy with. Once they were gone, she moved over to her feed and ate some with Patricia. Then, they drank together. They'd said all they could to each other, as well as to all the other elephants around them. Mary was afraid of the blandness making fog in her mind. The narrowing of her capacity to imagine left black voids inside her thoughts, which she worried would fill with nightmares or worse, empty numbness. Her mind was like her trunk; the more she used it, the more dexterous it was, the more things it could grasp at once. But lacking stimulation, it had become weak and limp. She'd forget things. Names, seasons, the coming of light or the falling of the sun. She secretly wished they could swap enclosures, be rotated or something so that she could meet new elephants from the other side of the stables. But they were always the same; Patricia, Joan, Rachel, and Elizabeth. They mostly passed the day complaining.

'My feed is too dry,' Elizabeth spat.

'The water is dirty!' lamented Rachel.

'I want to walk now,' Patricia stomped her foot. Mary stomped too, but she always wanted to walk. She wanted to walk and just keep walking. They all did, and they all knew it of each other. Rachel didn't really care that her water was dirty, if anything she wished it was dirtier, like it would be out there, where the sun shone, and the grass rustled. Elizabeth's food was always dry, all their food was, but they didn't complain about that, they complained because they missed the lush, juicy, leafy greens that grew on trees, rather than the yellow straw that was towed about in carts by people. Mary could tell, because she felt that formless, dull ache simmering inside her heart as well, where something else once had glowed and warmed and filled her, where now she was dark, cold and empty. She never forgot the other places she'd been; that hot, dark little cage inside the rocking machine that carried her over the sea haunted the shadowy places of her imagination and sprung to life often while she slept. She'd feel the walls pressed against her, the ceiling touching her back and the top of her head and hear the screams and moans of all the other creatures sharing her torment, and wake crying, imagining that she'd find herself back there again. Times like that, she even loved this new place. But her contentment never took away that distant hurt for a precious thing that had disappeared.

Retired to her corner, Mary began to sway her head, trying to form memories of sweeter things. It upset her. She always felt tears stinging the back of her eyes when her mind carried her back to the feeling of her horse's soft nose against her side. Then, when she remembered the relentless rains, the open spaces, the distance between herself and the curve of the earth and the warm, protective, watchful eyes of the herd and her mother, she'd cry openly. The other elephants wouldn't stop her. They were too busy swaying their heads and crying as well, for whatever worlds they were stolen from and whatever love they felt along the way being ripped from them and destroyed before their eyes.

Slowly the shadowy form of her mother returned to her. Mary could see the lonely trees with her watery eyes closed, could smell the freshness of the greenery and even began to feel the eyes of the herd, the presence of a figure formed of pure love and enforced with might and the will to protect her from all the world. The pain spread from her heart and seeped through her entire body, but she didn't want it to stop or go away. She wanted to huddle it, hold it close to her, and keep it safe. It was her reminder. It was a poison inside her that filled her heart with all the things she knew she loved but couldn't reach out and touch anymore. She wanted more than her mother, more than her eyes, her face, and the touch of trunk. She wanted scent. The coolness of her shadow. She wanted presence. She wanted something to hold and hug and keep warm and alive. As she swayed her head, she felt her there, but couldn't touch her. Couldn't just turn and look at her. Every time she felt, just for a moment, that she could begin to feel some of that powerful love tingling through her again in a way that was true and alive, she'd hear the explosions from the people's guns.

A cold shudder shot through her with the sound and swept it away like a wave.

Mary had fallen asleep. Patricia was nudging her head with her trunk, trying to wake her. Mary touched her side and assured her not to worry. She was awake.

'You were having a nightmare.'

'No, I wasn't. I was having a beautiful dream.'

'But you're crying!'

'That's how beautiful it was.'

Patricia knowingly caressed Mary's trunk again. It settled Mary's sorrow and kept her heart full enough of friendly contentment that she could face her time in here. She'd grown accustomed to her time anywhere being brief and knew that before long, this would come to an end, and Patricia would join the horse and the tiger with the misty fragments that only came to her when she forced her dreams to come. Patricia knew the same, and Mary could tell that she'd lost as much on her way to this place. The question of why remained unanswered, but the elephants didn't talk about it, and Mary had given up thinking about it.

Though people haunted her every memory and even frightened her out of the dreams where she chased the shadow of her mother around her own unconsciousness, she didn't want to hate them. She wanted to find more like Philip and the workers. More who seemed to understand her. She'd resigned to the fact that this was their world.

'I want to walk,' Patricia stomped.

'I want to walk too.'

It was a game they'd developed. They'd complain about wanting to walk until their minds took them out into the open, where they were walking all the time. There were no such things as structures or walls that could keep them enclosed. Only open space. Flowing breeze. The soft caress of the hot season, the serene shimmer of the wet. The endless call of the migration.

Philip, Benjamin, and the workers returned as the day grew hotter to put the cuffs around their ankles, which linked Mary, Patricia, Joan and Rachel together, and out into the sunlight they walked.

'Good afternoon, Mary!'

The workers, Philip and Benjamin stayed in a loose circle around them and led them over the stony ground around and around the paddocks. The elephants remained silent, the only noise was their crunching footsteps and the slithering of their chains. They didn't have time to talk to each other; this was the precious time of the day when they could see the vastness that they dreamed about. The endless sky, the rolling world, the blazing sun and the billowing trees. The air was ripe with all of its sweetness and openness. They could almost imagine walking over it, seeking out some distant watering hole or lush field of sweet grass.

Then, they came to the furthest structure in the yard from their stables. It looked just like all the others, but Mary had hated it since the first time she walked by it. It was like a cold, foul air hovered about it. It felt like the presence of Old Boy or the pink person. She quickened her pace, being at the front of the line, and the others joined in. None of them could pass it wide enough, though Mary only knew that for her it evoked the looming presence of Old Boy's stick, and the lightning bolts of pain it could shoot through her skin at the slightest misstep. Her flesh began to tremble, the way it used to. She remembered, to herself, the walking, the turning, the halt, the lean back, raising her trunk in the air...how cruel, she thought, that pain could bring back memories so much faster than love.

Haunted, they passed by the structure, and their pace slowed down again. The cold tendrils slithering at Mary's spine eased beneath the warm sunlight. They kept walking and dreaming of the open.

#

'Good morning, Mary,' Philip said, as Mary awoke from another long sleep. Her head ached, they still weren't normal to her. She was surprised to find that it was still dark. Philip had come with only a few workers, no Benjamin. He entered her enclosure, carrying a long length of rope coiled up at his hip.

She looked at Patricia. Still asleep.

This wasn't right. The routine had changed, and Mary didn't like it. She felt the icy tendrils coiling gently around her spine again. Fear. Real fear, not faceless phantoms courting the dark corners of her mind whenever she thought she heard the screams or walked past that structure on the far side of the grounds. She shrank away from Philip.

'It's okay, Mary,' Philip said, and he raised his hand. Mary reached out her trunk to touch it, but he pulled away and quickly looped the end of the rope around her neck. Last time this happened, she was small. But she knew she was bigger now; she stood higher than Philip's head. Still, she was afraid. There was something carried in the imposing form of the people that frightened Mary into submission, as if she was still a little baby at the mercy of Old Boy and his stick. Philip only had to give the rope a gentle tug and she followed him.

But she remembered, this time, to look properly at Patricia. She was sleeping, still. There was nothing to see, but Mary made sure she took down every wrinkle and imagined the way they moved when her eyes were open when she raised her trunk, and while she chewed food. Every detail she could register in those short moments before she was led right out of her enclosure. She didn't want to forget Patricia the way she forgot the horse or the appearance of her own mother. There was just some whisper amongst the gathering terror that crept through Mary's flesh that told her she'd never see her friend again.

Philip led Mary, while the workers encircled her. They walked right out of the stable and onto the grounds. Mary wanted to turn left like they always did, but another gentle tug ordered her to keep going straight. They were walking directly across the compound. Directly toward the frightful stable that had haunted her all her time in this place. She didn't want to, but she was too afraid to stop. She saw that the workers were carrying sticks, like Old Boy's, and though they were much smaller to her now, she knew the pain of them only as a baby, and her frightened mind could not differentiate.

Clouds covered the sky and tempered the sunrise, the vibrant colours that had been blossoming around the compound yesterday were reduced to washed-out tones of grey. The dawn buzzed with the soft current of a coming storm. It was just like Mary's first day here. Her mouth began to dry, and her flesh weakened. Her breathing became sharp and fast. Tears gathered. She didn't want to get any closer to that stable...but they were leading her there. She was powerless.

The earth seemed harsher at the doors to the stable, as they waited while two workers heaved them open. It felt uneasy. Mary knew elephants had shed blood here, even died. She could taste their pain in the air that seeped out of the stable once the doors were opened.

Inside was like the inside of the other structure, but instead of many rows of stables for two elephants at a time, this one had only one in the corner, with five elephants in it. They were all different ages and sizes, and there was grey as well as her darker brown. But they weren't interacting with each other. They were like the calves on the train; each huddled away from the other, alone and frightened, staring into nothing, disconnected from any communication with their own kind. Mary could see one had blood running from a tear in her ear. Another centred her weight to one side, a sure sign that there was too much pain in one of her feet for her to put her weight on it.

Philip opened the enclosure door and led Mary in, where he and a worker untied her rope. There she was, in the centre of the enclosure, surrounded by elephants who might just as well have been mindless. She tried to raise her trunk to them, to signal a greeting or a salute, but they didn't respond. They didn't even look at her. She quickly turned back to Philip. He and the worker were closing the enclosure door.

'I'll be back later on today, Mary,' he said. His voice sounded heavy. There was a slurred sadness in his drawl, and Mary could sense his discomfort. His shoulders were slumped, and his head hung low. 'Don't you worry.'

He followed the worker out, leaving her alone with the others. She tried moaning. They ignored her. She tried growling. They ignored her. Their utter disregard frightened her all the more. It was like they were the machine that substituted horses for the people. Like the train. Lifeless. Just a form that could move things about for the people when activated. With all the signs of life, and yet seeming dead. She sobbed, trembling, afraid to move in case something shot out from the darkness and ripped into her flesh, the way it obviously had for these poor creatures.

All she could do was wait.

CHAPTER 15

When the small side door next to the barn door opened, golden daylight flooded into a small space right in front of it, and then Mary saw the silhouette step in. Short for an adult person, stocky and thick, with a cold air of power about him that not only recalled Old Boy but made him seem weak. He carried a stick in his hand, the tip of it glistened as it caught the sunlight shining in through the door with each of his strides until he reached the centre of the stable, where he stopped. He was dressed in all white again, even his hat. Mary was frozen with fear.

Philip entered behind him and came running across the stable to her enclosure. She knew he was coming for her.

The pink-skinned person watched her with his tiny, black little eyes. Philip opened the gate to her new enclosure. 'Come on, Mary.'

'Don't talk to it, son,' the flat, steely voice of the pink-skinned person said. Mary had heard other people telling Philip the same thing and it always seemed to upset him. This time, he shivered with fright before his shoulders slumped and his eyes cast down at Mary's feet. A moment passed, then the pink-skinned person said something else. Philip looked up at Mary. He looked through her eyes, and straight into her. The sorrow, the regret, the guilt she saw in his face was a perfect reflection of all the things swirling about in the aching depths of her own heart. But why on Philip?

The pink-skinned man walked slowly over to Philip and nudged his arm with the stick he was holding. Mary saw that it was different to the one Old Boy had used; it was thicker, shinier, and the end of it was sharpened and bent into a hook. She saw Philip gingerly reach up and take the device from the pink-skinned man, who then simply walked back to the centre of the stable, turned, and watched. Mary felt Philip's flesh trembling. Like he was in pain. So, she realized with a white flash of horror, the people torture each other as well. How many times had Philip been whipped before he performed whatever it was he was about to correctly? For just one moment, Mary thought she'd defend Philip if he continued to hesitate. She'd take that fat little pink man in her trunk and snap him across the middle...

...the pain hit her before she realized what was happening. Like a bolt of lightning, right through her ear, hammering through her flesh and rattling through her bones until she thought they might shatter like the shell of an egg. She screamed. It was only a small force pulling her forward, but the agony was so intense that her vision rippled and blurred, and her mind numbed. White mist filled her eyes and blocked out any thought or rational response. All she could do was follow the tug.

When it finally released, the whole side of her head was throbbing. Her eye felt like it had exploded. Her jaw ached. Philip stood before her with the stick at his side, and tears streamed down his cheeks.

It was Philip. He hit her with that thing! He pulled her from her enclosure! The pain, the betrayal, swelled in her heart and eclipsed the throbbing in her ear and face. All her body burned on the pyre of her trust for the boy. She wanted to collapse. To fall into the ground and be swallowed by it. She wanted to mist to blacken and absorb her like the darkness of death. How could he? How could her Philip? Suddenly, quickly, his every cheerful "Good morning, Mary" flashed through her mind like poison, and stabbed at her. His friendly gestures scorched her skin. All the memories of his smiles seared her flesh. The food she ate, the water she drank, churned in her stomach, phantoms of the one pale-skinned person who'd ever shown her kindness. Like standing on the edge of the precipice and looking into the deepest abyss, she awed in horror at their capacity for cruelty. Their monstrousness.

Yet, though it all, she could not take her eyes off the stick in his hand. Through all her misery, aching inside her every muscle, she remembered the pain Old Boy had inflicted on her and remembered that the pain Philip could inflict on her was so much worse. Heartbroken, alone, adrift again, wishing that sorrow could kill as would a tiger's jaws or a shot from a gun, she was still under his command. Mary was at Philip's mercy.

Philip was gesturing with the stick, while the pink-skinned person shouted at him in a high, shrill voice. But Mary didn't know what the gestures meant. She remembered what it meant to raise the stick in front of her eyes; lean back on her hindlimbs. She remembered what pointing it at her face meant; raise her trunk. She remembered a tap on the back meant walk, and a bark of 'Halt!' meant stop. But this was something new. Philip was pointing the stick beside her and moving it in a half-circle around his body. Mary didn't understand. Panic began to shoot through her, as she sensed Philip's heart beating faster. She saw the redness in his face and the tears in his eyes. Desperation was holding him. But Mary didn't know what he meant. She raised her trunk to make a friendly gesture, a peace offering even though he never understood it.

'Hit her!' the pink-skinned person was barking.

Philip kept trying to make her understand the gesture. But she couldn't. In her rattled mind, though shuddering with terror, she knew he was going to have to hit her. She understood the pink-skinned person's words. But Philip was responding to training as much as he was wanting her to. She understood this as well. Maybe, Mary thought, just...

Another bark from the pink-skinned man and Philip transformed before Mary's eyes. The mercy, the fear, the innocence faded from him like life does from a dying body, and with cold, furious eyes and a body rigid with fury he charged her. The hook stabbed under her trunk, scratched her lip and dug into her flesh. The pain made her want to curl into a ball. For a moment she thought her whole body would shrivel up around that one agonizing spot. Again, he dragged her. He dragged her in a half-circle, midway across the stable, then let her go.

The pink-skinned person was making a terrible cackling sound. Even his laugh was cold and sickening.

Philip was moving the stick around his body again, but this time Mary knew what it meant. She quickly obeyed his order and walked in a quarter-circle back to her original position, front, and centre to the pink-skinned person. All her instincts centred on avoiding the pain, as they had many times before. It was second nature, now. Subconscious. Her body just acted, though her mind was a heavy fog of fear and hurt. Avoid the pain. Avoid the pain.

Philip raised the stick again. Mary knew their day had just begun.

#

'Keep her walking,' Colonel Breaker said. Anger and exhaustion kept Philip from catching his breath. 'Keep her walking!'

For how long? How many times?

'Stab her now and then,' Colonel Breaker instructed him. 'Not any regular like. So she don't expect it. Elephants got good memories. Hit her good!'

Philip swung the bullhook and struck her in the ear. He dragged her to the spot, then stopped her. He sent her back. He got her walking again. He saw the dark patches swelling under her eyes. Tears staining her wrinkly, grey face. He got her walking again. She seemed off balance, she leaned toward him.

'Hit her, boy!' the Colonel cried. 'Stab her foot, she comes too close!'

Philip swung at her foot. Mary screamed, retreated.

'She'll tear you limb from limb, she don't know who's boss. Hit her proper like. Make her scream!'

Philip led her in the arch. His arm was hurting from hitting her with the heavy bullhook. He saw she was suffering. His heart ached. He wanted it to stop. Tears pushed at his eyes, but he kept them down. She'd been wary of him but had never threatened him. He'd warmed to her. He'd been warned it would happen. He could not afford to let the Colonel see him cry, or his father would never let him work with the elephants at all. Then, what would he do? He had to persevere.

'Boys don't cry, son,' his father had said. 'Men aren't careless and emotional. Men have to take command.'

He swung the bullhook at Mary, feeling it sink into the soft flesh of her armpit. She screamed this time. Loudly. It frightened Philip. The sound rang in his ears. He wanted to fall against her and beg her forgiveness. But he'd been taught about that. Animals don't feel emotions.

But he could see it in her eyes. They were wide and full of fear and distress.

'That's just your emotions, reflected back at you. Now pull yourself together.'

Philip directed her back to the starting position. He was exhausted. Holding back tears and suppressing the fright of her screams had stolen the breath from him. He felt sweat soaking his clothes. It dripped over his brow and stung his eyes. He let himself cry. Colonel Breaker wouldn't see. He couldn't tell the tears from the sweat.

'Alright, gimme the hook,' the Colonel's voice demanded. Philip retreated a few paces and held the bullhook out. The Colonel took it from him, and he instinctively turned his face away. He'd made a mistake earlier and turned his back to Mary. He'd done it a thousand times when she'd been under five years. But now she was older. Now she was an adult elephant. Seemingly docile, but able to snap. Just like any wild animal. But he'd known her since he was twelve...

'Naming them's gone and got to your head, boy.'

Colonel Breaker walked up to Mary and rammed the bullhook into her ear. One swift stroke. She cried out, and he dragged her over to the resting bars. Philip dragged himself quickly over to the leash and collar and hurried, sweaty and panting, over to Mary. He threw the collar over her neck, and fastened, before trying the other end of her leash to the resting bars. The Colonel reached up to check the buckle of her collar and whistled.

'Sure is big, this one,' he said. He tapped the side of her face with the hook, and she recoiled so quickly her head hit the tin wall with a resonant thud. 'Been trained before, too. Not s'well, though.'

He was tapping the bullhook against the crowning tusks on either side of her trunk. Philip had never seen an Indian cow elephant that grew tusks, but he'd heard they existed. Colonel Breaker was right on one thing though; she was big. Bigger than the other elephants of Stable 6, and some of them were at full maturity; ten to twelve years old.

Colonel Breaker whistled through his teeth. Philip knew what it meant, and he hurried across to the other four elephants to unbuckle their collars. They'd spent long hours training these ones. Philip had forgotten their names. Once they were in Stable 6, they were usually gone shortly after. He directed the four into the centre of the stable, and they knew already to form a semi-circle around him. Colonel Breaker joined him and handed him the bullhook.

Already the big animals were shrinking. They were nine, ten feet tall, while Philip was barely five foot six, but with the bullhook, he might as well be twenty feet tall. Their size and visible power did not intimidate him. He wondered how much time he'd spent with them in their younger years. Or if that had anything to do with why they didn't attack. More likely, it was the bullhook. He felt silly, being so emotional over Mary. He didn't like the days with the Colonel, but as he guided the elephants through a simple routine, he could see the rewards of their labours. Elephants that were obedient and didn't need to be struck. He had them walk in a full circle around them. Turn twice on the spot. Face outward. Sit back. Raise their trunks and front legs. Fall forward, into a brief headstand. They did it all, fluidly and without a fuss. It was a simple routine, but they spent years drilling it into them. When the circus owners came to select elephants for their tours, they always wanted to see that they were at least a little bit trained. The rest, the barrel-walking, the waving flags, the being ridden by showgirls, that was up to the circus. This was just a show to make the owners want to hire or buy the elephants. A simple routine.

They also had to do it without too much correction. When the circus owners came to visit, they'd have to trade the bullhook for a regular stick, which both the Colonel and both Misters Junor insisted to Philip wouldn't do any good if one of the elephants lost their temper. But some circus owners didn't like the bullhook.

'They'll get 'emselves killed one day,' the Colonel always said.

Philip had them run through the routine again. One of them stepped out. He quickly beat its armpit, and it fell back into line without screaming or limping afterward. He looked at Mary. He hoped somehow, she'd see, and learn. Like these elephants learned not to scream.

'They're just dumb animals.'

Still, he hoped. Somehow. She'd learn not to defy, or scream. Maybe even learn some of the routines. But she was just standing there, chewing on some hay she'd scooped up from the floor.

'They're just dumb animals.'

CHAPTER 16

Seasons changed and changed again. Mary forgot.

She forgot hate. She forgot hope. She forgot the touch of the rain, as they only took her out walking when it was dry outside. Even when they did, she felt only somewhat aware of things. The sun on her back. The dirt and grass against her feet. She didn't eat when she was hungry, only when they fed her. Eventually, she forgot hunger. Forgot the humid mornings and lush evenings of her home country, the sense of her mother, the security, the love and that stability. These were ideas, but nothing she had ever grasped. Nothing she had ever known or would ever know again. She forgot those days when she'd frolic with the horse. Seeing horses, she saw only creatures that aided the people. They did not remind her of anything. She forgot the days when Philip was anything but a cruel person with a bullhook. She grew bigger but felt small. Tiny. Insignificant. She'd watch flying creatures and wish she was one. Able to fly away. Leave Philip and the Colonel. But she forgot that too, eventually.

But she learned as well. She learned the relief of getting the routine right. Mary even felt happy when Philip didn't hit her. The way she might have felt, once, when children cheered for her. Attention that was happy, not painful. It became a sweet feeling, then euphoric, then an addiction. Not to be hit was the greatest part of her day. It was more exciting than the soft muzzle of a horse, more than the open country, more than fresh water or warm sunlight. It was even more important than beautiful, painful memories. She'd wake up craving the applause that was a relieved smile from Philip and content silence from Colonel Breaker.

The Colonel's bull hook hurt more than Philip's, at first. But gradually, as Philip and Mary both grew bigger, Philip used it more and more, while the Colonel stood back and watched. Mary saw the same pattern of training passed from the Colonel to Philip as Philip passed to Mary. She even saw the Colonel hit Philip a few times, to stop him from crying. Mary never thought it would work. Philip only cried silently, when hit. But one day, the Colonel stepped in a swiped him across the head with the back of his hand, and Philip's eyes dried and his face lost its sorrowful contortion and even the red faded from his skin, and he was cold and predatory as a tiger. It was so sudden! Mary realized that people learned through pain, and that was how they were teaching her.

Eventually, she decided they were helping her. The people were teaching her ways to perform tricks. She learned to stand on her head, to balance on a giant ball and walk around on it, to stand on a little platform, to sit back with her forelimbs and trunk in the air, to spin on the spot and even to let a worker ride on her back. They taught her how to do all these things, synchronized with three other elephants, who didn't go by names.

'They're hurting me!' the new ones would complain, when they stepped out of line and were hit with the bullhook under the arm, or on the ear, to drag them back into step.

'They're teaching us!' Mary would always answer. 'They're helping us!'

Mary alone seemed to know that doing tricks endeared elephants to humans, just like performing Old Boy's tricks in front of the children made them cheer and show their teeth to her.

'If they cheer and show their teeth,' Mary would explain in their enclosure at night, 'they don't hit you.'

'They won't kill us if we learn their tricks.'

'This is how we survive in their world.'

Mary came to like that it was their world. Even tigers could be controlled by the people, and if the people wanted to keep the elephants performing their tricks, they couldn't let the tigers hurt them. They'd killed her mother, but her mother never had a chance to understand. Nothing was stronger or more lethal than a person, Mary realized, so under their protection, she was safe. The calf who died from his wounds, that day so long ago, would have been safe from the tiger had he learned to do tricks for people.

'All you have to do is learn to avoid the pain,' Mary reassured the newcomers, before they'd disappear again.

She never had time to make friends. The elephants came and went too quickly. Mary was the only one that stayed. She grew big. Always bigger than those that came in to join her in Stable 6. She knew her mother had been big; bigger than all the other elephants of her herd. But she couldn't remember how much bigger. Once, she swayed her head to try and dream herself back to being by her mother's side, but she was so small then that there was no comparison now.

Mary did feel lonely. Mostly when Philip and the Colonel weren't there, and she was left with the other elephants, who'd sway their heads as they tried to remember things, leaving Mary with nothing to do but join them. Her isolation remained a constant cold darkness that lurked in her periphery like some entity, stroking its cold talons over her flesh now and then when she wasn't looking, and leaving sad thoughts in her heart. Eventually, even the loneliness became part of her. Like a piece of herself that she couldn't remember not having. She just accepted its dull ache, its sad thoughts, the heaviness of mourning, the prickles of fear and vulnerability without people around, and the gentle malaise that felt soft as a whisper and lived with it as one does a heartbeat or breathing. There was no such thing as life without it.

She'd still reach into her mind to try and find pictures, sensations or even just emotions of what she used to have. Openness. Wilderness. The lonely trees. The looming mountains. The infinite security of her mother's gaze. But it came forever tinged with fear.

It wasn't security, she told herself, because she lost it. It was stolen from her by people. Nothing stole from people, though. They were too strong.

One morning, Philip entered without the Colonel. Without a word, he opened the gate and called out the elephants, and had them run through a routine. With experienced Mary leading, all went perfectly. He only hit one of the others, twice, and that might have only been warning strikes. When all of them had returned to the semi-circle, Mary on the far right, Philip held up the bullhook threateningly.

'Now y'all don't screw this up, now, y'hear?' he warned. Mary knew what that meant. That was all he said to them, these days, except for the usual orders for their performances. He'd grown bigger too; he was tall for a person, and thin. Narrow shoulders and skinny legs. Nothing like the Colonel. From a distance, they would have seemed like different species. But in their eyes, it was the same; that authoritarian malice. That cold, calculating stare they had. Discerning the elephants. That was how Mary knew Philip and the Colonel were the same creatures.

The doors were opened, and in walked a man in a ragged suit with a black jacket. He carried a hat in his hands and had tufts of blonde hair left on a scraggy head. Philip gave the order, and the elephants ran through the routine again. But something went wrong.

Mary's thoughts went elsewhere. Maybe she hadn't been disciplined in too long and had grown complacent, or maybe there was simply too much else on her mind. She wasn't thinking much. One of the lonely trees had occurred to her, during a daydream, and it had seemed magnificently detailed; it's bulbous trunk, its thin canopy which rustled in a light breeze, the green that shot out of its winding branches when the wind carried those slivers of cold that hinted of a cold season soon. Whatever it was, she walked in a straight line, instead of a circle.

The furious pain of the bullhook bit her ear sharply, and Philip pulled her back into line. But it was too late; the other elephants followed Mary and Mary had gotten off track. Without her, they simply meandered about. Philip had to call for help. Two workers came, also with bullhook, and pulled the elephants back into line.

'Actually, I hear Ringling's putting one up for auction,' the man said after they talked for a while. 'Thanks all the same.'

Philip looked at Mary with white rage blazing out of his face. The workers mustered the other elephants back into the enclosure, but Mary was kept out. Philip attacked her. He beat her again and again, until her heart shook, and sorrow flowed out of her eyes and mouth in the form of tears and wailing. The agony shot through her like a lance each time; through her face, her eye, her ear, her jaw, her leg...over and over. She thought he'd never stop.

Finally, he did.

'You're the oldest one here, Mary!' Philip shouted as he tried to catch his breath. 'We done this routine five hundred times if we done it once! So, the only thing I can think is, you done this on purpose! You done screweded it all up on purpose! Just to get at me! That's all I can think, Mary!'

He worked himself up into a fevered state and attacked her again. Mary screamed and cried. She hurried back to her enclosure and cried after he left. All through the night, she wept openly, while the other elephants tried to dream. She was sorry to Philip. She was sorry to ruin his routine.

She knew what was supposed to happen. The man in the
suit was supposed to pick an elephant, and that elephant would
be taken away. Gone forever. But this time it didn't happen.
Mary knew it was her fault. She hated herself. She hated
herself so much she imagined more beatings. The bullhook
became her mother's trunk, flailing her for her abandonment.
She was a terrible elephant, she thought. A failed daughter, a
failed member of a herd, she couldn't stay captive in one
place, she couldn't do Old Boy's routines properly, and now
she'd failed this one. She might as well die, she thought. Just
die.

Next time, she was so afraid she almost pre-empted what
Philip wanted her to do. The man picked out his elephant,
and that was that. Mary didn't get beaten. She felt good but was
still sorry to Philip.

Another time, they were out for their walk, and a breeze
carried across from stable one the fresh, powdery smell of little
calves. Mary didn't know why, but her heart swelled suddenly
with sorrow and she started crying and walking toward Stable
1, instead of where she was supposed to. She wanted to find
the source of them smell, to touch them, to caress their little
heads and hold their little trunks in hers, to protect and guide
and care for them. For the first time in her life, Mary felt truly
dangerous. It was a desperate anger at first, but then she saw

198

the little creatures as they beat her with their bullhook. She perceived herself crushing them with her feet or bashing their heads off with her trunk. She could do it, she thought. One swift stroke, it would break that little neck easily.

Horrified with herself, she cried that night as well.

The world around her changed. Philip stopped arriving at the stables in a wagon pulled by horses and instead came in a wagon with no horses, which ticked loudly. She finally learned these things were called automobiles. The stables had objects fitted high on the walls which made light, even at night.

Mary tried to imagine where the picked elephants went. She couldn't imagine anywhere more bland, painful and exhaustingly stressful than here. Sometimes the thought of upsetting Philip kept her from sleeping all night. She'd just stand there, swaying and hearing her own heartbeat, to the point where it became painful, as though it was smacking against her ribs. Every time she breathed in, a sharp pain would shoot through her chest. She'd lose her breath, just standing there. The thought of upsetting Philip would revolve around in her mind, over and over and over. She'd be dry-mouthed and frozen with fear. The next day, she'd be so tired she knew she'd get at least one bite from the bullhook, either for being too slow or just appearing too shabby.

Then, one day, Philip took her out of the enclosure alone. Outside of Stable 6, a whole lot of workers joined them. Mary wondered if she was being taken away, but then they didn't lead her out through the gates. They led her to the stable directly behind 6. One she'd never even been near before. She tried to feel relief that, in some small way, her usual, measured, symmetrical and straight day was being broken up by something, but she couldn't. Though she knew she was grateful, she felt hollow. Empty. The fog in her mind had finally consumed her. She wasn't an elephant anymore. Even that thought didn't make her feel too sad. She only worried about disappointing Philip, at whatever it was she was being taken away to do.

They pulled the doors open for her, and she was blasted by an unfamiliar smell. It was intimidating. Her heart was beating at last. The giant elephant, towering over her captives, felt helpless and weak. She felt deep parts of herself come alive where she'd never felt alive before, as far as she knew. Sensations she could not even place in the memory of a dream. They led her into the stable, and she saw the elephants they had in here. They were bigger than she was. They had long, white tusks on either side of their trunks. Not like her little things. They were huge. They smelled strong. They moved, and stomped their feet at the sight of her, as Philip led her in. Mary felt short of breath. Her chest was tightening. She felt again. She was relieved for that. She was trembling, she was frightened, she was intimidated, she felt.

Feeling awoke another thing she'd forgotten; bulls. She'd not thought of bulls in so long that they'd stopped even occurring to her. But now, here they were. One of the assistants had untethered one of the larger bulls and it moved toward her. She quickly evaded. But something else had been awoken. Some tingling amidst the fear. The tightness in her chest was not altogether from her intimidation...or it was the intimidation she felt exciting? Like the tingle before an electrical storm. A soft current flowing on the breeze. She remembered something, then.

It was a sparse place. Open and grassy. The sun was hot, not like today. Today it was cold and frigid, and the sky was grey, heralding the coming snowfall. But she felt that heat. She remembered a giant elephant, casting a shadow that was like night itself, how it covered so much of the land. Giant. Bigger than any structure a sir could build. It had tusks, this monster. It was an elephant. It frightened her. It intimidated her. But it excited her, and she never knew why.

The bull in the stable moved closer and she evaded again. Philip was standing nearby her, holding the bullhook. The bull moved again, and she tried to evade, but the sight of the bullhook suddenly thrust at her halted her still. She turned back toward the other elephant.

It kept its distance as well. It raised its trunk, up and down, as though trying to remember some custom, or something that was supposed to be done, to make it known. The bull, like her, must have forgotten about being an elephant. She knew this. She knew the bull knew this as well. So, she just did what he did. She raised her trunk at him. They grunted to each other. Back and forth. Again, and again. The bull finally moved in closer. She didn't back away. She felt her blood run hot. She was scared, but not chilled. Her trembling wasn't because of slivers of cold that normally came when she was terrified. This terror was hot. It was comfortable. It was almost sweet.

The bull got close enough to reach out with his trunk. She withdrew. But Philip did not strike her with the hook. He kept out of the way. The currents had gotten stronger. The bull reverted to raising his trunk at her. She raised hers back. He grunted. She grunted. His smell was overpowering. Dizzying. She felt her mind awash with strange sensations. Sweet sensations.

The bull moved in closer again, and this time his trunk touched hers. It was warm against her skin. She felt herself flushing. A cascade of warmth soaking through her. She felt soft and vulnerable. He moved in closer. Touched her more. She touched him, feeling more of his warmth. The currents grew intense. The heat was like a deluge.

She was not in control, but control was not taken from her. She surrendered.

CHAPTER 17

Ernie Grimes died in June of 1907. Philip Junor knew, as soon as Benjamin's letter arrived with the date for the funeral, that he would be unable to attend. He hadn't spoken to the crazy old man in years anyway, or so Philip reasoned in his responding letter, and he'd been useless around the compound since 1902 when he had the first stroke. How old was he anyway? Ninety? What if Philip was asked to speak about him? He couldn't! He hardly remembered what the guy looked like, let alone anything he said or did. Other than breakfast. He remembered the odd breakfast when Philip was a kid. But that was years ago. He'd be embarrassed. Benjamin was the one who kept in touch and kept the useless old negro employed, even though he couldn't even lift a broom. It was enough that Benjamin would go. More than enough that Junor Brothers were paying for the damn funeral because Grimes was penniless.

Philip omitted from the letter and, so much as it was possible, from his own mind that there was a guest coming today to inspect that damn Mary.

'Honey, breakfast is ready!' Angeline called from downstairs. Philip quickly crumpled the letter announcing the funeral into his trash basket and stood up from his writing desk. He'd kept it there until today, in case anybody went into his office. They'd see it, and think he intended to go.

She sat with their newborn daughter on her lap, her dress thin and loose for the Missouri summer. The little one, Deborah, was feeding from her. Seeing his wife caked in sweat, stretched and torn out of shape, her hair a matted mess about her salty head, Philip couldn't help but cringe. Even her soft French accent disturbed him now. As an eighteen-year-old taking a post-graduation tour of the South, he'd found the Creole women of New Orleans devastatingly attractive. But it wasn't long after he brought Angeline up to meet his family that it started to occur to him how popular she'd been around Bourbon Street. How many others had enjoyed the better days of Angeline's body, before Deborah came along and destroyed it? He had sworn it would never be a problem for him. He was so madly taken by lust, he thought he meant his word. It would be their secret forever. Forever lasted two years.

Philip sat down to his bacon and eggs. There was a side of oatmeal, which Angeline still hadn't figured out how to make properly. It was like cement. She smiled at him, looking dejected, as she always did since he stopped kissing her good morning.

The Colonel had seen through the façade. 'Them N'awlins folk ought to be sent back where they come from,' he'd warned. 'Won't be long, boy. You'll be layin' wi'that wummun, an' it'll pop into yo' head where you found her. What she was doin' there before you came. You'll think of all those other men, and what they done t'that body a'hers. Then, once the baby stretches it out, rips it all up like, you'll wish y'left her in that whorehouse.'

As usual, the old breaker was right.

Philip watched the back of Deborah's near-hairless head throb slightly as it sucked the milk out of Angeline. He wanted to be sick.

'You're sure you won't come today?' Angeline asked.

'I told them already,' Philip scoffed, shaking his head. He avoided looking at her.

'He spoke about you, near the end,' she said. Philip had objected to her spending so much time at his bedside, as old man Grimes withered away. Still, she mentioned doing it. 'What a good boy you used to be.'

'Useless then as he is now,' Philip mumbled, through a mouthful of bacon.

Angeline sighed. 'What are you doing today, then?'

'Got someone coming to look at Mary,' he was eating quicker, eager to end the conversation and be on his way. Away from the sight of her.

'Oh, she's such a nice elephant!' Angeline said, as Deborah, having finished suckling, promptly vomited over her mother's shoulder. 'Oh, dear.'

'She'd be nice if she could breed,' Philip said, as he watched Angeline set Deborah on the benchtop. She wiped her neck and shoulder with a wet cloth. 'Elephant that size would make a fine litter.'

'Who's going to buy her?' Angeline asked, turning to look at him. For a moment, he saw her hazel eyes and remembered something about her...a hot sensation touched him as it passed by. But it was momentary. Her dress was clinging to the sweat coating her body.

'If I told you a name, would you know it?'

Angeline shrugged.

'Then what difference does it make?'

'I just asked.'

'Well, what the hell for?' Philip threw the last piece of bacon down and stood up. 'Charlie Sparks, you happy? Do you know who that is? Are you wiser now?'

She sulked at him, then turned to pick up Deborah. Philip took his white jacket and hat and headed out the front door. He managed to curse his wife the whole hour and a half walk, as the blazing sun unleashed its full fury onto the green hills. The leather on his boots had loosened, and he felt blisters forming. Angeline should have kept an eye on that.

He did regret one thing about missing the funeral. Mary Parker's younger sister Celeste had come of age, at last, Philip couldn't take his eyes off her smooth, supple sides and delicate, white neck at the last family gathering...it might have been Mary's funeral, he didn't remember. But what could he do? Angeline was there. Bulging with a baby inside her. Junor Brothers needed an heir. Someone to take up training and grow accustomed to the animals. Benjamin wasn't going to produce a son any time soon, having moped about over the death of Mary Parker a whole year and a half now. Angeline had pushed out a daughter. Now he was going to have to make love to her again. Her...body, if anyone can call it that anymore.

Sheriff Donoghue was standing at the gates to the facility, with the retiring night watchman, Billy. Philip cursed Angeline again, though he couldn't quite figure how this was her fault. 'Morning, Sheriff!'

'Morning Mister Junor,' Donoghue said, touching the rim of his hat. 'Thought I'd drop by, see if you were expecting any visitors today.'

'That I am, Sheriff, but only Charlie Sparks.'

'Who's that?'

'Circus owner,' Philip said, before seeing he'd need to give up more than that. 'You might not have heard of John H. Sparks' World-Famous Shows. Not a big outfit. Comes by Springfield about twice a year. Usually passes right on through.'

'Sure,' Donoghue said. 'I heard Ernie Grimes was being buried today.'

'At the expense of Junor Brothers,' Philip said, through his teeth.

'Any old friends in town for that?' Donoghue asked.

'Not the fella you're thinking of,' Philip said. 'They weren't exactly close.'

'Who am I thinking of?'

'Breaker Croft,' Philip said, stopping himself from saying 'Colonel'. He felt confident, nonetheless.

'S'pose he's still in Ethiopia, or Sandtopia, or...where was it?' the Sheriff was saying.

'Congo,' Philip said, only able to guess himself. He was eager to move the Sheriff along, lest Charlie Sparks walk in on a questioning.

'Well, good day,' the Sheriff said and touched his hat again. He cranked up his automobile, and was on his way, popping and spluttering down the trail toward town. It was no secret Sheriff Donoghue never got over his suspicion of the Colonel in the murder of Mary Parker. He'd been the one to find her at the bottom of Red Stone Creek. The suspender strap used to strangle her was still around her neck. Of course, he reported it immediately. But for whatever reason, the law turned against him. Harassed him night and day, despite the fact that two ex-con negros had come to work at Junor Brothers and run off only nine months beforehand. The Klan saw a potential miscarriage of justice from all the way over in Little Rock Arkansas and rode into town to lynch the negros and a few others who'd been hiding them in Criswell, just a half mile west. All of Springfield had been satisfied, except Sheriff Donoghue. Something about an unsolved murder in northern New Mexico, a twelve-year-old girl killed just the same way. Donoghue thought they were connected. He never gave up, even when Colonel Breaker was harassed right out of the country. Donoghue hadn't counted on the Colonel's contacts in Africa. But the Sheriff still held hope that the Colonel would slip up and return to Springfield, someday. What he'd charge him for, only he knew. The case of Mary Parker was long solved, in everyone else's eyes, including Philip's.

'All the bull hooks out of Stable 6?' Philip asked Billy, as the Sheriff's exhaust cloud disappeared over the hill.

'What's that, sir?'

'God damn it!' Philip spat. 'I told you to make sure the bull hooks were taken out of Stable 6 by morning!'

'Taken where?'

'Anywhere not Stable 6,' Philip was shouting. 'Get the boys you have left here together, and get it done, will you?'

'I got to go home!'

'Well you had ten hours to do your damn job, so now you're gonna be late! Get!' Philip almost kicked Billy's pants, as he hurried through the gates. Philip followed as he heard the carload of day workers rolling up behind him.

No sooner had an exhausted Billy finally reported that the bull hooks were hidden did Philip hear the sound of another car cracking and creaking its way through the gates of the facility.

'Alright, get on home,' Philip said, sending Billy out of his office. He quickly checked his appearance in the mirror off to the side, and there was a knock at his door. 'Come on in.'

The door cracked first, then opened all the way. Charlie Sparks was never off. As his slender frame, wrapped in a bright yellow waistcoat, black blazer and tall top hat, stepped through the door. He puffed on his cigar and carried an air that would be suited to a crowd of hundreds. His smile was broad, posture was open, and gestures just that little bit exaggerated beyond the normal. When he took his hat off he practically pirouetted to face the hat stand and hang it up. He had a black moustache, was short in stature, and still had the faint politeness of his English ancestry to his speech.

'How do you do, Philip Junor,' he said, as he took a long stride to shake Philip's hand. 'What a fine day it is!'

'That it is,' Philip said, taking a seat at his desk. Sparks sat opposite. 'You well?'

'Well,' the smile escaped Sparks' face so suddenly and completely that Philip almost felt his heart sink. 'You know, Addie and I lost our beloved elephant just this month gone. An infection, of all things. Where could she have got that? She was with us since birth, you know. Jumbo wasn't born in America, I'll venture to guess.'

Philip shook his head. Sparks' rivals, the giant Barnum & Bailey, had bought Jumbo from Philip's father. But Sparks didn't need to know that.

'Anyway,' Sparks waved a cloud of exhaled smoke out of his face. 'They've got that Jumbo, you know, and they always manage to tour when we're kicking off, by Jove. We have horses, five lions and a tiger! But the audiences want an elephant. Oh, I'm so sorry our beloved Geordie's gone.'

Geordie was Sparks' elephant. Philip remembered seeing their circus as a boy, and Geordie was just a baby. But he was too amused by Sparks' exclamations to say anything; the way he raised his hands to the heavens whenever he mentioned his dead elephant, and the way the man's emotions seemed to have complete control over him.

Sparks was slumped in his chair, stroking his brow and making a strange, whining noise. 'Oh, Geordie...'

'Well, that's what we're here for, Mister Sparks,' Philip finally said, seeing the show was probably over. 'I'm sure nobody can replace Geordie, but we might just have a specimen that would give Barnum & Bailey a run for their money.'

'Oh, please don't use that word, specimen,' Sparks said, waking from his trance and holding both hands up before him. 'They aren't tissue samples, young man. They're beautiful creatures. Just magnificent!'

Philip smiled to remember the Colonel's constant warnings about being too kind to the elephants. Sparks was one who was defiantly and aggressively opposed to the bullhook. Or any kind of discipline whatever, it seemed.

'Do you really?' Sparks said, as though Philip had repeated himself. 'Addie is terribly nervous, you know.'

Addie meant Adelaide Sparks, whom Philip had only read about. Sparks' wife, whom he allows to co-manage the circus. Philip had no doubt in his mind why they were on the verge of bankruptcy.

'I understand Misses Sparks' concerns, that's why I kept this big darling in reserve, just for you,' Philip said. 'When I heard Geordie had passed away, I knew you'd need the comfort of a really special elephant.'

'Barnum & Bailey would have snapped her up if she was really special,' Sparks waved him off, correctly guessing the elephant's sex. Most people say 'he' whether it's a cow or not.

'Barnum & Bailey came snooping,' Philip lied. They had, but it was while he was still trying to get Mary to breed, and make others like her. 'But I said to myself, Philip, Charlie Sparks needs this elephant. Nobody but Charlie Sparks should have this mighty elephant.'

'Oh, you're a darling young man, a true gentleman,' Sparks said, reaching across the desk. 'Please, can we see her? Oh, she's not been reared with those dreadful bullhooks, has she?'

'Absolutely not!' Philip said, standing.

'Bless you, boy, bless you, bless you.'

Philip walked the little man out of his office and across the compound. He saw that the hood was drawn over Sparks' car and Adelaide Sparks was sitting in the back seat, dressed in a frilly gown that Philip thought would be unbearably hot. But from the distance, she seemed composed. Her make-up clung to her face perfectly. Her hair was up, under her hat. She was a figure of elegance, seeming cool against the heat. He didn't know how old she was, but she was a picture of beauty. He wished he could meet her. But he couldn't ask. It would be inappropriate, and he knew he'd only go home even more bitter at Angeline than when he'd left her.

They walked to Stable 6 and a labourer got the side door for them. Philip held his breath. If one bull hook was hanging in sight, he'd use it on Billy. But it really wasn't too much of a problem. The mention of Barnum & Bailey had given him an idea. They could easily afford Mary. More easily than Sparks, who was doubtless pledging his last remaining scraps.

He paused at the door, a dramatic effect he figured Sparks would appreciate. 'Mister Charlie Sparks meet Mary the Elephant.'

'Mary, oh a lovely name, just absolutely lovely name.'

They walked into the tempered light of Stable 6, and Mary was the only elephant present. Philip exhaled, seeing Billy had left not one bull hook in sight. She stood at the far end of the stable, watching them approach. Labourers hurried past Philip and Sparks to let her out of the enclosure. Philip stopped Sparks right where he and the Colonel stood while he was learning his trade. He could see Sparks was already taken. The circus owner stared, wide-eyed, at the giant creature before him, his mouth slightly open.

Philip took a few paces forward. He beckoned Mary and she took a few strides closer, then turned slightly to one side, showing her full size and girth. A man like Sparks was completely dwarfed. His mouth hung agape.

'Massive, absolutely massive!' Sparks wheezed.

Philip beamed, knowing he had the sale. He gestured Mary to walk. She did a quick lap around them and Sparks stared fixedly at her all the way, utterly enraptured. She stopped.

216

Turned around once. She sat down, as ordered, then raised
her trunk and forelimbs into the air. Then rolled forward into
a perfect headstand, looking back at Sparks as she did. At the
end, she took a few paces back to the front-centre and stood
still.

'Five-point-three tons,' Philip said. 'Twelve years old. Born
and raised right here in Springfield, Missouri. Asian elephant,
Indian parents. That's from India, by the way,' he winked at
Sparks, but it went ignored. 'Trained by professional circus
handlers on loan from Cedric and Co., without bullhooks, of
course. She stands eleven feet, nine inches tall. Name, as
stated, is Mary.'

'Mary,' Sparks said, as he stepped in towards her. 'Mary,
hello Mary. My name is Charlie Sparks. It is truly a pleasure to
meet you. I'm Charlie Sparks, Mary.'

She watched him approach with her trunk obediently
wrapped under her chin. He held out his hand and gently
touched her between the eyes.

'Mary, you are magnificent, do you know that?' Sparks
asked her. Philip forced himself not to laugh. 'Magnificent
Mary. No, what was the word you used, Mister Junor?'

Philip opened his mouth but couldn't remember.

'Mighty!' Sparks said, as he reached up and patted Mary's face, adoringly. 'Mighty Mary. Mighty Mary. I cannot wait to show you to the world, Mighty Mary.'

CHAPTER 18

Mary held her breath as the little person who kept saying her name, this Charlie Sparks, approached her. He raised his hands to his sides as he did, speaking to her gently, and then he touched her. She felt her flesh tighten upon the first contact. Charlie Sparks didn't seem to notice. He just kept petting her and saying she was Mighty Mary over and over again. She looked at Philip, who just stood there with a faint smile on his lips and a predatory glint in his eyes as he watched Charlie Sparks. Neither of them had noticed her flinch. Then, neither of them noticed how her skin flushed with sudden heat from a surge of emotion. Vulnerability, mourning, grief, yearning, needing, loneliness and desire all came together in one great eruption that forced tears to her eyes, which also went unnoticed. For a moment, Mary didn't understand, but then she realized, as her body relaxed, and Charlie Sparks kept petting her, that she couldn't remember being touched.

She'd been hit with a cane, hit with a bullhook, she'd been lashed with a rope, cuffed with chains and pushed and shoved and had her trunk slapped, but a person had never touched her. Even Philip had never touched her. Through her mind flashed all the bull elephants as well. Touching her with their trunks, with their feet, their bellies on her back as they'd entered her, one after the other, for days and days unending.

That had been touching, but they had wanted something from her. This was a different kind of touching. Charlie Sparks touched her for no reason but to calm her and make her feel good. It wasn't punishment, it wasn't needy, it wasn't selfish or cruel or false, though she'd learned that people could beguile as effectively as they could kill and destroy. There was something about the touch, and the soft, gentle words, that assured this was true. This was genuinely just for her.

It had been so long. It had been since...her mother.

For a moment, she felt light and small and vulnerable. Soft and weak and in the care of great, watchful sentries whose hearts beat for her. She remembered the forest's edge. Rows of trees with fat trunks. Stifling heat that made breathing difficult. Creek beds with thin vapours wafting over them just before the heavy rain fell. Creeper vines brushing her back gently as she passed under them. It was a place where the sky never ended, where she could walk forever in any direction she pleased and never see a fence or a house or a stable or a person at all. It was a place where the constant ache in her heart, the pieces that were broken and cracked, could come alive and form the presence of her mother; above her, behind her and around her. Never in front, never where she could see, but there all the same.

It was all over in a few breath-taking moments. Charlie
Sparks was back with Philip and they were talking, all the while
Charlie Sparks' eyes kept moving back over to her as he
looked her up and down. He seemed somewhat melancholy
himself, with shoulders that slumped and eyes that seemed too
heavy for him. He was only small. Mary knew she was going
with him.

She dreaded the possibilities ahead of her; some other
confined space, another Stables that popped and rattled under
the morning sun, that got blazingly hot in the warm months
and numbingly freezing when the snow fell and that was
overseen by cruel people that beat her with bullhooks, or
another water-machine, where the suffering of animals formed
a constant, deafening backdrop of raging torment. They all
floated around in her mind. Possibilities, like nightmares, but
rooted in memories instead of in dreams. Yet, her heart
remained open and vulnerable. It was even frightening, even
frustrating, that the terrors in her head couldn't stay the
affection swelling in her heart. The suspicions she had forged
inside herself, like stone walls against the innocence, fragility,
and friendliness people like Philip were capable of exhibiting
before they turned violent and cruel, were crumbling beneath
the delicate hands of Charlie Sparks. Mary could not help but
trust and want to go with, her new master and protector. He
didn't carry a cane or a bullhook, though he dressed in

symmetrical, well-fitted second skins. He didn't stand over her
or bark sharply. But more than anything, gone was the cold
indifference of the average person, that which had been the
constant of Old Boy and the Colonel, and which Philip had
learned from the latter. There was just a gentle, slightly sad
face. More like the apes than any person Mary had yet come
across, not just in physicality, but in the peaceful, serene
benevolence he radiated.

The surrounding workers ushered Mary back into the
enclosure and closed the gate on her, while Philip walked with
Charlie Sparks back to the door, and out into the warm
morning sunlight. Already, she was excited to see him again.
She knew her time with Philip was soon to end, and she would
miss him, but the anticipation of going away from here with
Charlie Sparks was an enrapturing feeling she couldn't recall
experiencing before, and so it drowned out her concerns.

Mary strutted around the pen, buzzing and quivering while
other elephants were brought in to join her. They ran through
their routines, went for their walks, and swayed in their
enclosure at night, as always, but Mary kept the light glowing
inside her heart. She just couldn't imagine that anywhere
Charlie Sparks would take her could be worse than this place,
and this place had become her home. She'd grown

accustomed to pain but daring to let herself believe that there might be no more felt too good to deny herself.

They didn't take her to the bulls anymore, either. That didn't bother her, at first, but on one of their walks, she caught their scent on a soft breeze as the column passed by their stable, and Mary grew uncomfortably agitated. Hot flushes made her dizzy. She ground her teeth that night, trying to weather the tide of lust roiling in her loins. By morning, she found herself swaying her trunk from side to side, unable to break the aggression hardening her flesh.

Then, she noticed the workers running around in the grey light of early morning. They were gathering up the bullhooks. They'd done that the morning Charlie Sparks had visited, and never before or since. She forgot all about her base needs and watched the door with waiting eyes. The soft rustle of the other elephants swaying their heads, brushing their trunks against the floor, became irritating, as though it was slowing down time and delaying Charlie Sparks from reaching her. She wanted to hit them. To shut them up. But then, finally, the door opened. Philip stood aside, and in stepped Charlie Sparks, his hands out to his sides and a warm smile again on his face.

'Mary!' he cried.

Behind him walked another person, this one Mary could tell was a female. A woman. Her second skin billowed out

223

from her middle, like an upside-down tree, and was all frilly. Her hat was frilly as well, and a translucent layer of frills thinly veiled her face, so Mary couldn't quite make out her eyes or nose or mouth. But her top half and arms were both bound tightly in the second skin, which was pure white all over except for the boots, which were black, so Mary could see the more delicate shape of her. She was soft and curved where Philip and Charlie Sparks were sharp and angular. The woman stood so the light from the door seemed to light up her dress, as though she was shining her own light. She was smaller than both of them, narrower and shorter, and looked so delicate that Mary was afraid she'd frighten the poor little thing...she realized she had never seen a person female up close before. Yet, this one was oddly familiar. The woman radiated a presence, almost uncomfortable in its sweetness, oddly troubling in its immediate intimacy. Though her face remained enshrouded in the veil, there was just something about the way Mary felt as the woman stared at her through it, the way she held herself so upright and so tender and so calm, in spite of her obvious fragility, that made Mary want to cry. Like Charlie Sparks' petting, but more so, it made her feel soft and vulnerable.

'Come,' Philip ordered, so Mary gingerly stepped out of her enclosure and took the space she always took, front and centre. The workers closed the gates and locked the other elephants inside.

The woman smelled strange. It was a pleasant smell, but one that felt so artificial, so unnatural, that Mary found it unsettling. The people, it seemed, not only created their own habitats, they created their own smells as well. But still, Mary could not but be fixated with the woman. She didn't recoil the slightest bit when Mary stepped closer to them. She just stayed right beside Charlie Sparks, watching devotedly.

'Mary,' Charlie Sparks said, 'this is Miss Addy.'

Miss Addy lifted the veil off her face, and Mary almost shivered. The skin was somewhere between the brown of the workers from her homeland, and the white of the cruel overlords. Her eyes were big for her little face, and they were brown and seemed to have a sparkling, glossy sheen. It was then that Mary placed what made her so unsettled by Miss Addy; it was that watchfulness. A love so devoted and yet so quiet that it never announced itself, and yet was as powerful as gravity. Mary felt it flooding her heart.

Something crept out of the mists of her mind. Something that gently wafted about inside her, and softly whispered 'mother'.

Mary longed to touch Miss Addy. She had to force herself to keep her trunk pointed straight to the ground. She didn't want to be punished by Philip, but she also didn't want Miss Addy to break, she was so small, and yet without saying or doing a thing was able to completely fill a sensation she had longed for such a length of time that it frightened her to feel it again. A sense of total security... of... love. Mary wasn't even sure if she was recalling it right, or if this was something new she was just mistaking for love. Either way, it called to those dark corners of herself that she hadn't yet had the will or the energy to explore, try though she did.

'Mary,' Miss Addy said, with a voice that was like the song of a single bird cooing in the early morning. Sweet, comfortable, and promising warmth and light. 'Pleased to meet you, Mary.'

Miss Addie held out her gentle, delicate hand. Mary thought she could almost see right through it. She touched Mary's trunk with it. It felt so soft and so warm Mary wanted to climb into that tiny little patch and curl up and stay there forever. She closed her eyes, so nothing would keep her from experiencing every moment of this Addie's touch. She felt a vibration through it. More of her mother came to her. The sentinel, watching her. The warm body curled around her at night. The towering defender, guarding her against danger. Somehow, the Miss Addie was all of them, and yet Mary's mother was never so frail and so small. How this beautiful creature could be so much to Mary, so soon, and with so small a frame to in which to exist in the world, was baffling, but in a way that Mary wanted to be confused by. It was not confusion. It was awe. A pure light that channelled out of Miss Addie and into Mary, and shone into all her haunted hollows, where there lurked the nameless pieces of her existence that she hid from herself or that hid from her. The rigor of training, the paralyzing boredom of being held inside enclosures and stables and paddocks, seemed to melt away. She felt the vastness of the earth again. She felt the world open before her. Miss Addie was her doorway.

Mary hadn't even noticed the workers fixing her leash around her neck.

Miss Addy stepped away, still smiling at Mary, and Philip gave her the end of the rope. She took it, so delicately that Mary almost wanted to push Philip away; he was too abrasive and coarse to come so near to her pure softness. Charlie Sparks tapped her forelimb, which meant he wanted to ride her, so she lifted her leg and he climbed up until his legs hung down either side of her neck. He was laughing. Mary was surprised at how light he was. Then, Miss Addy, still smiling, led her toward the stable doors. Mary was breathless with anticipation. She knew she was leaving not only the stables but the compound. For a while at least, that meant openness. No fences surrounding her. No walls. No ceiling. Her body began to ache for it, the closer she got. Once she was under the sky, she could barely contain herself. Only the gentle strides of Miss Addy, who walked as though she was floating on a cloud, kept Mary pacing herself. Every now and then, she looked back to smile at Mary. Mary had never seen a person's smile look so beautiful.

The compound gates were already open, so Mary just had to walk right through. Soon enough, the fresh grass was swishing by her ankles again. Little flowers softened her steps and the sun warmed her skin. Thin white clouds rolled slowly by above through an azure sky. In the distance, trees stood tall and majestic. Mary felt like she was flying; she could look at it all, without a fence or a pole or a stable obstructing her view. She was no longer watching the world, she was part of it. Out there, in the open. She never even looked back at the place she'd grown big in. Already, Philip was fading into the mists of her painful memories. Every breath took all the fresh, shining, green scenery into her and lit her up with green and gold and sunlight yellow. Like a dissipating cloud, she felt rays of warmth bursting through her flesh.

It was brief.

Soon, they were back in town. Mary was so shocked she broke her stride. Everything was so small! Houses had shrunk, as had horses and wagons, and automobiles which ticked and coughed as they rattled past, leaving that cloud of black acrid, foul-smelling black smoke in their wake. People hurried to the sidewalks to watch the elephant go by, and they waved their hands and smiled and cheered, and Mary felt life pulsing through her vividly. She'd done it! She'd learned their tricks, she'd performed for them, and she'd earned their affections. Mary was one of the people! For a moment, she thought all the pain and suffering was worth it. Now she was safe, as well as free.

Then, the train station again, where a long, black train was waiting. Even that seemed tiny compared to the giant, chugging serpent-beasts which haunted her dreams, tearing through the landscape and ripping down trees and smashing through mountains which lay in its way, devouring creatures and spiriting them off to alien worlds. It had been so long since Mary experienced artificial motion, she was excited to see if it had changed for her, the way everything else seemed to have gotten smaller and friendlier.

There was even a little worker child sitting behind a box where pale people put their feet to have them rubbed down with a cloth who stopped to smile at Mary, once she climbed up the ramp and onto the platform. She remembered the person who'd been making the beautiful sounds with his instrument. At last, she had become like him. Making them happy, so they'd accept her. At long last, she felt safe again. She didn't dare raise her trunk or show any sign of excitement, but Mary knew she was destined for better things.

Miss Addy stopped in at the side of a carriage with no walls, just thick bars. A steel frame supported them. Workers standing by hurried up the ramp and heaved the creaky door open. Miss Addy tapped Mary's leg, and she raised her forelimb again, so Charlie Sparks could climb down. He turned to the happy people immediately and held his hand in his hand and made broad gestures toward them.

'Thank you! Thank you!' he bellowed, loudly. Mary was surprised he could make such a noise with his little mouth.

But she was more perplexed by the carriage. She'd wanted openness and freedom, but she'd never imagined such a thing as this!

'Come, Mary,' Miss Addy said. Mary took a breath and walked across the ramp, into the enclosure of steel bars. It was just big enough for her to stand comfortably in. A flash of horror cut through the excitement of the moment as her back touched the bars of the ceiling and, for just a moment, she was taken back to the horrible little cage on the water-machine. But she wasn't. She told herself she wasn't. She was going somewhere new, somewhere her hard work and devotion to Philip's training had finally earned her.

The intermittent hissing of the train pushed memories through Mary's mind as well.

The workers closed the cage on her and carried the ramp away. Charlie Sparks was bowing to the people gathered on the platform as he sidestepped toward the front of the train and gradually disappeared from Mary's sight. Miss Addy gave them a wave, but she turned to Mary for one last beautiful smile before she followed Charlie Sparks.

It was enough to still the little jolts of unease running through Mary, pale though they were compared to her enthusiasm...though she had to insist more and more upon it.

Before long, she was riding by train through that vast and many-coloured and multi-layered landscape again, the wind whipping about her only slightly tempered by the bitter odour of the train's breath.

CHAPTER 19

Daylight came and went, and air that whipped around
Mary's head and body warmed under the sun and cooled in
the twilight and chilled her at night. The landscape seemed to
go on and on forever and the train spewed its horrible, bitter
air out the entire time. Mary found herself wishing with all her
might the journey would end soon. She could barely believe
they hadn't gone all the way around the world and come back
to where they'd started from again. The exhaust of the train's
chimney had coated her in grime, which didn't come off when
she sprayed herself with water, whenever they stopped to feed
and clean her, and to refill the back tray of the train's head
with stinking black stuff. If only, she thought, she was still small
enough to travel in the enclosed carriages. She smelled the
scent of various animals issuing from them when the train was
still, and as the days grew hotter the smells became more
potent. The bitter, sickly odour of predators was strong. But
Mary could tell they weren't along for this voyage. They were
waiting, wherever she was going.

She began to pass the time imagining what sort of person
Charlie Sparks was, why he would have so many different
animals belonging to him. It was still too alien for Mary to
understand the way people kept animals as their own and used
them as servants or for entertainment. She grasped that they

232

did it but couldn't understand why nature had granted them the powers to do so, and what inclinations the people had that compelled them to use this unnatural gift.

Gradually, the landscape around them changed. The hills flattened out and the forests grew thicker, rich with treetops of red and gold. Grassy fields and flat prairies were crisscrossed by rivers, or by flattened paths what were paved black, so automobiles or horses could travel along them. Towns and villages grew bigger. There were fields of small houses, sometimes whizzing by them for a whole day, before the bigger structures came into view, and the train would pass between them and Mary felt so small and insignificant that it frightened her. But she always remembered that the mountains were bigger, and the trees were taller.

Some of the villages seemed to be crumbling back into the earth, as though nature itself had a way of reabsorbing the structures people made, after a time. They were usually rows and rows of bland, wooden houses and only the workers lived there, nobody had pale skin.

But every day, they would stop and let Mary walk around a bit. Every time, Miss Addy and Charlie Sparks would touch her skin and speak her in sweet tones that made her feel strong and comfortable again. Without them, Mary didn't think she'd have made it.

It was a warm twilight when the train started to slow down, at long last. A few of the brightest stars were already twinkling in the darkening blue dome, while the sun cast a fiery yawn across the horizon far behind them. In the last traces of light, Mary could see the yellow glow of electric lights shining through the windows of houses all clustered across an open field. Ahead, the scattered stands of trees converged into a woodland, but from somewhere deep inside of it, Mary could see another strong, yellow electric glow issuing, accompanied by the pulsing red of firelight and the smell of smoke. Beneath the dulling chugging of the train, she could also hear a beautiful lulling sound that she knew she'd heard once before, coming from an instrument held by a worker man on a train platform. Sound that told story without words and seemed to caress her ears and tickle her heart. She hoped they were going into the woods to find the source of the light and sound.

The train stopped on the tracks for a moment. There was a sharp squeak from up ahead, and they were going again, but even slower this time. They turned a corner and veered onto a bed of stones where the tracks broke off into countless different directions, and all around were other carriages disconnected from the train, waiting for use. There, they came to a stop. The woods blocked out the sunset and the sky plunged into darkness alighted by the most brilliant explosion of twinkling stars Mary thought she'd ever seen in her life. The cold of the night made her muscles tense, but she was excited to see where they were going. She could still hear the beautiful melodies fluttering from the trees.

Workers again hurried to her open carriage and put the ramp in place. Charlie Sparks and Miss Addy appeared as one of the workers heaved Mary's gate open and Miss Addy quickly floated up to touch Mary's face with her tiny, delicate hand.

'Hello, Mary,' she said, radiating the soft, soothing light through the elephant again. 'We're home!'

Workers had come hurrying from near the woods as well and they quickly set to work on the other carriages behind and in front of Mary's. Charlie Sparks touched their shoulders and greeted them with smiles, handshakes and happy cries which Mary thought must be their names. She realized that she'd never seen a pale-skinned ape do that. She'd seen the workers in both this land and her own labor for them, but she'd never seen them acknowledged with any warmth of kindness in return. But Charlie Sparks was smiling and happy to all of them. She knew already she was with a different kind of person, with these ones, but she was only just learning exactly how different. A homely sense came over her. There was no malice or cruelty hanging in the air, as it had when she'd arrived at her previous home. There was nothing like the

235

Colonel. Just happy people, happy to see each other, and happy to work for each other. While Miss Addy gently took her lead, Mary felt herself beginning to glow, just the way Miss Addy did.

Workers filled Mary's cage and began to clean it as Mary climbed down the flimsy ramp, which caused her knees to buckle, to the cold stones below.

She helped Charlie Sparks climb up onto her neck again and they walked across the stones to the cold, wet grass which instantly numbed Mary's feet. A few workers escorted, Miss Addy led, and Charlie Sparks rode while Mary walked. They moved along the woods' edge until they came to an opening which led into the clearing from which the light was shining. Mary stopped in her tracks when she saw what was there.

A column of black smoke rose into the stars from a huge, bright fire that was contained in a ring of stones, and all around were structures, but nothing like the towns and villages and cities Mary had seen. They were small, wooden, and set on wheels, and scattered without symmetry or order around the central fire. Some were larger than others, but none were particularly big, except for a large barn off on the far side of the clearing, nestled amongst the trees. Between the structures were canvas sheets, stretched from rooftop to rooftop, and all throughout were lengths of wire that had little shining lights running along them, like a spider's web that had caught a whole swarm of fireflies. Around the fire moved the residents and Mary could already see there were men and women, pale and dark, and they were all gathered around the source of the heart-melting sound.

Miss Addy gave a patient tug on the lead and Mary knew she was holding them up. She wasn't afraid, she knew that the people could control fire. She'd just never seen such a sight before. Something so serene, that felt so hidden and had such an ambience of otherworldliness that Mary felt the land around seem to be blocked out, or cease to be, as she stepped into the ethereal vision in the woods before her.

They passed underneath the web of lights and Mary lifted her trunk. A firm tap on her head stopped her. 'No, Mary!' Charlie Sparks was saying. 'Mustn't touch!'

They continued to the warmth and light of the fire, where the people were gathered. The sounds came from a group of workers and pale-skinned people, mixed together, all with different kinds of instruments with which they made the sound, but Mary immediately picked out the gold-coloured tool that was blown through, the way she remembered it. The others sounded wonderful, but that was her favorite. Its wavering sadness and soft-but-metallic whine led the others, which were either struck, held upright and plucked or held up

237

under the chin and rubbed with a long bow. Together, the sound made Mary want to cry. She stood behind the group of onlookers, who were sitting in chairs and eating from steaming bowls, feeling tears of joy welling in her eyes.

'That's music, Mary,' Miss Addy said, and she looked up and smiled in a way that perfectly complimented the way the sound stirred Mary's emotions and warmed her heart. 'Music!'

The onlookers had noticed Mary and were turning away from the music band to smile and look at their new friend. Mary wanted to shake her trunk at them, but was careful not to, remembering how it frightened people, and being scared could make even kind people hurt her. Her first instinct remained to avoid the pain. But they stood and came toward her, one at a time. The first was big, a man who seemed to barely fit inside his second skin. He had a bald head, but hair across the top of his mouth, which showed his teeth.

'Ladies and gentlemen!' Charlie Sparks bellowed from on top of Mary, and the band stopped. Mary immediately felt a chill. Not only because she wanted the band to keep playing, but also because she'd heard those words before; they often preceded a routine and a beating. She tucked her trunk in and braced herself for pain. She didn't notice the first tap on her side, the signal for her to let Charlie Sparks down. The second sent a wave of nausea through her. Forgetting meant a beating.

She quickly did as she was told, but Charlie Sparks just climbed down, and turned to his audience, arms outstretched. 'Ladies and gentlemen, I want you all to meet Mighty Mary!'

'Hello Mary!' said the big person. 'I'm Cole, that's my name,' he petted his own stomach, 'Cole.'

The gathering all started talking at once, so Mary couldn't understand them.

'Hey!' one voice cut through them all. 'Hey!'

The people slowly turned their attention back toward where the band had played, where a female person was standing, and holding big, circular rings in her hands. Mary was immediately struck by her appearance; she wore a tight second skin, with only a short skirt to cover her legs, which were long and muscular, just like the rest of her body. Firm, but delicate. Little beads all over her glittered and sparkled as they caught the lights crisscrossed on the web above her. She had a thick, black mane that cascaded wildly down her back, her lips shone they were so red, there was a black spot on her pure white cheek, and her eyes were big and blue and full of ferocious focus. Mary saw the disdain in those eyes, the contempt, but for once it wasn't just for her. The woman regarded them all, and all of them the same.

'Are you going to play so I can practice, or not?'

239

'We just meetin' the new elephant, wummun!' one of the band people argued. 'We was playin' for an hour, waitin' on you!'

'Well, I'm here now.'

The crowd dispersed with a series of sighs and head shakes, and the band took up their instruments again. The others gathered their bowls and took them to a tent that had no walls, it was just a ceiling with tables and chairs all set up under it. The band picked up their lively music. The woman started to dance.

Mary was dazzled by her. With the hoops over her arms, she swung them delicately about. They made patterns and stayed on her body as she moved and pranced and spun them about as though they were part of her. She seemed to flow, the way she moved. There was nothing in machinery or nature that Mary had ever seen move so fluidly but rivers or waterfalls. She spun the hoops off her arms, over her neck, around her waist and even over her thighs. It was as though she was the music, like the sounds created life and there it was moving and dancing for them.

Then, just like that, it was all over. The band stopped, the woman stopped, and Charlie Sparks slapped his hands together for them. But she didn't smile back, or wave, like most people did, or like Mary had when she'd got clapped at.

She just gathered up her hoops, snarled at Charlie Sparks and walked back off into the darkness amongst the wheeled structures whence she had come.

There was silence while the people dragged their chairs back into the sheltered area. Charlie Sparks said something quietly to Miss Addy, and then Miss Addy smiled at Mary and started to lead her away. Mary wanted to stay, she wanted to see more! She hoped this was not just a once-off thing. She hoped that the hoops woman danced all the time. More than this, she wanted to be able to make her dance. She wanted to be able to make the beautiful music. Somehow, she had to get the instrument for herself and make music for the woman to dance to. Mary hoped she'd dream about it.

Miss Addy led her to the barn, where workers opened the door for them. They went into the darkness, and Miss Addy slipped the leash from around her neck. There was food and water, which made Mary realize how hungry she was. She quickly began to gorge herself.

'Good night Mary,' Miss Addy whispered, as she left. 'See you in the morning!'

#

As usual, the communal task of washing up was left to poor Indira and Jessica. They had started as Charlie served himself the last scraps of sausage and beans from the cooking pot, and as he sat down, he noticed Marvin's habit of leaving his plate and cutlery at the table where he sat had communicated itself over to George and John. The three of them were gathered around the fire, smoking and urging the band to play another song. Yashi had set up her knives and was practicing. He appreciated her exhaustive efforts to be ready for the tour, but he wished she'd help her fellow showgirls cleaning up.

It meant he'd have to talk with them all again. Charlie Sparks hated calling those meetings, he hated lecturing his performers, but they had to learn to live together if they were going to work together.

Cole sat down beside Charlie and jabbed his hip with a huge thumb. 'That's some elephant, you got there.'

'No kidding,' Charlie agreed, fondly, though he could see Cole's avoidance of helping Indira and Jessica. 'What are those three doing?'

Cole looked at Marvin, George, and John, as they pleaded with the band as they packed up their instruments. 'They're clowns, whaddya expect?'

'Has it been like this since we left?'

'Like what?'

'Everyone helps clean up,' Charlie repeated himself, looking at Cole, as though to give him the hint as well. 'It's the deal. Addy is happy to cook, and when she's not here Yashi, but everyone has to clean up their own dishes!' he flicked a little bean over at the clowns' soiled bowls and cutlery.

'What've you got those niggers for anyway?' Cole asked, and Charlie cringed. He knew how some of them felt, despicable as he found it, but he wished they'd found a way to keep themselves from expressing it.

'Those labourers are working at the depot, they're not here to do everyone's dishes.'

'Well, you're gonna have to tell the gang, Charlie boy!' Cole jabbed him again. 'We saved you and Miss Addy some of the strudel. Leave room, right?' he made the A-Okay gesture with his thumb and index finger.

That calmed Charlie a little. He rarely got any of Yashi's strudel, being that she only cooked when Addy was away, and when Addy was away, invariably so was Charlie. But then Indira came over to gather up the clowns' dishes, and he snapped his finger, sharply, as though she was one of the lions. 'Don't touch those!'

'But it's cleaning time, Charlie,' Indira said, with her rich Indian accent.

'No! The clowns are going to clean up their own dishes, I'm tired of this!'

'Then they won't get done.'

'Then they'll eat off of the dirty dishes,' Charlie insisted. Indira shrugged and left them there. He immediately felt bad, talking to her like that. Indira had those big, black eyes full of naïve innocence, and he wished she'd wear her Indian belly-dancer's costume all the time. It just didn't look right, seeing her beautiful skin and shapely form hidden beneath slacks and a shirt.

Marvin raised his voice as he reached a punch line. The other clowns laughed.

'Well anyway, that's it for me,' Cole said. 'Welcome back, Mister Sparks.'

'Wait a moment, please,' Charlie called him back. 'Did Christina eat anything tonight?'

Cole shook his head, no. 'You can see she's fighting fit, though, Charlie. Enough to run a full-dress rehearsal on the hoops for us tonight,' he chuckled and slapped Charlie's arm.

'What's got into her?' Charlie asked. 'She doesn't like Mary?'

'Of course, she doesn't like Mary,' Cole said. 'Mary takes the attention away from her!'

'Is that why she's on a hunger strike?'

'I think it's got more to do with us not touring a whole summer like we were supposed to!' Cole protested.

'I didn't expect my elephant to die,' Charlie said, tears stinging his eyes.

'Well, Christina doesn't think we need an elephant,' Cole said. 'She thinks she's enough, and I tend to agree with her.'

'You don't like Mary?'

'I like Mary fine, Charlie, beautiful creature. But we got all down here, and all for nothing. Are we going to be paid?'

Charlie spooned his beans around, having suddenly lost his appetite. 'Next summer. We'll start early. Get one up on Ringling. I'll book twice as many shows.'

'Next summer isn't going to keep us warm through this winter, Charlie,' Cole said, then stood. 'I'll go talk to Christina. She might appreciate that news better coming from me.'

Make sure you remember to give her that news, Charlie wanted to say, but he knew he'd be overstepping his boundary.

Addy joined him at his side, already with a plate of strudel and two cups of coffee. 'Join me?'

'Of course, I'll join you,' Charlie beamed, and he pushed his bowl aside.

'We can't tour with an unfamiliar elephant,' she insisted, reading his thoughts again. 'She needs to be broken in with us.'

'I suspect mutiny first,' Charlie said.

'It's going to be fine,' Addy said. She stroked his thigh. 'Just look at Mary. Isn't she something? People will pay just to look at a creature that size.

'She's something,' Charlie nodded. 'Christina DeRosa is something.'

'Yeah, some piece of work,' Addy scoffed. Charlie giggled. Indira came back to gather up the clowns' plates.

CHAPTER 20

Mary woke feeling as though there was someone there with her. She felt eyes beyond the darkness, a presence just outside her field of vision. She quickly stood up and looked around. Her heart anticipated something, but she couldn't predict what. Joy? Love? Fear? Pain? She searched for it anyway. The gentle sunrise filled the barn with milky light, but other than herself, the place was empty. Her head ached, and her legs wobbled, the way they always did when she slept for a long time. She was still sure someone was there.

'Hey!' she cried out. 'Hey!'

Emotions swilled inside. Wants she couldn't pin down. She wanted someone to be there. Maybe just outside, out in the open...where she could run into.

'Mother,' she cooed, in a shaky, painful voice. It grated her, this emotional insistence that if she just looked, or just went outside, there would be her mother, her herd, her freedom, all returned to her. She hated herself for not being over them yet. Why, she thought, must she ache for something that's gone forever? Why couldn't she convince her subconsciousness that they're never coming back? It had been long enough! So why couldn't she forget? Why did the openness still call to her heart, when she knew she couldn't go to it? Why did the pain

247

still hurt so much, when it was all she'd known for so long?
Why did the night still fill her with dreams she could never
fulfill?

'Stupid Mary,' she said to herself. 'Stupid, stupid Mary!'

Then, with a rattle and a thud, the barn door opened just a
little, and let the pure morning light in. Appearing in it was
Miss Addy.

'Good morning, Mary,' she said, as she approached the
elephant without a trace of fear or reservation. She stroked
Mary's trunk and spoke to her soothingly. 'There, there, Mary.
Did you have a dream? It's alright, darling. It's alright.'

In a softening moment, Mary realized there was someone
there. Someone who watched over her, who touched her
without want and who spoke to her in ways she'd never
imagined a person could.

'You're never alone here, Mary,' Miss Addy said. 'This is
one big, beautiful family you've joined, and we're all sorts of
different. But you're never alone here. You're one of us now.'

\#

Christina had fallen asleep. Cole almost didn't know what to
do with himself; she never fell asleep! But this time, after their
bodies had melted over each other and they'd shuddered in

each other's arms, she'd turned away, mumbled that he should leave, and dozed right off. Cole had thought, for a moment, that he should have done as she wanted. But there she was, laying naked beside him, her body next to his in the damp spot where they'd had each other. He knew he should have left her, but something would not permit him. His heart? Well, whatever. It was one thing to be naked with Christina DeRosa, that was luck for a man enough, but it was quite another to be intimate with her. He'd tasted and touched all she had, but he didn't know her. He didn't reside in her mind, the way he wanted to. She had him, but she didn't need him. He wanted her to need him. Maybe the intimacy with her body could become confused with the intimacy of her heart, and secrets beneath clothing could melt with the secrets beneath the vales of faux personality, the graces of strength and the airs of control?

So, he'd spent the night gently running his fingers up and down the gentle curves of her side and watched as the corner of her lips had twitched into peaceful smiles now and then. He'd watched her chest rise and fall and listened as she breathed deeply and rhythmically. He'd felt their sweat dry. He'd even mustered the courage to embrace her from behind, at which she'd made a faint moan; slight and soft and vulnerable like she never was.

Daylight came too quickly.

A sharp, frantic knock at the door startled him from his dozing. He looked up into the waking light. He felt Christina tense beside him. Suddenly, the sheets were ripped from him, and she bunched them up over herself, those blue eyes aflame with fury.

'Who said you could stay here?' she spat, with her heavy Jersey drawl.

'I...you fell asleep...' Cole answered, a deer stuck in the headlights.

The knocking at the door continued.

'Get out!' she snapped. 'Get the hell out!'

She started kicking him. He scrambled to avoid her hard, little feet.

'Who said you could stay here anyways?' she growled as he dressed quickly. 'Who d'you think you are?'

'I think I'm your lover!' Cole answered, feeling stupid.

'Uh-uh,' she said, and she shook her head slowly. 'Love's got nothin' to do with this, get that straight, mistuh!'

The knocking again.

'What?' Christina shrieked. The cabin door opened slowly, and Yashi sheepishly peeked in. When she saw what was happening, her featureless face flushed with wry joy.

'That Mister Grubb is coming,' she said, suppressing a chuckle.

'Get out!' Christina shrieked, with that birdlike caw. 'Get out, both a'yous! Get out! Get out! Get the hell out!'

Cole fumbled his shirt off the ground and quickly threw it on. He buttoned as he slid passed Yashi. She closed the door behind them, but it was too late. Whoever Mister Grubb was to Christina, he was stopped in his tracks only a few feet away from them. Yashi just smiled and walked away, but Cole froze. Right there, in front of Christina's door, he saw a tall, narrow-shouldered man he never met before try to hide behind a stoic face a heartache that was turning him to dust inside. It was all in the eyes. The pain that shot through them when he looked up at Cole was almost too much for either man to bare. Neither could say anything.

He was carrying a bouquet of roses.

Cole quickly stepped out of the way, as he heard Christina's door opening. Grubb and Christina stared at each other. Cole saw the skinny guy's chest heaving as he held back tears.

'I heard the tour was cancelled,' Mister Grubb said. 'I thought I'd come pick you up. I...who is this?'

Christina put her hand on her hip. She'd managed to get a bathrobe on, but the hardness of her face was penetrating. Cole couldn't believe it belonged to the same woman who'd gasped breaths over his neck just the night before.

'What do you want me to say, Marty?' she said. 'What aren't you figuring out here?'

'I don't believe it,' Marty breathed, weakly.

'If you still want to put me up for the winter...'

'I don't want to put you up for anything! You lied to me! Christina, how could you?'

'Needed a place to stay,' she shrugged.

Grubb's mouth fell open. Cole couldn't believe it either. Grubb took a few more sharp breaths, slumped, dropped the bouquet, turned and walked. All the way across the grounds, he went, before Christina turned to Cole, her face tight, her lips compacted and those eyes livid. They were blue, but Cole was sure he saw a white flame in them.

'You stupid muscle head!' she shrieked. 'You just cost me a place to stay!'

'Who was that?' Cole asked, though he wasn't sure why. Maybe he just wanted to know how cold her heart truly was.

'A putz!' she shouted. 'I told him I was Catholic! Every winter, for four years, he gives me his bed and sleeps on the couch. Now how the hell am I supposed to find a replacement for that, huh?'

Cole was frozen, mouth ajar, shirt hanging off, shoes in his hands. He couldn't believe it. He could not accept that this was his Christina. He knew she was assertive...maybe a little nasty...but this was something else.

'You ruined it, you idiot!' she seethed at him, turning red. 'Go on and get away from me, and don't dare touch me again until I say it's okay.'

She turned, went back inside, and slammed the door shut. Cole gathered his senses. He was hurting, but the shock numbed him. Maybe he did just get to know the confines of Christina's heart. Could anybody that beautiful, he wondered, be that ugly?

He'd never know why, but he stopped and picked up the flowers.

'Hey!' Christina's voice called. He turned. She was looking out through her door. 'Give me those.'

Cole brought the flowers to her. She snatched them out of his hand. The door slammed in his face again. His heart sunk low, he turned and walked back toward his cabin. His bare feet swished in the dry summer grass. The sun heated it steadily.

#

'Don't you want to go see what that is?' Jessica asked, in her sparkling leotard, while she and Charlie waited for Miss Addy and the handlers to get Mary ready for her full-dress rehearsal. Yashi, it seemed, was already doing just that.

'I've seen more than my share of Christina's tantrums, my dear.' Charlie assured her. 'You'll get used to it, in time.'

Finally, Yashi appeared, a strange, smug look spread across her narrow, normally expressionless face. Charlie squinted suspiciously but decided it was better not to know. Christina was too valuable to lose over some spat, and as long as Charlie himself was not involved, he felt assured it would not come to that. Yashi was, however, dressed in jeans and a button shirt.

'Good morning, Mademoiselle Renoir,' Charlie said, as Yashi smiled at Jessica. 'Or is it afternoon?'

'Good morning...and sorry. Christina, you know,' she answered, and her eyes again feel on Jessica, but this time fluttered up and down, and the smile melted away. 'I didn't think...'

'It's a rehearsal, my dear,' Charlie said, also in his full ringmaster costume. 'Never mind, I suppose you've got enough experience to run a routine comfortably without your dress.'

'If she's not wearing the dress, I don't want to,' Jessica said, pinching the shoulder strap. 'I hate these things.'

'I love them,' Yashi shrugged. 'Want to just swap?'

Jessica nodded and immediately started pulling at the straps of her costume.

'Not here!' Charlie interrupted. 'Do you want to give those police patrols a reason to kick us off this land?'

He pointed his walking stick toward the seemingly empty trees, but everyone knew he meant the police who were known to walk by the camp at all hours, just itching for a reason to have them evicted or, if possible, arrested. Public lewdness was flirted with enough by their leotards.

Yashi gestured toward the mess tent, and they turned to walk toward it. A loud clunk called their attention back towards Mary's stable.

The labourers had got the door open. Mary was wearing her clown cap and short cloak. She came out, timidly, led by Miss Addy. Yashi and Jessica both immediately forgot their discomfort and stared at the elephant as it came shyly over and stopped before them.

'Golly, she sure is big,' Jessica said, breathlessly. 'I'd forgot already.'

'Biggest I've ever seen.' Charlie took the opportunity to boast. 'Probably the biggest there ever was. Say, Miss Addy dear, how big were those dinosaur statues? The ones near Crystal Palace Lake?'

'Not as big as our Mary,' she answered, as she petted the shy giant's side. Mary turned her head toward Addy, shyly, but Addy gently pushed it back, facing her forward.

'Why, she might be the largest land animal on earth,' Charlie said, watching Yashi and Jessica, arms linked, look at each other in surprised belief. 'Say, Miss Addy dear, how tall was Jumbo?'

'Twelve feet tall,' Addy answered.

'Well, that does it!' Charlie turned to Yashi and Jessica, seeing he was having an effect. 'I distinctly remember the supplier tell me Mary is all of twelve feet, three inches. Three whole inches taller than Jumbo!'

'She's a little scary,' Jessica said, shying away.

'Well,' Charlie looked over at Mary. 'She's gentle as a mouse, really, but if you two feel uncomfortable...we can run through a couple of routines without you first, until you feel a little better?'

Nearby, Christina had emerged. She walked over to the high bar, pulled herself up, and swung from it. She curled upside down, whipped her legs over it, and hoisted herself up to the top, all in one, fluid motion.

Yashi glanced over at her and saw her watching.

'No, come on,' she said, tugging on Jessica's arm. 'It's tame, look at it! It's just big, is all.'

Jessica perked up, channelling a little confidence from Yashi.

'You stay here Mary,' Miss Addy was saying as she moved away, toward the mess tent. She kissed Charlie's cheek as she passed. 'I'll go start breakfast.'

'Okay, then,' Charlie said, smiling. He looked at Mary, who stood still. Waiting. 'You ready, Mary?' he heard Christina's piercing giggle. Ignoring her, he turned to his imaginary audience. 'Ladies and gentlemen! Boys and girls of all ages! Brace yourself for an encounter, the likes of which many will never experience in all their lives! Not since the time of the dinosaurs has such a creature existed! From the depths of darkest Africa, we brought her to you. From the wilds of the mighty green inferno, where she ruled as a Queen, to the Big Top in Carthage, Ohio, where she is your humble servant. The largest land animal that ever lived! Five whole tons of Mighty Mary!'

He gestured the stick toward her, and she flinched. He took a breath and gave her the direction. She followed perfectly; walking in a semi-circle. He stopped her, near Yashi and Jessica, and tapped her leg with the cane. She raised her foot. Yashi climbed up first, straddling her behind the ears. Charlie gave her Mary the prompt, and she turned outward and reared up on her hind legs. Yashi raised her free hand and smiled to the air.

Perfect, Charlie thought. It couldn't be more perfect.

Charlie gave her another prompt, and Mary walked back around the circle, carrying Yashi, who climbed onto her feet, and then out onto Mary's back. When Charlie stopped her, she tilted into a headstand, and Yashi cartwheeled over Mary's head and landed on her feet. Then, Jessica quickly mounted Mary before she stood upright again. Then, the whole routine again, in reverse.

Christina was watching. She lifted herself up onto her feet and stood upright, balancing perfectly on the thin bar. With arms crossed, she scowled at the elephant.

Charlie was beaming with joy.

CHAPTER 21

For a while, Mary kept waiting for the pain to come. She didn't make mistakes, but she knew sometimes they'd hit her anyway, so she was braced for it. Ready for the paralyzing sting of a bullhook from Charlie Sparks. As soon as she'd seen him holding a stick, she'd known what it was and what it was for, as well as who he really was and what he wanted. She didn't want Miss Addy to leave her. For some reason, she felt like Charlie Sparks wouldn't hit her if Miss Addy was still there. But she did. So, Mary knew nothing else but to focus on avoiding the pain. The delicate, feathery women climbed onto her back and rode her through the routine, and Mary was terrified of dropping one. Whenever they rolled off her head, she tensed, ready for the beating.

But they never came. Routine after routine, he never hit her. He used the stick to give direction, but never to strike her.

It went on like this. The sun chased the moon across the sky again and again, and each time Mary would be woken just before the dawn by the workers. The beautiful Miss Addy would welcome her to the day, then put her cap and cloak on. They'd go outside, and Charlie Sparks would direct her through a routine. She'd wait for him to hit her, but he never did.

It wasn't called a routine here, it was called a dance, and instead of performing it with other elephants, Mary had to learn to cope with two people women climbing up on her and riding her, then rolling off and swapping over. They were called Yashi and Jessica. The other one, with the black hair and the hoops, who would perch up on the high bar and watch them like a giant, long, delicate bird, was called Christina. There was one who was darker-skinned, just like the people she remembered from home and who spat fire during her dances; she was called Indira. There were three pale men, who Mary had seen setting little white twigs asmoulder and sucking on the smoke, or staggering about strangely, as though they were dizzy, with bottles in their hands while they shouted at each other and broke into hoarse cackles; they were called Marvin, George, and John, but Mary didn't know which was which. It seemed as though nobody did. Then, of course, there was Cole.

The mornings were Mary's time to rehearse. After that, Christina would make the band play, and she'd do all kinds of different dances; they changed all the time. Mary found a crack in her barn, through which she could watch, but sometimes the workers would take her for a walk, and she'd miss out. She hated missing out on Christina's dances. Then, the other animals would come out to run through their routines, but

Mary never saw them. They were kept in cages somewhere across the camp from her barn.

Mary felt more and more like one of them. She almost began to wonder if this was how being part of a herd had felt, but she wasn't sure. She'd sway her head, during her idle times, and try to figure it out. During a dance, one day, she got confident enough to take a closer look at Charlie Sparks' stick and realized that it wasn't a bullhook at all. After that, she started to love playing with her new friends. Even though it was rehearsed carefully, and she had to follow rules, she took to the games and even looked forward to the mornings with excitement.

Gradually, as the golden leaves fell from the trees and left them bare, and the days grew shorter and colder, the people started to leave. Cole was first. He stopped by Mary's barn, petted her gently behind the ear, and then was gone. After that, Charlie Sparks seemed to grow increasingly worried. He'd watch the landscape with fearful eyes, as though something was prowling around there, hunting him, ready to strike. Jessica and Yashi left them as well, soon after. By the time the icy slivers of winter were prickling through the air, and the grass became hard and frosty, it was only Charlie Sparks, Miss Addy, and Mary, as well as the yet unseen other animals in the cages. Mary knew they were predators; she could always smell them. Sometimes, the scent would get to her at night, and she'd wake in fear, ready to take flight or fight for her survival. But they never bothered her. Even the cold didn't bother her as much as it used to.

Every day, Mary was taken for a long walk. Usually, just before the sunset, either Charlie Sparks or Miss Addy would come to her barn with a few workers, they would fit her leash, and she'd go out of the woods and walk along the train tracks. From there, she could watch the sun fade and the electric lights inside the houses across the fields begin to alight. Every now and then, there was a heavy gonging sound, which Mary pinpointed to the taller building, often just a silhouette in the winter mist that had pointed spikes on its rooftops.

One day, when the daylight hours were at their shortest, Charlie Sparks took her for a walk around the grounds and showed her to the other animals. He talked to her a lot, now with fog blowing out of his mouth as he did, and that made Mary think that she should talk to him, even though there was no way he could understand her. She liked to try it anyway.

'These are our horses, Mary,' he said, when they got to a barn, not unlike Mary's across the way. Mary remembered her companion, with the innocent eyes and the soft, nudging nose, and wanted to cry. She wished she knew what became of him. She hoped that he was still galloping about somewhere.

Without Old Boy on his back, but maybe with another elephant friend. Another elephant that reminds him of her. She doubted it, there was an obvious vacancy about his gaze that suggested he didn't have much of a memory, but it warmed her a little, against the colder times, to think that maybe she was just special enough. Maybe. Somehow.

Charlie sparks led her along, and from the warmth of remembering her horse friend, her blood instantly ran cold as another memory burst through her with an icy, violent shudder. She froze, next to Charlie Sparks. Her heart was raging. Tears filled her eyes and felt almost frozen on her cheeks.

'This is our tiger!'

It was in a small cage, just barely longer than would be its body, if it were stretched all the way out. It's cold, cruel eyes forever searching, as it paced up and down, rapidly, from one end of the little cage to the other. When it finally realized it was being watched, it stopped pacing and crouched low to the cage floor. It was staring at Mary. Maybe it smelled her fear. Maybe it knew creatures like her, in the life it had before it too was caged, held captive, forced over a sea in the belly of a giant vessel, and trained with a bullhook by a Colonel or a Philip. She remembered the tiger in the water machine...

A wave of hatred passed through her. Even for Charlie Sparks. He may not hit her with anything, but he wielded a weapon nonetheless, and he may be kind to her, but he was a person. They kill, they capture, they enslave. That is what has happened to this predator before her. It was no longer a predator. It was just another victim of a cruel person, who stole and reshaped it like they do everything, intent on collecting all the world.

'Hello, Tiger,' she said. She wanted to touch it. 'I'm sorry for what has happened to you. I wish we could be free.'

But she knew it would not listen. It just got up and resumed pacing, as though Mary wasn't even there. She watched it, back and forth, back and forth, ceaselessly. She wondered why. It banged its head against the bars as it met them on either side, then changed direction, and Charlie Sparks moved in closer to the bars. He banged his stick against them, sharply.

'Amelia, Amelia,' he was calling. 'Don't knock your head about!'

She wasn't sure what he'd said, but then something else dawned on her. Something more chilling than the thought of Charlie Sparks being just another cruel person. There was something in his tone. In the ignorant manner in which he stood, fleshy and exposed, within arm's reach of a dangerous predator. There were bars, but Mary saw it could get its paw through. It could make one swipe, and eviscerate Charlie Sparks where he stood, like a fool. But it was clear. Clear and horrifying. Charlie Sparks didn't realize he was a monster.

Mary swayed her head to ease her queasiness. It was true, then. They didn't know they were monsters. They didn't realize they were inflicting such awful pain on the other creatures. That's how people carried such commanding confidence before her. That's how Philip had changed, having befriended her, into a brutal overlord. That's how Charlie Sparks stood before the cage now, talking casually at an animal that could in no way understand him. He didn't realize it was torture to be kept in a cage. He didn't realize their hearts were full of the wilderness, and the warm southern breeze, and the blankets of life which grew up from the endless earth, and which he and his kind stole them from, and denied their ever returning to it.

He didn't know. He acted kindly because he thought he was kindly.

Finally, he got Amelia to stop still in front of him. He made a gesture with the stick. She sat down. He made another. She lay down.

'Now you just rest a bit,' he said, in a sickeningly pleasant voice, to a creature that was losing its grip on its mind, which was fractured inside, and was spilling out over the cage floor.

266

That's why it paced. Its mind had been smashed to a thousand little shards. It was pouring out, little broken pieces of instinct, of desire, of a will to live and hunt and roam and see the sunrise across one plane and set across another. Pouring out in sharp little pieces all over the cage floor. Out of her eyes, out of her mouth, out of her nose. She was pacing so they would distribute evenly. So they wouldn't pile up so much, they'd bury her.

Mary followed Charlie Sparks to another cage. This one was a large dome structure, with bars that held four predators. She knew they were predators, because they looked like tigers, and had that same cold, lurking stare. But these were the colour of barren earth. There was another one, with a great brown mane over its head and neck, in another small cage, off in the corner. All of them were lying on their bellies. Their heads were upright, and they were faced away from each other, staring into nothing. They didn't move or acknowledge Mary or Charlie Sparks, as they walked slowly by.

'There are our lions, Mary!'

These ones had already been buried in the shards.

They went for a long walk through the woods and out across the paddocks, where they watched as the sun set and the houses lit up with electric light under the starry sky. Charlie Sparks didn't want to ride her, he just walked along beside her, gently guiding her with her leash. She wasn't in any mood to wander. It was cold, but serene and oddly sweet, even though Mary had discovered a newfound fear of Charlie Sparks.

The twinkle lights and the bonfire welcomed them back to the camp, though only the workers remained to enjoy it. Two of them were sitting by the fire with the band's musical instruments in their hands. One of them was the gold-coloured blowing instrument and the worker who played it, while different to the worker from the band, still sounded beautiful.

'Here you go, Mary,' the other labourer said, as he dropped an armful of hay at her feet. 'You sit up with us a'while t'nite.'

She looked into the mess tent, which was the structure with no walls, and saw Miss Addy standing over the stove, stirring a steaming pot while Charlie Sparks talked with her and watched the fire. Mary ate the hay, though she longed for something fresh and juicy, and listened to the slightly squeaky blowing instrument. The warmth of the fire crept through Mary's flesh the same way the lone music instrument's sound did her heart, and her mind began to wander. She thought about the workers, and whether or not they had been wild once as well, and whether or not the pale apes had been free and wild once too, but something happened, and one of them became cruel and strong, and started to make others like him, until gradually, the whole species became what they were, their habits so ingrained now that they didn't even realize their own unnaturalness.

The biting feelings of guilt again hovered around her. She had submitted to the people in order to survive. Their punishments had been a way of teaching her to not be punished by them. But there were others who were being punished as well, more brutally than she. Mary was not kept in a cage. Not here. But the same person who gave her this mercy locked other animals in cages, just like the ones on the machine that crossed the water. She began to feel sickly thinking about it, as she remembered the tiger and the sloth bear. The tiger had tried to talk to her, as she had to it. The sloth bear, meanwhile, had let itself die. Two creatures that knew all the freedom she had once, even more so, because she felt that they were older than she was, and probably grieved their families the way she did, and here she as, warmed by a fire and listening to a song by the same creatures that had done that to them. The same man who kept their cousins locked in cages in this freezing night, while she was warm.

'It's their own fault,' she told herself. 'They didn't learn their routines. They haven't submitted enough that they can be trusted to roam free about the camp.'

But her heart didn't believe her. She felt the sickening unease swirling inside her like the mists that followed the river back in her own land. Mary wasn't small anymore. She didn't need to conform to avoid the pain. She could defend herself. These people were so small and frail, their bodies would break easily. There were wild creatures in this world. Even as she was thinking to herself, a small, furry animal with a brushy tail came bolting past. It zigzagged between them, not eliciting a flinch from the workers, and disappeared into the trees on the far side of the camp. Mary heard the quick scratching of it climbing up a tree trunk. She wished she was that small, so small the people didn't even notice her running around. Or that she could fly! If she could fly, she could just go home. She saw the flying birds in the skies and tried to dream of the places they went to. All her mind could ever conjure was the grasslands with the lonely trees, or the swollen river that she kept locked inside.

The music kept her still. She wanted to listen, and to stay where she was, part of the group. She didn't want to hurt the workers. If she tried to break free now, they'd be hurt by her. Betrayed. She knew it. However guilty and rotten her heart felt, Mary just couldn't hold any thoughts of escape, of breaking the predators out of their cages and setting them loose or running off into the woods and smashing any little person who tried to stop her. Like soft clouds in her mind, the music and the serenity simply floated through her and drifted off with any aggression or sorrow she could have inside her.

Mary felt eyes watching her. They pulled her attention towards the high bar, where Christina was perched, crouching and watching from a distance. Her long, warm second skin hung down over the bars and dangled above the ground. Mary had thought Christina left some time ago, with the others. She hadn't seen her around the camp at all...

She could tell Christina didn't like her. The way she glared had that open contempt that was universal amongst all living things and visible no matter how subtly each species expressed it. That, Mary began to think, was why she hadn't seen her around. Mary knew Charlie Sparks liked her a lot. So, had Philip, and the Colonel, none of them had glared at her the way Christina always did. But Philip and the Colonel hit her, and Charlie Sparks kept animals in cages. It was all so confusing! If they hated her, would they leave her alone, like Christina did? Was Mary bad or good? Were they bad or good? Why did they treat her so nicely, but not let her be free?

Why did she want Christina to stop hating her so much?

'Christina!' Miss Addy called from the mess tent. 'Supper's up!'

Christina ignored her. Mary felt those blazing eyes still glaring at her, all the while.

Miss Addy sighed. 'You boys want something to eat, then?' she asked the two workers. They both got up to follow her to the pot and left their music instruments by the fire.

In the silence, Mary found herself swaying her head. She wanted her mother. Someone who could tell her what she was doing was wrong or right, without piercing her with a bullhook or beating her with anything. She wanted to know what these routines were that won her praise and affection, and why they were so important that her mother had to be killed so that Mary could do them. Guidance from another like her. An elephant. She wanted something to say what she should do. But nothing came. There was only the crackle of the bonfire, and its warming glow, and the gentle murmur of the people eating their steaming food.

Christina wasn't glaring at her anymore. Mary looked over at her and saw as she glided down from the high bar, wrapped her arms tightly around herself, and slowly walked over to the mess tent. She stopped just short of entering but Miss Addy quickly climbed to her feet and hurried over to her. Mary could hear the sweet voice and see the soothing touch only Miss Addy could give both being given to Christina. They both went toward the food and Charlie Sparks clapped his hands and cheered.

Mary felt a spike of jealousy. Her mother wouldn't come to her, and now Christina, who hated her, was stealing the radiance of Miss Addy and the applause of Charlie Sparks!

The music, Mary thought, forgetting everything else she'd thought about that night, except the threat of pain and how it would happen to her if she didn't do her routine right and impress the people. She quickly picked up the golden music instrument and held it in her trunk. It was so light! How could something so delicate make such a beautiful sound? A sound able to possess and captivate her entirely! But it was small and so fine she was afraid she might break it. She knew she had to be careful as she inspected it.

It was big at one end and thin on the other. Mary remembered how she'd seen the people play it, that the thin end goes in the mouth.

Slowly and gently, Mary put the thin end in her lips and blew. The sound startled her so much she almost dropped it. It was not the sweet tune that intoxicated her, but a piercing, awful shriek, like a dying rat. But it was enough. Charlie Sparks came running out of the mess tent, with Miss Addy and the workers behind him. He was showing all his teeth at once and his eyes were big and wide. Encouraged, Mary blew again. The sound was hideous; it seemed to ripple inside Mary's gut. But the excitement of the people vibrated off their frames and

273

filled the air around her, so Mary kept trying, defying her own ears.

She felt Christina glaring at her again.

CHAPTER 22

'It's the most astonishing thing I've ever seen!' Charlie was shouting, excitedly. Miss Addy lay wrapped in her covers, hopelessly trying to sleep. 'I'd like to see Jumbo do a trick like that!'

It was a freezing night. The first webs of winter's frost were creeping like cracks across the thin windows and the walls of the collapsible trailer home did nothing to keep all but the rain and wind of the elements out. Adelaide was curled tight, waiting for the warmth of her husband's body next to her. She dozed, somewhere between wake and sleep, but his sudden exclamations kept fetching her back into cold reality.

'Mighty Mary,' he hollered. 'The largest living land animal on earth! Watch her dance, watch her play a trumpet! A trumpet! Did you ever see such a thing!'

'You're not in the Big Top,' Adelaide managed to drawl, 'now, darling...'

'We don't need a Big Top!' he cried. 'We've got an elephant that plays the horn!'

Adelaide was used to this. As much as anyone can get used to a husband who spontaneously breaks into practice routines throughout the nights. But when the harsh light above his desk suddenly snapped on, blasting the merciful sleepiness out of

her eyes, she could take no more. She sat up and saw that he
was only in his pyjamas. No robe, no slippers, just the thin,
cheap flannel.

'Darling, you're going to catch your death!' she croaked,
remembering to swallow the balled fist of emotions threatening
to punch up out of her throat. Instead, she wrapped herself in
the sheets, climbed out of bed, and quickly draped his robe
over his shoulders. The fibres of the rug felt like ice on the
soles of her feet!

He had his fountain pen and was drawing up potential
posters. He was no visual artist, but Adelaide could see the
attempted elephant taking the majority of the space. Mary,
dominant, trunk in the air, one foot raised. A trumpet at her
mouth. She couldn't figure which of the stick figures,
suspended in midair, was supposed to be Christina, but she
knew their star aerialist wouldn't like this. Cole Waxman
didn't even seem to feature.

'Are you sure you can get Mary to play the trumpet again?'
Adelaide asked, gently squeezing Charlie's shoulders.

'Get her?' boomed, still using his stage voice. 'She just did it
herself!'

'She is an animal, honey,' Adelaide insisted. She bit her
tongue immediately, hiding her frustrations deep. This man

gave her a home. This man gave her a life. Without him, she had nothing. Was nobody.

'This is no ordinary animal,' Charlie shouted, and she could see there would be no getting through to him tonight. The bed was already oppressively cold again, but she crawled in, shivering. She kept to herself the longing she felt for the warmth of the South, and for the old wintering spots that had no electricity for them to plug into. Even if Charlie was restless, she could always sleep by lamplight. Electricity was another matter. It was coarse, harsh, and somehow cold as the night. Adelaide hated it. She curled tightly again and waited. 'She's going to keep us warm next winter, my darling.'

As she was used to, Adelaide woke up alone. The soft, gentle touch of the late autumn sunrise, shining through the lightly frosted windows, pulled her from her sleep, and the fading patch of warmth beside her was all she had to tell her Charlie had been in bed last night at all. She dressed quickly, in the thickest gown she had, fixed her hair and make-up, and stepped out into the crisp morning. Shimmering dew covered the grass and the grounds. She hurried to the mess tent and lit the kindling under the stove.

The camp was quiet. Normally, on the first truly wintery morning of the winter, the lionesses would become restless, and she'd wake to the sounds of their grumbling and groaning.

But even they were subdued. A slight chill ran through Adelaide. It was like there was nobody there at all. Just a collection of empty trailers and tents. In her early days as a circus trapeze artist, she'd had recurring nightmares in which the lions escaped their cage. In that first circus, they were all males. Four of them. She'd dream that she'd wake in the night, and there would be nothing but silence. She'd feel alone. An orphan just like Charlie, she'd learned the trapeze and joined a circus so as not to feel alone. Nobody is ever completely alone in the circus. But she'd feel the aloneness around her like all the world had fallen away. Like being lost and naked in the middle of the ocean, with no land in sight and no way of knowing just how far she was from anything. Sometimes she'd leave her trailer, looking for someone. Sometimes she'd stay where she was, curled up in her bed, her guardian Vera having disappeared. Either way, they'd get her. In the first instance, she'd be walking about the grounds, and there'd be no sign of anyone, but she'd hear it stalking behind her. A deep purring in the dark. Then, a flash of hot breath against her throat, and the massive weight smashing into her body, and she'd wake in terror, bathed in sweat, Vera already holding her tight. In the other, it would just push slowly in through the door, prowl up to the foot of her bed, and drag her into the night.

Adelaide shuddered. She wished someone would appear. Even Mary. Even Christina.

Having managed to get the oats and coffee pot over the fire, she quickly set out some syrups and fruit. No pancakes today. She wanted to be back inside her trailer. The aloneness was beginning to creep up her spine and chill her flesh. She kept thinking about lions. Kept seeing their eyes. Adelaide moved away from the mess tent.

She'd have to stir the oats.

Adelaide stopped, cursing under her breath. Then, she saw Christina's high bar. Practice for her aerial stunts and trapeze. Aerials had been a means of escape for Adelaide. Something to give all her attention to and calm the tumult that threatened to overwhelm her mind whenever she was alone. Which, as a girl, was often. Up there, she'd say, I am at peace. The high bar also resembled the platform Colonel Patterson wrote about, to shoot the lions from. So, lions couldn't get up there.

She hurried over and jumped up to grab the bar. Immediately she swung upside down in her nightgown. Lions and aloneness disappeared, as all her mind and all her body synchronized into the sole intention of pulling off the manoeuvres, maintaining strong lines, and moving with fluidity and grace. Suddenly, she was aware of herself. Every fibre of every muscle, every view from every angle, she heard the rhythm that she moved to, a beat that nobody else would ever

hear. They'd only see it, through her. She pulled herself up
and sat on the top of the bar.

Christina was watching, arms folded. Even scowling, even
without a hint of makeup, her long hair wild and frazzled from
having been slept on, she was strikingly beautiful, and her ice
blue glare froze Adelaide where she sat. 'Don't you have your
own?'

'Can you make your own coffee, and fix your own
breakfast?' Adelaide snapped back.

Christina softened. Her arms dropped down beside her,
and she stepped over near Adelaide's feet and leaned on the
frame. 'I suppose I'll have to soon.'

'Don't talk like that,' Adelaide said. It was she who'd picked
Christina out of a rejected class of aspiring ballerinas and
brought her to audition for their founder John H. Sparks'
travelling show. Her full hips and womanly endowments had
cost her a dream. But her exotic beauty, her tall physique and
her rapid ability to learn gravity-defying stunts won Sparks'
heart. She was their star ever since. Though the prestige had
somewhat gotten to her head, over the years, and a marriage to
a dancer had been plagued by his flagrant infidelity and violent
disposition, leaving her bitter and promiscuous, times like this,
when Christina would lash out at Adelaide, and be promptly
put in her place and start sulking thusly, warmed Adelaide's

heart. From up on the high bar, she even looked the girl she was when Adelaide had taken her under her wing. They had drifted far apart, it was true, and these encounters were all too rare now, but Adelaide loved her. 'Charlie will come through for us, he always does.'

'I miss John,' Christina mumbled, her voice sounding shaky. Adelaide quickly leaped down and touched her coarse, wiry hair.

'We all miss John,' she said. 'But Charlie does a good job! He...'

'Doesn't know the half of what he's doing,' Christina said, snapping back into her scowling, discontent manner, and driving that invisible wedge between herself and her mentor. The showgirl turned and walked toward the mess tent. Adelaide watched her. Christina, aside from Charlie and Adelaide, was the only one here who had toured with John, before his untimely death. She was now in her mid-thirties, though it was easy to forget.

The spoiled brat sat down at the table, arms crossed, waiting. Adelaide wanted to slap her. But then she remembered the oats and hurried to stir them. While she was there, she thought she might as well serve Christina's breakfast as well.

They were in a transitional phase. Christina would catch on, soon enough. John H. Sparks had run a wagon-based show, dating back to the era of Buffalo Bill Cody. But times had changed when Charlie took over. The travelling carnival, with their gypsies and freak-shows, had faded in the smoke of the locomotive. Circuses were the new age, and circuses travelled by rail. Charlie was building a rail-based circus. Only with the rails, the bigger circuses could travel faster, and be put on nearly all year-round. Giants like Barnum and Bailey were swallowing businesses like Sparks Shows. Charlie just had to assert himself. He had to make sure the Sparks name stood up, even if that was in Ringling's wake.

He was hinging an awful lot on that new elephant, though.

Adelaide put Christina's bowl in front of her, no syrup, just how she liked it, and only a glass of water to drink. Christina snorted and started eating.

'Did you happen to see where Charlie went?' Adelaide asked. Christina shook her head, no.

Adelaide certainly didn't enjoy the idea of eating breakfast alone with her while she was in that awful mood of hers. With her bowl and coffee cup expertly held in one hand, she walked back into her trailer to eat.

The trails of steam had long since stopped wafting up from the coffee pot and oats, Adelaide had already washed up after Christina and herself, and Christina had begun her daily ritual on the high bar. The camp remained silent. Adelaide sat in the mess tent, drumming her fingers on the table top, trying to think of where Charlie might have got to. She started having deranged fantasies; he climbed into the lion's cage, dazzled by a sleep-deprived state, perhaps with a half a mind to tell them about his new plans for Mary, and they rushed him.

She shuddered at the thought. One of the four labourers, eating their oats and drinking their coffee cold, must have noticed her looking anxious.

'You feelin' okay, Miss Addy?' he asked.

'Perfectly,' she croaked back, unconvincingly. How could they not have noticed Charlie was gone? 'Check the lion cage today, will you?'

'Sure thing, Miss Addy,' one of the others said, without turning around.

Only then, she realized something about the door to Mary's shed. The latch. It was hanging open!

'Oh, dear lord!' she cried and leapt to her feet, a thousand morbid scenarios running through her mind, all at once.

The labourers overtook her on the way to the shed and got the door open first. One of them held her back, just in case a rabid elephant was inside.

'Nothin' here,' a worker's voice called out.

'What do you mean, nothing?' Addy shrieked, having worked herself into quite a state. 'What do you mean?'

'He must've taken her for a walk,' the labourer said, reemerging. 'They're gone.'

'Charlie doesn't take Mary walking all day long!'

'It's only nine-thirty,' one of the labourers said, as he checked his fob.

'Boy, yo' watch is stopped. It's ten!' another corrected.

'They've been gone since before sunrise!' Addy cried. She covered her eyes and turned away. 'Oh, nononoooo, what has happened? What has happened to my Charlie?'

'You ain't even got a watch, how can you tell?'

'I's lookin' at the sun!'

'Oh! What are you now, part Injun?'

'Just shut up all of you!' Addy shrieked. They did. Immediately. They stared at her, mouths open. She never lost her temper. Not ever. But her hands were shaking. She was frightened for Charlie. She'd lost herself.

'Hey!' the voice of Christina cried, as she was squatting on top of her high bar. 'They're back.'

Sure enough, there sat Charlie Sparks, atop Mary, in his full Ringmaster's tuxedo, holding his top hat high above his head, and with swarms of children, probably from all across Carthage, following behind and beside him. Like some pachydermian distortion of the Pied Piper, he led them right toward into the grounds.

Relief flooded through Addy first, followed closely by the necessary persona, which she wore in the presence of the animals just as much as the children. There was a kinship between the two, she always found. So, it was the graceful, gentle, angelic Miss Addy who welcomed the children into the centre of the camp, in front of the mess tent, next to the fire pit; rather than the devoted wife who wanted to cuff her husband.

Charlie tapped Mary with his cane and stopped her where Miss Addy stood and had her turn in a quick circle for all their little adoring eyes.

'Gather round children! Gather round!' Charlie was bellowing. 'Free admission, only today. See the amazing

Mighty Mary! The most enormous land animal alive today! That's three whole inches taller than Jumbo, kids, three whole inches! Come one, come all! See her perform the most astonishing, most unprecedented, most awe-inspiring trick ever performed by an animal!'

Miss Addy buried deep the questions running through her mind. Did he get a permit to march that elephant up and down the streets, collecting people's children? Do the parents of these kids know where they are? Is it not a school day? But all of it disappeared in that instant. She knew he wanted Mary to play the trumpet again. She doubted he'd taken the time to make sure she would, when presented a trumpet, play it at all.

Charlie Sparks climbed down from Mary's neck and quickly pulled the trumpet out of its case, which at least he'd had the presence of mind to preset by the fire pit.

'Mary, take a bow!' he called and gestured her with his cane. She reared up, and the children retreated a few steps as she raised her trunk in the air. When she came down, she rolled forward in a headstand. The children screamed and applauded.

Then, Charlie handed Mary the trumpet. She hesitated for one heart-seizing moment, but then took the instrument in her trunk, and started blowing on it again.

'Music sounds a little different to animals than it does to humans, folks,' Charlie excused. 'Mary is giving us a taste of the cultural songs of Mabbadad, her home country, in the deepest, darkest forests of Africa!'

Miss Addy smiled and presented herself. From the corner of her eye, she saw Christina watching them.

Charlie must have seen her too. 'Hey, kids! What do you say we get Christina DeRosa over here, and show us how they dance to this kind of hokey music, over in Muddadad, where she once danced for the great Sultan Huggaboo! You all know Christina DeRosa, right!'

The children cheered. One kid, with a tilted beret and a cigarette between his teeth, wolf whistled. Christina just perched there, arms crossed.

When the cheers finally died, and Mary's trumpet kept squeaking and grinding, Christina lowered herself to the ground. 'I don't perform with animals.'

Christina turned her heel and strutted back toward her trailer.

'Well, Christina hasn't been feeling well lately, kids, but let's say Miss Addy does it for us today, and we'll see how Christina feels tomorrow?'

There was a complacent moan. Miss Addy rose to the occasion, doing her best impersonation of Indira Chopra's pre-belly dance routine to the nonsensical trumpet.

'One quarter entry after today, kids,' Charlie said, as they applauded. 'Come see Mighty Mary perform again, right here tomorrow! Tell your friends about this magnificent beast! Born in the wilds of Africa! Tamed right here in Ohio!'

CHAPTER 23

The days and nights grew colder and colder, but Mary was finding her days fuller and much less fragmented between routines than they had been, which made them pass more quickly. She was also growing accustomed to the dry, sluggish feeling that eating nothing but hay and grain gave her and was getting used to the long periods of sleep, which she'd now known longer in her life than what still felt right and natural to her. Every morning, Charlie Sparks would wake her before the sunrise, climb onto her back, walk her to the paved ground where the houses stood, and wave his arm around and shout as they walked up and down the streets, and gathered swarms of children as they went.

One day, a few people in rigid looking, symmetrical blue skins that matched each other hurried over and made awful, shrill squealing sounds through metal things in their mouths. Mary was shivering with fear, as they both carried black sticks that looked like bullhooks at their sides. At first, she thought they were coming to discipline her. When she saw they were shouting at Charlie Sparks, up on her back, she thought maybe he was going to get a beating himself! It would have confirmed what she suspected; that people passed on the cruelty they learned from others.

But Charlie Sparks was calm as he climbed down, and even as the two people shouted and pointed their fingers at him furiously. Their faces went all red. Charlie Sparks had his own routine, and he must have run through it perfectly, with his gentle smile, his soft words and the tender gesturing of his hands, because the two people calmed right down, and one of them even stopped to pet Mary's trunk as they both kept walking on their way. Charlie Sparks smiled at Mary before he climbed back onto her neck.

She was relieved, that day, to have him, and felt less concerned with his innate cruelty. She didn't forget the animals in the cages, but Mary again wondered if there was no right or wrong, and maybe if that was the case then it was truly their own fault that they found themselves in cages. If even Charlie Sparks had to run through routines, then why couldn't they?

Mary also didn't like the children, at first. She couldn't understand why they wanted to charge at her, screaming and waving their little hands in the air. She didn't like them touching her and was afraid whenever they'd run under her, in case she accidentally hurt one. Mary knew that would get her a beating that would most likely kill her. Maybe from the blue people, with their black sticks.

She began to get used to the children, as the days went by and even began to feel warmed by their appreciation. Mary

290

noticed their innocence, the vacant simplicity in their eyes that
was so close to the wild creatures Mary remembered, and so
distant from the foggy haze of the captive ones, or the
calculating cruelty of the adult people. It made her regard
Charlie Sparks with a greater fondness. After all, they all had to
have been children once. Mary learned to be more careful
how she walked and where she stood because there was no
directing them where to run, once they started.

'It's a teaser, Mary,' Charlie Sparks explained. 'Sort of an
appetizer for the real show!'

He'd ride her around town, gathering up the children and,
as days went by, their parents as well, and lead them back to
the wintering grounds. Once there, Mary ran through a basic
version of her dance; she wouldn't rear up, headstand or sit
down, she'd only spin around once, raise her trunk, and play
the horn. That was all, at first.

One night, blankets of frost covered all the grounds and
even clumped in the treetops. It was snow, and it stayed for
days and days, softly sparkling under the sunlight of each day,
and looking like a frozen ocean beneath the silvery moonlight
at night. Mothers began to accompany their children and
follow Mary and Charlie Sparks back to the camp, where
they'd watch Miss Addy dance while Mary played the trumpet,
as she found out it was called. The mothers would hold their

children's shoulders at first, keeping them back, but they'd have to stop to clap their hands. Soon enough, they gave up holding their children at all, and some of them joined in with Miss Addy's dance, able to mirror her, they'd come to know it so well.

Then, as the days grew warmer, the frost melted away, and life and colour began to blossom in the land and the trees again, from the pink little flower buds to the rich, green grass shoots and the dazzling splendour of the treetops as they caught the sunlight. It was then that familiar faces began to return to the camp. Indira was the first. She returned to her trailer quietly and soon after began to join in with the teasers. Mary would walk back to the wintering grounds with the children, as usual, and do her spin and raise her trunk, and then Indira stepped in, and she waved sticks with fire at the ends around, so it looked like she was spinning giant red circles around with her hands. Then, while Mary played her trumpet, Indira would put the fire to her lips and spit something out, and it would light up and look like she was breathing fire. Mary saw that it was a trick, but the children and even their parents seemed stunned and bewildered. Once, when a child started crying, Mary tried to tell her it wasn't real.

'It's only a trick!' Mary said. 'Indira can't really breathe fire!'

But the little girl's father came and pulled her away by the hand and looked nervously back at Mary as he did. It hurt Mary that he was unnerved by her trying to communicate with his child. He didn't mind Mary entertaining his child and himself. It didn't make sense. She could show them her silly tricks, but if she tried to talk to them she was frightening?

She decided to just be glad she didn't get beaten for it.

Soon after Indira, Jessica came back. She'd ride Mary instead of Charlie Sparks, who'd instead walk in front of them, leading with a long stick in his hand that he waved at people as he shouted at them from the middle of the road. Then, Yashi came back as well, and they'd both ride Mary together, and dance on either side of Indira and Mary while Indira breathed fire and Mary played the trumpet. Sometimes, Mary would see mothers covering their little boys' eyes while Jessica and Yashi danced. She even saw a woman cover a grown man's eyes once! Though she couldn't understand why, she couldn't help but feel spitefully gratified that it wasn't just her the people outside this new herd of hers regarded with distrust.

Then Cole returned, and though they were running out of room in their little wintering grounds, he found a place to lift his huge bar, with two big, hard balls stuck on either end, above his head. Mary saw some of the women covering their own eyes when he did that.

293

'This is Cincinnati!' Charlie Sparks shouted, one day when their walk had taken them far from the rows of houses and into the deeper viscera of the city, where structures stood taller than Mary could believe, and blocked out large portions of the sky, so she couldn't even see it. 'Don't get used to it, Mary. We won't be wintering here much longer.'

She was beginning to understand what Charlie Sparks said quite well, but sometimes she couldn't figure out what he meant by it.

When they returned from that walk, the clowns were back, and days had grown warm and the full beauty and colour of life had returned to the woods. Their teasers quickly descended into total chaos. Mary felt frustrated at the lack of order, with clowns running about, falling over and shouting to each other while the others performed. But the onlookers still smiled and slapped their hands together with joy, so Mary tolerated it by grinding her teeth together.

The only one who never joined in the teasers was Christina. While Jessica and Yashi danced, Miss Addy played with the band, Charlie Sparks shouted, Cole lifted things, the clowns tore the place apart and Mary played her horn, Christina either hid away entirely or would watch from her perch upon the high bar. Mary could sense that she was unhappy. She felt cold whenever she saw Christina, sitting in her self-imposed isolation, watching them as though she couldn't join in even if she wanted to. It was as though there was some kind of hurt that stopped her, like the hurt inside Mary that always kept her that little it distant, even when she was part of the fun, that little bit alone when she was surrounded by the herd, and that little bit frightened even when the people were happy with her performance.

It made Mary want to be closer to Christina.

With her new herd, Mary had come to feel a comfort she might have forgotten, or never have truly known, but there remained something amiss. In her heart, she felt the pieces missing. There was the pain, the grief, they still throbbed there, gently but persistently, and the longing to feel the muggy weather and the blazing sun she'd known first. But there was something else as well. Mary didn't quite fit amongst this new setting. This herd was not composed to creatures she understood, or that understood her. She loved Miss Addy, and was grateful to Charlie Sparks, but never without the tinge of fear that came with their pale complexions, elicited by the control that radiated from their little bodies. Even the workers, with their more strained, burdened demeanours, seemed fearsome. It was a respect she'd learned by hand, or with weapons. One that could not but come with resentment. Then, there was Christina.

It was a night like any of the others; they went for their walk
in the afternoon, they gathered up the children of Carthage
and Cincinnati, they led them back to the wintering grounds
and performed into the dusk, until their little faces were flush
with excitement. Mary played her trumpet, then watched as the
clowns fooled around with each other. One of them stood up
to the other two and delivered a slap to another's face. The
slapped clown fell backward, into the arms of the clown
behind him. The two of them then tumbled down, formed a
wheel composed of their own bodies, and went into a graceful
roll. Into that leaped the third clown, who'd delivered the slap,
and made the clown-wheel even bigger. Then, they crashed
into the rocks surrounding the bonfire pit and fell into a heap.
The children laughed and laughed. Mary wondered why they
found it so exciting. She'd spent too many nights trying to
figure out what had caused the initial slap; had that clown put
his foot in the wrong place? Maybe he'd stepped out of line?
After she'd realized it was part of the routine, she'd given up
trying to understand what people did in secret, and what they
liked to show each other.

Nevertheless, it always caused a warm sensation to roll
through her body and leave in its wake a dream about little calf
elephants rolling around in mud and playing rough by a
swollen river. How difficult it had been for one of those calves
to get water into her trunk and spray it out like the others did.

How lonely that little calf had felt. How could she have known what her life would become?

The world had got warmer again, so there didn't need to be a fire that night. Into the darkness, beyond the fairy lights, the children disappeared with their parents, until Mary heard the last whining tone fade into the chirping of crickets and the soft scratching of the squirrel who had made a home in one of the nearby trees. Miss Addy led Mary back to her stable to settle her for the night and sang her a lullaby that made Mary cry. She couldn't understand what it meant, but there was a comforting, maternal feel to it that only made her miss some distant place and some long-lost company she could only think she might have had once.

'Whatever is the matter, Mary?' Miss Addy asked, interrupting her song.

'I hurt,' Mary said, though she knew Miss Addy couldn't understand her the way Mary could understand Miss Addy now. 'I feel lonely.'

'Hmm,' Miss Addy said, and she touched Mary's trunk. 'You're such a special elephant, you know that?'

She continued her song until Mary started to doze, but as soon as she was gone Mary stirred again, unable to sleep. She'd realized what she was feeling, whenever she looked at

Christina. It was more than just contempt for Mary, more than anger at the rest of the herd, even more than a mysterious sadness Mary wanted to know and understand, because she had her sadness too that she didn't understand herself. It was what Mary felt whenever Christina went away and wasn't staring at her anymore. It was loneliness. Mary was sure of it. Christina was lonely.

Mary thought of the tiger. It was lonely too, no doubt, but it made no attempt to communicate with her. Christina did, even if it was just by staring from a distance. Mary wondered if Christina had a mother she missed, had a herd and little children around her when she was a child. Mary wanted to know. She wanted Christina to tell her, and to tell Christina so that they both shared their loneliness and weren't lonely anymore.

But they couldn't. Even if Christina was there with Mary, there was no way they could speak to each other completely.

So, remembering the dream which occurred to her earlier, Mary swayed her head and tried to remember a swollen river, a mountain range, long reeds and the sounds of calves playing in the muddy water. She tried to remember tall birds and chilly breezes that felt like the icy mountaintop's breath. She tried to remember speaking and being spoken back to. She swayed herself to sleep and dreamed about a forest. Christina was running through it, tears flowing from her eyes. Mary called to her. She bellowed with all her might. Christina kept running and crying. They were both lost but couldn't see each other.

There was a presence. Something following. Old Boy? No, something fouler. A stout man on a white horse, a bullhook in his hand, a hat on his head. Chasing her. Tiger's fangs in his mouth.

#

Charlie was standing in the trailer, running through the motions as though he were silently presenting to an almighty grandstand, packed out as they hadn't been for some time. Miss Addy sighed and sat down to take her makeup off.

'Don't you just want to rest, dear?'

'You know I never can, the night before,' he answered.

Well, we don't have to rest, she wanted to say, flirtatiously. But she couldn't. She was a lady. She had to wait until he asked.

She sat in front of the mirror and began to wipe off her makeup. Inadvertently, Adelaide found herself seeking out the imperfections he must see, that put him off so. A husband is supposed to want his wife. A wife isn't supposed to go so long without being wanted that she has to figure out ways of

coercing him, without being unladylike. She spotted the
wrinkles at the corners of her eyes and around her lips. She
tensed with jealousy that Miss Renoir and Miss Hoffmann got
to spend so much time with Charlie. Their tight, firm, plump
features made her look positively ancient.

That must be it, she decided, holding back the sudden flood
of hot tears. Charlie was spending so much time with those
gorgeous young women, that he'd lost interest in his darling
wife. Even the Indian, Miss Chopra, was enchantingly
beautiful, in an exotic way, she thought. He would never stray,
she knew her husband. He was a man of character, if an
eccentric one. But a man can fantasize without straying.
Fantasies can carry a man away.

Adelaide had seen Charlie having another one of his
conversations with their tiger that morning. She reminded
herself of it, and told herself, under her breath, that her
husband was just different, and that she had to adjust certain
preconceptions about married life to suit the reality. She
conveniently put out of mind just how many years she'd been
doing this.

'You know, I almost fell asleep singing to that blessed
elephant tonight,' she said, as she wished he'd at least turn
around and look at her.

Her face flushed with warmth when he did, and he broke into that joyful, boyish smile. 'Just an animal, you said.'

'Well, I'm not going to start reading to her from The Times.'

'Nor would I,' he said. He put his cane aside and sat on their little sofa bench. 'But animals are marvellous to talk to, don't you think yet? You could sing bum note after bum note, Mary would never know. You could be cursing, belching, you could pick your nose. Mary wouldn't care one bit.'

'I certainly hope you're not suggesting I would do those things, Mary or no,' Adelaide covered her hand and affected being shocked by him.

'Not at all.' Charlie mocked.

'And I do hope you're not.'

'Not with Mary,' he winked.

'Not with that tiger either!' she said, using the burst of energy as an excuse to get up and sit beside him. But he was up, just as quickly.

'I want Christina to dance with Mary.'

Adelaide sighed. 'You know she won't.'

'Can't you get her used to Mary? Just get them together.'

'What should I do? Coerce Christina into the shed and lock her in there, until the two make peace? The woman has a powerful back, I'll remind you.'

'Shoulder too,' Charlie said, touching his jaw.

Suddenly, the very woman burst through the door, holding a newspaper out in a clenched fist, her skin purple with fury. 'What is this?'

'Looks like a copy of the newspaper, my dear,' Charlie said, winking.

Christina violently ripped it open and found the page upon which was printed their poster. It was a week-old paper, and the poster was advertising for their show in Charlotte, North Carolina, that weekend's date.

'Ah, you found our poster,' Charlie said, his voice darkening.

'I had it mailed in,' Christina said. She shook as she held it up.

'Know a fellow? Local? Do you?' Charlie mocked. Adelaide wished he'd stop.

'Doesn't matter how!' she shrieked, in that rusty-nail voice. 'Why is that elephant taking up the whole damn advert? Where am I?'

Charlie waved a finger in the air and zeroed in on one of the silhouettes of showgirls, up behind Mary's head. 'Right there.'

'On the elephant?' she screeched. 'I don't ride animals. I don't perform with animals.'

'Christina...' Adelaide began, standing up.

'If I'm not important enough to this circus that I'm big and clear on the poster, then this circus isn't important enough for me to perform in,' she said, as though reciting something she'd read. Then, she turned and stormed out.

'Will you?' Charlie said, pointing at their slammed door.

'Better if we give her a minute to calm down,' Adelaide said. 'She won't pack her own bags, we have that much grace.'

She held out her hand. Charlie picked up his cane.

CHAPTER 24

Christina stormed back into her trailer, ready to rip all her clothes out of the chest, stuff them into her travel case, and walk into town...to the first safe place she could find. Had she not leaned back against the door for just a moment to catch her breath, she might have started. But in that fleeting pause, she realized she was not alone.

The sight of his silhouette against the electric light from her back window ripped a shriek from her. He didn't move. She backed up and tripped over the edge of her mattress. He got up, slowly walked toward her. Her heart was racing. She'd burst out in cold sweat. Christina scurried across her mattress and curled up against the back wall.

Finally, he spoke. 'Come back to see you, Christina.'

At the sound of his voice, all the icy fear pulsing through her suddenly ignited into a furious rage.

'Grubb! Get the hell out!' she cried, still trembling, but finding herself. 'What's the matter with you? Breaking into a woman's home.'

'Don't talk like that,' he was still advancing, ever so slowly. 'Here I thought you were a good girl. Catholic. But I guess you weren't playing paddy-cake with that strongman fella there, were you?'

Through the rage, a sickly feeling slowly moved through her. The dawning of what he intended of her. 'Hey, listen...'

'You LIED to me!' he suddenly roared, stopping at the foot of her bed.

'No, really,' she said, frantically. 'I mean...I really wanted to be good. For you. I wanted to. I was really thinking I'd change my ways, you know? I really did. That's as close as I've ever come...'

'SHUT UP!' he roared, sliding off his jacket. 'You going to go around, giving it to every guy but me? When I'm the one who put in the hours? I'm the one who showed you he cared?'

'Don't do it, Grubb,' she pleaded. 'You're a better man than this.'

'You aren't a better woman,' he seethed, then leaped toward her. She raised her feet and kicked him in the shoulder. Her powerful leg sent him reeling. She sat up and leaned over to punch him in the face, but her door suddenly burst open.

Cole charged in. He took one look at the writhing man on the floor, seized him by the collar, and hurled him right out onto the wet grass, dark blue in the moonlight. 'Don't you come back around here neither, y'hear?'

The panicked Grubb got to his feet and dashed across the camp into the darkness toward town. Christina got up off her bed. 'I had it under control.'

Cole suddenly spun around, grabbed her and pinned her against the wall between his enormous hands. She was trapped between the great, bulging pillars that were his arms. He spoke so close she could feel his nose against her cheek. 'I ought to have left you to him.'

'Get out of here,' she whispered, sharply.

'Yeah,' he said, releasing her. 'Yeah, I'm gonna get outta here. All the way over to my trailer, outta here. Tomorrow we're gonna leave on that train, and out on the rails, all across the South, just you and I.'

'You touch me, I'll have Charlie fire you,' she threatened.

'Oh, don't worry, you're safe, so long as you're with me,' Cole promised, stepping toward her open door. 'Heck, even a man like Grubb's got friends. Maybe friends all over town. Maybe even law-friends. But I won't hurt you, you stay with me. Not in any way you won't like. Or not in any way you'll be telling Charlie about, anyhow.'

He turned and stepped out. Christina quickly reached out and slammed her door shut. She leaned against it, feeling the tide of tremors and tears sweep through her. But she had to hold it a little longer. There came the gentle knock that could only be Adelaide. Christina took a few deep breaths, squeezed her eyelids shut a few times, and threw the door open. She immediately turned her back to the old lady.

'Christina, what's wrong?'

'They all hate me,' Christina said, automatically, biting her knuckles to stop herself from crying. 'All of them.'

'Oh, don't be silly,' Adelaide touched her shoulder.

Christina quickly pulled away, not wanting to submit to her affections. She fought against the desire to.

'You don't see it!' Christina barked. 'You don't! They hate me here. Even Charlie's replacing me with a damn elephant! And you! You care more about that thing than you do me. I hate that elephant!'

'He's just excited about it, that's all!' Adelaide urged. She reached out but withdrew just as quickly. 'It's Charlie's new toy. He'll calm down soon. You're a star, Christina, you're our star.' Christina had turned away again. 'How's an elephant going to upstage you anyway? Huh? Can Mary swing on a trapeze? Honey, you're crying!'

'I'm not!' Christina wheezed.

'Don't leave us, sweetie,' Adelaide said, though she noticed Christina's trunk was still tucked under her nightstand. 'We're family.'

'I'm not leaving! Just get out, will you?'

'What's got into you?'

'Oh, please get out! Please, oh, please just go...'

'I love you, Christina.'

'Leave me alone,' the dancer whispered. Adelaide gently opened the door and retreated back into the cool night.

Finally, alone. Christina bolted her door and collapsed into her mattress to cry.

#

Sunrise bathed the morning in copper light while a soft, chilly breeze carried the smell of fresh grass and blooming flowers through the woods and over the wintering grounds, where Mary stood beside her stable, watching as workers dismantled the village she'd known as home for two seasons and carried the pieces off toward the nearby railyard. That was where trains slept when they weren't being used. Mary knew they were moving somewhere, but she didn't expect they'd take their homes with them! But she did realize why the houses that the performers lived in had wheels; the workers didn't have to take them apart too much, they could just pull them over the grass, up through the clearing, and out over the hills and into the waiting train carriages.

Though she hated the open-air carriage she knew she'd soon be on it, getting that foul breath from the train's head blown over her while the sun circled the world time and time again, she couldn't help but tingle with excitement.

It was a migration!

Mary truly was in a herd, then. There was comfort in that, some cold recess of her being that was warmed by the idea of travelling with her herd, even if it wasn't on foot. It was another of those phantom urges which slept inside her sometimes and woke during dreams or when she felt emotional and shook her mind up and spiked her with guilty prongs that made her think she was a bad elephant.

Charlie Sparks came strutting over in his most symmetrical and brightly coloured second skin. He waved broadly. 'Good morning, Mary!' In his hand was one of the posters for the show. Mary had come to know them while Charlie Sparks had been designing them. At first, she'd thought that people had grown dissatisfied with the leaves on trees, the way they must have with being outside and amongst growing things, and decided to repaint them a different colour! But slowly, listening to the people talk, she'd figured out what they were. Why they existed was another matter.

'Let me up, will you?' Charlie Sparks was tapping her foot with his cane. For a moment, a searing wave of panic rolled through her. She'd let her guard down. She thought, just for the blink of her eye, that Charlie Spark's cane was a bullhook. In that moment, heat swelled behind the panic. She gritted her teeth. Her muscles tensed. It passed, just as quickly, and Mary lifted her leg to let Charlie Sparks climb up. She had to catch her breath, once he did.

She'd felt something new. Or something she'd forgotten. It wasn't fear. She wasn't afraid of the bullhook, or what she thought was a bullhook. In that moment where she thought he was going to hit her, she didn't even recoil. She was ready. What she felt was power. All at once, quicker than she could register, the size of her, compared to him, occurred to Mary. The fragility of him, next to her sheer power. His weakness, her strength. His reliance on aura and authority, and her brute force. What she felt was rage. Her heart beat quickly, and burning arrows of guilt shot through her flesh, with Charlie Sparks on her back, as she realized that in that moment, she could have killed him.

She was ready to kill him.

Mary didn't want to think about it. She swallowed hard, in her dry mouth. She forced back her tears. She pushed the wicked thoughts deep down, deep into her chest, where they hurt, but where they were safely buried. Miss Addy could see her, from near the mess tent. Mary felt that Miss Addy could see inside her and was afraid she'd see a burning ball of rage directed at her mate. These were people, and they had the weapons that killed her mother somewhere, Mary knew it. But more frightening for Mary than the thought of getting shot was the thought of being disowned by her herd.

A tear came to Mary's eye, while she stood still and let Charlie Sparks survey his village being pulled apart and moved away by workers from atop her back, as she realized she loved her new herd. Maybe it was the familiarity of them. The absence of obvious cruelty toward her, if not altogether, compared to others she would surely come across in this world that was never going to be her home. Or just that she had come to care about them for who they were. Mary didn't want to leave them. She never wanted to hurt them. Not one of them. Not even Charlie Sparks.

Miss Addy eventually followed the workers. The cages with the lions and the tiger, as well as the horses from the other stable, were already on the train. All that was left was the two structures, one of which had been Mary's, the other belonged to the horses. She couldn't figure why they weren't taking those too, but she knew she was going with them. There was no way they were leaving her behind. Her heart felt assured, even though everyone else had sent her off to somewhere else, either deliberately or by accident.

Charlie Sparks gave her a tap on the side. 'Let's go, Mary!'

Off they went. Mary felt another piece of the world move away from her, another constant fade into the darkness of her memories, and a new and mysterious expanse welcoming her. She climbed aboard the train, onto her carriage which was between the lions and the tiger in front of her, and the horses behind her. Charlie Sparks disappeared. That old familiar chugging, the clunking, and rolling, and before long life was moving by her again, so endless and so varied that she didn't dare imagine where they might find themselves.

But this time, she knew they'd find it together.

In front of her, the lionesses cuddled up to each other, while the lion, confined to his little cage in the corner, paced rapidly up and down, as did the tiger, also isolated. Mary found herself staring at the tiger until the sun went down. Strange feelings stirred inside her. A warmth, and yet a fear. A comfort, and yet grief. She wanted to touch it and hold it gently, and yet she was afraid of it, but she loved it, but it made her want to cry, all at once. So much feeling hit her that she didn't realize time passing and the stars alighting the velvety night sky. She forced herself to stop. She wished she could turn around and look at the horses. There were happier memories in their big, vacant, bulbous eyes. The tiger was a relic of a life she'd lost. As sure as if she'd died there with her mother, that world was gone to her. So should everything in it be, she thought. But she remembered the tiger on the water machine as well. How it had looked at her. Maybe thinking the same thing.

Mary stared off into the night, trying to imagine that she was looking in the direction of her horse friend from Old Boy's village. Out across rolling hills, through towering mountain ranges, around gigantic trees and across endless water that heaved and swayed like it was breathing. Up the sandy beach. Thought the wafting mists. Past the hanging creeper vines. Across the plains where the lonely trees stood. There he was. Tall and muscular and beautiful. Away from fences and canes and Old Boy. His vacant eyes taking in nothing but the endlessness and openness of eternity. Free.

Morning brought the green and golden vistas back. The rivers which cut through the lands, and the cities and villages and towns which flattened them and blocked out the skies. Mary saw that they were growing. Cities reached out into towns and made them into bigger cities, all the while they pushed the towns out further into wilderness and turned wilderness into towns. Each city and town was like a teardrop onto dry dirt; it spread, slowly but surely, through the light brown grains, flattening them and turning them dark.

Thoughts of freedom had flashed through Mary's mind. Ideas of abandoning her herd, even though the thought made her heart hurt, and running into the chaos, away from all this alien order. But she knew, as she watched the way people spread their symmetry and their straight lines out over the world that she would run out of places to hide eventually. Mary remembered she was in the safest place she could be; making them happy. Performing for them, as one of them. Avoiding the pain.

Days grew warmer. The air grew thicker and wetter, the way Mary used to remember it when she was little and belonged to a herd she couldn't bear thinking about. Now, as well as the tiger, she had the atmosphere itself to remind her of the holes ripped through her heart. She began to cry. They crossed prairies of browned grass and ran over lakes where trees had branches that hung limp and concealed their trunks. It was a denser, harsher world, Mary could tell. It was a world like home. She couldn't help but look at the tiger. But it didn't seem to notice. It was standing still with its head against the bars, watching as it had for a few days since they'd stopped over in a village to feed it. In the growing heat, the predators stunk of rotten meat.

Mary hated that smell. She didn't want to think of what happened to flesh when it died. She never ever wanted to think about that.

Up ahead, the sky grew darker. As the train moved, they cut through a dull electrical current, and in the twilight flashes of light and rolling thunder reached across the flatlands towards them. By morning, they were under heavy rainfall. It came down so hard, Mary couldn't open her mouth without it getting filled with water. She was soon up to her ankles, but the carrier couldn't flood any more than that. It went on after nightfall. Like nights in her dreams, whenever she spent enough time trying to recall the sense of love and protection of her mother, as though to use it for a blanket at night, there was not a star above, not a trace of light, just the constant flow of drenching downpour. All the while, Mary's sleepy mind played tricks on her. Moment after moment she felt like she could reach into the abyss and touch her mother's side. She even anticipated feeling the warmth of her flesh, the enormous power of her body, towering over her as though Mary was still just a calf. Every moment ended with the crushing reminder that however much it felt like it, this wasn't home.

After they stopped, a flood of yellow false-light pooled next to the train, which made the rainfall shimmer and revealed a road running alongside the train tracks and then across that a fence with a gate, and a small portion of what must have been a swampy paddock beyond.

The soft ticking of an automobile gently arose amidst the torrents of falling water. It appeared out of the darkness, first two round lights like eyes, and then the machine itself, which stopped beside the train, on the road. A worker ran out, hunched over as though the weight of the rain was too much, and paused by the side of the automobile for a while. Then, the automobile turned around and took off again, and disappeared into the darkness beyond the light from inside the train. The worker ran along to the gate and Mary heard a click, then he opened it.

Then, under the unrelenting deluge, the small army of workers appeared. Just like they had disassembled and packed up the village, they began unpacking it and assembling it again in the paddocks. Mary watched as they slipped and slid around in the mud, fell over, got back up, and just kept working. They sank upon their knees in the mud. They grunted and shouted, but all the while they toiled. Flashes of lightning showed their labouring bodies, now and then.

All through the night, they worked.

CHAPTER 25

Mary didn't remember falling asleep, but she woke in shock to find the rain suddenly gone, and the shafts of sunlight that pierced through the parting clouds and shone down over the paddocks. She could see them all now, but the first thing that caught her eye was what the workers had built in the rain and darkness. There was no way to avoid it; it consumed the otherwise flat, near featureless landscape around it. A giant structure, its skin walls flapping slightly in the nearly undetectable breeze, while sheets atop poles flapped upon peaks all across it's top. It was orange and red and blue, striped in perfect vertical lines, and was shaped like a dome with a great, gaping mouth flanked by two shoulders that seemed designed to funnel something right into it. Scattered all around it, but presumably mostly behind it, were the houses on wheels and the cages for the animals and whatever else the herd brought along with them. All the familiar things. Plus that giant thing in the middle.

Mary had never seen anything like it before. It was as though the excess of Charlie Sparks' personality had been recreated as a structure on the edge of a paddock that felt like the middle of nowhere. Besides their village, the road, the fence, and the train, there was a row of evenly spaced trees, growing in perfect lines and disappearing into the light grey

317

mists left by the rain clouds off in the distance either side of
the camp. On the breeze, Mary could smell the bitter, acrid
odour of decay and stagnation that usually issued from cities. It
must have been at the end of the road, though she couldn't see
it. Maybe it was just beyond the veil of fog.

Down at the foot of the giant dome, Mary could see the
workers sitting in a cluster, just plonked in the mud there, and
holding each other. Like her herd used to when they slept on
cold nights. She could see how exhausted they were.

The remaining crews were helping the performers off the
train. It was a long way down without a station to step onto.
Cole helped a person, a handler, collar the lions and the tiger
and lead them, at the end of a whip, off toward the cages just
behind the dome. Once they were safely locked up, the
horses were brought out, saddled, and rode. Jessica, Yashi and
Indira each had horses, as did the clowns. They didn't go off
to cages or stables, instead, they rode around along the side of
the fence, just meandering about. All the while, automobiles
were appearing from the mist, mostly from the direction Mary
had smelled the city from. They stopped along the sides of the
road and people climbed out, mostly men. Some children and
women, but not many. Most of the men were holding large
boxes with rods on the side, and devices mounted on top of

them. Only when they appeared did Christina step out of the train.

Immediately, a handful of the men rushed to her. They held up their boxes, and the devices on the ends of the rods let out a blinding flash. For a moment, Mary was seized with horror, but she didn't hear the deathly sound of a weapon, nor did Christina fall down dead. Instead, she touched her hair and smiled, and struck poses while more flashes went off and emitted little puffs of stinking smoke into the air.

'Good morning, Mary!' Charlie Sparks said, gleefully, as he climbed up her ramp and into her carriage. 'Bet you never saw the Big Top before, hey!'

'Never,' Mary said, as she looked at the dome. That's what it was. A Big Top.

Charlie Sparks climbed up onto her back and Miss Addy led them down the ramp. The people with the flashing boxes quickly directed their lights at Mary. She knew that if she got too scared and did something wrong, she'd be punished, or cast out. So she held herself as best she could, and held her breath whenever the bolts of panic shot through her. Miss Addy led them to where the clowns had strapped large music instruments to themselves and joined a number of workers who held other instruments. Slowly, Mary began to see what was happening.

319

'Come one, come all!' Charlie Sparks was bellowing. 'See the ferocious lions, straight from the African Savannah, where they ruled the jungle as kings. Witness the incredible, ravenous tiger, lord and ruler of his homeland, a servant here for you. And this! The largest land mammal that ever lived! Three whole inches taller than Jumbo, five awe-inspiring tons of powerful beast, Mighty Mary!'

The flashing became frenzied and fast. For a moment, Mary lost herself, raised her trunk, and released a slight squeal, before she managed to subdue herself. The crowd made a shocked sound, but it only made the flashes increase. A few of the women were clapping. Mary still didn't want to do it again.

But in front and behind her, the rest of the herd had formed a line. The music band was at the front, with the clowns behind them, and then the horses with Jessica and Yashi and Indira on them, then Christina and Miss Addy, and then Mary, while the handlers followed her. Christina had her hoops and was spinning them around. The band began to play their music. Everyone walked along the road toward the gate to the paddock.

Sheer emotion stole Mary's attention from the cameras. It had been so long since she moved properly with a herd that doing so almost made her faint with dizzying joy and erupting sorrow. But she held on to the happiness of belonging. There she was, in a herd, migrating.

Finally. At long last. A herd. A moving herd.

They didn't move far, but it was enough to fill Mary with melancholy happiness so that she could face the tumultuous flashing again. They migrated to the mouth of the Big Top, between the two shoulders, and then spread out. Everyone turned to face the flashes and pose for them. Mary kept very still, having sensed that this was somehow important. Charlie Sparks climbed down from her into a wagon drawn by four horses, which pulled him around in circles while he waved to the flashes and the people.

Then, just as quickly, it was over. The crowds dispersed, the automobiles shuddered to life and rolled back off in the direction they had come from, and the herd broke off and started taking their horses off behind the Big Top or just walking off with whatever they were carrying. All of a sudden, it was oddly quiet. Nobody spoke, nobody even acknowledged each other.

The air remained moist and the sky was still threateningly dark and angry looking. Mary was looking forward to getting back inside her stable. She could smell the fresh hay from inside the dome and was curious to see what was inside. But she didn't want to just walk into it. Charlie Sparks had gone off

with his horses in the wagon with Miss Addy, so it was just a
worker holding Mary's leash. She didn't like the silence. It felt
awkward and almost threatening. Herds spoke constantly, even
if they had nothing to say, each elephant kept a constant flow
of information.

'Come along now, Mary!' the worker cheerfully said, and he
gave a slight tug on Mary's leash. She followed him, but not
into the Big Top.

Instead, their feet squelched in the mud as he guided her
around the shoulder, past the edge of the dome, and deeper
into the paddock. They walked right past the houses, where
Mary saw Jessica and Cole shutting themselves in their
respective homes, as well as a few workers doing the same in
their communal cottage. Mary still couldn't see her stable.
They kept walking and soon passed by the little village
altogether. Mary was out in the paddock, with her herd and
their structures shrinking behind her. Ahead, there were only
vast puddles reflecting the vibrant sunrays and one lonely tree
standing with a pile of hay thrown down at the base of its
trunk. It didn't look like the lonely trees from Mary's home,
but just seeing it there made her sad. It looked so alone,
especially in a country where all the trees stood together. They
got closer and closer, while the camp got further and further

away, and finally, Mary saw that the hay at the base of the tree trunk was dry. It had been left there after the rain.

It was for her.

Mary was hungry. Her stomach had been groaning for some time, but she'd also found herself experiencing the hot flushes and swelling discomfort between her back legs for the last bit of the train ride, which tended to overcome any other discomforts. She found them regular, but irritating and often painful. Cramps, a soggy feeling, and grogginess usually sweltered inside her. Then, she'd think of bulls. She'd dream about them coming up behind her, investigating her, following her, and with their power and might mounting her and entering her. She'd wake up hot, and still feeling as though a bull was there somewhere, watching her from the dark. She'd look for him but never find him. Then, she'd have to return to sleep still trembling and roiling with hot flushes. It had only been the discomfort on the train, but the hot flushes had begun to threaten her during the night she watched the workers build the new camp. She knew tonight would be bad for sleep.

She didn't know what the large chain was wrapped around the tree for until she started eating and the worker quickly picked up a large cuff on the end of it, with a painful heave, and snapped it around her ankle. Mary watched him do it and

looked from the cuff to the tree trunk while she chewed the
hay. A dark feeling crept through her.

'No!' she said to the worker, and she lifted her cuffed foot
and rattled the chain.

'Well, Mary, g'night,' the worker smiled warmly and tipped
his hat. 'Sweet dreams.'

With that, he turned and started walking back to the camp.
Mary felt her heart sinking and tears filled her eyes. She raised
her trunk and trumpeted, and the worker stopped to look back
at her.

'No!' she cried. 'I don't want to stay here!'

'Eat up Mary!' the worker called out to her. He was already
a distance away. 'Don't be fussin' over it now.'

He turned and continued off on his way until Mary couldn't
see him amongst the wheeled homes and the cages anymore,
through the blur of her tears. Crying, she tugged at the chain
until her ankle hurt too much to stand on. Every time she put
weight on it, sharp, hot pain sliced through her. She trumpeted
toward the camp a few times, but they didn't seem to hear. She
couldn't see anyone around, other than a slight yellow fuzz that
might have been the lions resting in their cage.

The sky rumbled, and cold slivers that cut up the buzzing atmosphere promised another heavy downfall. Mary had never slept under the rain alone before. She didn't want to. She wanted to be inside like they'd kept her at the old camp. Why? Why this, now? What had she done wrong? She couldn't figure it...she'd moved with the herd, when they wanted her to move. She'd stood still for the flashing boxes like Christina had. Mary had done everything right. Why were they leaving her out here?

Mary looked back at the Big Top, with its strips of fabric fluttering high atop its roof, longingly. She wanted an answer, but she didn't know how to ask for it. She understood them, but as always, they never tried to understand her. Why? Why could they not understand? Why did they bring her into their herd, and feed her and keep her inside, only to tie her up so far away from them in this new place? Had she done something wrong?

She thought about it until her stomach twisted up with phantom guilt, and that brought on the cramps harder and stronger than she could ever remember them being. She felt so soft and weak. She wanted to sleep laying down but couldn't with the chain so tight around her ankle. So, Mary just stood there, and sobbed and waited for the rain.

No, she thought. Miss Addy will come. Miss Addy was always there when she had a bad dream, or when her memories consumed her, and she felt like she was drowning in a sea of sorrowful voices, images, and sensations. Miss Addy would come to her now. She'd get this cuff of her ankle and take her into the Big Top, where it was warm and smelled nice. That's where Mary wanted to be. More than anything, she wanted to be closer to them. It was natural! A herd slept together, always! The rest were close together...why was Mary not? No, Miss Addy would come and set things right.

But night began to fall first. It was deep and heavy under the tormenting clouds. Mary cried again, as the weight of despair fell upon her heart. Miss Addy wasn't coming. Mary looked back at the Big Top long enough to see the last of the yellow lights go out, and the night was plunged into inky blackness that enclosed around Mary like the sickening groans and cramps in her belly and the ripping, tearing sorrow in her heart. The rain only fell in intermittent showers, which only seemed to encourage the chorus of night things that lived beneath the muddy grass. With each cool gust, Mary was snapped out of her attempts at sleep, and whatever fantasy she was managing to conjure about bulls, the one thing that could distract her was blotted out. All that was left, then, was cramps and sogginess. Without the four walls she had gotten used to, the night was alive and pestilent. Mary could hear the tiger

326

moaning in its cage, under the brief showers, and without vision, the sound was immediate and terrifying. Like a nightmare, it seemed to come from all around. Mary kept thinking it had escaped and was stalking. She could imagine it, low down in the grass, prowling as it had by the swollen river.

Mary was too big for it, now. She had to keep telling herself. But as her mind wavered between wake and sleep, she thought she even smelled the bitter infection of an old wound again.

The night crawled by. Mary tried to distract herself by eating the greens off the tree, but first, she had to feel it out in the darkness with her trunk. Once she did, she found the leaves bitter. She gagged on the mouthful and spat it out.

For some reason, she started thinking about Christina. Mary wanted to be nearer to Christina. As the first light grey tones flirted with the horizon and slowly illuminated the paddocks, Mary told herself that Christina would understand her. Christina didn't like Mary, which was easy to see. But Mary didn't need to be liked now, she needed to be understood. Children, workers, and Charlie Sparks liked her, but they tied her to trees. Even Philip liked her, and he beat her with a bullhook. But Christina didn't like her, so all she did was understand her. Mary wished more people didn't like her.

The smell of cooking wafted out to Mary from the camp, as horses pulled the wagon out toward Mary. She could see there were only workers aboard, but her stomach folded over itself again and again in anticipation anyway. She couldn't imagine what they were going to do to her next, good or bad.

'Good morning, Mary!' the worker who'd tied her out for the night said, while the other uncuffed her ankle. She still struggled to stand on it, feeling like little insects were crawling about under the skin of her foot. 'Oh, now, was that too tight? I'll remember that for next time. No wonder you was makin' such a racket, last night! I saw-ry, Mary.'

Slowly they walked her, behind the horse-drawn wagon, back to the camp. Her mind bombarded with questions, each one struck her like a stone, but she anchored herself with the memory of how nonchalantly Charlie Sparks had acted around his lions and tiger, who all obviously suffered for him. Mary remembered how sweetly he had spoken to them, uncomprehending of their pain and suffering, all of which were easily evident to Mary. But Charlie Sparks was oblivious.

She gritted her teeth, suddenly flushed with rage over the thought that the people were unaware of their own cruelty. That they didn't even know how awfully she had suffered through the night. They didn't know. They thought they'd done her good!

Finally, they brought Mary into the Big Top. Inside, it smelled strongly of hay and horse dropping. Mary walked

down a narrow corridor after she entered through the mouth
of the dome, and at the end found herself in a big circle,
surrounded by hundreds of chairs, all in big rings, row after
row. Charlie Sparks, Jessica, and Yashi were waiting there, all
in their fancy skins.

'Good morning, Mary,' Charlie Sparks said, and confirmed
Mary's earlier aggression, but she was too awestruck now to do
anything about it. Up above them were crisscrosses of cables,
some higher than others, and perched upon a platform on a
pole, high up at the end of one of the cables, was Christina.
Quietly watching, as always.

It was Yashi who tapped Mary's foot. But Mary was too
interested in the cables and Christina. The elephant raised her
trunk to the dancer and aerialist, but she didn't respond with
any gesture at all. She just sat there, watching. Yashi tapped
Mary's leg again. It irritated her. She grunted and took a step
away.

'Mary, come on!' Charlie Sparks said. He had his cane, but
he'd never hit Mary with it. She didn't want to, just yet. None
of these people had ever hit her. There were no consequences
for not doing as she was told, or none she knew of yet anyway.
Besides, she'd been beaten before. What could these little
things do to her, now that she was so much bigger than them?

Workers had begun to gather around the perimeter, and they watched. Mary ignored them. She wanted to see how far this could go.

'Mary, we've got to run a routine before we do the parade!' Yashi said. 'They're waiting for us, outside!'

But Mary hadn't heard her words. She'd only heard the slight tremor in her voice. The breathy hesitation behind each word. Mary knew what it was; fear. For the first time in her life, a person was afraid of her. And Mary liked it.

Maybe they were all afraid of her?

Another first quickly followed; she wished she could see Old Boy again. Have him here. Maybe the Colonel. She wanted to see how afraid she could make them. She felt strong and powerful, with fear about her. She liked it.

'Mary, do as Yashi says,' Charlie Sparks said. 'Come along now, my dear. ... Mary! ... Now!'

He had the tremor too. Mary heard it. A man was afraid of her. It almost made her heart skip. He shouldn't have chained her out there, to that tree. He should have let her sleep in here, with the others. Now Mary had power. Mary liked power.

Then, a cooling wave of hesitation washed through Mary. She thought of Christina, up there. She thought of Miss Addy. She thought of being turned away, sent off, or simply cast out. Out into the wilderness. Paddocks were just embryonic villages, about to become towns, and then cities. Out there, Mary had nowhere to be. The trees tasted toxic to her. And she'd have no Miss Addy to comfort her, after bad dreams.

No sooner had Mary thought of her than Miss Addy stepped out from behind a fold of the skins draped over one small section of the central circle. She carried Mary's trumpet to her and held it up with a warm, loving, radiant smile.

'Come on now, Mary,' she said. 'We're waiting.'

'I don't want to,' Mary answered. But Miss Addy showed no sign of understanding. Mary thought it with all her might.

'Mary!' Charlie Sparks barked, firmer than she'd ever heard him. 'Come along!'

'I don't want to be tied to the tree anymore,' Mary grunted, and she turned away from them both, toward Yashi.

Yashi yelped fearfully and leaped a few strides backward in terror. A spike of adrenalin shot through Mary. For just one moment, she had a person entirely at her mercy. So afraid! Terrified! Of her!

'Stay where you are, Miss Renoir!' Mary heard Charlie Sparks shout.

'I don't like it!' Yashi whimpered.

Mary held still, confused and frightened of herself.

Then, just like that, she felt the warm, soothing, delicate little hands of Miss Addy stroking her ear, ever so gently, the way she did when she knew somehow that Mary was having trouble sleeping or had suffered a nightmare.

'Shush, there, there,' Miss Addy was saying. Her voice was like a soft breeze. 'Mary's just a bit confused, that's all. She's nothing to be afraid of! She's our friend. She's our family.'

'Ha!' Christina yapped.

Mary melted in those tiny little hands. Before she knew it, she had her leg raised, but it was Jessica who climbed up. Still, her straddle didn't feel as confident or assured as it had before. Mary knew she'd frightened them, even shaken their confidence. She also had seen that without confidence, people were just frightened little animals, easier to kill than a rat.

Though guilt plagued her, Mary couldn't help but like the revelation. She hated herself for it, for how could she dream of harming Miss Addy? But then, she knew she could...

Mary moved with the herd again, as they had yesterday, but it was a long migration this time. Charlie Sparks and Miss Addy were at the front, in their wagon, while the band and clowns marched behind them, and then the horses with Indira and Yashi on them, then Mary with Jessica riding her, and then the handlers.

Christina hadn't joined them.

CHAPTER 26

'Open this damn door, Christina, or I'm gonna rip it off!' Cole thundered from outside, over the savage beating he was giving the thin wooden entrance to Christina's carriage.

'Go away, goddamn it!' she shouted. Christina refused to let herself move from right in front of it. She wouldn't be afraid of the nights, she told herself. Not on account of some man. Not again. That was her life as a young dance student in New York City. That was why she had run to the circus. That was not her life now. She was in control. Nobody else would control her again. Not Cole, not anybody.

She was not afraid.

Cole's blows were rocking the whole trailer. Christina could hear the wood around the door frame beginning to splinter.

'Cole, I told you not to bother me unless I said it was okay!' she screeched. But his giant fist suddenly burst through the wood, his fingers spread out, and in one swift motion, he ripped the door open. Cole was inside her trailer.

He pulled the smashed door shut behind him and Christina felt his huge hands clasp around her shoulders. The wall behind her struck her in the back of her head and shoulders, but it didn't hurt. Her heart was pounding too hard. Her whole body buzzed with furious anger. Even while his enormous frame cast a shadow over every inch of her.

'What are you gonna do, huh?' she snarled. 'Bruise me up the night before our first show? I'd like to see what Charlie has in store for you after that, boy, would I.'

'Shut up!' he barked and shook her. She hit the wall again and finally looked up into his eyes. She knew Cole. She knew him intimately. There was a time, not long ago, when a confrontation like this, and having his giant body pressing hers against a wall and feeling helpless in his grip, would have excited her. But now, in those eyes, Cole wasn't there. They were vacant, empty pits staring from a tumultuous place of fury and determination. He was like one of the animals. She'd expected lust. When she didn't see it, only hate and spite, her steel melted, her fortitude crumbled, and she was overcome with terror.

'Please don't, Cole,' she had to force herself to remember his name. It wasn't him. But the shock of looking at him had stolen her voice away. All she could do was whimper. 'I don't want to.'

'Well, that there's a cryin' shame,' he said, and he nuzzled her ear and neck and sent her skin crawling. ''Cos, I got me a hankerin'. And I gets what I wants.'

'You got enough,' she squirmed out while he licked her neck, her sheer revulsion gave her volume. 'Got more'n Grubb did.'

'So, what's it to you, if I want me a little more?' Cole said as he groped her so hard it hurt. 'What's it to you, huh? I'm just another guy.'

'I'll tell Charlie...'

'Oh, come on now!' he seized a fistful of her hair. Christina felt like fire was raging through her scalp. She screamed, but he hurled her at the bed so hard it knocked the wind from her. She choked and gasped, trying to make some kind of noise, but nothing came. He was quickly upon her. With one hand to took both her wrists and pinned them above her head. With the other, he was able to knock her knees aside and force his pelvis between her legs. Cold, sickly shivers ran through Christina, with her body open to him. Vulnerable and trembling with a familiar horror, her stomach twisted and knotted in disgust.

'Oh, please, no!' she wheezed. 'God...please, Cole, don't...'

'God?' he chuckled and stopped to stare at her in the softly pulsing lantern light. 'Who're you to be praying to God now, huh? You think God's gonna help you? You think anyone's gonna help a whore like you?'

'Charlie's gonna fire your ass!' she choked out.

'Charlie?' Cole spat. 'I'll crush that little bastard's skull between the palms of my hands, say it was that damn elephant. What would you do about it, if I did that, huh? Tell the law? Who'd believe you? They'd more likely lock you up! They got special institutions for a wicked woman like you, all across this fine country of ours! Who'd believe you, huh?' he slapped her face. 'Who? You're worse than a whore. You're a gypsy! A circus folk! A freak! Hell, what judge... after you gone and offered yourself all over town, corrupted good Christian boys and such... what judge would believe that you turned a man like me down, huh? Huh?' he started to shout into her ear. 'Who? Who'd think that? A hussy like you, turning me down? Who'd think? Who'd believe you? Nobody! That's who? Nobody would believe a whore like you would turn me down. What was I to do, huh? You giving it here there an' everywhere. Corrupting good Christian boys. What was I to do? Nobody would believe a carnival tramp. A whore. A gypsy. You're not good for society, even if you wasn't a whore.'

Christina had caught her breath, but no longer had the will to scream. She felt his bulging trousers pressing against her crotch. She felt his strength pinning her down, bearing over her. She tried not to cry, but she couldn't stop it. 'Cole...let me go...'

'Oh, lookee! Tears!' Cole taunted, and he leaned in a licked them off her cheeks. 'Yum-mee! Look at those! Tears from Christina DeRosa! Who'd have thunk it? Say, Christina DeRosa, you know who's coming onto this land, after us? Once we pack up, who's got the lease on this here place? Temperance folk! A good-ol'-fashioned revival! I wonder what they'd think, a whore like you sayin' she was forced. I wonder what they'd make of Charlie Sparks, keepin' you for show. I wonder what they'd make of your case. Hell, if they didn't lock you up, they'd lynch you. Then, I wonder what they'd think, if they found you and that little bastard Charlie Sparks all naked and twisted up around each other in the field, all because you felt you had to tell? Two dead sinners? Hell, they'd burn you both on a pyre just to make sure you stayed dead.'

'Alright, shut up!' she coughed. 'Get it over with.'

'What's that, honey?'

'I said get it over with!' she cried. She cried the whole time and never stopped. She let the pain make her cry, she let the sorrow weigh down on her, she let the sickening, disgusting feeling of her whole body being dragged over filth. Her blood and bones and flesh and soul being polluted and contaminated with some awful, acidic, vile essence that she could never wash off, as long as she lived. She was soft, and still, and weeping as he had his fun. She hoped, all the time, that he'd feel her that he'd realize his disgrace, and stop. That her tears would reach the good heart she thought he had. But nothing. Nothing got through. He hurt her deeply, he shamed her, and he burst into her and filled her with his disease until he was finished. Then, he lay breathless beside her. She immediately turned away, curled up, and trembled and wanted to be sick.

'Go on, now, get out.'

He caught his breath, and stood up, dressed in whatever clothing he'd lost. 'Same time tomorrow darling?'

She ignored him. Christina cried silently into her curtains.

'I like it this way,' he said, as he closed the door behind him. Christina cried long and hard. She cried until her eyes stung, and she was blinded by tears. She cried until her throat was tight and sore. Then, she felt the slime. She felt the dirt. She quickly put on a robe and hurried outside. She fled to her wash bucket and scrubbed herself, but she couldn't get it out. She felt it in there, coursing through her.

Breathless, she stopped. She held herself against the bucket. Her whole body was trembling. Her legs couldn't hold her up. Finally, she vomited.

'A woman has to be strong,' the soft voice of the headmistress at her dance school cooed, from deep within a memory. 'If she wants to get her way in this world, she has to first learn how to give men theirs.'

Those were the words she'd heard when she'd told the headmistress what the instructor was doing to her. She remembered them. She told them to herself whenever she allowed herself into a position that she felt violated her, or abused the body she lived in. For food or shelter, sometimes it was necessary. But they never forced. Only her instructor had forced. Now Cole had forced himself. A piece of her, something she thought was already gone, was stolen again. Ripped from her, and again left a great, sickly, bleeding edifice, painful as death. All over her skin. All through her flesh.

Nobody would ever believe her.

'A woman has to be strong.'

She vomited again and pulled herself up. In the night, the back window of her trailer reflected her face. She looked at her big, crystal-blue eyes. Her thick, soft black hair. The spot on her cheek, natural, while most women paint a spot there. Her full lips. The delicate curve of her jaw. Her slender, soft neck. She felt a burst of rage again, this time at that reflection. That's what they wanted. She wished she could tear her hair out. Rip out her eyelashes. Cut her lips off. Break her own jaw. Slash her slender throat. Smash the window and use the shards of broken glass. They'd leave her alone, then.

She felt eyes looking out from the night. The light grew stronger. She thought she saw them all. Staring at her. There she is. There's that whore.

Christina backed away. Their eyes burned her. Their pointed fingers scorned her. She saw the Big Top, all full of people, all filled to the brim. All full of civilized people, waiting for her. To put her on trial. To judge her. To point their fingers, click their tongues, and say how glad they are that this tramp doesn't belong in society. How glad they are that even the circus, the gypsies of the new world, saw fit to cast her out. She ran. They'd find her wherever she fell. She wouldn't be so beautiful anymore. Not by then. She'd be bloated, and grey, and half pecked away by buzzards.

Then, in the darkness in the fields, Christina heard Mary's chain softly slithering from side to side, as she came up behind the big elephant. Swaying, from side to side.

Christina meant to walk right on past Mary. She couldn't stand to see another set of eyes staring at her. She turned her head and kept walking past.

Mud was splattered up to Christina's knees. The whole bottom half of her robe was stained brown. The day was brightening. Christina felt the elephant watching her. She turned and looked back. Immediately, she froze.

Mary stopped swaying. She was watching Christina, but not with the judgement in her eyes that Christina had expected. Christina felt silly, then, expecting an animal to be staring at her, judging her. She felt silly to have thought the Big Top, and the circus were judging her. It was her imagination. But Mary was also not staring at her with that animal vacancy that Christina felt she should have expected, as a rational human being.

Animals don't have souls. Only man is made in God's image. Christina thought it, but she didn't believe it. Certainly not looking at Mary now.

There was a presence to her gaze. A curiosity, not a knowing. A blankness that asked to be filled, rather than a blankness for lack of intuition or comprehension. Christina felt she was being comprehended. Even just standing there, she felt that she was teaching Mary something about herself. There was something in Mary's gaze that asked. Questioned, and considered. If an animal can question and consider, then it can learn.

Animals don't have souls. So, they say about gypsies. Only man is made in God's image. Does that include women?

Warmth slowly dripped through Christina's heart. She felt the sickly poison melting away. She walked closer to Mary.

Something about that gaze beckoned her. Something hard caught her toe.

The chain. Mary was cuffed, by the ankle, to the tree. Christina could see how the cuff dug into her skin. Up close, she saw marks and scars all over Mary; mostly on her ears, but there were some white lines around her armpits, and her feet as well. Christina took the whole picture in. Tears filled her eyes again.

Mary's trunk came up and gently touched Christina's hip. Christina touched the rough skin, petting her gently. She still couldn't bring herself to talk to animals, the way Charlie did. But she found that if she whispered, she felt less silly. 'Oh, Mary. Hello Mary.'

Mary's big, innocent eyes just stared, absorbingly.

'I guess they've got their ways of keeping us both stuck here,' Christina whispered. She slid down the tree trunk and sat against the cold, hard chain keeping Mary stuck. She felt he wet mud seeping over her backside. Before she knew it, she was humming a lullaby.

#

That was where Charlie Sparks found them, a few hours later, when it was time to prepare for the show. The crowds were already gathering out front. They had to run through

343

their routine, iron out any faults, and be ready by three o'clock. Surely it was a sell-out. The first Sparks Travelling Shows had enjoyed since the death of its founder.

'See, now, I told you you'd warm up to Mary, eventually,' Charlie said, jovially, while he gently touched Christina's arm.

'Leave me alone,' she snapped. They rode back in the wagon together. She was huddling herself, shivering. He asked if she was okay. 'Leave me alone, I said.'

'Will you ride Mary, with Jessica?' Charlie asked. 'Yashi's got a bit scared of her, since yesterday. Would you?'

'No.'

Back in the Big Top Mary did as Charlie asked with either Jessica or Yashi, or both, riding her at various times. She walked in a circle, stood up on a pedestal and reared backward, did her headstand, and her pirouette. Finally, she played her trumpet. Then, the clowns let the audience in. People flooded the grandstand. The Big Top was full.

'Ladies and Gentlemen,' Charlie began. The clowns raced around in a car that was too small for them. They fooled with horses. Yashi, Jessica, and Indira rode horses out, striking poses on their backs, and doing tricks. Indira did her belly dance, and spat fire, as Jessica and Yashi rode horses around behind her, balancing on their backs and twirling hoops off their arms or legs at the same time. Jessica and Yashi dismounted their horses, and did a dance, while Cole took to the ring, and lifted a heavy barbell, then lifted a plank of wood with clowns on either end. Then, he lifted a plank of wood with Jessica and Yashi on it. Indira reappeared, spitting fire. Charlie lied about capturing Cole in the depths of the Amazon Rainforest. Christina rode a horse out, standing on its back. From there, she grabbed her trapeze, and weightlessly hung upside down, twirled around it, hung from her legs, hung from one leg, swung to another trapeze, then back again, hung upside down by her hands, her body turned upward. She came down, played with hoops, then swung in the air again, this time from a hoop, which climbed atop, hung from, and struck beautiful poses with. Charlie lied about her being from Norway. Nobody knew why. He then climbed into the cage with the lionesses. He cracked a whip. He put his head in the lion's mouth. He swapped the lions for the tiger. He cracked a whip. He put his head in its mouth. He pulled children out of the audience and had them hold out pieces of paper, between their hands. Then, with his whip, he cut the papers in two, right in the children's hands. He brought the lionesses back out and had them jump around, performing an obstacle course. Cole came back and played with the lion. The clowns came back and pretended to be afraid of the lion.

Mary stood backstage. The clowns were performing again. Yashi was a whiter shade of pale. Christina gently touched Mary's flank. Miss Addy caught her and gave her a smile. Christina turned away. Cole was standing nearby, shirtless, arms crossed.

'Good show,' he winked at her.

'Drop dead,' she said. She hurried back to her trailer.

Mary went out, into the screaming crowds. She performed her routine. Walk in a circle. Stand on the pedestal. Rear back, trunk in the air. Walk back. Sit on the pedestal. Raise forelimbs and trunk. Walk back. Stop in the middle. Headstand. Carry Yashi. Carry Jessica. Carry both. Rear up. Headstand. Trumpet. Play the trumpet.

The audience was overwhelmingly loud. But Mary kept herself. Charlie and Adelaide breathed a sigh of relief.

So the shows went, again and again. Christina never came out for curtain call. But otherwise, everything went smoothly. Audiences came in greater and greater masses. When it was time to move on to Charlotte, Charlie had to order a bigger grandstand. It was the same from Charlotte to Knoxville. From Knoxville to Chattanooga, he ordered a bigger tent. From Chattanooga to Atlanta, he needs another rail car. He booked extra dates in Savannah, Jacksonville, Tallahassee,

Montgomery and Meridian, all without missing his dates in
Atlanta, Memphis and Jackson along the way. He knew they'd
have to extend their tour. He knew what was different about
this tour that the others did not have.

Mary had saved Sparks Travelling Shows.

CHAPTER 27

The first time Mary saw the full grandstand, she froze midstride, halfway out from behind the curtains. She'd seen the countless seats and the way they were arranged, but still, in her mind she'd only ever been able to imagine a few children smiling and clapping at her from over a paddock fence, or at most a few families gathered by a bonfire. This was something else altogether. Even when they were silent, Mary could hear the soft rustle of them breathing. When they cheered, it was a booming uproar that would have muffled thunder. She stood before the waiting ring, where Charlie Sparks stood anticipant. Mary could feel the lithe, delicate form of Yashi straddling the back of her neck. The soft tremors of fear began to radiate from her flesh, through Mary's skin. She didn't want to frighten Yashi. But she was frightened herself.

'She's a little shy, folks!' Charlie Sparks cried out. 'First time in front of an audience and all. But just get a look at how enormous she is!'

The people started cheering. Softly, at first, but then the deafening battering ram of applause pounded Mary's body, and she turned to run away. Memories of awful pain stopped her. She couldn't run. But she couldn't walk into that wall of sound either. She was trapped.

Then, she felt the soft, delicate hands of Miss Addy touching her flank. 'It's alright, Mary. The show must go on!'

Mary's heart settled. The fear stopped shaking inside her. She knew how to avoid pain; she had to win people's applause. While Miss Addy's warmth steadied her tremors, Mary walked out into the ring, where Charlie Sparks directed her through the routine she'd practiced again and again, always with the revolting memory of sticks and bullhooks tearing through her.

Night after night, she did her routine for them. Every morning, she'd do it for Charlie Sparks. In between, she was tied to a tree or stuck on the open carriage of the train as they moved to their next destination. Many nights she couldn't sleep a wink because the sound of their applause and their screaming in awe still resonated inside her ears. She even barked into the darkness a few times, as though to quiet them down just for a little while.

With the repetition, the lack of sleep, and the sheer blandness of her daily routines, Mary felt the lights in her mind slowly fade beneath a blanket of heavy fog. When once she could stop and listen to the familiar sounds of insects, birds, and running water, or the soft breeze, and be reminded that she was still in her own world, albeit far from her home, all Mary heard was white noise. There were still insects, birds, running water and soft breezes, but she was numb to the memories and dreams their sounds inspired. When once she felt a constant weight inside her heart where grief, guilt, and loneliness throbbed and roiled, she began to feel nothing. That was something she'd hoped for during the lonely times when it would swell and threaten to consume her, but now feeling nothing where it should have been was terrifying. Mary felt that if that weight left her, so too would the memory of her mother, her herd, and her home. But in time, the fog covered them too. Mary stopped thinking of the lonely trees, of the swollen river, of her horse friend and even of the dead body of her mother as it quietly stopped bleeding under the dark blue rainclouds. For all the turmoil she carried inside her all her years, it was the stagnation of monotony that swept them all away.

Instead, Mary thought about how tired she was, how hungry, how lonely, she thought about bull elephants and how they used to feel, and how much she'd like to feel them again. She thought about the pain, now and then. She thought about her distrust for Charlie Sparks. But once he appeared before her, and it was time to run through the routine, or to put on the show again, she didn't think at all.

Every now and then, though, something would come back. Usually when they tied her to the tree at night, and Mary would wait for Christina to come to her. There, alone and in darkness, tinges of emotion would prickle her. In the silence between her thoughts, she'd hear the distant call of a herd of elephants wanting her to join them. In the formless shapes between her dreams, she'd see the eyes of her mother, looking down on her, wondering what her baby calf had become. Then, Mary would cry. The fog would lift, and Mary would holler into the night, calling out to phantoms, as though she could explain to them why she was this way, and earn their forgiveness. Sometimes, Mary would imagine her mother watching her from some distant shore, an eternity away and yet able to see her as clearly as if she was standing beside the tree Mary was tethered to. Her mother would see that there was no more grief or sorrow over losing her herd and then disappear. Her eyes would close, and she'd be gone. It was agony in Mary's heart, and yet she savoured it. It was emotion. It was life without the fog of monotony numbing, deafening and blinding her to everything she carried in the hollows of her heart and mind. She was an elephant again.

But day always came. The sheer length of daylight and the blandness of all that filled it would soothe Mary's tempest, and again she'd be no more alive than a train or an automobile.

Eventually, the train took them to a place where the air was thick and heavy with water. Mary felt the warmth on the train and let tiny vestiges of her memories, like single tiny stars in

the endless sky, begin to sparkle and stab at her again. When
the train stopped, it was in a clearing encircled by limp looking
trees that smelled of stagnant water, where light mist curled
and wafted beneath a forest of creeper vines. The heat was
sweltering. For one heart-stopping moment, Mary anticipated
seeing her herd come walking out of the mist. Ready to take
her back, away from all of this. Without ever having been to
this place before, Mary felt like she was home. It was so alive
and so immediate that Mary almost called to them while the
workers sweated and set up the Big Top.

'Come along now, Mary,' Mister Stephenson said. Handlers
for Mary had come and gone so quickly that she barely had
time to learn their names, but Mister Stephenson was different.
He was older than the others, she could tell from his more
seasoned gaze and the coldness of his personality. He was
almost like a taller, leaner Colonel. There was no expression
in his voice or on his face. He never showed his teeth. Worst
of all, whenever Charlie Sparks or Miss Addy wasn't around,
he carried a bullhook. His was holding on, as he held her gate
open and waited for her. 'Come on!'

Mary obediently disembarked her carriage, while a terrible
cold feeling ran like fluid beneath her skin over all her body.
All the dormant volcanoes on her flesh, where she'd been
struck by Philip and the Colonel's bullhooks, started to spew

phantom, fiery pain again. At the first chilling sight of the sharpened end of his stick, Mary forgot all about home. He climbed up onto her back and tapped her side to get her walking in the direction he wanted.

They walked along the road. Every time Mary felt the hard steel of the bullhook brush her side she held her breath and waited. But she never broke her stride. She knew better. She had learned, over the years.

They came to a bridge and Mary could smell running water. Mister Stephenson didn't have to tap her side, she knew what he wanted her to do. Carefully, she stepped down the slope and onto the soft bank of the brook, where she began to drink.

Mister Stephenson sat quietly. He was different from the other handlers in another way, too; he was a worker. He had the dark skin. But he dressed differently. His second skin fit him closer and was cleaner looking. And she never saw him working until his body ached, like the other workers. Beyond those inside her new herd, she'd seen workers in fields and in forests where the trees had been cut down, working and working. Even if they smelled sick or injured, they were working. But not Mister Stephenson. He did the job of pale people. Mary wondered if that was because of his cruelty.

Something soft hit her side. She heard a dull crack and then felt wet slime oozing down her skin. Mary stopped drinking and looked up at the bridge. Two boys, not unlike Philip when he was younger, were picking little round things out of a tray and throwing them. They mostly hit Mister Stephenson, and when they did, they'd crack to pieces, and yellow goo came splattering out. But Mister Stephenson didn't say a word. He merely raised his arm to shelter himself and waited. Mary knew what they were; they were eggs!

'What're you doin' ridin' that there elephant, nigger!' one of the boys shouted.

'What you doin' 'round here, boy?' the other shrieked.

They ran out of things to throw. Mister Stephenson sat quietly without response. He gently tapped Mary's side with the bullhook and she carried him back toward the Big Top. At the side of the road, another wet thing hit Mary in the backside. She stopped and turned back to look at the boys.

'Keep on going there, Mary!' Mister Stephenson ordered. But just then, another egg flew up and hit him in the back of the head. The boys shrieked and howled with laughter. Mister Stephenson rammed the bullhook into Mary's shoulder. She cried out as a barrage of painful, demeaning, humiliating and shameful memories flooded back through her mind. 'Get goin', I said!'

Instinct took control. Mary hurried them back to the Big Top, as an old, familiar agony seared through her side.

#

That night, they chained her to a far-off tree again. The moon and stars were out, but they only illuminated the clearing. Mary, the trees, and everything their canopies sheltered were plunged into solid walls of blackness. Her shoulder still hurt, and she sulked while the smells and feelings of Stable 6 haunted and tormented her. She swayed her head and tried to forget it. Mary had made them happy, she'd made them smile and slap their hands together, and she'd still got a bullhook.

Why couldn't she win? Why couldn't she feel safe again?

All the while, she remembered the boys as they tormented Mister Stephenson. She knew they were tormenting him. He, in turn, had ignored them. There was no crying, no obedience, no retort. Just total silence. The fog that swallowed her mind all the time frightened her, but Mary had never noticed it in another animal until she'd seen Mister Stephenson turn off his perception of the two boys throwing their eggs at him.

The velvet darkness beyond the canopies suddenly felt alive. Mary shivered. It carried a sound. A long, sorrowful howl like nothing she'd ever heard before. A cry from another world. A

355

moaning, haunting call. A chorus of them responded, but Mary couldn't imagine how many. Then, in turn, a greater number answered again. They were near. Mary could smell the bittersweet, rotting odour of predators. Their howls seemed right beside her. She felt so alone. So exposed. She kept straining her eyes to search the patches of silvery light that penetrated some of the treetops, but there was nothing there. The howling creatures were slinking about, somewhere in the dark.

Another horrible thought came to her. White fear fell upon Mary, as she remembered Christina. Christina had visited her almost every night, since that first time. Though she could not imagine what these moaning, sorrowful sounding beasts looked like, her mind conjured images of teeth and hunches and bulging muscles and drool and claws. Mary was afraid to look toward the camp, in case she saw Christina walking toward her. She couldn't imagine the heartache if she saw that beautiful creature set upon by such monsters...like a tiger...and a calf...by a swollen river...oh, the agony would kill her!

Mary yanked at her chain until the cuff hurt her again. She'd protect Christina if Christina was coming. But first, the chain had to go!

A shrill, rhythmic creaking was coming up behind her. Mary felt her breath turn cold. She looked back. It was Christina!

She was walking toward Mary, carrying a creaky lantern in her hand. Mary bellowed. She yanked and yanked until she felt warm fluid running over her foot. She didn't care. She'd rip her foot off and crawl to Christina to protect her from the monsters.

Christina broke into a run. 'Hey! Quiet down! What's wrong with you!'

Mary had to stop herself, or else risk hurting Christina. She stopped flailing and just kept a steely vigil over the darkness enshrouding them. The howling issued again.

'Now, don'tcha tell me you're scared of a few little ol' wolves now, will you?' Christina said, and she smiled at Mary. 'Oh, look what you've done to your foot! How are you gonna perform tomorrow, huh?'

'What are wolves?' Mary asked, though she knew she'd get no answer.

Instead, Christina turned and let out a howl of her own. There was a long, tense silence, and then a responsive howl, but it sounded far away. Much farther than it had been before.

'The size of you,' Christina chuckled, 'scared of that!'

She looked at Mary's ankle again.

'That must hurt.'

Mary told her it did. Christina sat down between Mary's forelimbs and gently pulled the cuff up away from the wound.

'We can at least let it breathe, right?' she sighed. 'Hey now! What's this?'

Christina shot upright and shone the lantern over Mary's shoulder. She was looking at the spot where Mister Stephenson hit her.

'I seen this before...a bullhook!' Christina cried out. 'Who hit you with a bullhook, Mary? Was it Gregory? Son of a bitch. If Charlie knew about that, I tell you this, that Gregory, he'd be out. That's for sure. Out.' Christina moved back to Mary's front and wiped her eye with her sleeve. 'I'm sorry, Mary. I'm sorry I'm so late tonight. I suppose the howl of a red wolf is pretty scary, even if you are the size of a bus...if you just got hit with a bullhook. Truth is, nothing that howls or walks around out here can hurt you. Nothing like a person can, anyway. I oughta know,' she sat down again and rested her back against the tree. 'I got a few freshies myself. He came again, tonight. He hit me more than usual. He's doing that a lot now. Getting to hitting me. Like he's getting braver, 'cos he's getting away with it, you know?'

She took a deep breath. Mary touched her shoulder, gently, with her trunk. Christina sighed and rested her head on it.

'I'm not scared of any wolves,' she said, her voice began to wobble. 'Not the four-legged kind. The kind who follows you home to grandma's house, that's the kind you gotta watch. I hear wolves go for the crotch when they attack a person. It gets you down quicker. Well, it can't be worse than what the kind that follow you home do to you. Am I right? There are worse things than being ripped apart by wolves, right? They get you down, bitin' your crotch, and then they all jump on you, and then it's done. Sooner or later. What's it matter anyway if you're gonna die? A little pain, it's not like you'll remember it. Or have to deal with it later,' she was rubbing her shoulders, and huddled herself, as though it was cold. But it wasn't cold. It was a heavy, muggy night. 'If it's the last thing you'll ever feel, well...who cares, am I right?'

Christina curled up with Mary's trunk and seemed to relax just a little bit.

'You'll protect me from wolves, Mary,' she said, softly. 'I wish you could come to my trailer with me and stay with me. Protect me from the real danger. The wolf that follows me home.'

Mary kept watch all night, while Christina slept. She realized, through tears of both sadness and happiness, that she hadn't found the kind of love she'd craved all this time, but a different kind of love. No longer in need of protection, she was the protector. No longer grieving or yearning for that loving, guiding shadow to stand in; that shadow was hers.

CHAPTER 28

"Dearest Charlie,

I don't believe it. You're not even halfway through your tour! Where did you pick up the four new cars? I want to check up on them. I know you will have, Charlie, and it's not that I don't trust you, but they're not selling anything to me. I'll be able to get more information. Really, though, I'm so very impressed that you've managed such a great comeback. Don't you worry about Carthage, I'll take care of them. They'll just have to understand; their wintering ground is great for a six-car show. Sparks' is a ten-car show now. As for the new place, I got your return address as Jefferson City, so this letter should reach you at Nashville, by late-Fall. I've managed to find a good spot that isn't a ridiculous distance from there since it'll be the last leg of your tour. Enclosed are the lease agreement and the specifics. For now, it's about fifteen miles east of Salisbury, North Carolina. No trees, but the local parks are state-run, so you can't be walking that elephant of yours around, letting it destroy everything. Don't worry, though, it's only temporary; the owners want to sell it for a golf course anyway. Will keep my eyes open for the next spot, but this should do for now.

My love to Adelaide.

Your loving brother,

Clifton."

Charlie sighed and folded the letter and slipped it into his scrapbook with all the others. He loved the way Clifton wrote, it was just the same way he spoke. Homesickness was not an affliction for those raised on the road, but even fond feelings of nostalgia had their own certain sting in the tail. That was why he kept the scrapbook; beneath his hands, there at his desk, was the entire legacy of John H. Sparks' Travelling Shows, later just Sparks' Travelling shows, from correspondence to poster designs, publicity photographs and newspaper articles, and a few odd bits of memoranda stuck in there along the way: a four-leaf clover from Ireland, a diecast Brooklyn Bridge from New York City and the last remaining flea from Charlie's Flea Circus, which was really just a painstakingly shaped bit of fabric, made to look like a flea. Pressed between those pages was home, for Charlie. There was the first photograph ever taken of him, as a homeless boy dancing for pennies on the street, there was his and Clifton's adoption papers, there was the legal papers which signed the business over from John to Charlie and another dancer named Adelaide Matthews, who would become Adelaide Sparks. There was John's death certificate. There was the first animal brought in, at Clifton's insistence, an elephant named Geordie.

'How is he?' Adelaide asked, from the bed where she applied her makeup under the glow of the electric lamp.

'Oh, fine, I suppose,' Charlie mumbled, then he slipped the scrapbook into the desk drawer it had to itself. 'You know Clifton.'

'He didn't say, did he?'

Charlie shook his head.

'I think he's well,' Adelaide said. She tossed her makeup kit and little mirror aside and started tracing circles in her blanket. 'I think he did the right thing.'

'Becoming a lawyer?'

'Settling down,' Adelaide said. Charlie straightened up, prepared for another one of these discussions. 'You know, if we sold...'

'Out of the question.'

'...but if.'

'If what?' Charlie snapped. 'What do you want to do? Sell everything. Buy a ranch in New Jersey?'

'It was Rhode Island.'

'Wherever! It's one place! Adelaide, I've never lived in one place. London was the longest I was anywhere, and even then,

I moved around all the time. The zoo. That's where I've been static. The zoo. Want to live in a zoo, Adelaide?'

'We wouldn't need to!' Adelaide said. 'We'd have our own little...animals. There's still time.'

'Adelaide,' Charlie stroked his face. 'You can't choose your children. Your children can't choose you! Heaven knows, they might hate us! What then? John...father...he chose us. Me and Clifton. We chose him. An average family doesn't get to choose each other. That's what makes us more special. Now, why would you want to downgrade, and leave it to chance?'

'You choose your wife,' Adelaide said. Charlie heard her swallowing the ball of emotion clogging her throat.

'And I chose you,' Charlie assured her. He got up and moved over to the bed to take her hand in his. 'And I'm glad I chose you.'

'Would our children be so awful...'

'Which children?' Charlie cut her off. 'Samira can be a handful, but gosh, she's got an inspiring roar. And Griffon, what a mane he has! Mary, she's far from awful. Mary is wonderful. I'm especially proud of her.'

"They're our pets, Charlie, not our children!'

'But they are, my dear,' Charlie rubbed her hand between both of his. 'We chose them. Just like my father chose me, and I chose you.'

Adelaide sighed.

'I know,' Charlie said, stroking her hair. 'You have certain urges. It's alright. If you could give me children like Samira, Griffon and Mary, then I assure you I'd think about it.'

'That might hurt,' Adelaide said as a weak smile crept across her teary face.

'It might,' Charlie chuckled. 'But lions are easier than humans. They obey a firm rule, and it my rule is not firm, they will try to kill me and eat me. Simple. Humans are quite another matter. I can be as pleasant as a butterfly, or firm as the Tsar, it won't make a difference. They might take a liking to me, but then they might not. They might act like the latter and be thinking the former. They might even act like the latter and plot to act on the former. It's really rather impossible.'

Charlie's face got hot and he felt tears burning his eyes. Adelaide, and Adelaide alone, knew that he remembered his birth parents. She quickly sat up and threw her arms around him.

'Come now,' Charlie said. 'Let's don't ruin our makeup.'

He stood up, picked up his top hat and cane, and held out his hand to Miss Addy. Together, they hurried across the camp into the back of the Big Top. Charlie Sparks took a few seconds to pace up and down and tap himself repeatedly in the forehead with his index finger, knocking out all the bad thoughts. Around him gathered his performers and Mary.

'Last one,' he said with a crooked smile. 'Then, to our new home. Ready?'

The performers gave silent, tense nods. All except Christina, who smirked from beside Mary. Charlie ignored her, blew a kiss to Adelaide, and stepped out into the ring and the gazes of a thousand eyes.

'Ladies and gentlemen! Boys and girls of all ages!'

#

Mary buzzed with excitement the moment she realized that Miss Addy was leading her toward another stable and not an isolated tree somewhere to be tethered for the night. She danced around inside, trumpeting until she got tired and had to sleep for a while. There was no Big Top anymore, just the old camp Mary remembered, and day by day, life returned to how it was before their great voyage on the chugging beast. Mary never knew whether they'd gone in a circle or a straight line, or if they'd zigzagged, but she knew they were somewhere else. There was no forest surrounding the camp, just more open paddocks beyond the fences. When Charlie Sparks took her for their morning walks, they had to travel much farther than they had before to get to the city, which he said was called Salisbury. Also, instead it just being the two of them, there were handlers as well, let by Mister Stephenson, albeit without his bullhook. He never let Charlie Sparks see the bullhook.

The handlers kept the children a distance back. It was much better that way, even though Mary was afraid of Mister Stephenson.

As the leaves began to fall, so the clowns, the music makers, Jessica, Yashi, Indira and Cole all departed, one by one. All except Christina, Charlie Sparks, Miss Addy, the workers, Mister Stephenson, the lions, tigers and horses, and Mary. She was excited to see them go and leave her Christina. It meant they could be closer to each other through the cold time.

But it was not to be. Christina was still there, but she stopped paying her visits after Cole left. Mary would run through her routine twice daily, and play for the children, expecting Christina that night all the while, but when the sun went down, and Miss Addy left Mary in her stable, upright and waiting excitedly, Christina never came. Instead, she became her old self. She watched from atop her high bar, she smirked, and she refused to eat. Mary went entirely ignored.

367

Mary confused and upset herself as she spent days trying to figure out what she'd done wrong. Maybe Christina was afraid. But Mary wanted her! Sometimes, when they went for water, Mister Stephenson would hit Mary with the bullhook because she'd get distracted thinking about Christina and why she didn't like Mary anymore and she'd get something wrong. She'd scream and feel alone and confused and sad. But Christina never came to cheer her up. Mary knew she had cheered Christina up. Was it like people, to just take until they were satisfied and then leave? She didn't understand.

At night, Mary dreamed of the show. That was all. There were no more memories before Christina's first visit, other than the odd flash of a bullhook and, of course, her routine.

But she was glad for the stable, which let her feel closer, and still part of, the herd. There were nights when she felt her heart glowing with content; when the labourers would pick up the musical instruments at night and play while Miss Addy and Charlie Sparks danced by the bonfire, and times when Mary could stop still and just listen to the subtle sounds of her herd moving about, shuffling or bumping around in their houses at night. Every little scratch reminded her that she wasn't alone anymore, even though she felt like she was without Christina.

She even knew it was odd, but as the snow melted again, Mary began to feel excited to go back on the road, as Miss

Addy called it. It meant nights isolated and in terrible
discomfort, it meant much more time just her and the awful
Mister Stephenson, and it meant having to perform for the
horrible crowds every sunset. But it also meant visits from
Christina. That was enough to make her forget not only all the
comforts Mary had at the wintering ground but also all the
hardship of the tour. When, one by one, the performers all
returned, Mary braced herself for what she knew was going to
be difficult. But she did so with a fondness in her heart. Her
friend would come back, she just knew it. People were
creatures of habit, like every living thing, it was just much more
complex and selfish than any other creature Mary had ever
encountered.

Then, they embarked the train.

Mary found other things to enjoy about the tour. Being in
the open. Being in new lands, from time to time. Seeing rolling
hills, forests, swamplands, rivers, and mountains, though she
was always chained up and prevented from exploring them.
She tried to drink as much as she could of them into her eyes,
so her heart may still just a little, and keep the longing at bay.
She had Christina's visits again, and Miss Addy would pet her
and sing to her in that syrupy-sweet voice before every routine.
She watched the train grow longer and longer. There were
more horses. One day, when they were in the hot, heavy, wet

land, the tiger died. Mary saw it being carried, limp and awfully still, from its cage by a team of workers. They dug a hole and threw it in, then they filled the dirt in again.

Mary wondered why they did that. The birds wouldn't be able to get to the carrion it left for them, with it buried. She was sad that it was dead, and that it had led such a life as what befell any creature that was admired or loved by people, but she was angry that they covered it beneath the ground like that. That was cruel to the birds, which the people had no interest in.

But Mary was reminded of the casual cruelty of people as well. One night while she was tied to her tree, a group of children came upon her. They started throwing things at her, which hurt when they hit. They were little stones. She bellowed at them, but they kept throwing. One hit her eye and filled her whole skull with an electrifying agony. She screamed and trumpeted at them. Still, they persisted, until Mister Stephenson came running and shouting and waving his bullhook in the air.

Mary didn't understand why they punished her when they didn't want her to run a routine. Otherwise, they surely would have taken the chain off her foot, so she could perform for them. But they didn't. They just came up and started pelting her with stones and cackling and hurting her. They didn't want

anything, she decided. They just wanted to hurt her.
Sometimes, people just wanted to cause hurt.

But she had her Christina back, and again she'd come in
various stages of pain or with bruises on her face or body.
Mary realized that she hadn't been bruised or hurt either,
during cold time, when they'd stayed in one place. She knew
that meant that whoever was hurting Christina was someone
who left during the winter. Maybe it was her handler? Did she
have a handler? Was there a Philip and Colonel for Christina?
Who was the wolf that Christina had spoken of? It couldn't
have been Charlie Sparks...could it? The thought made Mary
again feel a surge of aggression toward him. It frightened her,
so she forced herself not to think about it anymore. She just
had to be there for Christina, and care for her. While she
couldn't remember exactly, there was a time in Mary's life
when she had been like Christina was; bruised, scared, lonely
and confused. Mary had found solace in a friend...she could
remember big, innocent eyes and a soft snout. This time, she
was that friend.

Finally, there came the great surge of relief that radiated
over the whole herd when they knew they were soon to be
home again. This time, they returned to the same place. For
once, the stability this suggested was a welcome comfort to
Mary, although she dreaded being separate from Christina

371

again. But Mary had learned that all things change. Often, without a hint of warning.

Surprise still almost carried her away, however, when her stable doors opened, and another elephant walked in.

'Mary,' said Miss Addy, 'this is Regina!'

But Mary couldn't have cared less for the name they gave her, even if it was told to her in the Miss Addy's voice. She was staring at the elephant, smaller than she was, and lighter in colour. She knew they were both frightened. She just couldn't stop staring. It had been so long since she'd seen another of her kind, and so very much fog had passed through her mind since then, that she'd almost forgotten what they looked like. She was just a little bit repulsed.

'Hello!' Regina raised her trunk.

Mary ignored her.

After all, this thing had none of the grace of a Christina and none of the delicacy of the Miss Addy. It was not lean and light like a Yashi or a Jessica and it was not elegant and powerful like the Indira or the Cole. It did not even have the odd nature of the clowns. It was big and saggy, and uncouth. Its head was enormous and inclined somewhat to one side. It had no tusks, but baggy, wrinkled skin, and eyes that were an odd colour; not the big, empty brown of the horses, the blazing coldness of the lions or the expressive shapes of people. It had a lumbering gait as it took a few cautious steps into the stable and it flicked its trunk around nonsensically.

Mary had to think twice before she remembered that she was staring at another, if slightly smaller, animal like herself. She looked like that. That was her kin. She was disheartened. She even began to consider that this was why they kept her isolated from the others; in a stable at their home and chained to a far-off tree on the road. She was too ugly to be one of them. Too big and bulky to be near them all the time.

They spent the winter doing their routine together, but only Mary got to play the trumpet. Yashi rode on Mary, while Jessica got switched to this other elephant, this Regina.

Suddenly, the stable was a cramped place. Regina kept wanting to huddle close to Mary at night. Mary wasn't used to it and kept trying to move away, searching for cold pockets where she could be as she had been for such a long time beforehand. When they went on tour, Regina was chained up with Mary, away from the giant tent. Though Mary did find this comforting, it cost her the company of the Christina. She stopped her visits, now that there were two elephants to be with. Mary missed her so much her heart felt stabbed with pain. She found herself tearily wishing that the Regina would go away, back to wherever she came from.

Because of Regina, they even had to find a new home for
the cold times. Mary knew it was all Regina's fault. There was
no room in that stable for the two of them. Their new home
never got snowed over. It never got as cold as their old homes.
It was hot, all the time, and it evoked memories which Mary
could not properly explore, because even in their new, huge
stable, Regina kept trying huddle up with her, or stroke her
with its annoying trunk. But that didn't stop yet another
surprise. The barn doors opened one balmy morning, and in
walked another elephant.

'Mary, Regina,' the Miss Addy said. 'This is Bernadette!'

'Hello!' Bernadette said.

'Hello!' Regina said.

Mary grumbled and held her trunk tight under her chin.

'What's wrong with her?' Bernadette asked.

'I'm so glad you're here now,' Regina said. 'Mary is a nasty
elephant! I've felt so alone!'

She didn't care what they said or thought. While they played
with each other, Mary huddled up in a corner and tried to
ignore them. She wanted to send them away and get Christina
back. Even Miss Addy was no longer visiting Mary, now that
she had two more elephants to share her space with. She never

dreamed more vividly of escape. Strangely, in some of her dreams, the two elephants accompanied her.

Lonely winter came with its crystalline mantle and naked tree branches reaching into the azure skies, followed by the Spring when the colours returned, and the circus went back on the road. Now with their three elephants, they were formidable. Mary did not escape. She stayed. Year after year. Tour after tour. Sparks' Travelling Shows became Sparks Circus. They were an event, whatever town they rolled in to. Ten cars became fifteen and then twenty. Four showgirls became twelve. Three clowns became fifteen. Eleven horses. Three elephants. Four lions, no lionesses anymore. A zebra, though it proved impossible to train. A crew of fifty labourers. A nine-piece marching band. Trapeze superstar Jasmine Clark left Ringling to join Sparks, as did renowned elephant handler Paul Jacoby. Barnum and Bailey saw the only rival they would ever have for the Greatest Show on Earth. The circus truly was a family. Everything John H. Sparks had set out to do was slowly coming to fruition. It truly became, to the mind of an elephant, a herd. It seemed as though the future had a golden hue...but all things change.

Like a nightmare, it all began to unravel...

CHAPTER 29

Charlie Sparks' eyes darted side to side as he walked across the wintering grounds in Central City Park, Macon. He didn't know exactly what he was expecting...a stone to come flying out? An angry mob to march on through the gates? More eggs and rotten fruit? It had all happened over the summer. The quiet summer, which had passed without a single booking. They needn't have bothered repairing the torched Big Top. Between his frightened glances, he saw what he'd seen in his nightmares for almost two years; the life of Sparks Circus flashing before his eyes.

The silence was terrifying. Charlie was sure it either meant they were planning another attack or had done something he'd failed to notice yet.

Ahead was his office. He couldn't see any of the windows smashed, or the door kicked in. It all seemed intact. But as he passed by Yashi's trailer, the sight of Jessica's caught his eye. For a moment, there was a flood of relief; the boards on the windows hadn't been ripped off, nor had the door. It was okay. It was all okay...

...something fluttered from the side window. Charlie's back tightened. Tensely, he paced over to see what it was.

Newspaper clippings. Articles cut out and stuck to the glass with glue. Charlie ripped on off and looked at it. He might have guessed. More about the Lusitania. More about German acts of piracy on the seas. More about the Kaiser's atrocities in Belgium, then France, and then the Russian Empire. In a fit of rage, he screwed them up and tossed them onto the soft grass. A warm southerly swept across the grounds and carried the little balls of paper away. From inside, he heard sobbing.

'I told you, you should have changed your name as soon as it started!' Charlie lectured, as he threw the door open and stepped inside. The sight of her stopped him in his tracks.

Jessica was crouched down at the foot of her bed, holding the sheets bunched up against her chest. She had a black eye, the corners of her lips were elongated by streaks of dried blood, her hair was in a fuzzy blonde ball around her head and her nose was battered, bloody and flattened against her face.

'Dear lor...ADELAIDE!' Charlie screamed. 'Dear Lord! What happened to you my dear?' he moved toward her. She recoiled. 'ADDY!'

Others were gathering around outside her trailer. Charlie could see them through the open door. Jessica crawled backward and hid beside her bed.

The tormenting hadn't stopped. It started over a year ago when the normally cheering crowds had taken to booing whenever Jessica Hoffmann got up on stage. Charlie had known immediately what had happened. He knew that Barnum and Bailey would take revenge somehow, even a decade later, for Miss Addy's acquisition of their most beloved showgirl, Jessica Hoffmann. But he never would have believed that Providence would hand them a golden opportunity, on a silver platter. The war had broken out two years ago. Barnum and Bailey only had to whisper to a journalist in Atlanta that the circus wintering in Macon was harbouring a German expat, and that was the end of their winning streak. The crowds stopped gathering as they went on their morning walk, even when Mary came out with the other elephants. The tickets stopped selling. Then came the attacks on their home.

Adelaide came running through the gathering crowd, small because it was an all-too-expected scene, and hurried in through the door. She paused beside Charlie and covered her mouth. 'Good God...' she whispered. Charlie saw her exhale, breathe in, and then move forward with a stoic but gentle assurance. 'Oh, my dear... I'm so sorry.'

Adelaide crouched beside Jessica, and gently put her arms around the sobbing dancer. Charlie turned away, unable to see his prized showgirl so badly broken.

'I tried to run...' he heard Jessica whimper. 'They were waiting...'

He could take no more. Charlie stepped out of the trailer and closed the door behind him. He shooed away the crowd. 'Go on, off with you!'

As he walked toward his office, his stomach churned with shame. He thought, in the beginning, he could prevent it all. He went into damage control. He made a stupid decision. Seeing his surging success threatened by the rivals he'd longed to overthrow for years, he went to the papers. He talked about his being an Englishman by birth. An Englishman more than happy to accommodate and employ Jessica Hoffmann, the German, even though it was England with whom Germany was at war. They didn't see border conflicts, in the circus, he'd said. There was no immigrant who ever became more American than Jessica Hoffmann, he'd said. The pro-British papers turned his words inside out, and upside down. Suddenly he was a traitor. She, a German spy. It had cost him any profit on his 1915 tour, and the 1916 season was reaching its end without them even boarding their train. Meanwhile, Barnum and Bailey had booked Ringling all over the South. It was like a victory lap, of some sort. A deliberate torment to their competitor.

Charlie opened his office door and slammed it shut behind him. He wiped the cold sweat off his brow with a trembling hand. Cole Waxman had been the first to jump ship. He'd said he was getting too old. Two weeks later, Charlie read about Ringling's new strongman, The Great Cole. Indira Chopra followed him. How many more, he thought. All of them? All but his beloved animals?

Molly had left a newspaper and a pot of coffee on his desk. He dragged his feet over and plonked down into his chair. For everything to fall apart over Jessica...it just wasn't fair. It just wasn't right. His mind started working automatically. He wouldn't be punishing her...he'd be saving the others. He wouldn't be conceding defeat...he'd be discarding unnecessary burdens. He rang the little bell on his desk.

Quick as lightning, ever-loyal Molly opened his office door and peeked in. 'Sir?'

'Have Adelaide come to my office, there's a good love.'

She was gone again.

The headlines of the newspaper were reporting on some new German atrocity. It was now inevitable, it said, that the United States would enter the war. He leafed through it anyway, curious to see if Ringling were making any show of support.

What was the point, he reasoned, of risking Jessica's safety by keeping her in the show? It was Fall, and they were looking at another starving winter, like the old days. Before Mary. She wouldn't be too hard done by. She...

...a Wild West fair in Kingsport, Tennessee. This September. Next month!

Charlie read on, something alighting in him again. He hadn't thought much about performing during the winter, despite the obvious benefits of the South's warmer climate. Why not? Why, all these years, had he retreated to snow country when there were relatively warm days all through the year? Traveling shows were a staple of the Old West, so John always told Charlie. What would an Old West fair be without one? It could be their chance! Their chance to announce themselves again; Sparks' World-Famous Shows, One-Hundred Per Cent Sunday School Circus, Now German Free!

He'd begun pacing about, announcing the banners to himself, when Adelaide finally appeared at his door. 'You wanted to see me, Darling?'

'Yes!' Charlie cried, busting with excitement. He quickly checked his insensitivity, cleared his throat, and sat solemnly at his desk. 'Yes, my dear. How is Jessica?'

'Quite beside herself,' Adelaide said. She sat down at his desk and freshened his coffee from the pot. 'She's lucky, they were just boys. But I'm afraid that nose shall be permanently disfigured.'

Charlie bit his finger. That gave him another idea.

'Let's say we send her home, shall we?' Charlie proposed. 'Give her time away from all this, maybe time to reassess her life?'

'You don't mean fire her, now?' Adelaide said, breathless. She saw right through him, as always.

'Of course not, my darling!' Charlie pleaded. 'It's just I've seen this show being advertised in Tennessee, an Old West show, and I think it would be good for us to get out there and give them something to remember us by before we go bankrupt.' He knew he was sounding a lot more vicious than he intended.

'Oh, Charlie,' Adelaide said, perhaps seeing the reality behind his unintended cruelty. 'What shall we do?'

'Send her home,' Charlie insisted. 'She has family in Vermont. We'll put her on a train, send one of Paul's men to accompany her so she feels safe, and give her time off to recover. The war will end before long, and everyone will forget about this whole thing. She'll be welcome back, with open arms.'

'I suppose there's no hope of Ringling snatching her up, in the meantime,' Adelaide replied, though a tear was gathering in the corner of her eye. 'She's a talented girl.'

'Wonderfully talented,' Charlie said. 'It's not like her name's Helga or Greta, all she has to do is disguise her surname, and she'll be able to make a fine living. She could dance in a parlour lounge, she could perform at a cabaret. Perhaps she'll settle down and get married! Who knows, it's never too late.'

'I suppose I'll be the one to tell her?'

Charlie reached across the desk and placed his hand on hers. 'Would you?'

'Of course, Charlie,' Adelaide stood. 'I'll try to make it easy on her.'

'Send in Molly, will you?' Charlie called after her, as she closed the door. Almost immediately, it opened again, and there were the beady eyes and thick spectacles of Molly staring in at him. The sacrifice of Jessica had to be worthwhile now. 'Come in, Molly.'

'Yes, sir,' she half-whispered, and closed the door behind her.

'Send a wire to Clifton, will you? I want this in the papers as soon as possible!' he ordered. Molly quickly sat down and took her notepad and pencil from her apron. 'Sparks World Famous Shows will be traveling to Tennessee this September, to join in the Old West show in Kingsport. We shall be dedicating our every performance to the American lives lost to the terrible acts of German Piracy of recent years. As a show of support to the Allied Nations fighting for their lives against the tide of German tyranny, Sparks World Famous Shows has dismissed all performers of German heritage. That's right, folks, Sparks World Famous Shows continues to uphold its all-American reputation as a one-hundred per cent Sunday School circus!' he heard her pen stop scratching as he paced around the room and caught her as she glanced up at him. But he continued, and so did she. 'Come witness the spectacular showgirls! Marvel in awe at the gravity-defying stunts of world-class trapeze artist Christina DeRosa! Stand awestruck as man tames beast, in the lion cage! And of course, only at Sparks World Famous Shows, come and see the living wonder of the natural world, the largest living land animal on earth, the trumpet-playing, dancing elephant, Mighty Mary!'

Molly scribbled frantically, trying to keep up with him. 'That all?'

'Yes,' Charlie said, breathless.

'Do the show organizers know that we'll be joining them in Kingsport?' she asked, in that flat, cynical tone that always arose when Molly suspected Charlie might be wafting.

'Not yet, no, but have Clifton organize it,' Charlie ordered. 'Clifton will save us.'

'Right,' Molly muttered, making the last note. She took the notepad and hurried back out into the grounds.

Charlie gripped the back of his chair; his heart was fluttering. They'd have their chance. This was how they'd come back. Only then, he remembered Jessica. She'd be hearing the news now. He thought he'd better be there for her. At least to see that she was okay.

He hurried across the grounds in time to see a labourer carrying her trunk out of her trailer. Adelaide was standing in the doorway while Jessica was outside, watching them move her life away from her circus. She seemed calmer, as Charlie approached. Her arms were folded, there was a serene look about her face, through her nose was certainly broken, quite badly. It was swollen, blue, and turned to one side.

'Jessica!' he said, relieved. She turned and charged at him. He felt her fists weakly rain down over his chest, as he clutched her shoulders, and tried to keep her back. The labourers dropped her trunk and hurried to pull her off.

'How could you!' she was screaming in a ragged, fearsome cry that Charlie had never imagined her capable of. 'How could you do this to me?'

'It's only temporary!' Charlie insisted. She collapsed from the arms of the labourers onto her trunk and wept openly. Charlie looked up at Adelaide who only shook her head and otherwise remained stoic. 'As soon as this is over, you'll be welcome back! Welcome back with open arms! Just as soon as the whole mess is over with.'

'I stayed by you,' she said, into the lid. 'I stayed by you when you had nothing!' she beat the side of the trunk. 'I stayed...I stayed...' She broke down into sobs, unable to continue.

Behind her, Charlie saw George and Paul taking the elephants for their morning walk, with Mary, as always, at the front. They were on the edge of a National Park here, with the Macon Centre more than twenty minutes down the road by automobile. Where their camp ended, and the park began, was hard to tell, but the rangers were happy for the elephants to wander about where they liked. As long as they didn't eat anything.

'Please, Jessica,' Charlie said. 'I promise you, we're not firing you. We're sending you home to recover.'

'I know better, Charlie,' Jessica said. She eased off her trunk and let the labourers pick it up again. 'I know what you do when something gets in your way. Even someone. Even someone who was ready to starve with you, in those years when it was like that.'

'That isn't true, Jessica,' Adelaide said. She stepped down to her and took her by the arm. 'Come on up out of the mud.'

Jessica slowly stood up. 'I was leaving when they got me. I was leaving, and I wasn't going to come back. Not because I wanted to. But because I know you, Charlie. I know you too, Miss Addy. All your warm smiles and gentle nature. I know you both. I was leaving so I wouldn't have to see you two turn against me like this.'

'Nobody's against you, Jessica,' Addy said, stroking her back.

'You're not talking sense, my dear,' Charlie said, softly as he could. 'We love you. You're a part of our family, and always will be.' He suppressed the frantic urges rising inside him. He had to make sure she was far away before his newspaper ads hit. If this was how she was going to take being sent away, then she'd surely explode when she saw their announcement.

Maybe even turn violent. Charlie couldn't have that. 'I'm even going to send an escort with you, to make sure nobody gives you any trouble.' He raised his cane toward Mary. 'George! Come here a moment, will you?'

She and George boarded the train without further fuss, and Jessica Hoffmann was gone before the evening from Sparks Circus forever. Charlie and Adelaide accompanied them to the station. Adelaide worked her charm to keep George's objections at bay. Somehow, she assured him that he was coming straight back, without letting on Jessica would surely be gone for good.

By the time Charlie returned to his office, the sun was already going down. Paul Jacoby was waiting for him. 'Hello, Paul!'

'Mister Sparks,' so Paul always insisted on calling him, despite Charlie's objections. 'You sent away Mary's personal handler.'

'You'll have to get a fill-in until we arrive at Kingsport,' Charlie said, knowing there was no way George could go all the way to Vermont and be back in time to depart with them. 'Someone with experience. Don't worry, Paul, Mary's been with us so long, she's the easiest of all.'

Paul agreed to have Molly put an ad out for a new trainer, while Clifton sent word to his performers to muster at their wintering ground. A special tour was being announced. They were booked for Kingsport before the next morning.

#

Five hundred miles away, a young man leaped aboard a freight train as it went by the farm he'd been labouring at. He had a small rucksack with him and a newspaper clipping. 'Seeking: Elephant trainer,' it said. 'Sparks World Famous Shows of Macon, GA.'

He knew this freighter went right past Macon. He curled up in the corner, between the boxes and the splinter-ridden walls, and tried to sleep. A hobo climbed aboard as they passed by Atlanta.

'Benjamin's muh name,' the black runaway said. 'Headed t' Florida fo' fo'est work.'

'Red Eldridge,' the young man answered, with a grin. 'I'm joining the circus.'

CHAPTER 30

Mary came to know the surroundings of their wintering ground so well she didn't have to walk out into them to see them. She could picture them, just perfectly. But they made her anyway. They took her out walking to the city, out through the parks, past every tree and every stone and every bend in the path that was the same as it was yesterday and the day before, and exactly how she knew it would be tomorrow. It never got too cold, gone was the shimmering snow. The trees were scattered and few and the same. The grass never hit the rich, green pitch it had in the old places. It just stayed off-brown and looked half-dead and dry.

She sensed the unrest in her herd. She almost knew it hadn't just felt like a long time since so many of them left for what should have been the cold times, it had actually been much too long. It made her grind her teeth at night, thinking about it. Staying here. In one place. The very air she breathed tasted stagnant and bland. Mary needed movement. Something fresh and new. The herd needed to muster and migrate. It was what herds did!

The salvation of the warmth was that Bernadette and Regina gave her space at night. No more trying to huddle.

Stuck in her stable, without even having run her morning routine for some time, Mary tried to remember the discomfort of the road. The way they chained her to a tree with Bernadette and Regina every night and left her alone with their irritating head-swaying. The way she missed Christina coming to visit her. But nothing could douse the desire to move and be mobile. The longing for the horizon was overpowering.

They were swaying their heads again, once they'd returned from their morning walk. Mary pushed herself into her corner and chewed on some hay. They kept swaying. Standing there, swaying. She remembered herself doing that, crying as she tried to remember. Finally, she spat the hay out.

'Stop it!' she said.

'Mary!' Bernadette said. Maybe it was Regina. 'I'm sad.'

Mary looked away.

'I'm sad too,' Regina said. Maybe it was Bernadette. 'I miss my home.'

'I do too.'

Mary grunted aloud. How many times could they have this conversation?

'I want to remember home. It makes me feel nice.'

'It makes you feel sad,' Mary said.

'But it feels nice first.'

'Do you miss home, Mary?'

'There's nothing worth remembering out there. I am home.'

The side door creaked open and Miss Addy stepped in.

'Hello Regina, hello Bernadette,' she said. Mary could already tell she was sad. The other elephants couldn't. 'Hello, Mary, my dear,' she said, and she stroked Mary's trunk.

That was how Mary knew Miss Addy liked her best. She got her own hello, and a stroke on the trunk. Mary looked at the other two gloatingly. They would never be as close to Miss Addy as Mary was. Gently, Mary touched Miss Addy's shoulder with her trunk.

'Oh, it's been a difficult morning,' Miss Addy said. Mary looked at the other two again. She'd taught Miss Addy to understand her, as much as she could.

Though Mary wondered why Christina had never learned. Why Christina never came to visit anymore. But then, why care? If Christina didn't want to see Mary, Mary didn't need Christina. She was leader of the elephants, she alone was allowed to play the trumpet, and it was her on the posters, not the other two. Not even Christina.

'But I have some good news!' Miss Addy continued.

392

The door opened. Jacoby stepped in. That old, familiar cold feeling swept through Mary and she could sense Bernadette and Regina tensing as well. A thousand memories of agonizing pain shot through Mary's mind. She stayed perfectly still, Miss Addy beside her, while Bernadette and Regina froze where they stood.

'Misses Sparks. I told you not to be in here alone with the animals,' Jacoby half-mumbled. He never raised his voice. But he carried that same coldness and radiated that same intense aura of absolute control that seemed to seize Mary by the flesh all over and hold her like a vice.

Even Miss Addy seemed to take a while to respond. 'I know these animals, Mister Jacoby. I've known Mary almost ten years.'

'They're animals, Misses Sparks. Billy Kemp knew his elephant all its life, didn't stop it from trampling him to death,' Jacoby said. Horror swilled inside Mary. She could never. How could he not know that she could never... 'I'd just hate t'see something like that happen to you, s'all.'

Miss Addy didn't say anything else. She just lifted the hem her skirt and marched out of the stable again. Jacoby moved over to where his bull hook was just peeking out from behind their water troth and gently nudged it back in with his foot.

393

As he did, a worker appeared at the open door with his hand held in his hands. 'Mister Jacoby, sir.'

'Hm?'

'There's a boy here to see you,' the worker said. 'A Mister Red Eldridge, here about the elephant job, sir.'

Without a word, Jacoby turned around and walked out. The worker followed him and they closed the doors behind them.

Mary heard the other two elephants gasp their first breaths, having held it all the while. She knew better than to forget to breathe, by now. It was a distraction and could lead to dizziness, which could lead to mistakes during a routine. Then, Charlie Sparks would make them run the routine again. But Jacoby would be watching and as soon as they'd be finished, and brought back to their stable, the bullhook would come out.

Mary missed Mister Stephenson. He only hit her when he was angry about something else. Jacoby was always perfectly calm. With sickening shudders, she always remembered the Colonel whenever he was around.

'I want to go home,' Regina said. Mary roiled, remembering how she'd have such fancies after a bad experience with people.

'We're safer here than home,' Mary told her again.

'I don't want to be safe!' Bernadette said. 'I want to be home!'

Mary sighed and resumed chewing on hay. It was pointless. She wondered if they'd ever learn. It hadn't taken Mary as long as these two to give up on emotions that only cause pain, she was sure of it.

'Avoid the pain,' Mary said. 'Remember, avoid the pain.'

They weren't listening. They were swaying their heads again, while tears ran down from their eyes.

#

There was a knock at the door. 'Hmm?'

'Someone to see you Charlie,' came the half-whisper of Molly. 'No appointment, but I thought I'd better check with you... a Riley Cotton. He says he's from Ringling.'

Charlie set his pen down and slide the posters he was drawing up for the massive 1917 tour aside, without folding them. If someone was from Ringling, he wanted them to see it would see them go over the winter, into 1918, and keep pushing on. He even had a mind to take some of his show overseas, even. Go where Barnum and Bailey were afraid to; right into the war. Entertain the troops. That would be something! Either way, the 1917 tour would be a spectacle. His spirits picked up again. He fixed his tie and collar. Perhaps they'd come to concede defeat? Even to beg Charlie not to play on their dates? 'Send him in.'

Charlie was raised right. He stood up when Cotton entered, a man in a black suit, carrying his hat by his side, thin spectacles on his nose and a grin that seemed wired on to his face. 'Hello Sparks!'

'Good day,' Charlie said, trying to remember if he'd met this Cotton fellow before. 'Can I get you a drink?'

'No, thank you!'

'Oh, I do mean water, or a sarsaparilla, of course. We know the laws of the land, eh?' he winked. Cotton gingerly sat down. 'What brings you here, Mister Cotton?'

'Well, as you know, Barnum and Bailey were always great admirers of John H. Sparks Shows, and when you took over, my employers were nothing but encouraging and supportive of your ambitions...'

'If I remember correctly, sir, your employers tried to buy me out the very day after my father's funeral.'

'A most generous offering, if I recall.' Cotton was fast. Sparks knew he was both patient and aggressive. He had to be careful. 'But you politely declined, and right you were to do so. Sparks World Famous Shows was the show of the South,' he scratched his ear and looked away, 'until this unfortunate Hoffmann incident.'

'We've dealt with it,' Charlie quickly said.

'So I've been informed,' Cotton nodded. 'Nevertheless, Barnum and Bailey would hate to see such a fine circus go down. Terrible, that would be just terrible. I agree. I've seen your show, Mister Sparks, in Shreveport. Fantastic! Just fantastic! You could have asked anyone, I was raving about it. Almost drove my employers crazy.'

'I think we'll be just fine, actually, Mister Cotton, now everything's been set to rights.'

'Barnum and Bailey understand the emotional attachment you have to this circus,' Cotton continued. He raised his gloved hand. 'My employers know already there's little to no hope of buying you out.'

'I emphasized the point on several occasions.' Charlie smiled. He could feel his own strength.

'And we couldn't annoy you, repeating ourselves,' Cotton finished for him. 'So, I'm not here to make an offer for the circus. We know full well you plan on making a show at the Old West fair, in Tennessee, and several of my colleagues are hoping to secure a ticket, let me tell you in confidence. But we do figure you could use a little grease, just to help you take on the world again. We know how expensive these comebacks can be. Between you and I, my employers know it intimately,' Cotton winked. 'I mean, you've gone a year with no income, and you've got fliers to print, you've got posters, you've got advertising spots to buy in the local newspapers...PR is hell, I tell you, just hell. on. earth.'

'I don't suppose your employers are offering to make a donation?' Charlie asked. He braced for it.

Cotton reached into his pocket and pulled out a crinkled, yellow envelope. He set it on the desk. He said nothing, as his hand rested on his knee, fingers drumming, impatiently. Charlie reached across and peaked inside. It was a stack of fifty-dollar bills.

'Five hundred dollars,' Cotton said. 'Twice what we've estimated she's worth.'

'What who's worth?'

'Mary,' Cotton said. 'Mighty Mary. Maintaining an elephant is expensive. Barnum and Bailey are offering to remove the burden while financing your advertising material for at least another eighteen months.'

'Meanwhile, you'd procure a rare and talented elephant,' Charlie said. He folded the envelope over and slid it back across the desk with his fingertips. 'She'll make ten times that on our tour next year, just on her name alone.'

'Come now, how old is she now?' Cotton objected, his voice cracking a little. 'Do you even know?'

'My father purchased her when she was four years old,' Charlie insisted, as was the story he'd been telling all these years. 'She's a family pet for eighteen years. As a matter of fact, yes, I do know how old she is. Young. Quite fit enough for several more years performing. She's the longest serving member of this circus, after Miss Addy and myself. You can go and tell your employers that they've no hope of acquiring Mary. Not over my grave.'

'Can I persuade you to be reasonable here...'

'I am being quite reasonable, Mister Cotton, I assure you,' Charlie said, unable to keep himself from grinning. 'Mary is accustomed to us. She is more than an elephant, she is a pet, a friend, and a companion. I wouldn't trust an elephant I don't know to Barnum and Bailey, let alone a pet, friend, and companion. I'm fully aware of your employers' liberal use of bullhooks in training. The conditions in which those elephants are crammed together, night after night. Out of love for Mary, I say unreservedly no. I am also aware of the business practices of your employers and know full well the extent of their philanthropic nature. You wouldn't have turned up here, all false charm and sleazy grin, waving an envelope of cash around if you didn't already know Mary was worth a hundred times the value. So, don't threaten my elephants, firstly, Mister Cotton. And secondly, dare not to insult my intelligence, in my own office. For God's sake, man.'

'You just don't get it, do you?' Cotton said. He snatched the envelope off the desk and rammed it back in his pocket. 'What do you think? You're just going to hit the ground running again? After sitting here, a whole summer, earning nothing? Not mentioned, outside of scandals? What do you think this is? America has forgotten you, Charlie Sparks. It's over.' He'd stood and was walking to the door. 'I'll show myself out. You'll be sorry you did this. You've been lucky, that's all. Luck. Luck ends for all of us. Barnum and Bailey are prepared, for when their luck turns sour. I don't know what you're going to do, Charlie Sparks. Good day to you, sir.'

'Good day,' Charlie said, to the slam of his office door.

#

'Where was it you said you were from?' Paul Jacoby asked the young man as he opened the door to the elephants' barn.

'Oh, I'm from all over,' he said. 'You know, once you're with Ringling, the tour never stops. Sorry, I don't know if that's okay to say.'

Paul waved it off and stepped in. Red followed him and quickly forced down the sudden surge of fear at seeing the three enormous animals looming in the dim barn. Two grey ones stood at one wall, on the other was one enormous, darker coloured one. That had to be Mary, he thought. Gee, she was big! He tried to cover the fact he was staring.

'I heard Jumbos about the same size,' Paul said, obviously seeing Red's shock.

'Sure, yeah,' Red said, bracing to take a chance. 'Jumbo's a male, though.'

Paul chuckled. 'Barnum and Bailey, huh?'

Red nodded.

'What the hell would you leave them to work for Sparks for, then?' Paul asked, looking over at the other two elephants. 'That's Regina and Bernadette by the way.'

'Sure, I know 'em,' Red winked. 'Ringling is a big circus. You know, everywhere you go, you feel like you're in this big ol' city of its own. Who's to say where you are really, you're always in Ringling, ya know? I figure this is a little smaller. I get to experience a little more of America, this way. Get paid for it too.'

'Not as much,' Paul said. 'I worked for Ringling myself. I never saw you there.'

'Why'd you leave?'

'Christina DeRosa. I didn't realize how old she was.'

Red laughed like he knew what Paul was talking about. 'Well, you know, I wasn't with Ringling long.'

'I can see that. You're shaking in your boots.'

'Well, there's only the two of us in here!'

'Two, ten, a hundred. Don't make any difference, one of these things loses its temper,' Paul said, good-naturedly. 'One thing you'll have to get used to. Old Charles hates bullhooks. He has me train his elephants with a clicker. We have the hooks, but only for show. The elephants know what they are, you wave one at them, and they back off. Whatever they're doing, they'll stop. But Sparks won't like you using them. Same isn't so when Charlie's not around, you follow?'

Red smiled. 'I follow.'

CHAPTER 31

Mary was brought out by her handlers the day after meeting Red to a sight she'd both longed for and dreaded. Workers were deconstructing the wintering grounds and loading the pieces onto the train. Her heart skipped a beat. They were moving! They were going on migration! At long last! Regina and Bernadette walked out behind her and saw what was happening as well.

'We're going on tour!' Bernadette said.

'Pay attention!' Mary nudged her. If one of them made a mistake, they'd all get the bullhook later. Charlie Sparks held his cane out, but Jacoby was watching from the sidelines. She could feel his eyes burning into her before she even knew he was there.

Under Charlie Sparks' direction, the elephants ran their routine and showed that they hadn't forgotten it over the dull period. After that, they were loaded onto the train together, and with a chugging and a buckle and a bump, they were rolling along the tracks again, chasing the infinite horizon. They left the familiar sights and smells of the wintering ground behind them, and the world was fresh and new again. But Mary had forgotten how stifling it was to stand still and just watch it all go sliding by. There were trees bursting with lush, juicy greenery, while she had nothing but hay to eat. There were rivers sparkling and fresh winding through the boundless wilderness, while Mary had to share her slimy, stagnant troth water with Regina and Bernadette. There were fields of dazzling colour that smelled sweet and dewy. Mary smelled only the acrid breath of the train blasting over her face day in, day out. Worst of all, there were rolling hills, bushy heaths, grassy prairies, rich woodlands and sparkling lakes surrounded by smooth, soft mud and Mary and Regina and Bernadette were stuck in their little carriage, unable not to be touching each other, unable to move more than a half-pace to either side, and not forward or back at all.

Somewhere along the way, while the air grew thicker and heavier, Mary felt a strange pinch in her heart. Like the first glimmer of sunlight as she'd open her eyes first thing in the morning, something had awoken inside her. She started to breathe heavily and felt her flank pressing against Bernadette's head. Mary was feeling something. It hurt but was sweet. There was an open wilderness before her, with brown grass swaying softly in a humid breeze and lonely trees dotted about. She was walking through it. Everything was larger, or she was smaller. There was a presence. A loving, protecting shadow that fell over her.

Mary recognized the memory that threatened to consume her and quickly forced it down deeper. But it had swollen as it woke. She felt her insides fit to burst with the sensations and emotions bubbling to life around them.

Eventually, they reached a train station and the workers quickly went about unloading the train. That was unusual. Normally they'd stop just somewhere, on the side of a road or near a paddock. Not at a station. Mary wondered where the Big Top would go.

'What's wrong Mary?' Bernadette was nudging Mary with her trunk.

'Leave me alone.'

The workers unloaded the camp and either carried or carted the pieces off the platform and into the town, where they disappeared into the labyrinth of structures. Mary's knees were shaking. She couldn't contain herself much longer and was afraid either Charlie Sparks or Jacoby would come by eventually and see her getting confused and distressed.

The clowns and the marching band were gathering on the far side of the station. Christina rode a horse back and forth while Yashi and Jasmine were standing beside theirs, waiting for something. A parade. A migration. But it wasn't a migration, because they weren't going anywhere. And they weren't Mary's herd.

Images began to flash through her mind. Her friend, the baby elephant who'd raised her trunk to her and brought her to play with the others. The wounded calf, after his scuffle with the tiger. The larger bulls. The playful cows. What they might look like now, had the bad things never happened. Older, bigger, with calves of their own. Their mothers, old and withered and fighting just to keep pace. Or wandering away in the night to die. Where were they? Mary saw them beside a misty river in the forest. Feasting and playing in the water, as they were the last time she saw them. So, so long ago.

Jacoby opened the elephant's carriage while workers set up the ramps. He and the other handlers didn't have bullhooks, which meant that Charlie Sparks and Miss Addy were somewhere nearby. Mary tried to focus.

Did they think of her, now and then? The herd she'd left behind, did they wonder if she was migrating over tiny distances, with some strange assortment of creatures? Did they know of what she'd endured at the hands of people? Did they remember her mother? Was their new alpha anything like her? As big? As strong? As wise?

Red tapped Mary's side. She raised her leg to let him up. Other handlers climbed up on Bernadette and Regina and they disembarked the carriage in a line, Mary led them like her mother once did.

Her heart smashed open and bled inside her as she suddenly realized her kinship with Bernadette and Regina. She wanted to turn around and embrace them. But that was impossible. She'd be beaten, if not now then later. Mary suppressed her yearning to touch them and beg their forgiveness. What a monster she'd been! To her own, to her flesh and blood! She felt Regina's trunk wrapped around her tail. It wasn't Regina's trunk. It wasn't an elephant's. They had no names. They just were.

The herd marched through the town with a band and the horses in front of the elephants. Jacoby rode a horse alongside Mary and handed Red a bullhook. He then fell back and gave the other two bullhooks to the other two handlers who rode on the other two elephants. They walked past the structures and along the road toward a sprawling village of tents, much bigger than any wintering ground or Big Top Mary had ever seen.

There were carriages, banners, flags, and tents all over the open grassland. Only a few trees stood, way out at the far end, so much so that the canopy of one could not be distinguished from the others. Beyond them, half faded in the milky distance, loomed a row of mountains. Mary couldn't help but stare. She remembered seeing such things, long ago. Giant, white-capped citadels of steely grey, watching silently and endlessly over their sparse curve of the world.

Mary remembered a swollen river. It was a day like today, an overcast sky with dark, ominous clouds rumbling behind fathomless mountain peaks. It was sweltering; thick, muggy air that she had to fight against to move through. Mud squelched at their feet. A river had swollen. Reeds stood tall all around her and the herd. They were not elephants. She was not Mary. They just were. That's all they needed to be. Silence had fallen about them. All was quiet but the rhythmic songs of the little things that lived unseen amongst the stems of the grass. Something prowled in their periphery. Something with cold, cruel eyes. A presence had watched over them, but it had fallen away. She was on her own.

At that moment, Mary was wild again.

Without control, without boundaries, without any sense of pain or punishment, she spotted a watermelon left on the side of the road. Mary wanted the watermelon. Something sweet and bursting and juicy to wash away all the dry, scratchy hay. She left the migration and walked toward it.

'Hey!' a voice cried. 'Back on track, Mary!'

Who was Mary? What was on her back?

Suddenly sharp, stabbing pain erupted in her jaw. He'd hit her with something and it pierced her skin and sent buzzing currents of agony through her face. Then, she remembered. Old Boy. He beat her. He hurt her all the time. He took her mother away!

Shooting guns flashed before her eyes. The cracking sounds that stole the life of her mother. All that she knew of love in the world was gone in an instant. Then, only pain. Because of him!

Rage seized her. Mary flung her trunk back and felt it hit the side of the frail little ape that was perched there. He screamed as he fell to the ground. Mary stepped back and felt one of his legs snap and crackle beneath the weight of her foot. Old Boy let out a shredded scream that filled the air and stopped every movement around them. She pushed him out from under her, but he wasn't Old Boy. He was Philip! The boy who'd befriended and cared for her, only to stab at her with bullhooks and hurt her!

Mary rammed her head down into the boy's stomach and pushed until she felt the dirt sinking beneath him. He was screaming and feebly pushing at her brow. She reared back, but he wasn't Philip. He was the Colonel! The ape who'd made her only friend cruel and aggressive.

She rammed her head down again. The tiny, fragile ribs of his chest gave out beneath her forehead and his screams became gurgled as blood splattered out of his gullet.

'Someone help me!' he screamed. He wasn't the Colonel. He was just another upright ape. A pale one. The cruelest and meanest of all.

'Get a gun!' voices cried. 'Get a gun and kill it!'

'Someone please help me!' the ape cried as he writhed and tried to crawl away from Mary. She gritted her teeth and kicked him. The body went hurtling through the air and smashed into a popcorn stand. Glass and popcorn showered down over him. He was still moving. Mary hated him. She charged toward him. He was screaming and waving his hands. With one foot she crushed his pelvis. He screamed and doubled over. With her other, she pressed down onto his head. It gave out beneath her weight and she felt warm, sticky goo come out. Finally, he was still.

Scores of people had encircled Mary but kept their distance. She recognized the objects they were holding; guns. Mary knew what guns were. She knew that was what killed her mother. All around them was chaos; people were running, screaming, they knocked over structures and tore right through tents. All to get away. Panic took her, and Mary let out a terrifying bellow that stirred her own heart.

'That's my elephant!' Charlie Sparks screamed as he ran toward the circle. But the clowns grabbed him and held him back. 'That's my elephant!'

With an almighty crescendo the guns let rip that terrifying crackle of shots and smoke filled the air. All over Mary's, stinging bullets burst through her flesh and vibrated sheer agony through her body. She screamed. It hurt. Sorrow and panic held her all at once as she realized what she had done, and reality came flowing back through her.

Red. She'd killed Red. One of the people. Her handlers. She'd killed one of her herd.

Cowering from the bullets she turned and ran toward Charlie Sparks. The shots stopped, and the people scurried out of her way.

'Kill the elephant!' the emboldened masses were shouting. 'Kill the elephant!'

Mary ran back to the town with the crowd following her, firing shots into her backside and legs. The pain was so much that her knees buckled, and she almost fell as she climbed onto the dirt road between the buildings. The train station was just ahead. A few bullets cut through her ears. She screamed. All her body was aflame. She saw Jacoby come riding out beside her. He fired shots at her head with his own gun. Mary felt them burst into her cheek and smash against the bone of her skull. But she ran. Adrenaline carried her. She stumbled again on the ramp but managed to get up. Then the boarding ramp. It was still there. She clambered into her carriage and cowered against the rails.

Where had she been going? What was her plan?

Avoid the pain.

The crowds amassed in front of her carried. The men with guns pushed to the front and took aim at her. But Charlie Sparks ran out in front of them. The clowns pushed the gates to her carriage shut. Charlie Sparks was shouting at them with his hands raised by his sides.

Mary's heart was pounding. She felt dizzy and her gullet became slimy and she wanted to vomit. All over her body, she felt warm blood running out of her hundreds of tiny wounds. Her vision blurred. She felt liquid seeping out of her mouth as she hung her head to try and catch her breath. Finally, Mary lost consciousness.

#

'She's not dead yet! She's still breathing! We have to shoot her dead now!' Paul Jacoby screamed. Charlie still clutched the nozzle his Winchester rifle. 'Do you hear me, Sparks? It's gone rabid! When it wakes up, it could break out of there and kill us all!'

'We can't!' Charlie screamed.

'Do you still think you're gonna make a buck out an elephant that's crushed a kid's head?'

'Do you have an elephant gun handy?' Charlie cried. He looked at one of the confused, sweaty labourers. 'Get everything back on the train, now!'

The black man nodded and hurried off, calling to the other labourers. The clowns were hurrying back into the train, obviously hoping for a quick getaway. Charlie knew they couldn't just make a break for it. He'd have to address the crowd. He'd have to talk to the police. He'd have to do something!

He let go of Paul, seeing he was just staring down at his useless little rifle. He looked up at Mary. She lay on her stomach, half-awake, watching the crowd with one bloody, groggy eye that still seemed somehow to comprehend what was happening.

Golly, he thought. That could have been him! Or Adelaide! Or anyone! It could have been the children she'd marched with! How could he have been so negligent, keeping such a crazed animal, and not even realized it?

Adelaide and Christina were pushing through the crowd on horseback towards them. 'Go back!' he cried. 'Get back inside!'

Christina looked over toward the crowd and grabbed Adelaide's arm. 'What? What is it?'

'I'll tell you what it is,' Paul spat out. 'That damned elephant just killed Eldridge.'

Adelaide cupped her hands over her mouth and stared up at Mary. Christina turned her away and pushed her back toward their passenger carriage.

'Alright, this has to be done,' Charlie said. The police had taken over the crowd, all with their guns ready. He walked over to the officer in charge, while the others collected raving testimony from the witnesses.

'That elephant just snapped, and speared that boy through with its tusks,' a whiny voice was screeching.

'I tell you this, that thing is mad! Murderous Mary! I tell you this, plum crazy! Plum crazy!'

'We ought to electry-cute it if our guns won't work! I seen 'em do that 'afor'n!'

'You Sparks?' the policeman said when Charlie was close enough. Immediately a rabble tried to rush him but officers held them back.

'There he is! That's the son'bit with the damn elephant!'

'He done brought that devil-thang 'ere!'

'I'm Sparks,' Charlie answered very quietly.

'Who was the kid? You know him?'

'Wilber Eldridge,' he said, he touched the brim of his hat. 'Red Eldridge. We don't know much, he was just filling in...'

'You better get that elephant out of here, Mister,' the policeman said. 'These folks are gonna tear y'all apart, an' I'm not inclined to stop them.'

'That there's Sparks,' someone said. A tall, burly man broke away from the police and pointed at him. 'You ain't gonna get away with this! This ain't never happened no-how with no other circus. You trained that elephant.'

'I didn't train her to kill anyone, sir,' Charlie answered. 'Not least my own employees.'

'You son of a bitch!' someone else said, joining his friend. 'That coulda been anyone!'

The officer in charge was pushing Charlie back, away from the increasingly belligerent crowd. 'Next town's Erwin, I suggest you get to it!'

Charlie turned and ran back to his train. Their train was loaded up again and they were ready to move on. Charlie quickly boarded the first passenger carriage and the order was given to go. They were at the nearest watering station before anyone said a word. It was Charlie.

'It will be okay,' he said. 'This does happen, time to time. It will be okay.'

'How will it be okay?' Adelaide asked.

'Barnum and Bailey made me an offer for Mary, right before we left,' Charlie said. 'We sell her, change her name, nobody's the wiser. We carry on with the tour, with the added money from the sale of Mary to bolster our advertising. It's called cutting out losses and we'll be just...'

'Charlie...' Yashi half-whispered. 'Did Mary really kill Red Eldridge?'

Charlie swallowed hard and nodded.

'She did,' said Christina. 'I saw her.'

Yashi turned ghostly white and huddled up in her seat.

'He hit her with a bullhook,' Christina continued. The other dancers were looking at her.

'We don't have bullhooks,' Charlie said. 'I don't allow them.'

'Mister Jacoby keeps them. Mister Stephenson used one too...'

'That's enough Christina!' Yashi finally screamed. 'A man is dead! Can't you understand that?'

Christina sat back in her seat and put her feet up. 'He shouldn't have hit her.'

'What? So, he deserved to die?' Yashi cried.

'He shouldn't have hit her.'

'My handlers don't have bullhooks!' Charlie thundered, and they all turned pale. Charlie had never shouted before. Not like that.

Adelaide was crying silently into her handkerchief. Charlie was glad Paul Jacoby was traveling in the other carriage.

The storm hit, and they travelled again in silence. It was not until nightfall they saw the lights of Erwin ahead. Along with them, scores of citizens standing out in the rain, all around the train station. As he peered through the window Charlie could see they were holding posters to his show. Once the train stopped, a man marched right across the platform and slapped the soaking poster against the window beside Christina's head.

The 'Mighty' of 'Mighty Mary' was scratched out and replaced with 'Murderous'. Murderous Mary.

CHAPTER 32

The night grew dark and the rain let up to a light patter. Charlie's feet had gone to sleep, he'd been sitting so long, turning his hot hat around and around by the band. Voices hummed constantly beyond the glass, behind his own reflection. Malaise might have carried him right off into a dream, had he not felt his wife's warm, loving arms sliding around his shoulders.

'Go to them, Charlie,' she said, softly and sweetly. The way she always did when she needed to get her way. 'We need our ringmaster now.'

'Find out what they want and for God's sake give it to them!' Marvin slurred. His bottle crashed to the floor with a loud clunk.

Adelaide didn't look away. She just stared with those big, twinkling, chocolate brown eyes. Charlie felt her strength moving through him.

'Whatever you have to do,' she said, suddenly not so sweet, 'nobody will judge you for it.'

Charlie looked over at Christina. She seemed to be half-dozing, dressed in a man's slacks and trench coat. He took a deep breath and stood up. Adelaide nodded to him. He put his hat on. A wall of water met him, when he opened the carriage door, along with it the voices of a hundred or more angry citizens. Their wild, wet faces flared up with rage as the light from inside the carriage fell upon them, and Charlie felt the surge of aggression rolling over him with a barrage of screams and pointed fingers.

'Get outta here wid yer murderin' ephelant!'

'We don't want yo' circus kind 'round here!'

'Devil worshippin' tramps got what's comin' to 'em!'

'Get on outta here, wid yo' wicked wummun!'

'Ladies and gentlemen,' Charlie Sparks shouted, but to no avail. The shouting only escalated into an unintelligible rabble. He could see what he thought were rifles or shotguns being waved in the air. 'Ladies and gentlemen, by now you will no doubt be aware of an incident which occurred in Kingsport, earlier today.... ladies and gentlemen!'

He didn't know whether he kept talking in order to get his point across, or because he thought they wouldn't shoot him as long as he was saying something. He could feel himself breaking into a sweat. Then, he noticed a small cluster of people moving through the crowd. Five or six. They were pushing their way through and the crowd was parting for them. The line of furious men before Charlie broke in two and revealed a fat man with a broad, smiling face and an escort of four men with tin deputy's stars on their breasts. He touched the rim of his hat. 'Howdy.'

Charlie made space for the man and he stepped up onto the carriage to shake Charlie's hand. There was an immediate uproar, but the deputies turned to face the crowd while the tips of their fingers teased the grips of their revolvers and the silence fell over them as though a great sheet was drawn over them.

'Mayor Kearns, Mister Sparks, pleasure to meet you, sir,' the fat man said as he continued to shake Charlie's sweaty hand. 'And let me be the first to welcome y'all to Erwin.' He spoke to Charlie, but half-faced the town, and projected his voice so they all could hear. 'Now we here is a civil place, just as hospitable as any good Christina town. But you must know, sir, that the safety of the people of Erwin must be our number one priority. So you'll understand if we don't want any insane ephelants hanging 'round this here place. You do understand, don't you Mister Sparks?'

'I...' Charlie couldn't conjure a sentence. It was the first time in his life.

'Good.' Kearns said. 'And that brings me to our number two priority here in Erwin; punishing injustice. Now we welcomed this here ephelant into our town not five years back.'

'I remember.'

'We weren't to know then, the terrible risk of having such a beast so near our loved ones and our children,' the Mayor said. 'We've come direct from a town meeting, called soon as we heard about the murder in Kingsport.'

'...murder?'

'That's right. And we hang murderers in Unicoi County, Mister Sparks. Hang 'em by the neck until they're dead.'

'It's...an animal.'

'That being the case...we are hesitant. We've thought of a number of things we could do. Shooting. Electrocution.' Kearns took his hat off. 'Now you can carry right on past this town if you want to. That would be Johnson City. Now I have personal word from the mayor of Johnson City that you won't be allowed in so long as Mary is with you. You can go on along. But there will be the next town, Mister Sparks. And the next. And maybe you'll high tail it out of Tennessee and keep your heels fore' of the news. But then there'll Kentucky or Mississippi or Alabama and...well, they won't take kindly to a murderin' elephant neither, Mister Sparks. And the rate news travels these days...you understand, don't you?'

'I'll be ruined.'

'Yes, you will. Or we can correct this miscarriage of justice here and now. End it. At last, you'll know you did all you could.'

'Excuse me for a moment,' Charlie said. He felt cold. A few carriages down, past the Mayor, he could see a portion of the crowd that kept their distance. Mary's carriage. Despairing, he stepped down from the carriage and shimmied past the silent mob down to her.

Bernadette and Regina were huddled at the back of the carriage, while Mary was at the front, riddled with little red holes and streaked with blood. But alive and upright. She looked down at Charlie. He looked up at her. She still had that knowing gaze in her eyes. Always did. He stared until hot tears stung his eyes and the ball in his throat threatened to choke him.

'Good evening, Mary,' he whispered. 'Mighty Mary.'

He knew what he had to do.

'We didn't come here to put Mary on display!' Charlie Sparks roared to the crowd and turned to them with a great sweep of his arm. 'We didn't come here to give Erwin any circus show, not after what happened today!

He started away from Mary, back toward the Mayor.

'In all my years, I've never seen such a barbaric act of savagery from an animal,' he said. 'Not one of my own. Not one reared with the love and devotion of myself and the beautiful, adoring Miss Addy. No. This is a betrayal. Like my own child has plunged a dagger into my breast. This elephant has turned on all of us! We came to Erwin to bring her justice, with your help, you good, honest, decent people, who know justice, and know truth, and know that I am speaking the truth, and seeking justice. We came here not to try her. But to execute Murderous Mary!'

There was a roar of brutal agreeance. Fists flew into the air. Charlie climbed back up, next to the mayor.

'If a good, decent Christian was murdered on Tennessee soil, they'd be hanged!' Charlie continued. 'So be it. You have brought us a guilty verdict. So be it. Who am I to stand before the just and good people of Erwin? Tomorrow, at noon, you will see an elephant hang!'

There was a second roar, louder than the first, and it didn't stop. Charlie stood before them, he could hear the difference between this applause and the applause of a circus arena. There was a cackle to this, a savagery he'd heard in nightmares.

'How do you plan on doing that?' Kearns said through his smile, as he clapped along with the dispersing crowd.

'It was before the sons and daughters of this great state of Tennessee that my elephant chose to commit this unthinkable crime,' Charlie said, matching the Mayor's earlier pomp. 'It is therefore by the ingenuity of the sons and daughters of this fair state dole out the sentence. We can wait until the necessary arrangements are made.'

They both looked at the satisfied crowd as it thinned and spread out. Both knew the Mayor was stuck to his word. The chilling chant rang out from somewhere in town:

'Kill the elephant!'

'Kill the elephant!'

'Kill the elephant!'

Mayor Kearns looked at Charlie with eyes of a stung predator. He wasn't done yet. 'There's a railyard two miles along. Clinchfield. Plenty of dormant tracks for you to rest overnight. We'll get back to you by noon tomorrow with our arrangements.'

'I look forward to seeing them,' Charlie said with a wry smile.

'Good night, Mister Sparks.' The Mayor touched his hat again and stepped down from the train. 'Don't let my lawmen catch any members of your circus around here, you understand?'

'You make yourself abundantly clear,' Charlie said, and he touched the rim of his hat. The Mayor and his deputies disappeared behind the station wall before Charlie climbed down and hurried to the driver.

'Clinchfield railyard?' he said.

'Stayin' on the train all night?' the driver asked.

'Yes. Nobody is to leave the train.'

Charlie made it back into his carriage just as the train started moving. He shut the door and, as though someone fired a shot through him, the adrenaline died, and he collapsed against it. He had to force back the tears. But when he stood up and stepped out before his performers, he couldn't stop himself. Adelaide hurried to his side and held him up. He felt his strength grow again. The performers were all staring at him, waiting. He took a few deep breaths.

'We have to kill her.'

There was a long, uneasy silence. Even Christina was just staring, flatly. Charlie wondered if they heard him.

'I've bought us some time. I promised the people a hanging. They're going to have to figure out how to do it. They might give up. I've put the mayor in quite a spot...'

'You said hang her?' Christina suddenly roared. Her face flushed purple with rage. 'She's an elephant! She doesn't know what she's done!'

'That's exactly the problem!' Charlie shouted back. 'She killed a man without a second thought. She has no idea the magnitude of her actions. She has no comprehension of consequences. That's part of training for most elephants. At Barnum and Bailey elephants know and understand the laws of man which they are obligated to obey. Ours don't. I have to let these people have their way if we're ever going to tour again.'

'Eldridge hit her,' Christina snapped. 'I was watching. He hit her with a bullhook. Hit her in the face.' She pointed at her own, 'right in the jaw!'

'Perhaps we should have done more of that,' Charlie said. He flopped into his seat. Adelaide curled up beside him and rested her head on his shoulder. 'We might not be in this fix.'

'You son of a bitch,' Christina said. She was glaring at him.

He looked at her, wanting to say, 'not now' or something, but he figured it was just easier to let her wear herself out.

'You're going to kill Mary for the same reason you cut Jessica!' she shrieked. 'Money. It's all you're worried about. You don't care about those people or the law! You're worried about the money you're going to lose if you pack up and go home now and sell her to Ringling, like you said you would. It'd cost too much, with things how they are now. That's all. You're killing her to save yourself a damn buck!'

'It's more than one damn buck!' Charlie roared.

'Well, you won't make your damn buck with me around.'

She marched to the door.

'Darling, the train is moving,' Adelaide said.

'I'm not getting off the train!' Christina said. 'I'm going to my trailer.'

'Sit down, will you? You're going to get hurt.'

'I'm not spending another minute in here with you people!' Christina shrieked again.

'Well then get on your way!' Charlie waved her off. He hoped she'd throw herself into the mud from the moving train.

'Oh, I'm not going just yet,' Christina said. 'I'm gonna stay and watch this. I'm gonna watch what happens. I'm gonna watch you kill one of your own family. That's what you always said we were, is family. Do families hang each other?'

'We aren't much to you, are we?' Charlie asked.

'I was about to ask you the same thing,' Christina said. She pushed the door open and let the rain and whipping wind flick up her hair.

Then, into the night she disappeared, and the door flapped shut behind her.

#

Mary felt as though her stomach might hurl itself right up out of her gullet at any moment. She was weak, tired, and her whole body throbbed and seared with pain. Bernadette and Regina kept huddled away from her and she couldn't stand up to move closer to them. Her knees were too weak. The motion of the train added to her nausea. Slime covered the back of her throat. Mary wondered how much more she could take before she died. She wished she could just close her eyes and be far away. Somewhere warm and sheltered. Or better, huddled with the bodies of her herd. Wherever they were. Under the giant, silver mountains by the swollen river, or amongst the tall grass where the little pigs ran around their feet.

The people hated her. Mary knew it. She wondered if they were right to. Had Mary betrayed them? They'd kept her safe. They'd taken her in. But they'd beat her and hurt her. Mary wasn't sorry. As the desolate cloud of doom hung over her, she didn't regret killing Red. Only the consequences it brought on her from the people.

But Charlie Sparks had saved her. He'd protected her. Mary was sure he was taking her somewhere safe again. Away from the angry crowd. She just wondered if she could make it there without dying on the way. And hoped that she hadn't hurt Miss Addy with her actions. Not too much, anyway.

'I'm sorry,' Mary tried to say to the others. But they were frightened of her and she couldn't muster the strength to get their attention.

Out of nowhere, Christina suddenly dropped into the carriage, right next to Mary's face. Mary was frightened for her, that she had climbed all the way down here with the train buckling and jolting along. Christina could have fallen. Strengthened by melancholy love and gratitude for seeing her friend again, Mary lifted her trunk and touched Christina's face. Blood smeared over Christina's shoulder, but she hugged the trunk like she used to and sat down beside Mary's bleeding head.

'I'm so sorry, Mary,' Christina said. 'I stopped visiting you, huh? It's just...I'm a terrible person, Mary. I know it. I love you though.' She started to cry. Mary heaved her trunk around her shoulders and Christina wept into it like she used to out by the tree on nights while they toured, while wolves howled in the distance. 'I thought you'd always be there. So sorry. I'm so sorry.'

'I'll be okay,' Mary tried to assure her, though she wasn't certain herself. 'I'll heal and be fine.'

The train rumbled to a stop. Mary couldn't figure out what they were doing. They weren't safe yet.

'I love you, Mary.'

#

The sun came up, the rain stopped, and the day ambled by while Charlie paced up and down the carriage, waiting for them to appear. What would it be? A rabble? A mob? The whole town? What would they do? Find a tall tree? Shoot her instead? Electrocute her?

'There isn't enough bloody electricity in all of Tennessee,' he said aloud. A few who were dozing in the humid morning sun awoke.

'Young lady, you get down from there!' another voice was shouting from outside. 'Don't you know what that thing did?'

'He's lost his mind!' Charlie said, with a hint of delirious glee. But as he hurried to the door, he heard the distinctive Yankee squawk of Christina, and it all made sense.

'I've been here all night!' she was screeching, as Charlie stepped off the train into the thick, squelching mud. 'She's been nothin' but kind to me.'

'That thing's a killer, don't you know?' the tall, deep-voiced man accompanying the Mayor said, while both of them watched the mad woman standing firm in protest beside the bleeding, pale-looking elephant. Their car was parked a few yards away with the deputies.

'Good God,' Charlie breathed when he saw Mary.

'Mister Sparks,' Mayor Kearns said. 'It looks to me you have a nut on board your train.'

'You're trespassing,' Charlie said to Christina.

'You don't know this woman?' the deep-voiced, tall man said. He was wearing a sheriff's badge.

'Miss DeRosa was fired from my shows last night,' Charlie seethed.

'Well now!' the Sheriff smiled. 'That means I'm within my rights to arrest you, ma'am, if the gentleman wishes to press charges.'

'We have a home for wayward women none too far from here,' Kearns said. 'They lobotomize the ones who don't listen when a man speaks.'

Christina turned around and threw her arms around Mary's trunk. Somehow, the elephant had stood up.

'What'll it be, Mister Sparks?' the Sheriff asked.

'If she's not down in five seconds,' Charlie said. He meant every word. Christina knew it. She looked at him with all the heat of pure hatred in her eyes, but she climbed down from the carriage.

'I hope you have somewhere to go, missy,' the Sheriff said. 'Wayward women, n'all.'

'Hell with all of you,' she seethed.

'Sheriff Buckley,' the Sheriff shook Charlie's hand. 'You had a stuck for a while there, Mister Sparks. At first, we thought this plan of yours was crazy, hanging an animal that large. We even thought about electrocuting her, but the town's electrical engineer warned us that an elephant would short out the entire county. But then I remembered; you're right outside a railyard!'

Charlie stared at them, breathless.

'The derricks, Mister Sparks,' Kearns said. 'They can lift about twelve tons.'

'Railyard worker said they couldn't bring one out in this weather, so we did the next best thing,' Buckley checked his

433

fob. 'In another two hours, the half of Erwin is going to come right on up in here and witness the execution in the railyard.'

'High noon,' Mayor Kearns said, as he patted Charlie's shoulder. 'Just like you promised.'

#

Mary watched the men talking. She felt waves of heat beneath her skin, while the surface broke out in cold shivers. She didn't understand what the men were doing, but her heart was kept beating by the sight of Christina. She'd walked a few paces away but stayed close enough to watch from the muddy paddocks which surrounded them.

Eventually, Charlie Sparks climbed back into the train and they were moving again. The automobile rode alongside them, in front of Mary, while Christina ran to keep up with both. They were carried through gates and into a place made of steel and stone. Train tracks crisscrossed and spread out in every direction, laid on top of pebbles. There was not a sign of life but for herself and the people. Huge structures of cold steel stood. They looked hard and sharp and dangerous. Workers were beginning their day, both dark and pale skinned. Mary noticed their bodies; bent and broken. As though they carried the strain of an immense weight with every step. She'd seen these places before. They'd passed by them at a distance. Mary had always been frightened she'd find herself in such a place one day.

The train stopped. The workers came to open her cage and set her boarding ramp. Charlie Sparks had his stick and he gestured her to come down while Paul kept Regina and Bernadette where they were. Mary climbed down onto the horrible, stony ground. She was weak and trembling and she stumbled and almost fell. But her fear kept her upright. She hadn't been this afraid since she was a baby, repeating a routine in a paddock with Old Boy.

She didn't know what was happening to her. But Mary followed Charlie Sparks. She knew he'd do his best to protect her.

Around them, the area was filling with people. Men, women and children. They were rolling up in automobiles and climbing out. Or riding horses. They were all gathered around an object to which Charlie Sparks led Mary.

It was a train carriage, but nothing like Mary had ever seen. One jagged, cruel steel arm reached high into the air and a chain hung down, all the way to the ground. The workers looped the end of the chain and fixed it, so it would stay that way. They had step ladders. Charlie Sparks directed Mary to stand before it.

She saw the audience. They were not shouting or spitting or shooting at her anymore. They were silent. Mary sensed a cold tension about them. Children gathered around the front to watch. Mary's breath quickened. Charlie Sparks was sombre as he watched. The workers looped the chain around Mary's neck. Once she had on her chain leash, they retreated. The thing behind her made a metallic whirring sound, and Mary felt the chain tighten.

The audience was wowed. Mary began to wonder what the horrible new trick was...

The chain tightened around her neck. It pinched her skin. Fear gripped her and held her still. She felt her breath, frantic and fast, slowly being cut off, and sharp talons felt to be sinking into the flesh around her throat. The pain was immense. She felt her whole spine was ready to explode. She felt herself lift off the ground. Her tongue popped out of her mouth. Her eyes felt like they were bursting from their sockets.

With a loud snap, the pain suddenly released. Mary felt herself falling. Her insides churned, right before she struck the ground, and hammering, blinding, agonizing pain burrowed into her hips, and she screamed and squirmed. She heard others scream. The children dashed into the crowds, which receded back a few paces, revealing Christina. She was watching, tears flowed from her eyes, her hands covered her mouth. She sank to her knees and doubled over and cried loudly.

Workers ran around while Mary cried out at the roaring agony between her hind limbs. She felt the chain smack against her flank and be dragged off. It felt like hours were passing. She screamed until she had no more scream left in her.

The clouds were breaking up and some dim sunlight shone down over Mary's face. Miss Addy stepped in close to her. She seemed to come from the light itself. Pain and sorrow were driving Mary to the point of delirium but in this moment of clarity, she reached out her trunk to that merciful Miss Addy, who'd been there for her so long. Her soothing voice touched Mary's ears, and Mary felt her hands on her head.

'Come now, Mary,' she sang, so sweetly. Just the way she had before Mary had to go out into the ring. 'There's nothing to be afraid of.'

Mary lifted her head. Miss Addy would save her. She'd stop this. She'd make them stop. It would be okay. Miss Addy would tell Charlie Sparks to stop this horrible new trick. Mary tried to stand, despite the horrific agony. But Miss Addy immediately stepped back. A second chain was looped around Mary's neck.

That finally, heart-shattering betrayal was the last thing Mary felt before the pain of the talons sinking through her throat gripped her again. Again, she was lifted off the ground. Again, the pain in her eyes, in her throat, her tongue. Somehow, she saw the Christina, crying up at her, while the other faces faded into a formless blur.

Slowly but surely, all Mary knew was pain. Then, there was only light and sound; bright, dazzling yellow that shone through the formless void of darkness and a cacophony of tuneless, unintelligible noise that frightened and confused her. A dark shadow moved amongst it. Something big, looming over her. She wanted to move toward it. Maybe it was the darkness, closing in around her.

Maybe it was her mother, waiting to take her home.

THE END

Dear Reader,

Thank you for taking the time to read this book. More than anything, I would appreciate an honest review on Amazon, Goodreads or any other online platform from where you purchased your copy.

If I may suggest, here is a list of some other good reads you might enjoy, all available on Amazon worldwide;

1. **Terra Domina**
2. **Angel Valence**
3. **The Red Legion**
4. **Off the Map**
5. **Dino Hunt**

Please visit my website at www.maxdavine.com to keep up with my latest published work and by monthly blog.

Once again, thank you.

Sincerely,
Max Davine

TAMARiND HiLL
.PRESS